CONNECTIONS

Neive Denis

Book four in the Sonoma Whittington series

COPYRIGHT

Cataloguing-in-publication data
Creator: Denis, Neive, author

Cataloguing-in-Publication details are available from the National Library of Australia
www.trove.nla.gov.au

ISBN:978-0-9750287-6-6 (paperback)
ISBN: 978-0-9750287-7-3 (eBook)

Contents

OTHER BOOKS BY THE AUTHOR

An Ancient Solution
A public Service
Missing!

Chapter 1

"Empty again! That's the third day in a row." I realised I was thinking aloud and quickly checked over my shoulders to see if anyone had heard. No one else around; I was standing alone in front of the banks of mailboxes at my local post office with not even a piece of unwanted advertising material to show for my trip. The thought that I couldn't have insulted the whole world occurred to me as I turned to head back to my office. Even for me, that would be quite a feat. It wasn't that I didn't have any work at all. I had plenty of small jobs, more than I wanted of that variety, but it was a while since I had a big case. Even my last couple of enquiries would be interesting if they turned into real jobs.

Deep into this line of thinking, I was enjoying misery for company when a woman loomed up out of nowhere in front of me. After nothing more than a cursory glance in her direction, I moved to walk around her. Something about her suggested I should give her a wide berth. My assessment after one brief glance was that she looked frantic, a bit frayed around the edges somehow, and that she dashed out in the middle of performing some domestic chore. That's what the flock of fluoro pink curlers adorning her bleached blonde hair and scuffed bilious green coloured fluffy slippers suggested.

It looked like we were in for one of those shall-we-dance manoeuvres. As I stepped aside to walk around her, she moved in the same direction to once more stand in front of me blocking my path. No worries; I moved in the opposite direction to go around her on the other side. Oh hello, here she is again. I'm beginning to think this might not be accidental.

"No you don't, Bitch. You're not going anywhere until I'm finished. We are going to have this out here and now. …Can't find one of your own, so you think it's okay to steal someone else's man. Well listen here girlie, I am warning you to leave him alone. If you don't keep your hands off him, you'll end up being sorry you ever laid eyes on him."

Who is this woman talking to? I looked to the left and right

1

behind me. No one; there was no one else in sight. O-k-a-y, I guess that means she's talking to me. Who the hell is this woman and, as there is no 'him' in my life at the moment, who is this 'him' she is talking about. Whoever he is, it's obvious she believes the 'him' in question belongs to her. This whole thing is starting to wear a bit thin and, after the kind of day I've had so far, I just want to get back to my office and hide in the corner. I'll try being polite, but I doubt it will do any good. "Excuse me Madam, would you mind if I go past. I really do need to get back to my office."

"… You deaf as well as everything else? You are not going anywhere till I'm finished with you and I haven't even started yet."

"Are you sure you have the right person? From what you have said so far, I have a rough idea of what you are on about. If you think your husband is playing away, I can assure you I'm not the person you should be talking to."

"Oh, no you don't... I'm not buying that line. You're messing about with my husband and I'm about to put a stop to it. Whatever it takes, it's going to end now."

I watched her slip her hand into the large pocket that stretched across the front of the garishly coloured pinafore she wore over a once white T-shirt and frayed jeans. There appeared to be something weighty in the pocket. Best I try to talk some sense into this situation before it becomes really unpleasant. "Look, I don't know who you are, but that's not important. And I'm pretty sure I don't know who your husband is either. Who is he?"

"Don't give me that. You know him all right. He is Terry Fielding and he is my husband, so leave him alone."

"Terry Fielding…," I murmured as I dredged my memory banks for anything on that name. "No, sorry, I don't know any Terry Fielding and I have no desire to meet him." A stupid thought occurred to me. In a moment of what can only be mental aberration, I voiced it. "However, Madam, if you have reason to believe your husband is unfaithful, I'd be happy to investigate his activities for you." I flicked a business card. "That's me. Give me a call if you want to find out what he is really up to."

"I know who you are, and so does he."

"Okay, I'm not particularly flattered, but if you know so much about me, then why are we having this conversation? I'm too busy to have any sort of life outside my work, so what makes you think I've got time to waste on your husband? You're right, we're not going anywhere until this is sorted out, and that will not be until you've told me why you think it's me – or anyone else – your husband is playing around with."

Oh God, now she's going to dissolve into tears. I really do have problems with the tears and tissues scenario. Bawling women are not my strong point, though God knows I see enough of them. Ah, I think she might have it all under control. That's something of a relief.

"He idolises you, knows all about you, keeps copies of everything in the paper about you, and never stops talking about you and fantasises what sort of person you must be."

"I'll grant you it does seem strange. But what makes you think there's anything more to it than just that – whatever 'that' is?"

After a little more spleen venting, her venom seemed to be losing some of its sting. I pressed her hard about how she had come to this conclusion about my involvement with her husband.

"I heard him on the phone…"

"Heard…? You mean 'overheard', as in eavesdropping."

"No … well, yes. I overheard him on the phone. I wasn't trying to listen. I just happened to hear."

"And what did you happen to hear that makes you think it involved me?"

"He told the person on the other end of the call that 'she' had started digging into things and that it looked as though it could develop into something big. If that were the case, she would be tied up for a while and wouldn't be around. Therefore, they had to make the best of the time they had."

"From that, you worked out he was up to no good with me! That's the trouble with one sided conversations. You only hear one side… and that gives your imagination plenty of scope to run riot. I can't believe you drew that conclusion from so little information. It doesn't say much for the trust that exists in your relationship." Perhaps I should have stopped while she was a little more subdued. My comments only served to encourage her to new heights of

3

character assassination. However, I detected a certain wavering in her conviction, so I let her run on a bit. After all, I didn't have any earth-shatteringly important case waiting for attention back at the office. After a moment or two of silence, she continued. She spoke so quietly, I looked around to see where the shrew I had been dealing with had gone.

"It wasn't just that conversation I overheard. He has been acting funny – no, not funny, differently – for a few weeks. He's been going out at odd times, sometimes staying out for quite a while, and he seems secretive and doesn't want to talk."

"Well, your suspicion of an affair is based on flimsy evidence. Instead of standing here screaming at me, maybe you should direct your questions to him. That way, you might even get to the truth. As I said, should you discover something that requires investigating, give me a call."

She seemed confused and searching for what to say next. About then, a woman and a child, followed by an elderly man, came in to check the mailboxes. I took advantage of the distraction, stepped around her and bolted. With my speed somewhat more than legal, I made it back to the office in near record time … only to find the entrance to the building blocked. A male and female were in the throes of a hearty brawl, she hurled abuse from inside the doorway while he tried to drag her outside. It must be something in the air. It's not full moon yet is it?

Not having a good day and a bit light-on for patience after my previous encounter, I wasn't about to wait around for them to sort out their differences. A solid kick behind his knee made him stumble. He started tumbling backwards. That precipitated various other actions which saw the pair of them end in a scrambled heap on the sidewalk. I stepped around the flailing arms and legs and rushed through the door. She must have had some sort of knickers on – surely – but, if she did, they were quite transparent. That view would haunt me for the rest of the day.

Back in the office, I checked my emails yet again … nothing new. What is wrong with me? I've been in this blue funk for the last few days, and for no good reason I can think of, and now I've started drawing all sorts of attention I can do without. Oh well, in the absence of something better to do, I should have a look at what those couple of insurance jobs are all about. It's either that or read a book, go fishing, take in a movie... throw myself off a bridge. I laughed aloud at the last possibility, startling myself back into reality. I was unlikely to do any of those things, but I have no enthusiasm for what few jobs I have. I opened the file holding the printouts of the insurance cases I'd been given. The file promptly flipped off the edge of the desk, landing on the floor and spilling its contents across a couple of square metres of carpet. I sat stock still for a couple of heartbeats – after delivering a string of expletives – before accepting no one else was going to pick up the mess.

While down my hands and knees under the desk retrieving pages, voices brought things to an abrupt halt. "She's still not here." From my hidey-hole, I couldn't identify the voice. It was female and I could detect a note of disappointment in it.

Another voice chimed in. "Like I said, probably out on a job. Leave a note this time. We should have dropped a note in the letter slot when we called before." This voice I recognised. Still down on all fours, I had managed to wriggle backwards out from under the desk and could hear more clearly. I bobbed up onto my knees and looked over the desk. Startled, Sandra Inneston let out a strangled shriek.

"Sandra, Emily, what brings you here. I do hope you have a murder most horrible for me to investigate."

"Are you all right?" Emily asked and accompanied the question with a strange look.

Before I could reply, Sandra said, "No, we are not here about a murder or any other crime. Emily is in town and wanted to catch up with you. I said you would be busy, but she insisted on dropping by on the off chance you were in the office – which you weren't the first time." This was Sandra at her starchiest best. Looks like I've offended her too.

"Ignore Mum. She's just had a run in with the manager of the shoe shop up the street – difference of opinion about what size shoes she needs."

"Oh, I see." It's hard to say much more when you are struggling to hold back a grin.

"Anyway, we thought you still weren't in," Emily continued "And I was just about to drop a note through your mail slot." She waved a small spiral notebook at me as proof of her intention. "By the way, where is the mail slot? It used to be there by the door? … And what were you doing down there on the floor?"

I managed a wry grin. "It's a long story of sorts. Would you like to hear it over a cup of coffee?"

"No. We would rather hear it over lunch. Do you have appointments during the next hour or two?" I shook my head and Emily continued, but with her eyebrows elevated questioningly at her mother as she spoke. "Good. It's lunchtime. Come on; let's have lunch at the coffee shop across the street."

With the bits of paper I had rescued from the floor dumped in a heap on the desk, I snagged my bag from the corner of the desk where I had dropped it and traipsed to the door after Emily and her mother. Sandra led the way out of the building and marched in a no nonsense way across to the coffee shop. The pair of us trailed along behind her. We were early. The usual lunchtime crowd hadn't started arriving yet. This also meant our meals arrived quickly, and were dispatched with much the same speed.

Conversation over lunch was the usual small talk exchanged by people who haven't been in contact for a while. As soon as we finished eating, Sandra announced she had something to do and someone she wanted to call in to see on the way home. Out the corner of my eye, I saw Emily sit up rigidly and place both hands palm down firmly on the table. "Then I suggest you go and do whatever it is you have to do, Mum. Sonny and I have plenty of catching up to do, and this looks like developing into a long lunch."

Sandra, standing with her bag over her shoulder by then, scowled at her daughter. "I wasn't planning on hanging around in town all day. How long do you think this catching up will take?"

This was not going well, and this certainly was not the Sandra I was familiar with. Whatever happened at the shoe shop must've been a sight to behold as it had left her in the foulest of moods. I felt obliged to step in. Besides, I didn't have anything urgent to continue with in the office. It would be good to just sit and chat to Emily for a while. "Sandra, why don't you go and do whatever it is you need to do. Don't worry about Emily. I'll drop her home later when she is ready. How does that suit you?"

She seemed relieved. "That would be good. It will free me up to do what I have to do without having to drag Emily all over town." With that, Sandra was on her way out of the place.

Emily heaved an audible sigh of relief and I watched her physically relax. "She was already in a foul mood when I arrived yesterday, but that was nothing compared to what she is now. Never mind, she is gone and we can get on with discussing more important stuff. So, tell me what's been happening. I must say you look a bit frazzled today. Is everything okay?"

"Okay… no, I don't think I'd describe it as that. I have had a lousy day. It started early this morning and it definitely hasn't improved as the day went by."

"Thank you very much. I'm pleased my visit fills you with joy and brightens your day so much." I looked up sharply at her response and was relieved to see her struggling to stifle a laugh. I apologised and made some comment about having 'foot in mouth disease'.

"Sometimes talking about it helps," she said with a giggle, "And I could do with a really good laugh after putting up with Mum for 24 hours. Come on, tell Emily all about it." I shot her a disapproving look. "Okay, okay," she held up her hands in resignation, "But what has gone wrong. You're not normally like this."

"Let's see… It all started at breakfast. I burnt the toast. Then spilt coffee down my blouse and had to change before I left for the office. Things were quiet this morning but I did have two phone calls from potential clients, both women, and both of whom wanted to know all the ins and outs of how I operated. In my current mood, after going through all the palaver of explaining how I work and providing quotes, being told by each of them that she 'would think about it' did nothing to improve my outlook. I felt inclined to tell them their problems couldn't be too serious if they had to think about whether to do anything or not."

"You didn't, of course. Anything else happened that I should know about?"

"Well, my mailbox was empty yet again today and there have been no emails requesting my services flooding into my inbox. Oh, and while I was at the post office checking for mail, some lunatic accused me of having it off with her husband. Come to think of it, even that would have been better than what my life is like at the moment. I think that's about it… ah, except for the file of a million bits of paper that fell on the floor just before you arrived in my office. I don't know what's wrong with me. I have got work. All little jobs, but I don't seem to be able to get on with them. I need something big, something I can get my teeth into."

"Right, so nothing serious then? Tell me, how is Ben Richards these days?"

"What are you on about? He's fine as far as I know."

"How long has Ben been gone and where is he?"

"Who said anything about Ben, or that he was away?"

"Oh, come on; you've got 'withdrawal' written all over you. How long before he comes back? All you need is a good dose of Ben to get you back on track again."

"I am not missing Ben. There is nothing to be suffering withdrawal over but, yes, he is away at the moment. He was one of a handful selected to attend a conference and then investigate policing methods in other places." At one time, when Ben Richards previously was stationed at Millhaven, he and I came close to being more than friends, but the timing wasn't right. Since then, we shared involvement in a few cases and scrapes. His recent promotion up the rankings ladder had him in charge of Millhaven's police department, and meant he was once more living here.

"Well, tell me the whole story, where has he gone and how long for?"

"The conference was four days in the UK followed by a few days looking at how they do policing, and then over to Europe to look at how policing works in a few selected areas over there. Altogether, he was going to be away for the best part of the month."

"How long has he been gone and when is he due back?"

"Uhmm, about two weeks now; I think he is due back sometime around the end of the month. I don't know why you think I'd be suffering withdrawal because he's been away for a while. There is nothing between Ben and I, we are just friends."

"Of course you are, and now that he's back in Millhaven, you might occasionally just bump into him on the street… and you're deluding yourself if you think I'm going to believe that."

"We do have a few meals together from time to time but, as I said, we are just friends."

At that point the phone rang. I put on my most exaggerated excited face and said, "Yippee, it might be a client." I didn't much care who it was. I was just thankful it rang when it did and brought any further discussion of Ben Richards to an end. Emily watched as I answered the phone. "Hello, this is…"

"Yes, hello Miss Whittington; this is Trish. We spoke earlier today."

God, am I losing it all together? I don't remember any Trish from this morning, but with the kind of day I've had I shouldn't be surprised. After the brief hesitation while I mined my memory banks for some recollection of Trish, I finally replied. "Trish…? I'm sorry, I don't seem to…"

"We spoke at post office. You gave me your card and said to ring you if I wanted some work done." Oh, that Trish… alarm bells began ringing. "Well, I think I might need you to do some investigating for me. It's about my husband."

"This is the Terry Fielding you mentioned earlier I assume."

"Yes, that's who I am concerned about. I think he might be up to something. How does all this work, this business of getting you to investigate someone?"

I spent a couple of minutes explaining how surveillance works, my schedule of fees, how I report back, and everything else I thought she might need to know. I also went to great lengths to explain that a surveillance job often stretches out over a long period of time and can become expensive depending on what the target did, where he went and how often it happened.

"Expense isn't an issue, but I am beginning to think I need to know what's going on. Look, I'm not sure … let's just say I need to think about a few things first. If I did decide to have you do some work for me, how should I go about it? When do I need to engage you, or whatever? Do I have to do something in advance? "

"The best time to start is the next time you notice something unusual in his behaviour. I would suggest not leaving it an open-ended arrangement, but that we set a period of about, say, a week in the first instance and see how it goes from there. It might be that we know all there is to know within a couple of days. The alternative is for you to contact me whenever you believe something is happening, and I will only undertake surveillance on those occasions. That way you won't be needlessly paying money to have me sitting around for no real outcome. So, it's up to you how we proceed and when we start."

The coffee machine was doing its thing as I wrote up my notes from the conversation with Trish and started a new case file. You never know, it might develop into a case at some time in the future and I couldn't rely on remembering everything from today. By the time I finished, a steaming mug of coffee was at my elbow and, when I looked up to thank Emily, I found her sitting forward on her chair watching me expectantly. "What...? Yes, it was a client; the lunatic from this morning."

"So, what do we have to do for her? I heard you mentioning surveillance..."

"What's this WE business? You are here to visit your mother. I might be undertaking surveillance for a client MAYBE sometime in the future. In the meantime, it amounted to just another 'I'll think about it' call."

Emily's phone rang. She checked the caller's number before indicating she would take the call outside. That's strange, but I nodded and she disappeared out the door. Perhaps she has found a man after all her mother's despair that neither of her daughters looked like ever marrying. It wasn't a long call. Her face when she returned suggested it wasn't a great call. Maybe not a man, I decided.

"That was Mum asking me if I thought I could manage to find myself something to eat tonight. The friend she visited has asked her to stay for dinner and, as you will be taking me home and she doesn't have to worry about me, she has agreed to stay with her friend." While Emily seemed a little put out about being fobbed off like that, I couldn't help laughing. At 29, Emily has been living alone for a lot of years and manages amongst other things to feed herself every day.

She flopped into the chair she vacated a few minutes earlier, leant forward and rested her forearms on the desk. "…So, I'm here with you for the rest of the afternoon. How about I help you with those jobs you're having trouble getting interested in? We'll get a bit done today, and then I could come back tomorrow to finish them off."

"Oh no, you're not avoiding time with your mother that easily. Anyway, the jobs I have are not the sort of thing you can hop into and knock over in an afternoon."

While Emily wasn't happy with my response, she seemed to accept it and we spent the remainder of the afternoon catching up on news of mutual friends. At about 5.30p.m., I suggested we take a drive to the harbour to try out one of the flock of new restaurants along the waterfront for dinner. Emily liked the look of a seafood place, so we had a white wine and ordered a kind of seafood buffet for two people. We agreed the seafood was average and expensive but there was plenty of it.

Lights were on at the Inneston residence. Sandra was already home. I dropped Emily off after turning down the invitation to come in for a nightcap. As I drove home, I realised the afternoon spent doing nothing with Emily proved a good tonic. I had shaken off my earlier blue funk.

Chapter 2

Friday found me in the office doing my routine end-of-week clear up of admin tasks. After a poor start, the week produced no significant drama. Two jobs I resisted making a start on were knocked over quickly once I got on with them. I finished the documentation for both cases and decided to take a coffee break before tackling something else. The soft 'whoosh' of my office door opening halted me mid-way to my kitchenette.

"Good, you are here … and about to make coffee, I hope," Emily said as she collapsed into what was becoming her customary chair.

"I thought about you earlier this morning and wondered whether you were still here or on your way back to Moxton."

"My thinking was to leave for home this morning, but I decided to stay the extra day."

"How's your mother, has her foul mood passed?"

"That's why I stayed the extra day. I'm not sure her mood hasn't gotten worse."

"Could it be a health problem, or something to do with money matters?"

"I asked about both those things."

"And…?"

"I'm still nursing my wounds. I doubt money is the problem. Mum is quite well off in her own right, and Dad made sure they were well provided for. Of course, the problem could be me upsetting her routine by being here. Anyway, I can't stay long. I need to spend the rest of the day being a dutiful daughter and getting ready to leave first thing in the morning."

*****

I completed another of the outstanding jobs over the weekend. It proved good money for not much work. I thought about it as I shoved my report, relevant photos and invoice into an envelope. On my way to the newsagent's last Sunday morning, I decided I wanted something to have with my coffee as I read the paper. My route to the baker's took me past the residence of the subject of my case, a man who allegedly suffered a serious back injury at work.

As I approached the house, the man barrelled down his driveway and out onto the street on an expensive looking pushbike. I parked briefly to let him get ahead a short distance, then followed him to the local squash centre. After watching him play a strenuous and lengthy game of squash, I followed as he pedalled home. I didn't think the insurance company would need much more than the photos to throw out his claim for a payout for a work-related permanently disabling back injury.

That left me with only one job to complete. Back in my office, I refreshed my memory of the case. Involving nothing more than trawling through records for particular information, this one will either take no time or prove frustrating and lengthy. No point in going anywhere until I explored everything the internet had to offer. I typed in the address of the first place on my list of likely places to investigate. It was one of those sites that thinks for ages before opening. I doodled while I waited and was admiring my efforts when my office door opened.

"Good morning, Sonny, could you spare me a few minutes, please?"

"Sandra…! Yes, I've got some time now. What brings you here on this fine Monday morning?"

"I think I have a … I was wondering if you might have time to do something for me."

"…As me, your friend, or as me, Sonoma Whittington the private investigator?"

"In your professional capacity … and I expect to pay your standard rates."

"Let me get you a coffee first, and then you can tell me what you want investigated."

We took our coffees to my couple of ancient lounge chairs that occupy space just inside the front door. From the moment she asked for my help, I suspected it was something personal and probably embarrassing for her to discuss. That was right on the money. Sandra struggled. It took much coaxing and encouragement before she opened up.

"As you are aware, my husband, Geoff, has been in prison for some time now, and will be there for many years to come. It has been difficult for me since his arrest. He was a leading public servant in this community; was held in high esteem. I think there is a certain faction in the town that has branded me guilty as well. By association, if you see what I mean."

"Aussies love to see a tall poppy brought down to earth. I don't doubt there are some who took pleasure from your husband's situation, but there has been many a wife who was just as unaware of what their husband was up to as you were. They stood resolute and, with the support of their friends, got on with their lives."

"I know all that, but I'm not coping with living in a community that has stigmatised me. So, after much soul-searching, I decided that moving from Millhaven might be for the best. A move back south to where I still have extended family and a daughter seemed a solution. I hadn't visited Geoff for a long time, but decided to share my thinking with him and discuss selling up. It seemed logical to me that, when Geoff finally was released, he would not be comfortable coming back to live in Millhaven, and it would be easier for him to assimilate into a different community where his past might not be known."

"What you propose makes sense, but there still could be complications when Geoff is released. How would you explain his appearance after not being around for all those years? It might mean another move – together as a couple – after his release."

"I don't think that's a consideration. We are only allowed to visit inmates once a month. My allocated visiting time was the third week of the month. I hated going there. It was horrible; the processes you had to go through and the way everyone looked at you. I went to visit him the first couple of months he was in that place, but I couldn't stand it and I was still coming to terms with what he had done and everything that happened. After those first two visits, I never went again until the third week of last month, just before Emily came to visit. I was refused entry."

"On what grounds…? Did they perceive you had done something wrong, or was there something wrong with Geoff that you couldn't see him?"

"No, nothing as simple as that, I would have understood if that were the case. They told me it was only three weeks since my last visit and that my week for visiting was the fourth week of the month. I… "

"The fourth week…? Had you forgotten which week? It had been a while since you visited, is it possible you were confused?"

"That was my immediate thinking, but I was sure I was right. That was the right week for me to visit. I fished around in my bag and found a note where I'd recorded all the dos and don'ts about visiting the prison. It clearly said the 'third week'. I showed it to them and argued the point, and eventually ended up getting myself escorted out to my car. As they bundled me into my car, they told me that as a result of my behaviour, they were tempted to block my next approved visit time."

"This doesn't make any sense, Sandra. There must be a mistake there somewhere, not necessarily yours, more like confused communication of some sort. What did you do after they escorted you out of the place?"

"What could I do? You know I'm not prone to tears, but I just sat there bawling. It was a terrible scene. Other visitors gawped at me as they went through the entry procedures and were let in. They must have thought I was the criminal, not the visitor. Anyway, when I ran out of tears, I just sat there. I suppose I was in shock, but I didn't know what to do and couldn't think straight. One of the guards just stood there watching me the whole time. After a while, one of the women who had been visiting someone inside came out. She noticed the state I was in and came to talk to me. At first, I couldn't make any sense of what she said. Her point seemed to be that I shouldn't pretend to be somebody else when I came to a place like that. I could get into serious trouble if they checked and discovered I wasn't who I claimed to be."

"I have a horrible feeling about where this is going, but carry on.

I take it you eventually sorted out what she was on about."

"Yes, but it took a while. Her son is an inmate and became seriously ill. He was in the infirmary or whatever it's called and they allowed her an extra visit to see him. Her normal week to visit is the fourth week of the month. I gather that the same group of women go there on the same day every month and, while some of them have become friends and support one another, others are only nodding acquaintances. After I finally got her to accept I was who I said I was, she explained what might have been behind the confusion. It seems that every month another Mrs Sandra Inneston visits Geoff. This … "

"I think you're about to confirm the idea I've been developing."

"She said the woman was much younger – too young for Geoff she thought – probably in late 40s. Always well dressed, usually in something like a business suit or smart pantsuit, the woman drove an expensive looking car – more expensive looking than mine she assured me."

"The obvious conclusion here is that Geoff has another woman in his life beside yourself and his two daughters. Is it possible that she is some sort of business associate, or worse still, that she is somehow connected to the business that landed him in gaol in the first place? Regardless, passing herself off as you does suggest guilt."

"I immediately thought the worst and then tried to dismiss it and find some other explanation. Not a particularly successful undertaking. The more I thought about what the woman told me, the angrier I became I decided that I was going to move south. If I couldn't get to see Geoff without all this fuss and bother being turned away again, I would write him a letter telling him what was happening."

"You haven't done that yet have you? We need to look into this a bit more I think before you commit anything in writing."

"No, not yet; I couldn't think of how to word it. I've been going through my things getting rid of anything no longer required. In the light of this new revelation and my response to it, I started going through Geoff's things as well. I was leaving Millhaven regardless of whether Geoff wanted to sell the house or not, so I was preparing for the move. Then I found it all. My suspicions were confirmed. The more I looked, the more I found; letters, emails, diary and photos. It was all there, everything you could possibly need to confirm a long running affair."

"You said there were photographs. Did you recognise the woman at all?"

"No, none showed her face. I know that sounds strange. I did think it strange at the time. There was one of a woman sunbaking on a towel at the beach. She was lying on her stomach on a beach towel and had a large sun hat covering her head. In another photo, he was adjusting his tie in front of a mirror in what looked like a hotel room. Women's clothes were laid out on the bed as if in preparation for a night out. Another shot appears to be taken from a balcony looking out over the ocean. You can just about make out the blurry reflection of a woman in one of the large glass sliding doors."

Sandra pushed an envelope across the desk and commented, "Those are copies. I've kept the originals."

Although it seemed straightforward, I spent the next 10 minutes questioning her about everything she had said, seen or thought since what had happened on her visit – attempted visit – to her husband. "I'm not sure why you're here, Sandra. What is it you want me to do for you?"

"I want to know who she is, what she does and what her connection is to my husband – apart from the obvious, of course."

"Okay, I think the likely starting point is when next she goes to see Geoff. I assume she visited him last week as that was the fourth week of the month. In that case, we will have to wait another three weeks before her next likely visit. I will do a bit of digging between now and then, but I'm not hopeful of finding anything as I don't know who the woman is. In the meantime, you must do nothing. Do not write to Geoff, don't talk to the girls about it – well, at least not until we know a bit more – and don't start talking to real estate agents. Okay?"

When she left, I felt confident she would do nothing to sabotage my investigation, but it took most of the morning to reach that point. After a quick flick through the photos, I typed up my notes from

Sandra's visit and created the new case file.

It was a bit earlier than my usual lunchbreak, but I decided to grab something now before returning to the case I started work on first thing this morning. For some perverse reason, a meatball sub appealed, so I walked the extra block. While my mind was miles away, I stood in the queue breathing in the aroma of freshly baked rolls.

I couldn't help wondering how Emily would react to her father's latest misdemeanour, if it proved to be that. Although I had met her sister twice, I didn't really know her. However, from Emily's comments in the past, I gathered that the sister was just as far from forgiving her father his criminal activity as Emily was. When her father was about to be arrested, I was the one who broke the news to Emily and sent her to support her mother when the news of his arrest broke. I suspect I might face a similar task sometime in the near future if current suspicions about her father prove true. The same concerns dogged me all through my lunch, and I found it difficult to settle down to work after I'd stretched my lunch break as long as possible.

Once I made a start, things flowed well. By four o'clock, I had exhausted all possible internet resources. While my research had been fruitful, it still lacked some details. My next target was the local newspaper archive. Some progress on digitising past copies of the local paper had been made, but it hadn't extended far enough yet to cover the period I needed. I rang the newspaper and arranged to research in their archives tomorrow morning.

It was still early. While I don't mind treating myself to an early finish occasionally, it didn't seem right to do that today. With nothing else screaming for attention to cloud my thinking, I returned to the Inneston case file. No miracles happened. Although I read through the notes again, and scrutinised each photograph using a magnifying glass, I found nothing to help identify the mystery woman. No point in staring at it any longer, I closed the file.

The frustration of not being able to get on with the investigation was overwhelming. I needed something to do, something to keep my mind off the case until the woman was due to visit the prison again. The problem is, apart from the research I hope to finish tomorrow, I have no other cases to work on. This time of the year often is quiet – although I've never worked out why – but I don't remember it being this quiet in the past. Should I just pack up and go home? Maybe going for a run or a workout at the gym would help.

I settled for yet another cup of coffee, opened the middle drawer of my desk, pushed my chair back and put my feet up on the drawer. With my eyes closed and lying back at an angle of about 45degrees in my chair, I sipped my coffee and tried to empty my mind of all thoughts. Apart from almost falling asleep, nothing happened until I was about halfway through the coffee. Then, a new question materialised to arouse me.

When arrested, Geoff Inneston was carrying his passport and other documentation indicating he was in the process of fleeing the country. He was tried and carted off to prison before Sandra knew about that part of the story. However, she knew about it by the time she first visited him in prison. She demanded an explanation. Later, she told me her husband said he planned taking a roundabout route to a country that afforded him the safety of non-extradition to Australia. He assured her that, as soon as he was safe and was set up in his new country, he would send for her.

In view of Sandra's story today, I have some doubts about the veracity of the promise to send for her once he was safely out of the country. If the affair, or whatever it is, with this other woman so openly continues, I suspect he planned a new life in another country with somebody other than Sandra. That thought led me back to the day Geoff Inneston was arrested at the airport. Was his lady friend also at the airport that day, and was she booked to fly with him? Perhaps she was to meet him somewhere along the way; Brisbane, Sydney, or even somewhere like Singapore. If I knew where she lived, I might get a better idea of how Geoff's exit from Australia was supposed to play out. I could be misjudging the man. At the time, he might have intended sending for Sandra as he told her.

My mind focused on Geoff Inneston's flit from Australia, as I packed up to go home. Somehow, I missed the worst of the afternoon traffic and had an easy run all the way.

It was just as well. The Inneston case never vacated my mind while I drove and later, when I retreated to my deck with a glass of cold white wine, the case came back with a vengeance to exercise my grey cells. I need to access records from back then but, after the best part of three years, my prospects were slim. I can't believe I am wishing Ben Richards was back here. He could prove useful in getting me access to some of the things I want to look at. There has to be something I can do in the meantime. Three weeks is a long time to wait before even a basic start on the investigation.

While I seemed unable to leave what little I knew of the case alone, I did manage to at least get it under control before I felt it safe to try for some sleep. It was a restless night. I woke several times although I don't think there was any time when I slept soundly. At some point during the wee small hours of the morning, a name came to me from the deep recesses of my memory banks – Sam – and that recall had me wide awake in an instance.

Sam Keller was a female detective attached to the Ralston squad. A few years back, she was seriously wounded protecting me. We had come into contact a few times in the intervening years and still kept in touch periodically by email. I knew instinctively that, sometime in the near future, Sam and I would be renewing our acquaintance, with or without Ben Richards' involvement.

Chapter 3

Tuesday brought two new jobs; nothing exciting but they would keep me occupied for two or three days. The first, an insurance job, involved surveillance but, as it was likely to be mostly daytime surveillance, it wouldn't be too difficult to suffer. Worried parents created the second job, which again looked like involving much surveillance work. Although their daughter was no longer a minor, they were concerned about her lifestyle choices. The girl already was wealthy in her own right thanks to an inheritance from a relative, and stood to benefit substantially in the near future from the imminent death of her grandmother.

This job looked as though it would involve mostly night time surveillance as the girl's practice was to sleep all day after being out all night. Isn't the saying something along the lines of 'beggars can't be choosers'? While I'm not exactly a beggar, a job is a job and means income … and might help keep my mind off the frustration of not being able to progress the Inneston case.

After spending Tuesday and Wednesday on surveillance for the insurance case, I was just about over this sitting-around-watching-people lark. Add into the mix Wednesday night spent watching a young girl behaving badly with an unsavoury looking group, and I am more than ready to spend Thursday in the office catching up on report writing.

I didn't hit the office until lunchtime. After being out all night, I figured three or four hours sleep might be useful before attacking the admin tasks. It still took me a while to settle into writing the report on the insurance job. I was mentally composing the concluding paragraphs when the phone rang.

"Sonny, it's Emily. I'm going to spend the next few days in Millhaven. As soon as I finish work this afternoon, I'll drive up. … Should be there about eight o'clock tonight."

"Take care with the driving. Has something happened that you're coming back to Millhaven so soon?"

21

"No… Well, yes… Oh, damn it, I don't know. Something is not right. I'll tell you about it when I'm there. Have you got time to see me tomorrow?"

"Yep, but not until about lunchtime. How about you come in around 12 o'clock and we start by having lunch together?"

Emily wasn't particularly thrilled about having to wait until lunchtime. I didn't bother explaining that I'd be out all night on surveillance work again. The risk was she would want to come to 'help'. That was to be avoided at all cost, and I did need a few hours' sleep before dealing with whatever situation had triggered her return.

Thursday night's surveillance went quite well. My target followed what seemed to be her regular routine, went out about eight o'clock, met up with a disreputable looking group of friends and spent the night nightclubbing. I took myself into one of the venues for a better look at what was happening. There were no surprises; much alcohol being consumed along with other illegal substances. A bonus was that I managed to chat to a few female patrons who were happy to dish the dirt on my target. By the time I followed her home at about 6.00a.m., I had enough to confirm her parents' concerns about their daughter. What they did with the information – if there was anything they could do – was up to them. My part, according to my brief, was done.

Friday followed Thursday's pattern. The only difference was that, after sleeping to almost lunchtime, I rushed into the office to meet up with Emily for lunch. My antennas twitched and my instinct went on high alert the moment Emily entered my office. This was not the confident exuberant woman I knew. This Emily seemed unsure and twitchy.

"Are you right to go somewhere for lunch, or do you have something to finish first?" She asked without wasting time on any greetings or preamble.

We walked to a small bistro in the next block. The food was good. Conversation was in short supply. In spite of my best efforts to get Emily talking, her sporadic contribution to conversation screamed 'not interested'. We didn't linger long over lunch before heading back to my office. On behalf of both of us, I had declined coffee at the bistro in a bid to end the situation.

As we started down the corridor to my office, I heard my phone ringing. There was no point in hurrying. I went straight to the kitchenette and put fresh coffee on to brew, casting an eye at the phone as I went past my desk. The red light was blinking in response to a new message. It could wait.

Armed with two steaming mugs of coffee, I made my way to the two battered lounge chairs and invited Emily to join me there. With no evident enthusiasm, she climbed out of her customary chair in front of my desk and slowly made her way across to the empty lounge chair. I had a distinct hollow feeling in the pit of my stomach. Whatever brought Emily back to Millhaven so soon would not be good news.

"Okay, it's talk time. Why have you come back so soon? ...No, I want the real reason, not something you think might fob me off. You asked to see me. So, come on, start talking."

"The trouble is, I don't know what to tell you. I just know something is not right – not right at home, I mean – not right with Mum. That mood she was in before hasn't gone away. It seems to be worse. Both my sister and I have been calling her regularly, thinking that might help with whatever was bothering her. It hasn't. Then my sister rang me a couple of days ago after speaking to Mum. She told me Mum said she would be moving back to Brisbane and maybe soon. She was talking about selling up and getting out of Millhaven."

In reply, I could only murmur a noncommittal, "Hmm..." Emily shot me a look that clearly indicated I should offer more of a response, so I obliged. "I suppose that does come as a surprise. It can't be easy for her living here with everyone knowing what happened with your father and where he is now."

"I suppose I understand that, but can she sell up without his authority? I'm sure everything here is in both names. Mum never wanted to live in Millhaven. It was Dad who took the job here and made it clear they were here to stay. I can't see him agreeing to sell up."

"It is going to be a lot of years yet before he has to decide where he wants to live but, when the time comes, I imagine it might be difficult for him to integrate back into the Millhaven community."

"Yeah, I suppose… If Mum would talk about what's at the bottom of all this, we might be able to help her."

"Sandra is an independent woman used to making her own decisions. She will struggle with this one, but she will need to deal with it in her own way."

I breathed a silent 'thank you' when the phone interrupted conversation. I was struggling to maintain Sandra's client confidentiality while watching Emily tie herself in knots with worry over her mother. I walked round my desk and flopped onto my chair as I answered the phone.

"Hello Sonoma, this is Trish, Trish Fielding. We spoke a week or so ago about my husband, Terry Fielding."

Only half my mind was dealing with the phone. I groped around in the murky regions of my memory for some previous reference to the name Trish Fielding. Bingo! Recollection finally clicked into place. "Of course, Trish, I remember your concern about what your husband might be up to. What can I do for you?"

"You explained everything to me about how you work and the costs and all that stuff the last time we spoke. You said that, if I wanted to do something about it, the best time to start was when something funny was about to happen."

"That's not quite what I said, but close enough. If you get some indication something that concerns you is about to go down, that's when you should call me. That way time and money won't be wasted sitting around in the off chance something might happen. So, if you are calling because of that sort of situation, this might be the right time to start an investigation."

"That's good. Can you start today? He's just rung to say he's working late tonight and might be gone all night. I find that hard to believe. It's completely out of character, although sometimes he does work late, it doesn't take all night."

"Yes, I can start this evening, but I need a whole lot of information beforehand. I don't even know what Terry Fielding looks like, where he works, or anything else about him."

"I took an envelope to the post office and asked them to put it in your mailbox. It contains a photo of Terry and a note providing his physical description. He works at Thornton Transport. Not a driver, he has some sort of office job, maybe a dispatcher or something similar, and only works normal daytime office hours."

"What sort of vehicle does he drive, and what is his standard finishing time in the afternoon?"

"He is supposed to finish at 4.30p.m., and leaves between then and five o'clock. He drives a little red Korean made sedan."

That came as a surprise. I expected him to drive something a bit more butch than that. Trish must've picked up on my surprise. She rushed on to explain. "He hates it, but it was his daughter's that is his daughter from his first marriage. She was going overseas, needed extra cash, and talked her father into buying it from her." Trish gave me the registration number.

I arranged to start surveillance today and suggested I report back in a couple of days. She vetoed that idea. She would contact me whenever she suspected something was happening and I could report back then. I understood that she didn't want me calling her. At some point during my conversation with Trish, Emily mimed 'refilling our coffee mugs'. I nodded enthusiastically. She disappeared into the kitchenette, which was no bigger than a cupboard and, when the doors were closed, that's exactly what it looked like: a built in cupboard.

A few minutes of silence followed while I read through my notes while we sipped our coffees. "Who was the caller? I gather you've got another case."

"It was… oh, you might remember her. It was the 'lunatic' – later know as Trish – who thought I was having it off with her husband. She has decided she does want to know what he is up to."

Emily gathered up the empty mugs, rinsed them and closed the kitchenette up again. When she regained her seat opposite me at the desk, I asked, "Do you feel like a drive?" She nodded. "I need to go to a couple of places in preparation for tonight. By the way, where have you left your car? I don't want you to get a parking ticket for staying there too long."

"It's okay. I didn't come into town in it. It is due for a major service and needed new tyres. On my way into town, I left it to have the work done and Mum dropped me here. Because I was so late dropping it in, I won't be able to collect it until tomorrow afternoon. Mum said to give her a call when I was ready to go home. She will pick me up."

"There's no need for that. I can drop you home later."

My first port of call was the post office. Emily remained in the car while I dashed across to retrieve Trish's envelope from my mailbox. Back in the car, I examined its contents while Emily finished a phone call.

"That was Mum. She asked whether it might be possible for you to drop me home. I didn't say you already volunteered. She has some things to do and won't be home until later this evening and suggested I either have dinner with you or bring something home for myself. Her abandoning me seems to be becoming a habit. It's out of character."

I couldn't work out whether Emily was offended or worried by her mother's actions. She shoved her phone back into her bag, snatched the envelope's contents from me and studied them as I drove off.

After a couple of minutes, she sat up and looked around. "Where are we going? This is not the most picturesque end of town."

"The place I'm looking for is up here somewhere I think. Yes, there it is, over there on the left."

There was no traffic on the street. I crawled along taking in as much as I could of the layout of Thornton Transport and other businesses in its immediate vicinity. A little further along the street, I made a U-turn and came back along the street to park in front of a car detailing business. On the opposite side of the street and back a bit from Thornton Transport's main entrance, I had a good view of vehicles in the Thornton employees' car park just inside their main gate. I decided this is where to park to watch vehicles leaving Thornton's. As I made moves to drive away. Emily announced she needed a sugar fix and asked me to stop at the diner a little further along the street so she could buy something to chew.

Her hunting and gathering expedition complete, she handed me a KitKat and, as she strapped herself in, commented, "You can't take anything at face value can you? That place is surprisingly nice inside; clean, and it doesn't have a bad menu. It might get plenty of custom from Thornton employees."

I munched one stick of my KitKat before driving back to the office. Once we were settled at my desk again and after I had dealt with the rest of the KitKat, I broached the subject of Sandra's filthy mood. "I know the last time you were here, you said she was upset by the woman in the shoe shop, but she's never been quite so abrupt with me before. Did I do something to upset her?" Since my meeting with Sandra, I understand the root cause of her 'mood', but I want to know if Emily has any ideas worthwhile knowing about.

"No, she was like that when I arrived last time, although she became worse after her run in at the shoe shop. She is treating me a bit like a leper as well. I intended spending the week here last time, but seriously considered leaving early when her mood didn't improve. My visit was to give her some knickknacks my sister and I bought for her while we were away."

"I didn't know you'd been away."

"Mum and my sister were supposed to do a 10-day tour of part of the US. My sister arranged to take leave and made all of the bookings. When she sent all the information home, Mum said she never agreed to go; only that she would think about it. The bottom line was, Mum flatly refused to go on the trip. Rather than let my sister lose money, I went instead. When we got back, I came straight up here and found Mother less than warm and welcoming. I thought she might be offside about my taking her place on the trip. I asked her a couple of times whether that was the case. She assured me it wasn't. She never wanted to do the trip in the first place."

"Have you been to see your father lately? Could he be something to do with what's upset your mother?" I thought back on that difficult time for the family some time ago now when Emily's father, Geoff Inneston, a high ranking public servant at the time, was arrested for his involvement in a drug trafficking network operating within the Public Service. He was apprehended as he was about to skip the country and received a lengthy prison sentence.

"No, I haven't been to see him since he went to prison. He went into a gaol up north but, a few weeks ago he was supposed to move to that new correctional centre down south somewhere. I don't think Mum's visited him either. She did go to see him a couple of times soon after his incarcerated because she needed to sort out a few things. I don't think she's been to see him since."

The whole sordid thing really rocked the family. While both of his daughters lived too far away, in reality neither of them displayed had any inclination to visit him in gaol.

Emily checked her watch. "What time are you going to start your surveillance this evening?"

Her question made me check the time. "Thanks for the heads up. I need to be in position a bit before half four. I'd better get myself organised." It was four o'clock.

I threw everything I needed into my bag and stood up to leave. Emily grabbed her bag from the floor beside her chair and stood as well. "I'm heading off now. Where are you going?" I asked.

"With you; I'm stranded here, remember. You are to take me home, and you don't have time to take me home before you start your surveillance. Therefore, I'm coming with you, and will stay with you until such time as you're finished and can take me home." She beamed at me, and I knew I wasn't in a position to argue. We headed for the car, me scowling and Emily smiling broadly.

I parked in the place I picked out earlier. Thornton's employee's car park didn't appear to have thinned out any during our absence. Emily made some comment about being prepared for the 'long haul', climbed out of the car and wandered along to the diner. On her return, she juggled chocolate bars, a couple of apples and a newspaper. "No bags…,"she offered by way of explanation as I reached across to open her door before she dropped everything. She read the newspaper, insisting it gave us some credibility while we waited. I'd never found it necessary in the past, but I didn't bother to argue the point.

A few minutes after 4.30p.m., the first of the cars exited the employee's carpark. At first a dribble, and then a continuous flow of cars departed, none of which included the red car we were interested in. By five o'clock, few vehicles remained. The red car now stood out from among the heavy duty 4x4s which were its only companions.

"Maybe he does have to work," Emily suggested. "He wouldn't hang around for long if he didn't have to."

She has a point but as I pondered her suggestion, at five o'clock, we watched a security guard come to the gates, and do something in a small box mounted on one of the gates' supporting pylons. The massive steel gates slid closed. After shaking them to make sure the gates locked properly, the guard disappeared. A couple of hours later, a loaded semi-trailer rolled up to the main gate. The locked gates barred its access.

The driver reached across to the other side of the cab, ducked down out of sight to reappear seconds later. He extended his arm across the cabin towards the gate pylon that had the small box attached. A moment later, the huge gates slid open. He must have used some kind of remote device.

"Doesn't that look like a loading dock over there?" Emily asked. She pointed to an area in the front right of the building. Its doors stood wide open revealing a well-lit tunnel stretching back into the bowels of the building. There was no mistaking it for what it was: a loading bay wide enough to take two semi-trailers side by side.

As we watched, the newly arrived semi drove past the loading bay and disappeared around the far side of the building. "Where's he going," Emily asked.

"He had a fair load on board. Maybe semi-trailers unload in another area, and the area we see from here is where they are loaded – not unloaded. It might need to be that way to ensure incoming and outgoing freight is kept separate."

"How do we find out? We can't drive in to carry out a tour of the facility. By the look of those gates, there is no way we can get in at all. Do you think our target might have stayed to help unload that semi? That would explain why he is still here so late. I wonder if he has to hang around to unload others arriving later."

Good questions and sound assumptions, but there was nothing we could do about any of it except sit and wait to see what else happened. It was six o'clock. Although it is spring, the days have not yet begun to lengthen. Darkness descended over the next quarter of an hour as we sat with our eyes glued to the transport company's massive building. To avoid fogging up the windows and making us conspicuous, our windows were about halfway down. The evening was cool, cooler than I expected. By seven o'clock, night was fully installed and I was beginning to wish I brought a jacket.

The only lights in the area were the security lights in the various businesses, and the diner and transport depot which were well-lit, street lights apparently not considered necessary in this part of the industrial estate. I raised the windows a little in a bid to keep out the night's damp chill. The orange blossom-like perfume from the flowering Murraya hedge across the front of the car detailing place wafted in on the heavy night air.

A few minutes later, Emily shivered as a cold gust of wind invaded the car. It brought with it another perfume, the sweet scent of jasmine. I hadn't seen any jasmine plants around here but there had to be one somewhere nearby. In the wake of the gust of wind, we became aware of a different aroma. The smell of onions frying taunted us.

"I've just realised that not only am I freezing, I'm also starving." Emily underlined her comment by sniffing in a lungful of eau-de-frying onions. "We could go and sit in that little diner. It's quite all right inside. I'm sure they would have coffee and, as nothing worth noting appears to be happening over the road, maybe we could have a meal while we wait."

"I'm sure the surveillance handbook says something about not doing that," I replied, adopting the high moral ground on the issue. I had to admit though that the smell of those onions reminded me I also was hungry. The chocolate bars and apples Emily bought earlier, and now sitting abandoned on the back seat, just would not do it for me. I needed something hot and solid. I was about to relent and agree to adjourn to the diner when a vehicle's headlights shone out from alongside the transport company building.

Chapter 4

"Sit tight, Emily. There's a vehicle on the move over the road; see, coming along the opposite side of the building from where our semi went." As I finished speaking, the nose of a prime mover came into view. Once the cabin cleared the front of the building, the driver hesitated. Then, instead of continuing straight ahead to the gate as I anticipated, it turned left, drove across the front of the building and reversed into the loading bay. It appeared to be the same prime mover and semitrailer that arrived earlier.

People materialised from nowhere and soon had the tarpaulins off and were unloading the freight. I grabbed a pair of night vision binoculars and began checking each of the bodies working in the loading bay. It was a hive of activity. A forklift ran around, an overhead crane lifted a huge crate and deposited it on some sort of trolley which a small tractor then towed out of sight. I jumped when Emily spoke.

"Look!" She yelped. "There are more headlights coming from where that semitrailer came out."

I swung the binoculars around to the far corner of the building. "Smaller vehicle this time; its headlights are lower and closer together. I stayed focused on the area where the vehicle would emerge from alongside the building. A light truck with a high enclosed canopy over its tray drove out and straight to the gates.

"It's coming out. What do we do now?" Emily asked.

"That depends on which way it goes when it exits those gates. If it turns left, we will be lit up by its headlights. Sit tight. If it looks like turning left, dive down below the level of the dashboard. If it turns right as it leaves the property, we will be invisible sitting in the car in this darkened street."

The truck stopped at the gates. We watched the driver use a remote device to open them. He drove out, paused briefly at the edge of the kerb, turned right and disappeared down the street.

"What do you make of that?" Emily asked.

"I don't know, but I think it was involved with whatever that semi was doing out the back where we couldn't see it." My binoculars were trained back on the loading bay. So far, there was no sign of Terry Fielding over there, or in the departing truck. While his car remained in the car park, it was reasonable to assume he was in there somewhere. We watched for about another 10 minutes after the truck left, but nothing of any consequence occurred. "This might be a good time for us to pay that diner a visit," I suggested.

"I'm not sure whether it's your stomach or mine that's rumbling, but a visit to the diner might make for a quieter evening if we are stuck in this car for a while longer tonight."

No time wasted, we soon were seated at a table and reading the menu. The staff didn't hide their surprise at two females dropping in unexpectedly at this time of the evening. Nevertheless, the service was good and the food arrived quickly. It was an excellent meal and our coffee afterwards was every bit as good. We lingered for quite a while. Aware that staying too long might arouse interest, with reluctance we returned to the freezing confines of my car.

"What's our game plan?" Emily asked. "What happens if our friend does spend the whole night at work, do we sit here all night as well?"

"That's a good question. I haven't seen him but I assume he is still on the premises. It's nearly 10.30p.m. I think I have to stay until at least midnight. Too bad it's not the exciting evening you expected. You'd probably prefer being tucked up in bed. If you can bear it, let's wait another half an hour. If nothing happens by then, I'll drive you a short distance away from here and call a cab to take you home."

"No you won't. If you're going to stay all night, so am I. Besides, it will be easier to explain things to Mother in the morning, rather than waking her up in the middle of the night and trying to explain where I've been."

Eleven o'clock came and went. Soon after that, the loading bay plunged into darkness and its huge doors rumbled closed. It was a while after that before any further activity occurred at the transport depot. Propped against the window and with the newspaper spread across her body as a makeshift rug, Emily had dozed off long before I saw someone make their way to one of the vehicles in the car park.

I retrieved the binoculars from where I'd dropped them on the floor. The man in the car park I recognised as one I saw earlier helping unload the semitrailer. He wasn't Terry Fielding. There was little chance of mistaking this burly big blonde bloke for the slight dark-haired Terry in the photograph. The man climbed into one of the SUVs and let himself out through the gate. I held my breath for a moment, but he too turned right and growled off down the street away from us.

My eyes felt heavy. I fought to keep them open and to resist the temptation to follow Emily's example. Thornton's was in darkness. That seemed to indicate no further trucks were expected tonight. If that were the case, surely the handful of men I'd seen in the loading bay would go home. I was contemplating getting out of the car and walking around it in the night air to wake myself up when movement in the car park made me freeze with my hand on the door handle.

Two groups of men came out from around the side of the building and walked towards the car park. The first group comprised four men. Three climbed into one of the SUVs while their fourth member went to another of the vehicles. The second group, trailing the first group by five or six metres, consisted of three people, one of whom could be a woman. One of the men in this last group went to the last remaining SUV.

I continued to focus on the member of the group I thought might be a woman. In a baggy high visibility work shirt, work trousers and boots, and wearing a cap, it was difficult to decide on the gender of that well-rounded third person. The other person of this pair I confirmed as Terry Fielding. Dark hair, swarthy skinned, shortish (170cm according to Trish), slim – make that 'skinny' – build, middle age paunch developing ('and going to seed' Trish had added) … Yep, this last man was Terry Fielding. "And will you look at that…," I murmured.

"Wha… what? … Look at what?" Emily asked drowsily as she fought to join me in the real world.

"Sssshh, Terry Fielding is heading for his car, and it looks like he has a passenger," I whispered.

The small red sedan was the only car left in the car park, and these last two people made their way over to it. An apparent gentleman,

Terry walked his companion to the passenger's side of the vehicle and opened the door. Before climbing into the car, the other person removed their cap and shook out a mane of light coloured hair. A mass of long (probably) blonde hair coupled with having the door opened for you... yeah, definitely female, I decided.

"Maybe the lunatic wife was right," Emily suggested. "Looks like darling Terry does have something going on away from home."

"That's called jumping to conclusions," I replied without much conviction. "There could be a simple explanation. He might be giving a fellow employee a lift home. Perhaps it's a regular occurrence. Ride sharing happens all the time in workplaces without any complicated contexts attached. The real test is what happens next. Remember, Trish expects he could be 'at work' all night."

"You think he gave Trish that story to clear him for not going home until after breakfast with his friend?"

"Could be.... But there is only one way to find out his plans for the rest of the night."

"Oh good, something is happening at last." In preparation for that 'something', Emily sat up straight, folded the newspaper and threw it onto the back seat. She rubbed her face to wake it up. As she ran her hand through her hair, she demanded, "Right, what do we do next?"

Terry had a problem opening the gates. He pointed his remote device at the box on the pillar several times, each time his action more emphatic than the last. Then, probably to his great relief, the gates slid open. I heard him gun the motor but underpowered, it was slow to respond. The scenario that flashed through my mind was the car being sandwiched between the gates if it didn't get through before they closed. It was a waste of a thought. The gates were calibrated to allow enough time for prime movers attached to semitrailers to pass through before closing automatically.

Once the car responded to Terry's heavy foot, it shot through the gates, rocketed across the footpath and bounced onto the street. Was that the slight screech of tyres I heard as he yanked it hard right before roaring off down the street? It was a relief that he turned right. At that speed, had he turned left, we wouldn't have time to slide from view. Again I marvelled at the silent operation of those enormous gates as they slid closed.

From the time I saw Terry and his companion heading for the little red car, I flexed my ankles, my wrists, my fingers and any other bits of me that seemed to have become numb from sitting too long. Now that it was time to move, I felt reasonably confident that all of me was in normal working condition again. I reached for the ignition as the taillights, now so far ahead, turned left and disappeared at the end of this long straight street. At this hour of the night, and with so little traffic around, tailing Terry would not be easy.

When we turned left at the end of the street, I was relieved to see Terry's taillights glowing red in the distance. So far, we hadn't lost him down some side street. There was an advantage in having so little traffic to contend with. The only vehicle we can see is Terry's. The downside is that, in the empty street, we stand out as a possible tail. Terry must be confident there are no Highway Patrols around at this hour as he headed towards the city heart at well above the speed limit and didn't slow down until he reached the first set of lights.

He travelled past the main shopping centre at a sedate pace until he crossed the bridge and was on the road leading to one of the beach suburbs. I was reasonably confident Terry wouldn't expect a tail and wouldn't be looking for one. Nevertheless, I felt it wise to employ some strategic manoeuvres rather than following him in a straight line from start to finish.

By the time we reached the city centre, the gap between our two cars had shortened. Then, at the road's junction with Queen Street, the main street running through the centre of town, instead of following Terry across Queen Street, I turned onto the street and drove a few blocks along it. Out of the corner of my eye, I saw Emily sit up. She looked from right to left as we headed along Queen Street.

"Where the hell are you going? We are going to lose him. What are we doing driving around the middle of town?"

"We won't lose him. He is heading for that new beachside suburb of Sandlands. At least, I think that's where he is heading. Anyway, if he does turn off, there is only that one small older suburb between here and Sandlands, so he shouldn't be too hard to find if we do lose him."

After a couple more blocks along Queen Street, I turned off towards the river and drove back along Riverside Drive to meet up once more with the road we had turned off a few minutes earlier. We crossed the bridge and I felt we were far enough out of the city heart to exceed the speed limit a bit. Emily had no faith in my tactics. She sat forward in her seat, straining the seatbelt, and peering into the darkness ahead for any sign of taillights.

The housing density increased as we approached the older suburb which sprawled along the left-hand side of the road. There was no sign of taillights. Even I was beginning to doubt the wisdom of my action. "We've lost him. I knew we would. We should drive through there to see if we can spot the car anywhere," Emily said. She made no effort to mask her disappointment.

"No, if we don't find him somewhere up ahead, we can come back and have a drive around in there." Almost convinced we would be coming back to search this suburb, I applied a little more speed. Although I didn't bother acquainting Emily with the fact, I was determined to go as far as Sandlands before turning back. It all became hypothetical a few minutes later when two pinpoints of red light appeared in the distance. I was travelling a bit faster than Terry. I managed to close the gap between our two cars until his taillights became clear.

A short distance after you drive under the fancy archway welcoming you to Sandlands, a long semicircular drive leads off to the left from the road that continues through the centre of the suburb. The other end of the drive joins the road again a short distance beyond the suburb's main shopping precinct. Terry turned onto the drive and disappeared around the curve. I drove through to the shopping precinct, went round the roundabout beyond the end of the built-up area of the suburb, and drove back out under the welcoming archway. A small parkland area prior to the entrance to the suburb provided easy access to the beach and a pleasant place to relax for non-suburb residents.

I drove into the park and parked facing the suburb's entrance. Emily shot her seat back and started to stretch out. "Don't get too comfortable, we might not be staying long."

"Aren't we going to sit here and wait for him to come out now we've lost him in there somewhere?" She said gesturing toward the suburb and I shook my head. "So, I assume we're going to wait here till he reappears."

"No. Think about what he might be doing. Trish might be right. He might intend spending the rest of the night with his passenger, or he might be dropping off his colleague. If the latter is the case, he should reappear after a few minutes on his way back to town. However, if he doesn't reappear after a reasonable period of time, it might be safe to assume he's spending the night. In that case, after the elapse of a reasonable period of time, we will take ourselves a trip along that drive in search of a little red car parked somewhere in there."

"Ah, I see. What's a reasonable period of time feel like?"

"Dunno; have to play it by ear."

Emily reached across to the back seat and delved into the pile of goodies she bought at the diner earlier. "Apple or chocolate bar…?" She asked and held up one of each. The apple still didn't do it for me, so I opted for the chocolate bar which, to my utter satisfaction, contained bits of nuts and layers of wafer. The only problem with eating it was that it dried my mouth out and I needed a drink of water afterwards.

We had emptied the small bottles of water I had in the centre console. I keep a couple of larger bottles of water in the luggage area in case I get stuck on a long surveillance job. A walk around to the rear of the car felt good after sitting cooped up for so long. It felt so good, I kept walking and wandered round in the park for a bit before returning to the car. After retrieving a large bottle of water from the luggage area, I climbed back in behind the steering wheel. "No sign of any cars while you were away," Emily assured me.

"No, I kept an eye out. I think it's time we went on a journey of exploration. Keep your eyes peeled for anything that looks like a little red car, and hope it's parked out in the open and not hidden in a garage somewhere."

An interesting mix of residences lined both sides of the drive. They ranged from exaggerated mansions sprawling over at least two blocks, to low-rise blocks of units and small cottages, with a number of small well-tended parks scattered in between. The four streets leading off from the drive all ended in cul-de-sacs. We explored each of them. There was no little red car. We had reached the other end of the drive and, as anticipated, Emily's question was, "Now what?"

I asked myself the same question but, so far, came up with only a vague answer. "I suppose it is possible he suspected he was being tailed. He might have turned onto the drive in a bid to lose any suspected tail. If that is the case, all he did was to employ much the same tactic as we used back in the city centre."

"What you're suggesting is that he drove all the way along the drive, came back onto the main road through the suburb, and continued on to somewhere further along in the suburb."

"Well, that's one explanation for why we didn't find the car anywhere along that drive. The other scenario is that the car is parked under cover – in a garage or something – where it is invisible to passers-by. I suppose the latter is plausible given that he might not want his illicit affair, if that's what it is, to become public knowledge."

With not much else to do, I drove to the far end of the suburb exploring every side street along the way. Still no sign of the little red car. I checked the time on the dashboard clock. It was now 2.00a.m. After negotiating the huge roundabout at the far end of the suburb, I drove back through Sandlands and pulled into the park where we waited previously. "Make yourself as comfortable as possible, Emily. This is where we will be in a few hours' time when the little red car comes out on its way to work."

"What time is that likely to happen?"

"Dunno exactly; Trish said he leaves for work about seven o'clock. I doubt he'll go home before going into work this morning, but he does have further to go from here to get to Thornton's. So, if he is going into work, it's possible he might leave a bit before seven o'clock. However, having supposedly worked all night, he might choose to go home first for a few hours' sleep before facing up to work."

"Great, that means we've got the best part of five hours to wait.

What if he leaves wherever he is earlier than that, say, before the neighbours are awake and might notice him leaving? If we are asleep, we won't see him leave. How is this supposed to work?"

"It won't be a problem, because I won't be asleep. However, I suggest you get some sleep. You're cranky when you've had a late night."

After my forthright comment, the vibes suggested the onset of a sulk. I abandoned the car and left Emily to indulge in her sulk alone. It wasn't such a bad thing. If she found nothing enjoyable about tonight, it might make her think twice before 'helping' me with my investigations in future.

Chapter 5

A watery moon appeared periodically from behind scudding clouds. I had no idea what the weather forecast was for tomorrow – which was now today – but I hoped it included no mention of any precipitation. The night was cold and damp and uncomfortable enough already without adding rain to the joy of being cooped up in a car all night. As I ventured into the park on foot, my bladder cramped, letting me know it was in need of urgent attention. With no facilities in sight and none that I knew of anywhere close by, I headed for a dense patch of plants a little further into the park.

With that taken care of and feeling more relaxed about life, I continued wandering aimlessly through the park, eventually finding myself at its eastern edge. Beyond the post and rail fence that marked the park boundary, the lush greenness of the park gave way to sand stretching down to the waves coming in from the Pacific Ocean. Not wanting to fill my boots with sand, I climbed up and sat on the top rail of the fence for a while, just listening to the gentle lapping of the waves and breathing in the briny sea air.

The next time I checked the time, it was after 3.00a.m. It was darker, the moon now blotted out by a thick cloud blanket that I hadn't noticed roll in. Off the fence, I turned to start back to the car. The park now loomed as a dark forbidding void in front of me. "Try not to fall over or into anything as you go," I told myself aloud as I began the return journey. This place that seemed so idyllic and calm before, now felt strangely intimidating as I forced myself to walk through it.

Where the hell is the car? I've no idea where I am, but I've been walking long enough to have walked right through the park and out the other side… and still no sign of the car. I giggled. I was beginning to sound like Emily. I had no trouble admitting to myself I was tired, cranky, and fed up with being cold and damp, but how the hell could I have lost the car? Just keep walking, I told myself. You must come out on the road soon. For a few moments, that weak moon appeared through a transient hole in the clouds. I took advantage of it to scan the area. A long way in the distance, I could make out a dark shape: Eureka, my missing car.

As I trudged towards it, the moon disappeared again, but I was homed in on the vehicle. Confident I would now find it even in the blackness, I marched on quickening my pace as I went. Apart from losing the car, it had all gone too well for too long not to have something happen. A rock firmly embedded in the ground was that 'something'. It made heavy contact with my boot as I strode along, and tipped me face first into the leaf litter surrounding it. I'd kicked the rock hard and now couldn't work out which hurt most, my foot, my ankle or my knee. After dusting myself off, I hobbled to the car. I was damp from the night air, my hands are filthy from where I'd used them to break my fall, and I suspect some of the leaf litter adorns my face as well.

I opened the luggage compartment to retrieve the other large bottle of water to wash off some of the grime. As I reached for the bottle, I spied the bag in the opposite corner. It was my wet weather bag containing a pair of gumboots, a flimsy plastic rain poncho and a large beach towel. I didn't need the boots or the poncho, but the towel would be handy. I wrestled it out of the bag, completed my clean up, and took the towel with me when I slid back into the driver's seat. Emily had her seat reclined and was sound asleep with her newspaper 'blanket' in place once more.

The cold water I splashed over my face worked wonders. I almost felt alive again, but there wasn't much I could to entertain myself without waking Emily. I decided to get out of the car again and go around to the luggage compartment. The small light that comes on when the compartment is open provides enough light for me to write up my notes. Not that there was much to record so far but, in the interests of accuracy, it is best to document everything as soon as possible after it happens… and it will help keep me awake.

A faint sound made me pause as I was about to pop the lock on the luggage compartment. It was a vehicle, still some way off but coming this way from the direction of town. I slipped back into the driver's seat and hunched down as the headlights drew closer. It didn't sound like a car. The headlights, much closer now, suggested it was something bigger than a car.

That's when the moon chose to make one of its periodic appearances for a few moments before the next cloud rolled over it. That was long enough to make out the light truck with the high, enclosed rear canopy coming my way. It went past at a sedate pace, the driver probably intent on avoiding unwanted attention by exceeding the speed limit.

As it passed, I slid out of the car and raced to the edge of the road. A quick look both ways and I was out in the centre of the road… in time to see the truck slow and turn off to the left before disappearing from sight. I stood there in the middle of the road for a few moments wondering what I should do – what I could do! The short answer came to me quickly: 'nothing'.

It was a coincidence beyond belief that, at that hour of the morning, a car drove along that drive so soon after the truck. Aware of my painful left leg, I limped back to the car. I hadn't noticed it hurt when I rushed out onto the road. My phone showed it was almost five o'clock. If that was 'our' truck that drove past, where had it been for the last few hours, and why?

The clouds hung around, but the sky was lightening, although still a while away from daylight. I decided to give it a bit longer, maybe half an hour or so, before taking another look along the semicircular drive. A small red car might be easy to hide, but hiding a truck with a high canopy on the back might be another matter. Perhaps it parked out in the open somewhere.

Patience not being one of my strong points, about 10 minutes later, I shook Emily awake and explained what I was about to do. Her mouth still numb from sleep, she mumbled something I couldn't understand. However, she hauled herself and her seat upright without complaint. She was still blinking and rubbing her face as I drove out onto the road and headed for the turnoff onto the drive. As I turned off, I noticed a street sign indicating the drive was called Grevillea Crescent. I was about to tell Emily to keep her eyes peeled for the red car or the truck, but one glance in her direction assured me she was already on the job.

"What's the time?" she asked. "Is it too early for Terry to leave for work, or home, or wherever he might go next?"

"It's not quite 5.30. I don't think he will be going anywhere yet. Perhaps he had to move his car to accommodate the truck in some way. We might get lucky if that happened. His car could be out in the open now."

As we approached the second side street off the Crescent, Emily jerk upright. "Stop, stop; pull over!" The urgency in her voice left me in no doubt I needed to do that.

"What's up... what did you see?" I had pulled up against the kerb about five metres from the entrance to the side street. I grabbed the newspaper and folded it to the size of a sheet of paper.

"What are you doing...?" Emily demanded.

"I'm creating what looks like a legitimate reason for us to stop here. The hope is that anyone watching will think we are trying to find an address. Now, stop fussing about what I'm doing and tell me why we are here."

"Look, over there..." She pointed towards a spot in the side street, ahead of us and slightly to our left. "See the second house on that side of the side street; it has a large shed down the back. Can you see the shed?"

"I can see the shed and I can see the truck parked inside. Kind of them to leave the shed doors open like that wasn't it? ...And that's not all I can see. I spy a small red car parked on the grass behind the house." That explains why we hadn't found the car earlier. It looks like it was in the shed, but had to move out when the truck arrived.

"Do you want me to photograph everything over there?" Emily asked and started reaching for my bag.

"No, don't do anything." I sensed the long hard look she gave me as I eased the car away from the kerb and drove off.

"Things are happening back at that house: the car has been moved, a truck has arrived. That means people are up and about. It is daylight and we stand out like the proverbial. The inhabitants of that house will not be happy to find a strange car stopped where it can observe them and showing interest in what's happening in their backyard."

"Yeah, I understand what you say, but what do we do now? Do we just go home and have breakfast?"

"I think we'll go back to the park and wait to see if the red car leaves here. More importantly, I think I noticed a coffee shop in that shopping precinct we drove through last night. I don't think Terry will leave just yet, so let's see if we can rustle up a quick coffee or something before we go to the park."

The coffee shop proprietor was opening for the day, so there was no waiting for service. Emily returned with piping hot ham and cheese croissants and large steaming coffees. We overcame the temptation to indulge immediately. The smell of our breakfast tormented us all the way to the park. Emily balanced the coffees as we drove to the park. After leaving Grevillea Drive, the trip back to the park took less than 20 minutes. "Are you sure we haven't missed him?" Emily mumbled through a mouthful of croissant.

I hoped I sounded more confident than I felt. "Yes. There was no activity around the car when we drove off. Terry wasn't about to leave when we were there, but I have no doubt he should be thinking about it by now."

By the time I dispatched my croissant, I harboured strong doubts about the reliability of my intuition. It wasn't until about half an hour later that the little red car sped out of Sandlands headed for town. After Terry was some distance away, I drove along Grevillea Crescent once more. No stopping this time, just a slow drive past for a check on that house of interest. No one about and no truck. I allowed myself the assumption that the truck was now concealed behind the closed shed doors. "Well, I suppose that proved something," Emily began. "At least we know where the truck is, or we think we do. ... Pity we don't know where the little red car went."

"You are a misery. It won't be hard to find out where Terry has gone." We were back on the road and heading for town again. "We will go by his unit first to see if he went home after his long night 'at work'."

45

"Do we know where Terry lives?"

"Yeah, I looked them up in the phone book and checked out the address when we drove to the Post Office yesterday to collect Trish's envelope. They're in one of those units across the road and along a bit from the Post office."

I turned into the street devoid of traffic except for us at this early hour and a woman on the refuge strip who waited for us to pass. "That's Trish...!" I yelped as we drove past. Emily swung around in her seat to look at the woman through the rear window.

"I think she is heading for the general store we just passed," Emily announced. That was not news to me. In the rear view mirror, I had watched Trish Fielding cross the street and enter the store. I was pulling in to the kerb as Emily spoke.

"Stay in the car please, Emily. I won't be long. I just want a quick word with Trish." Emily started to protest. "Stay here. I might want to move off quickly when I come back." I slammed the door closed behind me and strode to the store.

Trish was in the process of selecting a bottle of milk from the overwhelming range of the product in one of the fridge units. I sidled up to her and copied her actions. "Trish, did Terry arrive home within the last few minutes?" I whispered.

She looked startled but relaxed after giving me a hard look and realising who I was. "No he hasn't, not yet. He did ring about 20 minutes ago. He said he was too tired to drive home and was going to crash in one the rest rooms Thornton provide for drivers. I don't think I'll see him until after work today. Why are you asking, and what are you doing here at this hour of the morning?"

"I wanted to know if he did stay out all night as he said he might, that's all. Oh, and I'm here because I need bread. I'd better go. I've got a friend waiting in the car." She nodded her acceptance of my story, grabbed a bottle of milk and went to the counter.

I searched for the bread rack and selected a loaf. I did need bread. The bit of a loaf left at home already supported a good colony of colourful mould. By the time I was on my way back to the car and its unimpressed occupant, Trish was halfway home. Silence greeted me as I handed the bread to Emily and slid in behind the wheel. I tried easing the tension by way of a report on my chat to Trish. "Terry didn't go home, and indications are that he won't return here until after work this afternoon."

"Does that mean he has gone to work?"

"If we believe what he told Trish, that's where he is supposed to be. However, I don't know if he is a close acquaintance of the truth. After all, according to what he told Trish, he was at work all night."

"You don't think he has gone to Thornton Transport this morning? If he is not there, what's his excuse for taking the day off ... and, what's his lady friend's excuse for doing the same thing?"

"We don't know that she is taking the day off. She wasn't in the car with Terry when he left Sandlands this morning, but she could be going into work some other way today."

We drove in silence to the industrial area and cruised past Thornton Transport. As luck would have it, a semi pulled up at Thornton's gates as we drove up to it. We were forced to stop while the semi driver described a wide arc across both lanes of the street to line his rig up squarely with the gates. There was a bit of a pause while the driver appeared to be searching for his remote device to open the gates. As the driver sat up again, the security guard rushed up to the gate and opened it. The semi eased its way in through the gates and headed for the loading bay we observed last night.

The delay at the gates provided opportunity to scan the employee car park for the little red car without drawing attention to ourselves. With the street now clear again, we drove along to a lawnmower repair place and parked in its customer car park. "I'm sorry, Sonny, but I didn't see that red car anywhere in the car park," Emily apologised as soon as we parked.

"No need to apologise; I didn't see it either. The problem is, if it is there, it's such a small car, it gets lost amongst all the bigger vehicles. It could be there and we simply can't see it."

"Is it possible he parked it somewhere else this morning? Maybe we can't see it because it's not there to see. Maybe he didn't come in to work this morning."

I was busy with my own thoughts and didn't bother to interrupt them to respond to Emily's questions. Decision time, I told myself. I checked the time; almost eight o'clock. Too early, so I suggested, "Let's go for a drive."

"Where…? What for…?" Emily asked. Are we giving up on Terry and the red car, or have you thought of somewhere else he might be?"

"The short answer is 'no'. I want to fill in a bit of time before I try something to confirm whether Terry is at work or not."

Emily slumped back in her seat and I drove off, heading nowhere in particular. My meandering took us to the waterfront. I parked under a tree and persuaded Emily to walk along the breakwater with me. After walking the length of the breakwater and back, we wandered through the commercial strip that edged the marina. It was half eight, and I was about to suggest we head back to the car when Emily spotted a coffee shop tucked amongst the restaurants.

"I wouldn't mind another coffee. Does your master plan allow us time for a cup?" Although I wasn't in need of more coffee, I agreed to a coffee break. A few minutes after nine o'clock we left the coffee shop.

Not needing to waste more time, I drove to the industrial area and past Thornton's. An empty parking space in front of the car detailing business seemed a good place to park again today. I dragged out my phone and searched the local white pages for a phone number for Thornton Transport. Then, broadening my Aussie drawl a bit, I made a call. "Yes, hello; look Love, I was talking to one of your blokes yesterday about something to do with sending some freight interstate. I thought of something else I'd like to ask him if he's available. His name was Terry… uhmm… Terry Fielding, I think he said."

There was a short wait while she tried to locate Mr Fielding but she soon came back me. "I'm sorry, Mr fielding isn't in today. I could put you through to someone else who should help you."

"No thanks. It isn't urgent. I'd prefer to talk to Mr Fielding as he knows all about what I wanted to do. I'll try again some other time. Is he likely to be in tomorrow do you think?"

"I believe so. He took today off to attend to some personal matters but should be back here tomorrow from 7.30a.m." I ended the call and glanced across at Emily who sat watching me expectantly.

"That explains why we can't find the little red car. Mr Fielding is taking a personal day off today," I explained. "He should be back at work tomorrow."

"Is that dependent on his personal affairs not being too complicated and not requiring an extra day off to deal with them?"

"That's a real possibility, but we will accept it at face value and, until and unless something suggests otherwise, we will expect him to be back at work tomorrow."

"What's our next move?" Emily hesitated for a moment before continuing. "If he wasn't going in to work, why did he rush off so early this morning? If he had already arranged to take the day off, he could have enjoyed a long lie in this morning. What about the woman involved, is she taking the day off as well?"

"All very good questions, Emily, and ones I can't answer. Well, perhaps I can speculate about a couple of them. As it was never Terry's intention to go to work this morning, his early morning exodus from Sandlands might be because he had somewhere else to be and something else to do today. An alternate possibility is that his early morning departure was to keep his nocturnal activities – whatever they were – from being discovered."

"Found out by whom…?"

"Dunno yet, do we? As to your question about 'our' next move, I am taking you home before your mother starts raising hell about you being a missing person."

"No, that won't happen. I'll ring her. I'll tell her … I'll say … uhmm … I don't know what, but I'll think of something. So, ignoring that, what are you going to do now?"

"I could go home and get some sleep, but I think I'll take a quick drive past that house off Grevillea Crescent first."

"Okay, Grevillea Crescent it is. Now excuse me while I call my

Mother to let her know I won't be home until later today."

It had been a long night. I didn't have the strength to argue. After I stopped to fill up with fuel, we went to Sandlands for a slow drive along Grevillea Crescent. The suburb had come to life. Vehicles moved around the place, making us look less conspicuous. At the house, the shed doors remained closed. We had no way of knowing whether the truck remained in the shed or not. Nothing about the house's appearance told us whether anyone was at home.

I drove to the end of the suburb, went around the roundabout and came back along Grevillea Crescent on my way out of Sandlands. Nothing changed at the house in the short time since we last viewed it. With little to be gained from hanging about Sandlands, I drove to my office, dropping Emily off at her mother's house on the way. Coward that I am, I didn't go in, and left Emily to her own devices when it came to explaining what she had been up to all night.

Chapter 6

The blinking red light caught my attention as I entered the office. There were two messages. I returned the calls and made appointments to see the callers tomorrow. Then, with my two current case folders stuffed in my bag, I locked up and went home. I had felt a bit peckish before I left the office and told myself I would make some lunch at home. Now that I was home, lunch seemed an unnecessary chore. After a quick shower and setting the alarm, I fell into bed.

I slept soundly until the alarm woke me at three o'clock, giving me plenty of time eat something and be back to observe employees leaving Thornton's at 4.30p.m. The only parking space was in front of the diner. It wasn't where I would park by choice, but when necessity dictates... A bit early, I bought a coffee and a newspaper from the diner and settled down for at least the next hour to wait and watch.

No little red car exited Thornton's car park, and there was no sign of it amongst the stragglers that remained after the mass exodus. I kept an eye out for a woman with a mane of long blonde hair travelling in any of the vehicles, but drew a blank. It was a longshot. With nothing more to do at Thornton's, I took myself off to Sandlands for a leisurely drive along Grevillea Crescent.

The shed doors were open; nothing inside and no one in sight. I drove to the end of the Crescent, joined the road running through the suburb and continued along to the big roundabout. With no clear thought about what to do next, something possessed me to drive back along Grevillea Crescent. As I approached the house of interest, a woman with long blonde hair and wearing a skin tight blue singlet top over black stretch knee length pants checked the mailbox at the end of the driveway. Someone should tell her that outfit didn't suit her body type. She didn't look my way as I drove past and continued to the end of the Crescent.

Those open shed doors were intriguing. I parked in that now familiar parkland adjacent to the entrance to Sandlands. Was the shed open in anticipation of the arrival of Terry's little red car? If so, where was the truck… and when did it leave the house? Questions were easy to come by, logical answers were in short supply. There could be any reason the shed was open and empty. It might have nothing to do with Terry. After all, Trish seemed confident he would be at home tonight. If his intention was to return to the house at Sandlands, what plausible excuse could he give for not coming home again tonight?

After considering various scenarios, I was no wiser. I wanted to ring Trish, but I had agreed not to ring her. Right now, I want to know if Terry had arrived home as expected. I knew that, if he was at home, it would not be easy for Trish to ring me to confirm it. With not many options available, I decided to drive by the Fielding's' unit in the hope of spotting the red car. As I reached for the ignition, I glanced in the rear view mirror. A red car was coming towards Sandlands.

"That's interesting," I said aloud. "I wonder what he's told Trish." I watched the car drive past, Terry at the wheel. Perhaps he intends a short visit, and arriving at this hour has nothing to do with the shed being open. What is the relationship between Terry and the blonde if he can't go home without seeing her first? The temptation to ring Trish gnaws at me. With Terry at Sandlands, it would be safe to ring her… except I did say I wouldn't.

As I sat wrestling with temptation while watching Terry disappear onto Grevillea Crescent, my phone chirped, startling me. The caller ID didn't immediately register with me, but I answered it anyway. "Sonny, this is Trish, Trish Fielding. He hasn't come home again. He did say he didn't think he would be able to leave during the day – too busy and all that – but that he would be home after work this evening."

"Has he called to say what's happening? Something might have happened at work. He might have to work late again." I wasn't about to tell her where her Terry was or what I thought he might be up to. Besides, I wanted to see if she had any ideas about why he didn't return home as expected.

"No, I haven't heard from him since early this morning. I know it's still early and anything could have happened at work to delay him, but I don't think that's the case. I tried ringing his mobile. I was going to use the excuse of checking to see if he wanted an early dinner since he had worked all last night and probably needed to go to bed early tonight. It went through to voicemail. Then I tried ringing his work extension number. One of the other men answered and said he hadn't been at work today. I was pleased I hadn't said who I was. It would have been embarrassing."

"What do you think is happening, Trish? You know Terry better than anyone, so, what's your best take on what this is all about?"

"That's easy; I still think he's got a bit on the side somewhere. I'll admit though that the way he has behaved over the last couple of days suggests it is more than a passing fancy. It justifies my decision to call you in. I'll let you know if he comes home or if I hear anything else."

As soon as the call ended, I eased out of the park and drove the short distance to Grevillea Crescent. The red car was visible long before I reached the relevant side street. Terry had parked in the shed but the doors remained open. I eased up to the kerb in much the same place as I had stopped earlier with Emily. Aware that sitting here doing nothing but watching the house would raise unwanted interest, I dragged out my phone. I answered a non-existent call and went through the motions of carrying on a long conversation.

The performance involved much gesturing with my free hand, shaking and nodding my head at intervals, letting my eyes roam randomly over the surrounding area, and generally doing anything that did not suggest I was keeping an eye on a certain house and the contents of its shed. All went well until a woman walking her dog was coming my way. She was showing interest in the strange car parked on their street. I had a mental picture of her memorising my number plate in case she needed to report it later.

To add an extra realistic aspect to my non-phone call, I scratched around in my bag for a notebook and pen. By the time the woman drew level with me, I had the open notebook balanced on the steering wheel and was scribbling in it. She took a long hard look at me through the passenger's window. I gave her an exasperated look – that's what I hoped it looked like. That was followed up with a winding motion of the hand holding the pen and a roll of the eyes. The hope was she would buy the idea that this was a long and boring business call. She gave no indication whether she did or didn't buy it, so I went through the motions of wrapping up my imaginary call.

A few moments making a show of flicking through my supposed notes, followed by another good look at 'that' house, and I was easing away from the kerb and progressing along Grevillea Crescent. I felt exhausted after my marathon performance, but I assessed it as one of my best. …Pity they don't give acting awards to private investigators for such performances.

My time parked in Grevillea Crescent produced nothing of note. By the time I arrived there, Terry's car was parked in the shed and he had disappeared, presumably into the house. Nothing more happened until I started to ease away from the kerb. The temptation was to stop again, but I am hard-pressed to come up with another believable reason for it. As luck would have it, I saw enough in those few seconds of hesitation.

Terry strode the short distance across the backyard from house to shed and began closing the shed doors. One door was already closed by the time I crossed the side street intersection. The red car remained in the shed. I drove back to my favourite spot in the park and grabbed my phone from the passenger's seat where I had abandoned it at the conclusion of my charade in Grevillea Crescent. I needed to talk to Trish.

As I flicked through my contact numbers, a rogue thought jerked me to a standstill. What if I was wrong? What if that wasn't Terry driving the little red car we assumed to be the target vehicle? Everything did seem to fit. The driver fitted Trish's description of Terry, and the car was the right make and colour. Had I checked the car's number plate against the one Trish supplied? When the answer to that was negative, I was shocked. That was sloppy work. What if it wasn't the right vehicle? It could mean I've spent a lot of time on surveillance for nothing.

I took a couple of deep breaths, cleared my mind, closed my eyes and tried to picture the various times I had seen that red car. Not helpful; no results forthcoming. I tried again, this time focusing Grevillea Crescent less than an hour ago. The car was parked in the open shed. Focus on the rear of the car. Focus on the number plate. Running my mind in 'playback' mode like this doesn't always work but, when it does, it's a Eureka moment.

This was a Eureka moment. Today, this peculiar process of being able to recall things I didn't know I had even noticed worked. It was a struggle. At first, bits of the plate came to me. I forced myself to stay calm and to keep honing in on the number plate. I scribbled the registration number in my notebook and pulled the Fielding case file from my bag.

It took me a moment to find the information I wanted. Trish's note was long and comprehensive but not particularly well structured. ...But there it was, details of the car, including its registration. Bingo! For a moment jubilation ruled. Then reality set in. I had been following the right car, but was it Terry I had followed. A shock awaited me when I went to write up my notes. I checked the day and date on my watch. It's Saturday! God, where is my head at? Sloppy work followed by not knowing what day screams that I have lost my edge.

That revelation raised more questions. Not the one about me losing my edge, I mean the one about it being Saturday. Was Terry supposed to work on weekends? Somehow, it seemed unlikely. It also might explain why 'Blondie' – the woman from the house off Grevillea Crescent – wasn't at work today. "Damn! I need to talk to Trish... and soon," I said aloud, and then added, "...like now!" I reached for my phone.

Trish was a long time answering. I was about to kill the call when she answered. She was out of breath and sucking in great lungsful of air as she tried to speak. "Hi Trish; I know I said I would contact you, but I need some information, and I think I need it now. If Terry is there, make a fuss about telling a telemarketer not to ring you again, and then ring me as soon as you get a chance."

"It's okay, I can talk now. He hasn't come home – still, again, or both – however you want to look at it."

Maybe Trish wasn't happy about the fact that Terry hadn't come home, but it was good news for me. It helped dispel any lingering doubts about the identity of that car and its driver. "Today being Saturday, would Terry go into work?" There was silence rather than a response. I pressed on. "I just wondered whether his job often involved weekend work, or if Thornton Transport ran some sort of work roster that had the depot manned seven days a week."

"No-o-o, but sometimes – rarely though – he does have to go in. I assume there is something that requires urgent unloading. Quite a few people work on Saturdays as a regular thing. The workforce is divided into two groups. On alternate weeks, they work Saturday and have Sunday and Monday off. That arrangement doesn't apply to Terry's level unless something is happening that requires him to be there."

"I assume it would be unusual for anyone to work beyond normal hours on a Saturday, say, late into the night for example?"

"That's right; there would be no one there after their normal finishing time."

"Okay, one last question: has Terry contacted you to explain what he is doing?"

"No. That's how I know he is up to no good. He's not at work – I drove past to see – and he hasn't called to say why he hasn't come home like he said he would."

I ended the call and sat wondering what to do next. It was beginning to look like I would be sitting in this park again tonight. The thought didn't thrill me. Surveillance is a big part of what I do. As a rule, watching somebody all night doesn't bother me. The difference is, I usually know why I'm doing it, and it only takes a couple of days or nights, along with photographic evidence, to complete the job.

The Fielding case is different. I don't know what I'm watching for. Trish thinks he's playing away from home, but there's nothing that's happened so far that is solid evidence of that. My instinct, my gut feeling, is telling me there is something more afoot here than simply an unfaithful husband. Maybe it's just the curious involvement of that truck that's tweaking my antennas.

With my seat eased back, I settled in for what might be a long wait. As nothing to grab my attention was happening, I began thinking about something to eat... and I still hadn't replenished the car's water supplies. I considered risking a trip to the Sandlands shopping centre in search of bottled water and food – and food I could bring back to eat later. After considering it from all angles, it seemed a safe enough move. I started the car and waited for a couple of vehicles heading into Sandlands to pass before easing out of the park. My phone rang just as I nosed out onto the road.

It was Trish. I drove across the road and parked on the shoulder. "Sonny, Terry called. He said he was delayed at work but should be home in half an hour or so. I know he hasn't been at work, so what do I do?"

"Play it cool. Don't say anything that lets him know about you phoning him at work today. Be nice and see what tomorrow brings. I don't think anything out of the ordinary will happen tomorrow as it is Sunday, but I will need to know if it looks like something is going to happen. I think you and I should meet sometime early next week, but let's get this weekend out of the way first and then work out a time."

Sometimes the gods smile on you. Now I don't have to go for food. I drove into Sandlands and turned onto Grevillea Crescent. Not wanting to park in the same place as I had twice already, I turned into the side street and drove past what I had taken to thinking of as 'Blondie's house'. No obvious activity at the house and the shed remained closed. I drove out of the street and back onto Grevillea Crescent. The next few minutes involved driving some distance up and back along the Crescent, making a couple of U-turns along the way and, with caution ignored, parking in the same spot I should avoid. I fitted the long lens to my camera.

There was movement at Blondie's house. Terry came out and

opened the shed doors. One quick shot. The light level was just okay. I checked the image; good enough. The little red car left the shed and reversed down the driveway. I hunched down, thinking Terry was about to leave for home and would drive past me. Wrong; he parked the car out front and walked back up the driveway to disappear around the back of the house. As he made his way back to the house, I clicked off another couple of shots. I told myself that anyone who knew Terry intimately could identify him from his rear view.

A few minutes elapsed with no further sight of Terry. It shot down my theory that he went back inside only to collect something he had forgotten. If Terry were going to be home within the timeframe he gave Trish, he needs to make tracks now. Conscious of how long I had been conspicuous parked on Grevillea Crescent, I stowed everything back in my bag and started the car. I was about to ease away from the kerb when oncoming headlights lit up the bend in the Crescent behind me. I waited for the vehicle to pass.

It was the truck. Without paying me any obvious attention, it drove past, entered the side street, and went up the driveway to park in the shed. Another quick shot of the truck in the shed. As the driver climbed down from the truck, Blondie and Terry came out to meet him. A quick shot of the three of them standing behind the truck. Moments after the truck drove past me, another two cars came along the Crescent. Courteous as ever, I waited for them to pass. How obliging of them to come at the right time to allow me to take shots of the truck without appearing too obvious.

I signalled to pull out, but another set of headlight came around the bend. I waited … and watched as the rear doors on the truck's canopy were opened. It was difficult to make out what was inside. However, it was worth another couple of shots. Then, I had no excuse to linger any longer. I drove to the end of the Crescent and back through the suburb to the park. Less than ten minutes later, the little red car passed me on its way towards town.

With a couple of hundred metres between us, I followed it into town and watched it turn into Terry's street. After driving a grid pattern around three blocks, I drove past the Fielding's address. The red car was parked at the kerb in front of their unit. I hope Trish is up to playing her part and doesn't blow it tonight.

After weaving my way through that part of town, I found the right street and, with a sigh of relief, I was heading for home, a hot shower, food and a good night's sleep.

Chapter 7

After lunch on Sunday, I booted up my computer with the intention of entering all of my notes into the Fielding file. A couple of minutes into the task, my phone rang: Emily. Conversation hopped across inconsequential topics due I suspected to Sandra being within earshot. "Think of something to say that contains either the word 'yes' or 'no', then answer this question: are you babbling on because your mother is listening?"

"Yes, I heard she had moved but I didn't hear where she went."

Okay, as that statement had nothing to do with anything that went before, I'll take it as confirmation. The small talk continued for a bit before Emily's change in conversation indicated Sandra was no longer a problem.

"I called to let you know I think I'll be staying for a few days. I am concerned about Mum. Whatever is happening to make her like this has to be something serious."

"What about work, can you take more time off?"

"Yeah, I've got heaps of leave due. They're happy to see me using it. By the way, I don't know what you did to Mum, but you are well and truly on the outer with her. She told me in no uncertain terms that you have a business to run and I should leave you alone to get on with it. She also suggested that your work took you places where it was not appropriate for me to go. Any idea what she's on about?"

"I've no idea, unless she is put out about you staying out all night with me. She probably blames me for not taking you home when I should have. As for taking you to inappropriate places, I suppose it's possible she sees my work as happening in the shady underbelly of the community. Dunno what she's on about but, if you intend sticking around for a few days, you should give me a wide berth rather than upset her any further."

Although I didn't exactly laugh off Emily's comments about my being out of favour with her mother, I tried to convince her Sandra's view of me at the moment was consistent with Sandra's view of the whole world right now. However, the comments niggled at me for the rest of the afternoon. I told myself it might be a case of Sandra trying to let me get on with the Inneston case without Emily looking over my shoulder. Sandra still hasn't told her daughters of her recent prison visit experience, or that she has asked me to investigate.

With the Fielding file now up to date, I sat back to ponder what I had – not much – and how to proceed. Trish thought there was another woman involved. I haven't proved whether she is right or not. Another woman is involved, but I'm not sure in what way. A photo of Blondie with my photos of Terry at her house might confirm Trish's suspicions and close the case, but that did not sit comfortably with me. I had no evidence Terry was having an illicit affair. I couldn't keep racking up the cost of surveillance hours in the hope of catching them in a compromising situation. I need to discuss progress with Trish to establish how and whether to progress with the case.

With the Fielding case updated, I turned my attention to the Inneston file and my notes from Sandra's visit. It struck me how difficult it must have been for her to come to me, someone so close to the family for so long and who was partly instrumental in her husband's ending up in prison. After giving it some thought, I revised my thinking. Maybe it was easier for her to come to me than bring in an outsider. I already knew the history of the situation and, as a friend as well as an investigator, she was guaranteed extreme sensitivity.

It was a slim file, requiring little time to read it. The frustration at not being able to do anything returned. When all else fails, make a list of all the things you should or might do when opportunity occurs. I took my own advice and started a potential 'to do' list. The almost insurmountable first hurdle was that we knew nothing of the woman posing as Mrs Inneston. There was no opportunity to change that for at least another few days.

If the woman visits Geoff Inneston in gaol during the fourth week of every month, she is due to visit again this coming week. There are two visiting days; Tuesdays and Thursdays. As I don't know which one this woman prefers, I'm going to have to be there both days. I'm not sure how effective that will be, since I have no idea what she looks like. All I know is that she drives a large

By the time I finished with the Inneston file and dealt with a few other admin tasks, it was approaching four o'clock. An early afternoon had a certain appeal, but I decided to check for mail before going home. That was the mistake that wrecked any prospect of an early finish. As I drove down the street to the Post Office, I was tempted to drive past the Fieldings' unit. I collected my mail, drove past the unit and noted the red car was nowhere to be seen. Before I knew it, I was entering the industrial area of town and looking for a parking place with a good view of Thornton's gates.

The little red car wasn't obvious in the employees' car park; no surprise in that. After waiting about 10 minutes, the first of the employees left for the day. It was almost five o'clock when Terry's red car came out and raced off down the street away from me. He was all but last to leave the place. His blonde companion travelled with him again today. I got one quick shot – might be okay – as the car hesitated at the kerb before entering onto the street.

At the end of the street, Terry turned the corner to head across town. I followed. There was quite a bit of traffic, so it wasn't difficult to remain in a string of vehicles with a couple of cars between me and the red car. It was fortunate a few other vehicles took the same route but, beyond the older beach suburb, only one car remained between me and Terry. I pulled off and parked in Melaleuca Grove, the park I had frequented so often over the last few days.

I knew where Terry was going. Terry turned onto Grevillea Crescent. The second car drove straight on through Sandlands. I waited a couple of minutes before following Terry along the Crescent. I hadn't heard from Trish Fielding, so I assumed she had no word that Terry would be late home today. By my reckoning, this would make him late home. I drifted past the side street intersection. My assumption was wrong. I assumed that, as Terry had not told Trish he would be late, he was dropping Blondie home.

Instead of parking in front of the house or maybe in the driveway, parking the little red car parked on the back lawn, suggesting Terry intended staying longer than that. One of the shed doors was open. The truck was parked inside. A light in the shed flicked on as I lost sight of the place. Damn! I should be in one of my other vehicles. If I keep parking in the same spot in the same vehicle, I am bound to raise someone's interest. There was no other option but to return to Melaleuca Grove and wait to see what developed.

As I toyed with the idea of dashing home and swapping cars, my phone chirped. I expected it to be Trish, but was surprised by Sam Keller's voice. "A funny thing happened this morning and I thought I might share it with you. You might remember I said there were similarities between a current case and the one we worked on a while ago. At this afternoon's squad meeting, I casually threw in mention of that fact. It was a throwaway line, but I hoped Pete Messell might pick up on it. He did and asked me to hang back after the meeting. I'm lead detective on a case involving drug trafficking. One of our suspects at the moment is a public servant who does a fair bit of travelling."

"Oh, surely not... Don't tell me someone's resurrected that public service network."

"No, not exactly, and the bloke in question only travels through a fairly contained area. It happens that I'd requested copies of his phone records and financials last Friday. When I spoke to Pete after the meeting, I suggested that, although it was a long shot, it might be worth checking if he ever visited Inneston in prison. Pete didn't hesitate and told me to get a look at the register of Inneston's visitors and phone calls. As far as my case is concerned, it's a fair stretch of the imagination to think there is any connection but, in view of what's happening at your end, it could be interesting."

There wasn't much else to say and the call ended. Possible connections between the two cases sent my mind into hyperdrive. I felt the thrill of the chase building. Bring on Thursday! While my mind was preoccupied with the Inneston case, it grew dark. A check of the time showed it was approaching seven o'clock. Interesting; no sign of the red car going home, and no phone call from Trish about Terry being AWOL, something is not right. One more drive along Grevillea Crescent wouldn't hurt.

The light remained on in the shed. Both shed doors now stood open and people moved around the truck. As I cruised up to the side street intersection, the truck backed out of the shed and started down the driveway. Once I was out of sight of the house, I increased speed and did a fast circuit back to Melaleuca Grove. I wasn't quite hundreds who go through that process each year. By the way, have you decided how long you are staying here?"

"No, but it's looking like a couple of weeks at least. I'm not leaving until I know what's wrong with Mum."

"It seems to me, you might have to ask her outright as she doesn't appear keen to enlighten you. However, if it gets to the point where she has had enough of you hanging around, she might tell you just to get rid of you. In the meantime, if you are planning on staying a while, I suggest you don't do any more snooping and stop developing wild ideas. So, what are you going to do for two weeks, if that's how long you stay?"

"I was wondering if I could work with you. I've worked with you on a couple of occasions and we make a good team. What do you say?"

No surprise; I had half expected that request to come during her stay in Millhaven. If the Fielding job gets moving, I could use Emily to do surveillance while I was busy with her Mother's case. It would keep her occupied and make life easier for both Sandra and me. "There might be some surveillance work you could help with. It depends on what happens in the next day or so. I'll keep in touch. Will your mother mind your coming to stay with her but spending your time with me?"

Emily already had considered that situation and decided Sandra wouldn't mind, so long as she knew whether Emily would be home for meals. I decided it was time for Emily to go home and for me to go to bed. I planned an early morning patrol of key locations associated with the Fielding case. "Right, it's time for you to go home. We don't want to upset Sandra by your being out late before you start working for me, and you need a good night's sleep in case there is some late night surveillance tomorrow night."

I walked Emily to her car. She had a parting question before departing. "When's Ben back in town?" I shrugged. She drove off after giving me a disgusted look.

Although I took my book to bed, I knew I wouldn't read it. My mind was preoccupied with tomorrow's plans, something I avoid doing in bed because of its consequences. There wasn't much to plan for tomorrow, but it kept me awake until the small hours of the morning.

Tuesday morning I rolled out of bed early feeling as though I had barely slept. Without fuss or bother, I was soon on that familiar street in the industrial area, and checking on cars in Thornton Transport's employees' car park. As it wasn't yet seven o'clock, there a solitary vehicle. Its livery indicated it belonged to a well-known local security firm. Good to know Thornton uses a security service to check the place overnight. There might be temptation to explore the place some dark night. Meeting an unexpected security guard once you're over the fence can be embarrassing, not to mention complicated.

With no firm plan in mind, I headed back to town and drove past the Fieldings' unit. No red car visible, but it could be parked out of sight around the back in some garaging facility. Too early to do anything else, I headed for Sandlands. A cruise along Grevillea Crescent proved interesting. No sign of the red car there either but, the truck arrived home a few minutes before I drove past.

It was a few minutes past seven o'clock. "I wonder how Blondie is getting to work today," I murmured aloud. That question had me racing to exit Grevillea Crescent, negotiate the roundabout at the end of the suburb and get back to Melaleuca Grove. Parked in my usual spot and wishing I had brought a coffee with me, I lowered the window to better hear any vehicles moving about in the area.

This part of the park would not see sunlight until about mid-afternoon. I sucked in the musty smell of damp leaf litter with overtones of Melaleuca and sea air. Somewhere nearby someone cooked bacon for breakfast. The heady smell coupled with the pleasant chorus of birdsong had me drifting off. The sound of a car approaching interrupted my peaceful interlude. It took me a couple of moments to realise it was a vehicle coming from town and not a Sandlands local heading off to work. I mentally congratulated myself on my decision to use my spare car today instead of my usual vehicle.

Terry's little red car sped past. It turned onto Grevillea Crescent and disappeared from view. That he was so late arriving was a surprise. If he was on his way to collect Blondie, he had left it late. Even exceeding the speed limit wouldn't get them to work by 7:30.

Blondie must have been waiting for him. It wouldn't have been more than a couple of minutes later when Terry and passenger sped out of Sandlands. I assumed it would be at Thornton Transport for the day, so I didn't follow it. I left the park and turned onto Grevillea Crescent. It would be remiss to leave without one last drive past the house to see if anything was happening there.

The man I assumed to be the driver of the truck closed the shed doors as I cruised past along the Crescent. I glimpsed the truck inside the shed before the doors swung shut. Further on, I made a U-turn and drove by for another look at the house. Nothing happening and no sign of the man. I drove to my office with my mind wrestling a million questions about what Terry Fielding was involved in and the role Blondie's house had in it. This thing was about more than a cheating husband – if he was a cheating husband.

My early arrival at the office allowed a cup of coffee before starting work for the day. With my mind darting in a myriad of different directions, I sat nursing my mug in both hands as I waited for it to cool a little. One question kept returning to the forefront of my thinking: why hadn't I heard from Trish Fielding? There were a number of occasions over the last couple of days that should have caused her concern, yet she had not contacted me. …And she has forgotten or is ignoring my request for a meeting.

All morning, the Fielding case kept gnawing at me while I got on with other things. By ten o'clock, I had a case report ready to mail to the client. With nothing else requiring attention, I went to the Post Office. As I climbed back into my car to leave the Post Office, I looked across to the Fieldings' unit. Nothing indicated anyone was home. Then on a whim, I drove past Thornton Transport and confirmed my earlier assumption that Terry and Blondie had gone to work. The little red car was parked close to the fence.

Since I was already driving around, another trip along Grevillea Crescent wouldn't be a waste of time. Nothing had change at the house. The shed remained closed; no sign of anyone around outside. I needed a place to think, somewhere away from my office. On my way back to town, when I reached the older beach suburb, The Dunes, I drove down to the parking area at the beach and parked in the shade of a clump of trees.

Then, with my seat reclined and the windows down, I relaxed and let my mind drift wherever its fancy took it. At first, it didn't seem to go anywhere but, after a few minutes, it kicked into work mode, and perversely focused on the insurance jobs still awaiting attention.

One of those involved a man in his late-20s injured in a vehicle accident at one of the nearby mines. Injuries to his right arm and shoulder caused serious nerve damage and he remained off work months after the accident. The young man claimed it resulted in restricted use of the injured arm, and required hefty doses of medication just to get through each day. The insurance people doubted the man's degree of incapacitation.

Details of the case were in an email on my phone. The attached file didn't tell me anything new. Although I had his address, I had no information about his routine, or if he went out at all. Surveillance for this one could be long and frustrating. As I pondered the job, I watched a man carrying a surfboard walk along the beach towards this area of the beach where a few breakers rolled in around the point.

The surfer paddled out and, after sitting out there for a couple of minutes, rode a half decent wave into the beach. He flicked the hair back out of his eyes, bent to pick up his board ready to go again. My brain clicked into action. I checked the information emailed to me about the injured mine worker. There was an image of the young man ... and that young man just did a pretty professional looking job of riding a wave into the beach. With a long lens on my camera, I snapped off a couple of shots of him paddling out to wait for the next wave, and then a couple more shots of him riding it into the beach.

After thanking the gods for smiling on me, I decided to test my luck further. I hit the speed dial for Trish Fielding. My allocation of luck for today had run out. Trish did not answer. There were any number of explanations for that, or so I tried telling myself.

However, the day wasn't a complete loss. There would be income from the insurance job I had wrapped up. How much of my work over the last few days on the Fielding case would result in payment was a question I tried to ignore.

The absence of contact by Trish could be due to anything. She might have sorted out what Terry was up to and that he wasn't having an affair. Another possibility was that Terry found out about Trish investigating him and things turned sour at home. If the latter were the case, sending a bill for work done to date wasn't likely to go down well in the Fielding household. By the time I returned to the office, I had resolved to try calling Trish again this afternoon before Terry finished work for the day.

After grabbing some lunch from the deli in the next building, I spent the afternoon in my office completing the report on this morning's surfer. It was three o'clock when I stopped for coffee. I tried calling Trish again. Still no answer; the cone of silence surrounding her is beginning to worry me. The next half hour or so that it took to drink my coffee I devoted to mulling over the Fielding case.

I had to be missing something. Nothing added up. Something about that truck kept trying to elbow its way into my thoughts. All right, I know it's a part of the equation, I just don't know what part – or what the equation looks like for that matter. By four o'clock, I decided that, although without further direction from my client, I would go to Sandlands again this evening.

It was almost five o'clock when Terry and Blondie walked out to his car. With no doubts about where they were going, I headed for Sandlands before the red car left Thornton's. Terry didn't drop Blondie off at her house and then head home to Trish. I waited in Melaleuca Grove for almost an hour before driving along Grevillea Crescent to check.

An idea occurred to me as I approached the first side street off the Crescent. At the end of the cul-de-sac where it opened out into a large turning circle, was one of the several small parklands dotted through this part of the suburb. Parked at the edge of the turning circle, I wrestled the pram out of the back of the car. I wheeled it around to the far side of the car, and fussed around to give the impression of settling a baby in it. Then, after making sure the removable insect netting shroud was firmly attached, I strode into the park pushing the pram ahead of me.

This narrow strip of land separating the residential area from the wetland bordering a creek running some distance behind the development was too narrow for residential blocks and became parkland. It was with some satisfaction that I discovered the parkland strip followed the creek and continued along to the end of the second side street off the Crescent, the side street in which Blondie's house was located.

Although the terrain was difficult in a couple of places, and it was getting dark, I pushed the pram through to the end of the second side street. Once on the street, I stopped a couple of times like any concerned mother would to check on her baby before continuing to make my way towards the Crescent. One of those motherly checks occurred opposite the end of Blondie's driveway. Reassured that my 'baby' was okay, I went to move off … after a glance up the driveway towards the house and the shed beyond.

The red car on the back lawn I didn't see until after taking a few paces. I did see a bloke unlocking the shed. Intuition whacked me hard. After a great show of checking my watch and being amazed at the time, I stepped up my pace and was soon loading the pram back into the car. I did a U-turn across Grevillea Crescent and drove out of Sandlands while speaking to Emily hands-free as I drove.

"I have some surveillance for you if you are still interested."

"Of course I am. What do you want me to do?"

"How soon can you be at Melaleuca Grove, that park just before Sandlands where we spent the other night? Can you get away without upsetting your mother too much?"

"Mum's not home, so there's no problem there. I'll take the short cut and should be there in about 15 minutes." I suspect she didn't pay too much attention to speed limits as she arrived 11 minutes after she ended the call.

I greeted her with a string of questions. "Are you sure you want to do this? Did you bring food and drink? It might be cool again tonight, have you got a jacket?" She nodded in response to the first couple of questions, and held up a jacket in one hand and a rug in the other.

That's when the truck drove out of Grevillea Crescent heading for town. "I've got to go, Emily. Stay here. I'll call to explain what I want you to do as I follow that truck." I don't know if she responded because I was climbing into my car as I finished yelling my instructions at her. The truck was travelling fast as it went past. I didn't want to lose it. I roared out of the park and set off in pursuit.

Chapter 9

Tuesday is a slow night in Millhaven, or maybe it doesn't come to life until after dinner. Traffic was light as I chased down the truck at just above the speed limit. It had a head start resulting in a significant gap between us. The gap closed as the truck slowed down when it approached the town and went across the bridge and through the city centre at a sedate speed. I was careful to hang back so as not to stand out as a tail in the thin traffic.

So focused on the truck, I had forgotten about Emily waiting in the park for me to call her. As I was about to make that call, I realised I had entered familiar territory, the industrial estate. The call could wait a bit longer. We continued into an area I didn't know.

After crossing the street leading to Thornton transport, we were heading deeper into the industrial estate. Up ahead, the truck slowed and turned left. A street went off to my right a short distance prior to the one on the left that the truck took. I turned right onto an unknown street, hoping like hell the planners had laid out the industrial estate in a traditional grid pattern, and going around the block would take me back to where I started from. It didn't. After weaving my way through unknown country, I found the street I was travelling along before my rash move to avoid detection.

I was beginning to think I'd blown it by the time I again found the street where the truck had turned off. I parked in front of the first building on the street. Dull orange coloured street lights provided little illumination. However, I could see the street came to a dead end. I sat in the darkness watching the street for signs of activity anywhere that might indicate where the truck went.

As I sat there, I remembered the phone call to Emily. Nothing had happened at Sandlands and she hadn't seen the red car. "Okay, when last seen, Terry's little red car was parked behind Blondie's house. I don't know what his plans are for the evening. If he is planning to go home, he is going to be very late and must have fed Trish a very good line to explain it. Keep an eye out for that red car and give me a call the moment you see it on the move. I don't know when or if that will happen."

"I'll be fine. Should I go and check what's happening at that house occasionally?"

"No. Stay in the park for now. I don't know what my movements will be for the rest of the night. I was following that truck but I might have lost it. Our focus has been on Terry and the red car when perhaps we should have paid more attention to the truck. Depending on how things go here, I might relieve you later."

Throughout the phone call, I kept watch for any movement anywhere along the street; nothing. There were two possibilities. The truck went down the street and disappeared into a building or, while I was undertaking the scenic tour of the area, the truck exited the street and went elsewhere. The latter case might imply a couple of minutes spent dropping off or picking up something. Another explanation is that the driver ducked into the street to shake any tail he had before continuing to his appointed destination. None of those options appealed to me. My best hope was that the truck was here in one of the buildings along the street.

I locked the car and set off on foot, hugging the fronts of buildings to stay in the shadows. An eerie silence prevailed. A cricket chirped its tune and the cry of a curlew drifted in from far off. The only human sound in the street was that of my breathing and the soft fall of my rubber-soled shoes.

Hair stood up on the back of my neck. A sound, faint and close; metal scraping on concrete was followed by a loud bang. Startled, I jumped and then flattened myself against the split faced bricks of a building. My ears strained to pick up any further noise, any suggestion of movement. I struggled to hear anything above the beating of my heart. Out here on the street, I was exposed without even a doorway to squash myself into. These were industrial buildings with huge roller doors flush with the pavement.

With my back pushed hard against the wall, I slid sideways along the pavement and further away from where the sounds originated. I inched my way across the second last building on this side of the street. A couple more sideways slides and I noticed the bricks no longer caught threads in the back of my shirt. I now slid along the rendered front of the last building. My pulse was off the chart, my breathing shallow, and sweat trickled down my spine.

More noise, this time loud and persistent. Then I heard it: the familiar rattle and rumble of a roller door being raised. I quickened my pace to reach the corner of the building no more than a couple of metres away. Close enough to see the fence that barricaded the end of the street, "What then…," I asked myself. Invisible before as no street lighting penetrated this far along the street, the fence was chain wire. I could climb it, but then what? Did I want to be on the other side of that fence, and what might I find when I got there? Regardless, anything is better than being exposed like this.

I reached the corner of the building. To my relief, the fence, not flush with the corner of the building, was set back a couple of metres along the side wall. An industrial rubbish bin and a couple of empty drums awaited collection against the wall in the space between the pavement and the fence. This will do. I crouched beside the bin and peered around it into the street.

A rectangle of light lit up an area of the street out from the front of the third last building on this side of the street. Voices drifted out through the open door, male, relaxed and several of them. They reflected a hint of urgency or trepidation. Although I couldn't hear what was said, it suggested a group of blokes going about whatever they had to do. I didn't know what was happening or how long it would take, but the roller door being open suggested the impending departure of the truck. What could I do when it drove out of that building? How could I get back to my car ready to follow it when it exited the street? Time to explore my options… and quietly.

It was obvious I couldn't go back along the street. That left only one option: go over the fence and explore the opportunities beyond. I stood up and flexed my legs for a few moments to get circulation flowing again before moving over to the fence. The chain wire panels were stretched tightly but would 'sag' under my weight. A fair amount of noise would result if I scaled the wire. Anyway, climbing chain wire in bare feet hurts, and is impossible in boots because the toes of the boots don't fit in the mesh.

The empty drums adjacent to the fence posed an interesting proposition. With the larger of the two drums already almost up against the fence, I figured this was a good place from which to launch myself over the top. I used the small drum positioned beside the larger one as a stepping stone to climb up on top of the large drum. From up there, my head and shoulders were above the top of the fence. I could go over the top without having to touch the chain wire. I peered into the blackness on the other side of the fence. It was too dark to see my landing zone. I threw caution to the wind, placed both hands on the top rail of the fence and vaulted over.

Knee-high grass cushioned my landing and deadened the sound. After checking I remained intact, I found the side of the building again and started moving along it. Back here was pitch black. I prayed I wouldn't stumble into any abandoned equipment or rubbish as I picked my way towards the end of the wall. The building seemed to go on forever; surely I must come to the back corner soon. In fact, I was some way past the building's back corner before I noticed the change in the surface of the wall as I slid my hand along it.

I realised that, in this block, the large shed-like industrial buildings were built back to back and opened onto different streets. It felt like an eternity but I reached the front corner of the building that backed onto the one I had started from. After checking the street was empty, I took off at a gallop. My rubber soled trainers thudded on the bitumen as I ran but I decided the sound wasn't loud enough to be heard in the next street. As I started wondering how this street could be any longer than the one I had snuck down earlier, I came to the end of the block and reached the main street running through the area.

Caution prevailed. A quick check of the main street for any traffic about, and I was running again. I thanked the planner who laid out this part of the industrial estate in a neat grid pattern. As I ran to where I'd parked my car, I prayed no vehicles would come past. I was running alongside a building's brick side wall which had no doorway or niche of any kind that I could duck into to hide.

The last part was where I was likely to come unstuck. I pushed my back hard up against the bricks, slid round the corner and along the front wall of the building to my car. Things were happening at the other end of the street. That now familiar truck had reversed out of the building and stood in a blaze of light in the middle of the street.

Its headlights came on and the roller door of the building started to descend. Two long strides had me beside my vehicle. The truck turned to make its way out of the street. I crouched beside my car's passenger side rear wheel as the truck advanced. The sound of the roller door as it hit the concrete was deafening. It drowned out the purring of the truck crawling along at a speed nothing much above an idle. There was no urgency here; no fear of their nocturnal activities being disturbed or observed.

At last, the truck reached the end of the street, turned right and moved out of view, picking up speed as it went. I waited. The lack of traffic meant the truck had to be some distance away before I began following it. I also needed to avoid anyone from that building who might follow the truck out along the street. With the roller door closed, I doubted anyone planned to leave the building.

I darted around my vehicle, slid in behind the steering wheel and hit the ignition as I debated the question of whether to move away slowly and quietly, or to get the hell out of there as quickly as I could. The latter won out. I started the car, described a wide arc, and drove out of the street at normal speed. Although the sound of my car seemed deafening, I suspected it was quiet enough not to attract attention in that building at the other end of the street.

Out on the main street, my challenge was to find that truck. It was some distance ahead now. I went with instinct – and hope – and headed out of the industrial estate towards the centre of town. A bus proved my benefactor. At this hour of the night, the traffic lights remain green for extended periods on main arterial roads. The truck would encounter little hindrance in getting to and through the city centre quickly. However, an articulated late-night bus turning at an intersection delayed traffic until the lights turned red.

The bus was completing its slow wide turn through the intersection when the lights turned green against it. Thanks to the bus and the truck's slow gear changes as it moved through the intersection, I caught up to within a block of the truck. Its route was predictable:

out of the city and on to Sandlands and Grevillea Crescent. Once clear of the main urban area, I called Emily.

"The truck is coming your way. I am going to wander through that old suburb, The Dunes, to avoid following the truck all the way. Give me a call when you see it go past." After I ended the call, I realised I hadn't asked about our favourite little red car. Not a problem, I told myself. Emily would have called if it ventured out of Sandlands.

Most of The Dunes' residents appeared to be watching TV, the coloured images from their sets visible through windows along most of the streets. As I left The Dunes to again head towards Sandlands, Emily called. "The truck went past and turned onto Grevillea Crescent. What do you want me to do now?"

"Don't do anything for the moment." Emily reported no sign of the red car so far. "Okay; I'm on my way and should be there in a few minutes. Keep your eyes open now. Terry might decide to head home now the truck is back."

There was no point in exceeding the speed limit. We knew where everyone was at this time. Sometime during the few minutes it took to reach Melaleuca Grove and Emily parked there, an interesting thought occurred to me. It was the first thing I asked about when I spoke to Emily. "When the truck went past, did you happen to get a look at how many were in it?"

"Yeah, it was a bit hard to see, but there were definitely two people in the cabin. There might have been a third person, but I couldn't be sure there was someone sitting in the middle. In fact, I'm fairly confident there wasn't."

"Sit tight for a bit longer. I'm going for a quick drive along Grevillea Crescent. Call me if the red car or the truck reappears."

At Blondie's place, the shed doors were open, the lights were on and the truck was parked inside. Two men, one of them Terry, were undoing the back of the canopy. Damn! If I had been a couple of minutes later, I might have seen what was in the truck. I very much wanted to know what was in there. I drove as far as the next side street before deciding on a U-turn.

I drove back to the entrance to Grevillea Crescent and parked against the kerb. For a short distance along the Crescent there were no houses. It was left as natural bushland. After pulling on the black hoodie I had stashed under my seat, I jogged along the Crescent towards Blondie's house. This activity can trigger a chorus of barking dogs, but not tonight. Maybe cat lovers live along here.

Near the side street, I slowed to a walk. Then, when I was at a point offering a clear view of the shed, I stopped. Bent over with my hands on my knees, I imitated a runner pausing to regain his breath. A few stretching exercises followed by a bit more breathing recovery allowed me enough time to see all there was to see over at the shed.

The truck was empty. Terry stood watching while another man swept out the tray of the truck, occasionally running his broom over the inside of the canopy as well. Then the broom was abandoned and Terry handed the man a bucket and mop. Vigorous mopping followed. The unmistakable figure of Blondie wrapped in a robe came to observe.

My efforts were wasted. The truck was empty when it returned. The likely explanation was that its previous trip was a delivery run. Whatever it was delivering probably now resided in that warehouse building on the industrial estate. With nothing more to see at the shed, and with my performance as an exhausted runner having run its course, I jogged back to my car.

As I parked beside Emily's car, I heard a vehicle. Emily slid down in her seat. I did likewise. Within seconds, Terry's red car came out of Sandlands. I watched its taillights disappeared into the distance before joining Emily in her car. She greeted me with an all-too-familiar question, "Now what…? Do I follow Terry?"

"No, that would be a waste of time. He's off home. I think it's safe to abandon surveillance for tonight. Go home. I'll drive past the Fieldings' unit on my way home to make sure that's where he went."

"Can't I follow you home? I would like to know more about tonight and its outcomes. If I know what's going on, I could be more useful." I understood and suggested she come to the office for a chat tomorrow if possible.

Tomorrow is Wednesday. I have a few small jobs to knock over before becoming involved with the Inneston case on Thursday. If she was willing, Emily could keep an eye on the movements of those involved in the Fielding case. Anyway, a good night's sleep tonight won't do either of us any harm.

As I climbed into bed, I knew Emily would appear in my office sometime tomorrow. She wasn't a bad operator and would be useful if running the two cases simultaneously became complicated. My last thought as I turned off the light was about what story Emily would concoct for her mother to explain her absence tonight.

Chapter 10

After scrambling out of bed a bit late, my time until mid-morning was spent attending to domestic chores before leaving for the office. The downside of coming into town late was finding a parking spot. Although Whittington Investigations has a designated space behind the building, it was not uncommon to find someone else availing themselves of it if I arrived late. That's how it was today. I parked on the street and made a mental note that it was in a three-hour zone. As I unlocked my office, my phone rang: Emily. She would arrive in 20 minutes and would be at my disposal for the day.

By the time she arrived, I had planned the day and coffee was brewing. My task before she arrived was to work out what I wanted her to do. Emily walked into my office and took a long, deep breath.

"Ah, coffee; yes please. It was an early start accompanied by some weak coffee this morning. Mum and some of her mates are off to Ralston to compete – I think it's a competition – in some Mah-jong contest or something. They will be gone for a couple of days. So-o-o I am free to work with you without having to make up plausible stories to placate my mother about my absences."

"Okay, first thing, I want you to take a bit of a drive around to see who is where and perhaps what they are doing. It might not be possible to see what they are up to, but you never know your luck. Then, later, there will be some surveillance and another check on where people are and what they might be doing."

"That doesn't sound like anything I haven't done for you before, so I don't see any problems with that. What are your plans?"

"I've got a couple of insurance jobs to work on. Not very exciting, but they should be quick and easy. I'll probably be in and out of the office at various times during the day depending on how these jobs go."

Over the next half hour, I gave Emily details of what I wanted her to do and she made copious notes. In case I was out in the field, I gave her a spare key to the office so she could come and go as she needed to.

Her first task was to try to check if Terry's little red car was in Thornton Transport employees' car park. Then she was to check Blondie's house for any sign of activity, particularly anything to do with that truck. I needed to talk to Trish, or at least to know if she was at home. We discussed the Trish situation and agreed either of those outcomes was unlikely. Although aware of potential difficulties, Emily left the office brimming with enthusiasm.

Two of my jobs for today were routine insurance claim investigations. One involving a man with a back injury sustained at work seemed the easier of the two. I tackled it first. When I drove past his house he was mowing his lawn. I parked along the street a bit and watched as he abandoned the mowing to dig a hole in his attractive female neighbour's front yard and help her plant a shrub. My photos should see his claim for permanent disability thrown out.

The other job involved an insurance claim by a well-to-do couple. Their house was broken into and many expensive items stolen. The Police seemed to hit a dead end with their investigations, but the insurance company's investigator believed it was an inside job, or an attempted rip-off. Neither case was exciting, but they provided a good income stream.

How to tackle this second job required some thought. I went back to the office, wrote up and sent the report on the first one, before settling back to focus on the second case. There was no sign of Emily but my stomach began to rumble. I contemplated going in search of lunch when Emily came into the office. She looked very pleased with herself. I was tempted not to ask what she'd done, but I did anyway. She took out her notebook and flipped over a few pages as she sat down opposite me.

"Okay, let's see now; first up, I went out to the industrial estate and parked up the road a bit from Thornton's. I couldn't see the red car, so I walked along the street a fair way before crossing over and walking back beside Thornton's fence. Terry's car was there. He must've arrived early this morning because the car was towards the front of the carpark."

"Good work. Okay, so we can assume he is at work today."

"Next, I drove to Sandlands to check on Blondie's house. It

didn't look like anyone was around but you can't tell if there is when the house is all closed up like that. I went to that shopping precinct, wandered around to kill some time and then drove back along Grevillea Crescent. This time the shed was open, and a man appeared to be loading stuff into the back of the truck. Not wanting to stop, I drove by without seeing what he was loading."

"Looks like the truck might be out and about again this evening. We both might be on surveillance tonight. Now, what about Trish; is there anything to report there?"

Her grin almost split her face in two. "Ahem, I drove past the Fielding's unit twice, once on my way to the industrial estate, and later after Sandlands. There was no sign of Trish on either occasion. The unit was closed up, so I couldn't tell if she was home or not. I parked in that little car park next to the post office and waited for any sign of her. I didn't know how long I might be there, so I went to the little store where you bought the bread the other day and bought a paper and bottled water. I got chatting to the lass on the checkout."

"Whoa, hang on; am I going to be impressed with what you're going to tell me next? I have a feeling I might not be."

"A-a-w, don't be like that. It was okay. I mentioned to the chick on the checkout that I was from Millhaven but hadn't been back here for years. We chatted about the way the place has changed, and then I threw in that I had a friend who used to live somewhere around here and I wondered whether she was still in the neighbourhood. I said the friend's name was Trish but I couldn't remember her married name. After I gave her a bit of a description of what she looked like, the girl said someone called Trish living in the units across the road was a bit like the one I described. When I said I might drop over and surprise Trish with a visit, the girl said she wasn't sure Trish was around at the moment. It is usual for Trish to go to the shop every day for milk, bread, the paper, or whatever, but the girl hadn't seen her for a few days – maybe not at all this week."

"I do not like the way this is sounding. I haven't heard from Trish Fielding since last Friday. Plenty has happened to prompt her to call. And she didn't call about the meeting we discussed. Your news has me worried about her status."

Emily frowned and said, "Status…?

"Yeah, whether she is still around, whether she has been injured, whether she might have met with foul play… and, I suppose, whether I'll get paid for the work done so far."

"You think she might be dead?"

"No, I didn't say that, but it is a possibility that can't be dismissed. If Terry found out she was having him investigated, who knows what might have happened. I don't know yet what Terry is involved in, but I suspect it is not legal, and I remain unsure whether he is having it off with Blondie or not."

My stomach rumbled loudly. "Please can we get some lunch?" Emily asked. "Breakfast, such as it was, seems a long time ago. I'm starving and, by the sound of your stomach, so is it."

Although I thought to pick up something to bring back to the office to eat, Emily had other ideas. We walked to a little Italian place in the next block and dined out on pasta. Towards the end of our meal, conversation lapsed. After a couple of minutes, Emily broke the silence. "There's a bit more to report from this morning."

I heard the distant clang of alarm bells. "You only had the three things to do."

"Yes, I know, but … uhmm… there's a bit more to the Trish story." Alarm bells getting louder. "After I spoke with the girl in the store, I thought she would think it strange if I didn't go across the road to see if my 'friend Trish' was home."

"You didn't…?"

"I went across to the Fieldings' unit and knocked on the door. I worked out a story on my way there. If Trish answered the door, I would explain I was looking for someone else, apologise for my mistake and leave. Neither Trish nor Terry knew me, so there wouldn't be any connection to you. Anyway, I needn't have worried. I knocked a couple of times. An old woman eventually came to the door. She definitely was not Trish. I wasn't sure whether to use my prepared story, or tell the truth and say I'd come to see Trish. It didn't matter because, before I had worked that out, the woman said that, if I had come to see Trish, she wasn't home."

"Did this woman give you any indication of who she was or why she was in the Fieldings' unit?"

"She is a neighbour. Trish has a little hairy dog, one of those lapdog breeds. The neighbour was hanging out washing and heard the dog crying. When she couldn't raise Trish, she went to get the spare key Trish gave her to use in emergencies. The dog bolted outside as she opened the door. There was no one home, no food out for the dog and its water bowl was empty. By the look of the mess all through the place, she thought the dog hadn't been let out for days."

"I am liking this case less with every passing minute. At any stage, did you tell the woman why you called?"

"I told I had come to see if Trish was my old friend who used to live around here years ago when I lived in Millhaven. She said this Trish wasn't from Millhaven. She was from somewhere in New South Wales; grew up on a sheep property or something. I agreed it wasn't the woman I was looking for and asked her not to bother mentioning my visit to Trish when she returned."

"I don't think we need to worry about her telling Trish about you. My gut is telling me Trish is not going to return any time soon – if at all."

"What do we do now… about Trish I mean? How do we find out if she is okay and why she hasn't contacted you? You seem to be leaning towards some sort of foul play being involved. What do you think might have happened … and who is responsible?"

They were the big questions, and I didn't have answers. As Trish wasn't at home, I considered whether it was safe to call her, or if it might make a bad situation worse. Then, back at the office and ignoring my jittery instinct, I keyed in Trish's number. The phone rang for an eternity before switching to voicemail. I didn't leave a message. An hour and a half later, I tried again. The service provider announced that the number I was calling was no longer available.

I swore, slammed my chair back and stomped over to the kitchenette to make coffee. I probably didn't need coffee but it was something to do that didn't involve too much frustration. Emily, curled up in one of my ancient lounge chairs, was checking emails on her phone. "Yes, I will have a cup, thanks," she called out. I heard the hint of laughter in her voice. I spun around to face her. That did it. She started to laugh. I managed a wry grin and apologised. One thing clarified in my mind. I could not continue to involve Emily in anyway with the Fielding case.

Should I break the news to her now or later? Coward that I am, I decided later, after we had talked more about the case, was a better time. Although I didn't know what had happened to Trish or what was going on at Blondie's house, my gut told me this mess was too dangerous to involve Emily. And, in amongst all my other thoughts, I wished above all else that Ben Richards was back here in Millhaven.

At about four o'clock, Emily asked what our plans were for this evening. What she really wanted to know was what I had in mind for her to do. This seemed like a good time to break the bad news to her. It took me a while to answer as I tried to sort out the words that would do the least damage. After a rambling start, I improved.

"I'm a bit worried about continuing the Fielding case as I'm not confident about being paid. I guess this concern has strengthened in view of Trish's unknown whereabouts. My brief was to investigate whether Terry was involved in an affair with some other woman. That seemed to be what Trish blamed for his unusual behaviour and absences. I still don't know whether he is or isn't. What I think is that he's involved in something very shady if not downright illegal."

"Do you think Trish would want you to find out what it is he's involved in, or will she be happy if it's just not an affair that's happening?"

"That's why I wanted to meet with her to discuss my findings so far and my suspicions. It would be an opportunity for her to give me further directions, including whether to continue the investigation. Trish's unexplained disappearance makes me inclined to call a halt to the investigation until I hear from her. A lot of time could be invested for which there might be no payment. I run a business. Regardless of where my curiosity wants to take me, I have to approach operations realistically."

"Does that mean we're not doing anything more tonight?"

"Yeah, I guess that's the story. I will keep trying to contact Trish but, unless there is contact, this case is in abeyance. If nothing else, it means tonight we'll both get a good night's sleep. Sorry I don't have anything to fill in your time while your mother is away." She gave me a lopsided smile. I knew she was disappointed. While I sat trying to think of something to say to console her, my phone rang.

"Ben…! Where are you? When did you get back, isn't this early? Hang on a minute … No, no it's okay. I can talk."

Emily picked up her bag and stood beside her chair. "As we're not going to do anything tonight, I think I'll head home." Then, in a whisper, she added. "If Ben is home, you'll have other things to do tonight." After a wicked grin and a wink, she headed for the door.

I went back to the phone call with Ben. "I got back on an early flight this morning. You're right, I wasn't due back until the weekend, but we got finished early. I'd had enough. You know how it is when you've been away for a while, there's a pile of things for you to deal with when you get back. I came into the office this morning to catch up and have coffee with them and I'm still here. Unless you have other plans for this evening, what would you like to eat?"

"No plans for tonight, but I do have a couple of nice steaks in the fridge. Perhaps we could barbecue them on the deck and have bit a salad with them."

"A home-cooked meal sounds wonderful. See you about six-ish."

Just when I thought it was a shitty day, the gods smiled on me. I gathered up the Fielding file and everything else I wanted to take home and left the office. A quick stop at a supermarket to get some fresh salad fixings, and then I was on my way to the industrial estate. Although I told Emily the Fielding case was on hold, I decided to take one more look at things before going home.

I drove past Thornton Transport as employees were streaming out of the place, parked at the kerb further down the road and waited. Amongst the last to leave, Blondie accompanied Terry out to his little red car and I watched them exit Thornton's. Where they were going was a no-brainer. Regardless of what he was planning for the rest of the evening, Terry had to take Blondie home first. I didn't rush off to follow them, but waited until the last of the employees drove out of Thornton's gates before joining the end of the cavalcade.

The cavalcade thinned out leaving only two vehicles between Terry and me. What the…? Up ahead, I saw Terry's red car turn left into the street where the Post Office and the Fieldings' unit were located. I didn't follow him into the street but continued a little further along before pulling into a local pub's carpark.

My eyes watched the road for Terry's car coming back onto the road to Sandlands. After about 10 minutes I left the pub's carpark and drove back to the street. I assumed they were at the Fieldings' unit, but why would Terry take Blondie to his unit? If that's where they were, it indicated Terry knew Trish was not there.

I turned into the street and almost immediately swung a hard left and pulled up in the Post Office carpark. "I was not expecting that," I exclaimed. On the left-hand side at the beginning of this street, there is one house followed by the Post Office, a newsagent, and then the little general store both Emily and I had visited. The little red car was parked out front of the general store. From the Post Office's small carpark, I couldn't see what was happening further up the street. I grabbed my mailbox key and went to check my mail, taking my time as I sauntered around to the other side of the Post Office where the mailboxes were located.

There was a bit in my mailbox, most of it junk mail. Nevertheless, I bundled it up to take with me. A glass panel set in the outside wall of the mailbox area provided a good view along the street. Once you found the correct place to stand, you could see without being seen. A couple of women, one with a small child licking an ice cream, came out of the store. As items had begun slipping out of my bundle of mail, I dumped it all on the lid of the wheelie rubbish bin near the doorway and bundled it up again. I checked the street again just in time to see Blondie exit the store.

She carried a couple of weighty looking shopping bags and had a folded newspaper tucked under her arm. Terry leaned across and opened the passenger door from inside for her. After dumping the bags on the floor and throwing the paper onto the back seat, she climbed into the passenger's seat. As Blondie closed her door, Terry eased the car away from the kerb. He made an illegal U-turn over the double lines down the centre of the street before once more hitting the road to Sandlands.

The temptation was to follow him, but I asked myself why. I knew where he was going and, although I didn't know how long he would be there, did it matter? It was well after five o'clock and Ben would be at my house around six. Time to get myself home to freshen up before he arrives.

Chapter 11

Ben might think he is coming to socialise over a drink and a steak dinner, but I had extra entertainment planned as a surprise. With the salad prepared and the steak coming to room temperature, I took myself into my home office with the Fielding file and spread it out on the spare desk. I needed to refresh my memory about everything in that file and have it ready to discuss it with Ben. No doubt he would want to spend this evening talking about his trip overseas. My concerns about the Fielding case outweighed that and Ben needed to know about those concerns tonight.

He arrived armed with several carrier bags, one of which I recognised as coming from the local liquor barn. I discovered that another of the bags contained fine chocolates and an excellent brand of single malt, both of which probably came via the duty-free store. The final carry bag contained a number of gifts sourced from the various places Ben had visited. I have to admit, he has excellent taste, not only in alcohol but in the right gifts to buy a girl. And the powerful bear hug I received on his arrival wasn't bad either.

We drank toasts to the beautiful night, his safe arrival home and several other things that I don't remember too clearly before deciding we should cook the steaks before we were incapable of it. With tales of Ben's overseas tour exhausted and the food soaking up some of our alcohol intake, I felt the time was right to talk shop. We moved from the deck to the dining room and I placed the Fielding file on the table. Then, sitting side-by-side so we could both see the file, I took Ben through all that had happened over the last few days.

The process took longer than I expected. Ben asked endless questions as we picked our way through the file. But there was an end to it. At last, there was nothing more to read or to explain.

"This is not what your cases usually look like after this long," Ben commented on his way to the fridge to find a mineral water. "So when are you going to tell me what's got you concerned. I know it's not because you haven't got a firm line on the case yet. There is something else you haven't told me… and I have a horrible feeling that, whatever that is, I do need to know about it. What do you think you've uncovered and how will it throw my department into a whirlwind for God knows how long while we investigate it?"

"At the risk of giving rise to sarcastic comment, I'll say upfront some of it – most of it – bothering me comes from gut instinct rather than hard evidence. If the case were about investigating a wayward husband, it would be straightforward, although it might take a while to gather sufficient appropriate evidence. My client might be concerned about her husband playing away but, from what I've seen so far, while that might be true, there is more at play here than infidelity."

"How about you brew us a coffee while I go through the file again, and then you can tell me about all the things that I won't get from reading the file."

Over coffee, I told him what I had witnessed and my suspicions about the well-being of Trish Fielding. Again, Ben had endless questions. For many of them I didn't have answers, but I did have suggestions. Time raced away. A check of my watch showed it was 2.00a.m. Although Ben arrived back in Australia yesterday and spent the day in Brisbane before travelling to Millhaven today, he remained jetlagged.

"Ben, it's late. Are you supposed to be back at work tomorrow, or are you taking the day off?"

"I'm not due back at work until Monday, but I probably will go in again tomorrow for some time to get caught up a bit before jumping in again next week. What are your plans for tomorrow? Do we need to look into the Fielding case to see what we can uncover?"

"Tomorrow I'll be tied up all morning on another case. Maybe I'll have some time in the afternoon. I don't think I have any more to add to what I've told you tonight. However, it would be good to know if anything funny that interests your guys is happening around the place with possible links to what I've observed."

"Okay, I'll have a look at anything that is keeping my guys interested at the moment. I'll give you a call, say, about mid-afternoon." With nothing more to do or say, Ben left and I fell into bed… and slept past my intended wake-up time the next morning.

Damn! Today is Thursday, the fourth Thursday of the month, and

I need to be sitting in the prison car park a long way from Millhaven watching visitors arrive. I lost a half hour of my planned time by sleeping in. The next half hour was frantic as I made ready to leave for the four hour drive north to the Tulloch Correctional Centre. I managed to be on the road by five o'clock, accompanied by a vegemite and cheese roll and an insulated mug of black coffee to have for breakfast as I drove.

I was cutting it fine, but I drove into the prison carpark right on nine o'clock. According to my information, approved visitors were to present to the processing centre at least 45 minutes before the appointed visiting time. Visiting hours were from ten o'clock. Other vehicles already had arrived and a number of people made their way towards the main building. I pulled into a parking spot with a good view of the entire parking area and began scanning the parked cars.

No vehicle resembling the 'big, black, expensive-looking SUV' here yet. I settled down to wait and watch. About five minutes later, a vehicle matching that description roared into the parking lot. The driver wasted no time in abandoning the car to rush across to the building. I managed a quick photo of the woman near the front of her car, more shots of the car and its registration plate.

With no further arrivals and all of the visitors now safely in the processing centre, I took a slow wander through the car park. I tried to make it look as though I was filling in time while I waited for one of the visitors to return after visiting an inmate. The only problem was, I didn't quite know what I should look like as I did that. My wandering took me back towards the rear of the black SUV. There were a couple of bumper stickers on the rear fender. I made a mental note of them before continuing back to my car. I could see what Beryl meant when she suggested its owner had been watching too much TV. The vehicle did present as a big black ugly mass similar to what is portrayed in many TV shows as FBI vehicles.

From the bit of research I did, I knew visitors were allowed about 75 minutes with an inmate. By the time I included the additional 45 minutes or more of time spent in the processing centre, I was in for a long wait before the driver of the black SUV reappeared. I cursed myself for not having come better prepared, but a search of the vehicle produced the newspapers I'd bought over the last couple of days and not had a chance to read. I reclined my seat and began reading every printed word.

I finished the papers, including the crosswords. By my calculations I still had more than half an hour to wait for visiting time to finish. I was reaching for a bottle of water when I saw the door of the processing centre slide open. The woman in the charcoal grey two-piece outfit strode out. My thirst forgotten, I readied my camera. Stony faced and with eyes focused unwaveringly on her vehicle, the woman headed for the SUV. Her long swinging strides covered the distance quickly. I managed a couple of full frontal shots before she hitched her tight skirt up to an almost indecent height to climb into her vehicle. She turned through empty spaces in the carpark and roared out without as much as a glance in her mirrors.

This was a lady on a mission. Her early departure intrigued me. Had she encountered some problem being admitted today, or had things turned sour during her visit with Geoff Inneston? Perhaps Geoff was told about a woman posing as his wife trying to see him last week. Would such information create a problem for today's 'Mrs Inneston'? Lots of speculation but no answers involved in all that. I booted up my tablet and visited Google.

Google recognised the message on one of the bumper stickers. It was part of a radio station's recent promotional campaign. I wasn't interested in the campaign, but now I knew of one place the SUV was associated with, although the woman might not live there. I abandoned the tablet in favour of my camera and reviewed the shots I took.

Although I didn't recognise the woman, something kept hinting at some familiarity. I brought up this morning's images of the woman and carefully scanned each one. While something was familiar about her, studying the images produced nothing enlightening. I came back to the bumper sticker and the radio station it related to. The station had a wide listener area. Its promotional campaign offered substantial prizes to the driver of cars sporting said sticker if spotted at certain places at designated times. The campaign had run some 12 months previously and ended after only a couple of months.

The sound of chatter as visitors exited the building drew me back to the here and now. Although I had almost worn the pixels off my images of the woman by then, I was no closer to identifying her or recalling why she seemed vaguely familiar. There was nothing keeping me here and I still have a four hour drive home to look forward to. Where that black SUV might have gone wasn't a concern. I made my way onto the highway and headed for home.

Sustenance for the long drive to Millhaven seemed a priority. I remember seeing a diner attached to a service station about 15 or 20 minutes along the road. Half an hour later, I drove into the small carpark beside the diner. Three cars in the car park: mine, a sporty bright red coupe and a big black SUV sporting a couple of bumper stickers. Should I go in, or should I drive further along the highway to park and wait for the SUV to come past? No, damn it; I am starving, and I doubt the woman even noticed me at the Correctional Centre.

I pushed open the door and strode into the almost deserted diner. The woman in the charcoal grey two-piece was nowhere in sight. Amid the aroma of hamburgers on the grill and whatever was spitting and hissing in the deep fryer, I shouted my order for toasted sandwiches and coffee above the rattle and wheeze of the ancient airconditioner mounted high in the end wall.

It was a busy service station, but the procession of cars at the pumps couldn't be heard above the airconditioner. As I watched the driveway procession, the cook bellowed, "Two fish and chips", and plonked two plates down heavily on the servery. A young girl with azure blue dead straight hair and an abundance of tattoos and piercings scraped her chair back and went to collect the meals. What supposedly passed for her skirt didn't quite cover her knickers until she gave it a couple of good tugs on her way to the servery. She brought the plates back to the table and returned to the servery. While the girl collected cutlery, napkins and packets of condiments, the cook announced, "Hamburger and chips." She placed a plate containing a skyscraper burger and a basket of fries on the servery.

No guesswork was needed to work out whose order that was. A few moments later, a door bearing the traditional women's toilets sign banged closed. The grey two-piece marched out, collected burger and fries from the servery and sat down at a table right below the air-conditioner. There was no doubt about her choice of this table. It screamed 'I wish to be alone'.

I hadn't removed my sunglasses. There was advantage in keeping them on. If I pointed the sunglasses to somewhere else, I could move my eyes to focus on the woman without her being aware. While I waited for my food, I moved my head towards all the signs advertising various ice creams and fast foods while keeping my eyes firmly on the woman in the grey outfit.

While in the bathroom, she had applied fresh make up. The multistorey burger presented her with something of a challenge. Her jaws wouldn't open wide enough to bite into the burger and she might end up wearing most of it down the front of her outfit. She played it safe and opted for a plastic knife from the cutlery rack on the servery.

As I watched her sawing chunks off the burger, my sandwiches and coffee materialised. My lunch would not take long to dispose of, and I wondered how I might extend my time in the diner to avoid leaving before the woman. No bright ideas arrived, so I gathered up my rubbish and threw it in the bin on the way to my car. While waiting for some traffic to pass before proceeding onto the highway again, I remembered a rest area beside a creek some distance further along the highway. It was further than I thought. About an hour after I left the diner I pulled into the rest area.

It looked as though it had been created recently. Set beside the road in a cleared area of bushland on the creek bank, it was a pleasant stopping place. A toilet block, a tank providing fresh drinking water, two covered picnic tables with benches, and a couple of barbecues were provided for travellers. I drove around the gravel circular driveway to park facing the road and adjacent to one of the picnic tables. Armed with a bottle of water and one of the newspapers I had read, I made myself as comfortable as possible on a cast concrete bench at the table.

I was beginning to think it was a lost cause, when the black SUV flew past at what I estimated as well over the speed limit. Okay, that was good. I now knew she was continuing south... and so was I. There was no hope of catching her at the speed she was doing without risking being pulled over for a traffic offence. I resisted the temptation and set cruise control on the legal speed limit.

About 50 kilometres further on, I came round a bend to find a string of stationary vehicles up ahead. Way up ahead, dump trucks and rollers crisscrossed the highway. I remembered this area from my drive through here this morning. The bitumen was removed from a long stretch of the highway and new foundation material added in readiness for sealing. The hold-up was for workmen applying the bitumen coating to the area.

Like so many other drivers stretching their legs while they waited, I got out of my car and wandered around a bit. I wandered out into the other lane to check how many cars were ahead of me. About five cars and a small truck were between my vehicle and a big black SUV. I climbed back into the car and hoped that, when we finally started moving again, they let us all through at one time and I wasn't left until the next lot were let through.

After 20 minutes, I saw the lead cars moving across the newly laid tarmac. "Come on, come on, keep moving," I murmured repeatedly until at last I was on the new bitumen and once more on my way home. It took a little while for the line of cars to string out. I crawled along for a while before it was possible to apply any speed.

Not too far from the new roadworks was a major intersection. A small residential area had sprung up around the T-junction in recent years. A number of cars slipped out of our cavalcade there, slowing us down again. By the time we were once more sailing along the open highway, the black SUV was only a couple of cars ahead of me.

The remainder of the trip to Millhaven was uneventful. I kept watch on the black SUV closely as we approached town. There was no indication it would detour into Millhaven. It drove through town to the city limits and continued south. I turned off the highway at a set of lights just beyond the city limits and made my way back to my office in the city. It was late. My intention was to check my messages, collect a couple of files and head home.

There were several messages: the insurance company thanking me for the stuff I sent through, someone wanting information, and the last one was from Ben. As soon as I saw his number come up, I remembered. Oh God, I'd forgotten all about him. I should have called to say I would be late. After the usual information about date and time, the machine played his message. "Sorry, Sonny, I'm tied up with something here. See you this evening with take-away for dinner." That was convenient. Now I didn't have to feel guilty about not ringing him.

A couple of other calls went through to voicemail, but they were hang-ups. Many people don't like talking to a machine. They often hang up the moment the machine clicks on. Both these callers hung on for a few seconds. Nothing was said but background sounds and breathing were recorded. Somehow, I didn't think these calls were from people who didn't want to talk to a machine. I tried hard not to apply some sinister connotation to them. After spending a couple of minutes listening to them again, I picked up the things I was taking home and left.

Due to my late start this morning, I had left the kitchen in a bit of a mess when I departed. My priority was to tidy up before Ben arrived. By the time I dealt with the kitchen and showered, it was six o'clock. I didn't know quite when Ben might arrive. I was wondering what to do to fill in time when I heard him arrive. He came in carrying wine and a bag of Chinese takeaway. I was delighted to see both him and the food. I didn't feel like preparing dinner tonight.

We concentrated on eating and took the last of our wine out onto the deck before talking work. Ben looked tired. "You look as though you've had a long day. You should know better than to go into work when you're not supposed to be there. Would you like to escape and go home to bed? " I asked once we sat down.

"No, I'm fine. I just need to unwind a bit. I think I've just about done that. Anyway, how was your day?"

Tricky question; and one I wasn't sure how to answer. I didn't want to discuss the Inneston situation or where I'd been today, but there were some aspects I might want to discuss with him in the future. When in doubt, fob off the question as best you can. "I had a day of watching and waiting, and the surveillance stretched on much longer than I expected. And I have to admit, I don't know that I learnt a lot."

While we were chatting, the image of the woman I'd photographed this morning drifted into my mind. There was something familiar about her. What the hell was it, and why did I think that?

"Are you all right? Are you in need of an early night?" Ben asked.

"No, why do you ask? I'm fine."

"…Wasn't sure whether you were miles away or if you'd gone to sleep. I was talking to you but I knew you didn't hear a word I said. Is there something you'd like to share with me?"

Good question; truth is, I don't know whether I want to share or not. When I was slow responding, Ben through his hands up in resignation and moved to refill our glasses. I did notice the firm set to his jaw. "Don't be like that. It's just that what's on my mind stems from today's surveillance and is trivial, not worth mentioning."

Ben can be persuasive. We were soon in my office with my camera hooked up to my computer and viewing this morning's images on my large screen. I flicked through the images to the first front view image of the woman. Ben peered intently at the screen and enlarged the image until it began to pixelate. I don't know why I let him talk me into showing him the images. He was unlikely to recognise the woman. She did looked vaguely familiar but I still couldn't place her.

"She is not from Ralston but she used to spend some time there in the past. I interviewed her once. If I could just remember what case that was or why I interviewed her…"

I could see Ben was mining his memory banks for some connection with the woman. I kept quiet to let him get on with it and filled in the hiatus by staring at the image of the woman. It was a case of mind in neutral. I wasn't really looking at the image or thinking about the woman. Ben's words about interviewing her in Ralston in connection with a case kept running through my mind. From out of nowhere, the fog lifted… I knew who she was. Well, not exactly; I didn't know who she was but I knew why she seemed familiar.

"She was – and maybe still is – a Public Servant. I saw her on campus a couple of times when I visited Ralston. My then boss, Therese Melrose, introduced me to her once when the three of us shared the elevator to the top floor. The woman wasn't someone I was likely to deal with in the future. I didn't note her name as Therese's introduction was for the sake of politeness."

"Well done, old girl!" Ben said and slapped me on the back. "A-a-h, yes; I think I remember the case now. Her name will be in the case files, but it will be a bit of a challenge to locate those files without a bit more information."

"There might be an easier way of finding out her name." I flicked back through this morning's images to the one of the SUV's plate. "You could find out who that vehicle is registered to," I said… and made a show of flapping my eyelashes at him.

Ben pulled out his phone and ran through his speed dial numbers, before checking his watch. "It's a bit late and everyone is tied up on something else that I don't want to pull anyone off. I don't imagine the world will end if we don't know until I go into the office and look it up in the morning." He finished by miming my eyelash flapping performance.

Not having the name tonight was disappointing, but I contented myself with the fact that we had made progress. Ben was right. It was late. The effects of an early morning start and hours of driving were catching up with me. I stifled a yawn. Ben noticed.

"Right then, time to go; I'll give you a call in the morning when I know something more."

Chapter 12

A quick clean up before falling into bed; I was ready for sleep. My mind wouldn't stop working. It kept revisiting that day in the lift when Therese introduced me to a woman, the woman I photographed this morning. Try as I might to think of other things, my mind insisted this was what it wanted to focus on. I tossed and turned for about half an hour before it came to me. "Finance…" I yelped.

It came to me with such clarity and force, it was almost painful. The woman – there was no hope of remembering her name – had something to do with the Finance Section of our Department. Some years back, I found myself working at a technical training institute that came under the Department of Education and Training. When I moved into middle management, although I was based at the Millhaven campus, there were frequent trips to the Ralston campus where my boss sat. Our Director, Geoff Inneston, also was based on the Millhaven campus, but the institute's main administration function was based at Ralston. I saw the woman at Ralston a couple of times but, until the introduction, never spoke to her. She might have visited the Millhaven campus. If she did, I didn't know about it.

When I left the institute, the Department and the Public Service all in one foul swoop, Inneston was in the process of moving the major administration function to the Millhaven campus. He wanted them sitting outside his door to allow him a tighter rein on things. After I left, and the admin department was ensconced on Millhaven campus, the woman might have then become a regular visitor to Millhaven. Whatever the situation, I have no doubt Geoff Inneston knew her well… and possibly in the biblical sense too.

The department's employees became something of an ever-changing gallery of portraits as staff constantly changed. They changed jobs, climbed the ladder, changed sections, changed departments, in the hope of finding a position that gave them more money and, above all, offered something resembling security of employment – something that had become very rare indeed in the

Public Service. Perhaps this woman was one of those 'changelings'. Maybe she no longer worked for the Department.

My mind started to relax having reached that point, but one final question lingered as I drifted off to sleep. It seems likely Geoff Inneston knew her and they had developed a strong bond, whatever the nature of that bond, so it would not be too difficult to understand her visiting him occasionally. The fact that she visited him every month and posed as Inneston's wife begged the question that bothered me all day. What was the nature of that relationship then and what was it now? I didn't buy the notion that she was just a friend.

In spite of all the mental gymnastics before I fell asleep last night, I slept well. Over breakfast, I mulled over my plans for the day. I had nothing concrete to pass on to Sandra yet. Sometime in the past Sandra might have had contact with this woman, and might even know her name. However, I dismissed talking to Sandra about the woman until I had more information.

And there was the Fielding case to think about. Ben and I hadn't discussed it last night. I wasted a few moments on wondering whether that meant Ben had found no connection with any current police investigation, or whether he hadn't time to think about it yesterday. I could go for another drive today to see who was where, I told myself, and I knew that's what I would do first thing this morning. That left one insurance job begging for urgent attention. I thought about the job, was it something I could do during the day or was it an after dark activity. I decided I could do some preliminary scoping work for the job during the day.

My first port of call was the industrial estate. I drove past Thornton Transport and pulled into the car park beside the mower repair shop. I hadn't seen Terry's little red car in Thornton's carpark. The carpark was full. The red car could be hidden anywhere amongst the others. It was 7.25a.m. If Terry was coming into work today, he should have arrived.

It was wasting time watching Thornton's car park. I drove out onto the street. When I was only about 20 metres from the Thornton's entrance, a small red car careered towards me, bounced onto the footpath and roared through Thornton's gates. Although I slowed to a crawl when I recognised the car, I had nothing more than a fleeting glimpse of the car's occupants. Blondie accompanied Terry to work this morning.

That was easy and it was still early, too early to face my office yet. Besides, there was no point in only doing half the job. I drove through town and out to Sandlands. The world had come to life in the beachside suburb. Vehicles were streaming out of the place as residents made their way to work in town. I drove into Sandlands and immediately swung onto Grevillea Crescent. The truck was reversing down the driveway at Blondie's house as I drove past. I drove out the end of Grevillea Crescent and around the big roundabout before joining something of a procession heading out of Sandlands.

As I drove behind a gaggle of other cars along the main street, I could see the high canopy of the truck at the junction of the street and Grevillea Crescent. Something caused a small gap in the through traffic. The truck slid out of Grevillea Crescent and entered the vehicular procession about four cars ahead of me. I maintained my place in the convoy all the way into town. Numerous vehicles dropped off at various points as we approached town. With only two cars between us now, I followed the truck across town and out to the industrial estate.

I caught a red light at a major intersection while those ahead of me scraped through on the green. I addressed the universe in colourful language for a moment before realising the red light might be a godsend. It allowed a reasonable gap to open up between me and the others. When the light finally went green again, I maintained the gap but kept my eyes firmly on the tall canopy of the truck some distance ahead. From my distant vantage point, I watched the canopy turn left into a side street. I knew where it was headed. I turned right into a street before I reached the one the truck had turned into.

After fighting my way through the maze of back streets and alleys, I found the main road into area again, and drove sedately out of the industrial estate. Once outside the estate, I pulled up in front of a small store with the intention of buying a newspaper. While the place carried a limited range of grocery items, its main trade would have been as a café-cum-diner for workers in its surrounding area.

The aroma of freshly brewed coffee was overwhelming and convinced me that, although breakfast wasn't all that long ago, another cup of coffee so soon was okay. Besides, having someone else make it was a bonus. I took my coffee and newspaper to a small table beside the shop's plate glass window and waited.

It is difficult to spend more than a couple of minutes reading the local daily newspaper, even Friday's edition. The process can take a little longer if you are trying to read it with one eye on the traffic, but even that doesn't stretch it beyond several minutes. By the time I had to give up the pretence, it was past nine o'clock. I folded the newspaper and was about to get up from the table when my phone chirped: Ben.

I assumed his phone call was to give me the name of the person the SUV was registered to. To be ringing so early in the morning, he hadn't done himself any favours by having a lazy start to the day. "Ben, are you at work this early on such a fine morning? More importantly, what news do you have for me?"

"I had to come in early for something else, so I checked that registration for you. Does the name Gloria Purtell mean anything to you?"

"Not a thing; but if that's the name of the woman we looked at last night, I think I worked out why she seemed familiar. Did you get her address as well as her name?"

"Yeah, it's a long way south of here. She gave an address in the Gold Coast hinterland on the registration. It seems it is a private vehicle. I've got to go but, if I get a chance, I'll check her out further. Talk to you tonight maybe..."

He ended the call before I could tell him I was planning to undertake surveillance work tonight. I'll send him a text later when I know for sure what I'm doing. Ben's call gave me the excuse to remain at my table near the window a bit longer. Once the call ended, I made a show of making notes that I hoped looked like they related to Ben's call. As I still had my phone out, I decided to consult Mr Google. I keyed in 'Gloria Purtell' and waited for Google's response.

Google had a bit to offer, but I decided it was preferable to explore the information back at the office, where I could print bits if needed.

Where was my car key? I scratched around in my bag. I'm good with keys; never lose them. There was no key in my bag. I slung the bag over my shoulder and stood with my hands on my hips. The fingers of my right hand found a lump in my jeans pocket. Panic over; I found my key. With key in hand, I was about to step out onto the footpath when a certain truck with a high canopy on the back came out of the industrial estate and drove past.

I let a couple of vehicles go past before following the truck. We headed for Sandlands. As I approached the suburb's glorious entrance gateway, my phone chirped. I thought it probably was Ben ringing with more information. I let it ring out. When safe, I pulled off the road and I checked my phone. The missed call was Sam Keller. As I hit the speed dial button to call her back, I fished around in my bag for a notebook and pen. The danger was that she now wouldn't be in a position to talk to me.

"Sam, Sonny; Sorry I didn't answer your call, I was driving. Are you able to talk now, or should I leave it for you to call me back?"

"Give me five minutes. I have one quick call to make and then I'll call you."

It didn't think I would have time to drive to the office before she called back, so I drove to Melaleuca Grove parkland and parked under the trees. Sam rang back a few minutes later.

"Sonny, I looked into Geoff Inneston's visitors log. In recent times, his only visitor was his wife, Sandra Inneston. She has a permanent monthly booking. A couple of interesting things emerged around the time of his incarceration. Sandra Inneston visited him a couple of times at the beginning, before disappearing for a couple of months. Then she resumed regular monthly visits, but on a different week. There weren't many other visitors apart from his solicitor and his articled clerk on a few occasions over a period of several months, but nothing recently."

"I expected his solicitor would feature in the list of visitors, and I think I had worked out about the 'Mrs Inneston'. Were there any other visitors?"

"One other bloke has visited three times since Inneston was incarcerated. He is from the Education Department's HR section. His visits were all in the first year. There was one other visitor who appears a couple of times in the register. There were only about three visits I think and they were in the first three or four months. She also is an Education Department staffer, employed as something in the Finance Section."

"That one I am interested in. Do you have any of the information she supplied to become an authorised visitor?"

"Yeah, a bit; because she is with the Department of Education and Training, she didn't have to jump through the same hoops as everyone else. Her name is Gloria Purtell, she lives on the Gold Coast and she is a Public Servant. That drugs trafficking case involving Public Servants, including Inneston, threw the department into a spin. They ran audits on everything and everyone for months afterwards. I imagine her visiting Inneston would have been part of that 'accounting for the cash' operation that went on."

"You've done well. There were no other visitors at all?"

"There were two blokes, both of whom only visited once during the first few months. They turned out to be from the Department as well and I worked out they would have worked with Inneston in the past. I almost forgot. I managed to get a couple of images from Tulloch's processing centre's CCTV. They might be useful. One is of the Purtell woman, and the other is of the Sandra Inneston who is a regular visitor. Do you want copies?"

"O-o-h, yes please. At the risk of stretching the friendship, would it be possible to get me images of his other visitors as well?"

"Uhmm... yes, I probably could do that without raising too much attention. I need to do it now while I'm working this other angle. It might take a day or two. I'll send them to you from home rather than from work. Gotta go; I'll let you know if anything else crops up."

Yes please, I thought as I drove out of the park and onto Grevillea Crescent. I don't know why I'm doing this. I know the truck will be back at Blondie's and locked away in the shed. Nevertheless, I cruised the Crescent and proved what I already knew before heading for my office.

The blinking red light announced I had messages. "Not now… later," I told the machine Sam's email with the images from the Tulloch Correctional Centre's CCTV had arrived. The first one showed a woman with long blonde hair in an elaborate hairstyle and too much make-up. 'Stage make-up' came to mind.

While her face was the focus of the image, it took in down as far as her waist. The woman's dress appeared to be a floral knit fabric and devoid of shaping from shoulder to waist. A short buttoned opening at the centre neckline was buttoned up to the neck and was finished with a little collar in the same material as the dress. "That dress does not fit the head," I told an empty office.

Sam's captioned the image with 'Gloria Purtell'. Not a skilled attempt at hiding an identity, I decided. I enlarged the image and studied the facial features. After printing a copy, I turned my attention to Sam Keller's second image.

This was no surprises. The face staring at me from the screen was that of the charcoal grey two-piece driving the black SUV. Its caption announced it was Sandra Inneston. "In Sandra's dreams…" I told the image. The woman with short dark hair, minimal make-up skilfully applied, wore a navy blue jacket over a collarless high-necked white blouse. To confirm my assessment, I brought both images up onto the screen side-by-side. There was no doubt. The two images were of the same woman, Gloria Purtell.

What now, I thought as I printed off the second image. I had identified the woman passing herself off as Sandra Inneston, but that tiny part of the story only teased me. I needed to know her connection to Geoff Inneston, not since his incarceration, but prior to that. The copies of photos Sandra gave me suggested there was a long-standing well developed connection. I remembered all the mentions of Gloria Purtell Google found earlier for me. I asked Google to find them again.

I examined all the entries, printing off some and skimming over others. It took until lunchtime to peruse the list. Most of the entries were short and related to her position as a public servant. I stacked all the printed material, including Sam's two images, neatly in the centre of my desk ready review everything. It seemed a reasonable task to do over lunch so, with chicken and salad roll in hand, I began rereading everything I had on Gloria Purtell.

It seems she is a career public servant, who entered the Service years ago, although not clear whether that was straight from school or after university. She worked in a number of departments before moving to the Education and Training Department 15 years ago. It was a step-up for her and after that, she continued working her way along the promotions trail within that department. After a couple of years in the Admin Section of the department, she moved sideways to the Department's Finance Section (I congratulated myself on remembering that much from our introduction in the lift) and rose through the ranks in Finance over a few years.

The next printout was an attention-grabbing newsletter article announcing Gloria Purtell's appointment to the position of auditor within the Finance Section. It explained that, as its auditor, Gloria would be visiting all Department operations on a regular basis. In closing, the article encouraged all operational centres to make her welcome and assist her to settle into the position. Interesting…! Gloria's new position meant she spent her time travelling up and down and across the State. How convenient might that be for a drug trafficking network?

After thinking about what I knew about Gloria Purtell thus far, I scanned the remaining printouts. It seemed strange that Ms Purtell sought no further promotion after being appointed an auditor. It seems she remains an auditor with the Finance Section.

Even without further promotions, her grade level within the Public Service would have increased based on length of service. By now, she must have been on an auditor's top grade level for some years. Although I lacked current information, my knowledge of grade levels within the Department suggested her current annual salary crossed the six-figure threshold a few years ago. Whatever her salary now, in my mind it more than allowed for her wardrobe and choice of vehicles, especially as all her travel expenses are met by her employer.

If she is as clever as I believe she is, she could organise her travel to be able to slot in a visit to the Tulloch Correctional Centre every month. The questions remains: were the visits due to a personal relationship – 'personal' sounds less harsh than 'adulterous' – with

Inneston, or were they part of an ongoing 'business' relationship? Bugger! Now I've created another question for myself. If the latter is the case, is that drug trafficking network that involved so many public servants, including Geoff Inneston, still operational?

I tried to lose that idea. It didn't work. The question simply moved itself to the back of my mind and continued lingering there. My phone rang: Sam Keller. She asked if I was free, and launched into what she had to say before I had a chance to answer.

"I thought about your question regarding Geoff Inneston's other visitors and went back to the register. I've emailed you all the information I could get on his other visitors, with the exception of his solicitor and the solicitor's clerk. There were images, but they're not very clear. Apparently they had a lot of trouble with the CCTV system when first installed, which was around the time Inneston was sent there. Have you had a chance to look through what I sent before, and was it useful?"

"Yes, and I was just doing a bit more follow-up research. Is there anything so far to suggest something relates to your case at all?"

"I'm not sure... Something tells me there is a connection, but I can't see it. I haven't had time to think about it. I'm sure Pete Messell is going to ask me what I've found before too much longer and I want to feel confident about my answer when the time comes."

"I'll keep digging at my end because I think it might be relevant to my case. When I start pulling it all together, if it looks like there is a connection with whatever you're working on, I'll keep you in the loop."

As I turned to my computer to look at the latest information Sam sent me, the persistent blinking red light reminded me I had messages requiring attention. It made sense to deal with those first. There were two calls. The first was a potential client asking for information. I returned the call and obtained an email address so I could send her my various brochures. The other was Emily enquiring about progress on the Fielding case. That jolted me back to reality and brought on a fit of guilt. Since Sam's early morning phone call, I hadn't given a thought to the Fielding case, or to Trish Fielding's disappearance.

I couldn't use Emily on either of my investigations, but I couldn't be in two places at once. Although I'd planned to work tonight on another insurance case, I hadn't done any preparation for it. Perhaps I'd be better staying at home tonight and discussing my two major cases with Ben. I figured there was just enough time to look at Sam's latest email before indulging in my twice a day ritual of checking up on the movements of all the Fielding case players.

Sam's email was interesting. I printed out the email and its attachments and shoved them into the Inneston file. It took me a couple of minutes to sort out and make sure I had everything I wanted to take home with me before leaving the office. Ever hopeful there might be something from Trish, I checked my mailbox on my way to the industrial estate.

My routine for the next couple of hours echoed that of the last few days. Again, as I parked in a different area along the street from Thornton Transport, I asked myself the question: what is the point of wasting time and effort on a case that no one else seems interested in and that I probably won't get paid for? Nevertheless, I followed the little red car back to Blondie's house, and then hung around until about six o'clock when I followed the truck back to that same street in the industrial estate.

While I hung around waiting for the truck to leave Blondie's, I rang Ben. He thought he would be tied up at the precinct until after seven o'clock, but would pick up something for dinner on his way to my place after that. Good news; It meant I didn't have to be home until seven o'clock. I parked in a side street off the main road into the industrial estate and waited. Seven o'clock approached and I had seen nothing more of the truck. I started the car and was about to drive off when the truck flew past on its way out of the estate.

I followed it through town and over the bridge. It headed towards Sandlands. Perhaps he will have dinner and then do whatever else he has planned for tonight, I told myself. But, it was after seven o'clock and I should be at home. I half expected a phone call from Ben asking where I was. I arrived home about five minutes before Ben. I took a long way home which included driving past the Fielding's unit. There were no lights on. No one was home.

Chapter 13

Ben looked weary. He was loaded with food and wine. By the heady aroma filling the room, it was fish and chips tonight. I had no argument with that. We ate in the dining area as moving everything out to the deck seemed like too much pfaffing about. As usual, we didn't taint dinner by discussing work, confining ourselves to general small talk. Ben was tense, more so than I had seen in a long time. I wondered if discussion of my cases might exacerbate matters.

After dinner, we adjourned to the comfort of the lounge chairs and 'shop talk' began. I opened the conversation. "How come you are so late leaving the precinct tonight? The town seems pretty quiet at the moment."

"Yeah, there's nothing making the headlines, but we believe there is something happening. We haven't got a handle on it yet. What about your day? Anything interesting happen with that case you're working on?"

Somehow, discussing the Inneston case wasn't a priority right now. I had thought otherwise until I drove past the Fieldings' unit on my way home. I knew Terry wouldn't be there but Trish should be at home. Concern for her apparent disappearance outweighed anything else I might have wanted to discuss with Ben this evening.

"The Inneston case is progressing. I think that's about the only comment worth making. There is something else I'd like to discuss. I don't know if you feel up to it but, if you would rather not, just say so."

"It might be a breath of fresh air after the day I've had; fire away."

"It's another case I took on at the same time as the Inneston case. I thought it would fit in well. As I wasn't able to do much on the Inneston case until yesterday, I thought the other one would fill in and be settled by then. It hasn't worked out that way. The more I look into the Inneston case, the more convinced I am that it is about more than an unfaithful husband. The other case, also supposedly about an unfaithful husband, has developed worrying aspects."

"What exactly are 'worrying aspects'? Are they something that stem from your point of view regarding infidelity, or are there sinister overtones involved?"

I shot Ben a look. Was he being patronising? Although his face was fairly deadpan, I saw the laughter in his eyes. Damn the man, he can read me like a book. He knew I was trying to pick my way into this conversation and was needling me about it. Get on with it, I told myself, and launched into an overview of the Fielding case. When I'd given him the story, I indicated there were two issues haunting me.

"My gut is telling me that truck is involved in something illegal. I don't know how it fits together, but I feel the three people and the truck are involved, and Blondie's house and the industrial estate are fundamental to the operation."

"I take it you have discounted that it's nothing more than a bit of kinky threesome stuff going on." I gave him an 'oh, please' type eye roll. "Okay, scratch that. The truck driver could be Blondie's husband, son, brother, or simply an acquaintance, who you think lives in the house. He might be a bloke using his truck to operate a legal carrying business. Why do you think otherwise?"

"…Because of that strange incident involving the semi-trailer on that first night."

"What incident with a semi?"

"Oops, did I not mention that?" In my rush to roll out the story of the Fielding case, I seem to have omitted details of that first night's surveillance. Best I don't mention Emily's involvement I think. I explained seeing the semi arrive at Thornton's late at night and about how it disappeared behind the building before reappearing later to pull into the loading bay. "While they worked on the semi in the loading bay, a light truck with a high canopy on the back emerged from behind the building and left the premises. That was the first time I saw the truck. Although it was strange, I might have forgotten about it if that truck didn't continue to be involved with Terry and Blondie."

"You said the industrial estate was fundamental to whatever was happening. Does the truck continue to visit Thornton's? It's logical that a carrier might reasonably deliver goods to Thornton's for onforwarding by semi to some distant destination."

"It hasn't been back to Thornton's… well, not during the time I've been watching it. There's another address in the industrial estate it frequents. It's some sort of warehouse building with a huge roller door that they drop after the truck enters. There might be other places the truck goes at other times when I'm not watching, Blondie's, that warehouse, and that one time at Thornton's, are the only places I know about."

Ben's interest was tickled by my information. I could tell by his demeanour and the string of questions asked. After a while, it seems we exhausted the topic of the truck, and Ben started off on another tack. "You said there were two worrying issues associated with the case. The truck was one. What's the other one?"

His tone changed. Ben, business-like now, had taken over driving the discussion. For a fleeting moment, I wondered whether that was a good thing or not. I detected an increased interest in the Fielding case, and he looked less weary than when he arrived. My antennae were twitching. This was Ben being more than polite. Something else was behind the change in him. I felt my pulse quickening. I knew intrigue when it was afoot. Maybe I need to take care how I progress from here.

"The other thing that concerns me is the sudden and complete loss of contact with Trish Fielding. It's not just the loss of contact. It's more about her sudden inexplicable and ongoing disappearance. I haven't been able to contact her since the end of last week, and she seems to have abandoned their unit."

"I can think of a couple of scenarios that could account for that. Maybe she challenged him about an affair and he confessed, or maybe she found some evidence that confirmed an affair. Either way, she decided she was out of there, and packed up and left. Sometime along the way, she realised that, if you couldn't contact her, you couldn't get her to pay up."

"Yes, I could buy that except for the dog."

"The dog...? What dog and what about it?"

I explained about the neighbour finding the dog apparently abandoned and in a distressed state. Although I made sure Emily's name wasn't mentioned, I also avoided saying it was me who spoke to the neighbour. That would be too far removed from the truth. Ben studied his hands locked together in his lap as I spoke. He didn't look up when I ended the story, so I sought a 'punch line' in a bid to regain his attention. "The dog was a little hairy lapdog thing. It was a woman's dog rather than a man's pet. Regardless of whose dog it was, it was abandoned. If it was Trish's dog, why didn't she take it with her when she left... there seems little doubt she has left. If it was Terry's pet and he was sufficiently fond of it, he would have it with him – probably take it to Blondie's house. I don't think this is a case of Trish leaving Terry."

"There is the possibility that she couldn't take it with her. Maybe she left the district by train or plane and couldn't take the dog with her without hefty expense. They both might be fond of the dog, and she thought Terry would look after it after she left."

"Y-e-s, I can see the logic in that, but I think she would have left by car. Taking her things, including the dog, with her wouldn't be a problem."

"Did the Fieldings have a second car?"

"I don't know, but I think so. I never saw another car, but I got the impression the little red car was Terry's after he bought it from his daughter to help her out. I suspect they already had a car. Once the red one arrived, the other one became Trish's vehicle."

"Where does the vehicle live when it's at home: in a garage, in the street?"

"I don't know. It could be parked in the street, but I wouldn't know whose it was."

This inquisition had me feeling less than professional about my handling of the Fielding case. I was about to share that with Ben. When I looked over at him, he had changed. He now sat forward in his chair, his elbows planted on his thighs, as he locked and unlocked his hands between his knees. I bit my tongue. It was obvious Ben was deep in thought and wrestling with some gnarly problem. He heaved himself back up straight. "Coffee would be good about now," he suggested.

Oh, good; I'm looking for inspiration and help to make sense of the Fielding case, and he wants coffee. What else could I do but make coffee? Ben seemed more relaxed. During a long silence while we sipped our coffee, Ben disappeared into a world of his own. I had drunk half of my coffee when Ben startled me by saying, "Yeah, I think that might be what it's all about."

"Do enlighten me, please."

"My boys have been running an investigation for a couple of weeks. Since it started, I think almost everybody from the precinct has been involved at some time. The troubling thing about it is that nobody knows exactly what we are supposed to be looking for."

"That should make life interesting. Are you sure you do have something to investigate?"

"While I was away, intel came through about suspicious activity involving a number of locations. Millhaven was one of those locations. Our source didn't have many details to share. However, they believed it involves trafficking of some sort, but nobody knows what."

"How can you be sure trafficking is occurring if you don't know what is being trafficked?"

"Good question; the source of the intelligence that triggered the investigation received a tip off from another national authority about suspicious movements of transports. There was nothing concrete to indicate the activity they were monitoring was illegal. It was just that the activity deviated from past practice models."

"What does your brother have to say on the subject?"

"Neil has been away on a case, so I haven't been able to contact him. I did speak with the Federal Police. They claim to be as much in the dark as we are. I plan to ring Neil tomorrow. He should arrive home tonight. Knowing my brother, he will go into the office first thing in the morning. I'll try giving him a call late in the morning."

It will be interesting to see if Ben's brother, Neil Richards, knows any more than his fellow Federal Police officers. However, in a couple of previous cases where I have encountered Neil, he seemed to have access to sources other than those the Feds use. While what Ben shared was interesting, I couldn't see how it related to my case. I wonder if he absorbed any of what I told him. I was about to verbalise that thought when Ben started pacing about the room. After a few moments, he returned to his chair and began speaking hesitantly as gathering his thought as he spoke.

"There…just…might be… Sonny, what you told me tonight about your Fielding case makes me wonder if there might be some connection – however tenuous – between your case and our investigation. I'll give it some thought tonight. Tomorrow I'll go into the station to gather all the information we have so far… and to call my brother. Where will you be after lunch tomorrow?"

"I don't know, but either in my office here at home or at my office in town. I have an insurance case I was supposed to start work on a couple of days ago and I still haven't done any preparation for it."

"Okay, I'll call your mobile if I think we need to get together before tomorrow night. It's time I was gone. I'll talk to you sometime tomorrow."

He bounced up out of the chair and headed for the door. Conversations with Ben were akin to mental gymnastics. It keeps your mind exercised trying to keep up with all the chopping and changing of topics that occur. As I cleaned up, I wondered what tonight achieved in terms of my concern for Trish Fielding's wellbeing. On face value, it appeared I hadn't achieved anything, but I had gotten to know Ben Richards well over the many years of our friendship. What I told him about the case hit home. I had a feeling I would reap the benefits of tonight's discussion in the coming days.

As I drifted off to sleep, my last thoughts were about possible connections between my case and his brief information about a current police investigation.

****

Saturday mornings I devote to domestic chores (if I have to) and reading the paper at leisure over a cup of coffee. Today, there were a couple of chores to do at home before I headed to my office in town. I must make a start that insurance job. Instead of the weekend papers with my coffee, I read the case file.

It appears a well-to-do family home in an upmarket part of Millhaven was broken into over a week ago. The usual electronic gear and a few other expensive bits and pieces were taken. The theft was upsetting enough, but the thieves then expended much time and energy in trashing parts of the house and most of the front yard. This was a substantial house on an enormous block of land including magnificent landscaped grounds boasting several statues, a couple of fountains and a gravel circular driveway.

Statues and the fountains were damaged and several craters were left in the driveway. A circular bed of Proteas was trampled and then driven over several times rendering the survival of the plants unlikely. The French doors to a conservatory type area were rammed and pots containing orchid plants were upended on the floor. Assessment of the damage and loss amounted to hundreds of thousands of dollars. However, the insurance company's assessor was unconvinced it was a straightforward case of theft and vandalism.

In his report, he claimed the damage appeared too targeted and 'emotional'. The perpetrators appeared to know the loss of which things would cause the most distress for the owners. After studying the photos provided, I returned to the file in the hope of identifying a starting point for my investigation. I struck out and, resigning myself to the fact that I was no closer to starting this investigation than I was a week ago, I pushed the case file aside.

What did I know about the family? ... Short answer: not much. I remembered from newspaper articles that the husband made a packet out of civil construction projects. The wife, a big player on the local social scene, rated frequent mentioned in the 'society pages'. Time to boot up my computer get to know the family better.

An hour or so later, I knew the family was worth mega bucks. Apart from civil construction works, the husband had invested in mining in time to make a killing during the boom. The family company diversified and continued to do nicely thank you, while the husband served on a number of boards, further adding to the income stream. There were two children from his first marriage: a son with a couple of degrees who has an executive position in the company, and a much younger daughter.

After wading through irrelevant postings, I discovered the first wife died after a short battle with cancer. I calculated the daughter, Cynthia, was about 10 or 11 at the time. Her brother was already at university. Cynthia was packed off to boarding school until she was about 16. With some big project happening in Victoria, her father based himself in Melbourne after his wife's death. That's where he met his current wife and married her two years ago.

The daughter, not taking too well to the new arrangement, played up and was thrown out of her prestigious school last year. Sweet Cynthia went off the rails after that. The newspapers reported run-ins with the law, all for misdemeanours. Now, as one of a group of indulged youth, she is a fixture on the law enforcement's radar. Recent recorded public spats with her stepmother suggest things haven't improved at home.

I sat back, assembled the new information, and added it to the case file. As I reviewed this morning's efforts, my phone rang. It sounded deafening in the silent building. A cheery voice greeted me. "Got you on the first try; I thought you might go into the office today," Ben said. "What are you doing for lunch?"

Lunch... can it be that late already? I checked the time. Yep, definitely lunchtime. "I hadn't thought about it, so nothing planned at this time."

"Okay, you keep doing what you're doing and I'll see you in about 20 minutes – with lunch. You will have to let me in, since the building is closed today."

Ben's impending visit intrigued me. It was unusual for us to catch up in the middle of the day, let alone on a Saturday. My pulse quickened. I remembered Ben intended ringing his brother, Neil, this morning. The lunchtime visit might mean Neil gave Ben something relevant to my case... or perhaps it was something 'big' in relation to the Police's investigation.

After scrawling a few more notes for the insurance case file, I tidied up, filled the coffee machine and put it on to brew. As I retrieved a couple of mugs from the shelf above the coffee machine, Ben rang for me to let him in. Lunch smelled glorious and turned out to be chicken satay wraps. In spite of my – subtle – efforts, Ben avoided discussing his visit until after we dispatched the wraps and coffee.

"I rang Neil this morning. I thought you might be interested in what he had to say. Don't get excited. I'm not convinced it is of use to you, but there's always a chance I suppose."

If that were true, and he held genuine doubts about its relevance to my case, he would not be sitting in my office now. Anyway, that is what I told myself as I waited for him to get on with sharing his recent information. "Neil spoke to some 'unnamed sources' earlier. He gleaned some interesting information that helps explain why our investigation was something of a conundrum. Due to the lack of precise information, we worked on the assumption that, if trafficking was occurring, it would focus on one commodity. Logic and past experience suggested that commodity would be illegal drugs."

"I suppose that's the thought I had last night when you were talking about your investigation. Are you telling me now that's not the case?"

"Yes… and no. There is suggestion drugs are involved, but the surprise is that the trafficking is not confined to one commodity. The other factor emerging is that it's not just one highly organised trafficking network. From work done in other parts of the country, the latest theory is that the operation consists of small cells working around a hub servicing a particular area. The hubs might prove part of some overarching network, but there is insufficient evidence to run with that idea yet."

"I see that more as a variation on the theme rather than a major departure from what we encountered in the past. While I accept that it's different, I don't see it as being significant. Nevertheless, I am interested in how these cells and hubs operate, and why it's thought their business involves more than one commodity."

"That's where it gets a bit blurry. Details are sketchy, and it appears there could be variations in how the hubs operate and in the secondary commodities they choose to include in their operations. It appears the hubs have a high degree of autonomy within their own area, but they maintain some interaction, or cooperation, with hubs in other areas."

"What types of secondary commodities are we talking about? I can't think of much else that's in the same league dollar-wise as illegal drugs."

"That's the big question we don't have an answer to yet. A long list of possibilities exists, but the difficulty is in that each hub can make its own choices about what it deals in and how that occurs. There seems to be no doubt Millhaven is a part of the wider operation. Investigation to date failed to uncover anything resembling illegal activities happening around here."

"Are you thinking what I'm thinking... that my truck and Thornton Transport might be the key to the operation in Millhaven? I almost can see how that might work but, given all I know so far, I can't be sure whatever is going on isn't a legitimate commercial operation."

We worried the topic to death for the next while without reaching any sound conclusions. My gut told me what I observed during my Fielding case investigation might be the missing link in the Police's investigation. No point mentioning my gut instinct to Ben. He was not a believer. Nevertheless, I was itching for Ben to leave so I could devote some serious thought to how to proceed. He must have read my mind. He gathered up the coffee mugs and rinsed them, before heading for the door.

"Hang on, Ben, don't go yet." After wishing him gone, I now remembered something we never seem to get around to discussing: Trish Fielding's disappearance. "You don't seem to have any particular interest in this, but I am concerned about Trish Fielding. My intuition is telling me she might have met with foul play. If Thornton's, and Trish's husband Terry in particular, are involved in this trafficking thing, I'm all the more convinced her disappearance wasn't her own idea. Aren't you at all concerned that she might not be okay?"

"Not as concerned as you appear to be, because we have nothing to suggest we should be concerned. Without something more, we couldn't get a warrant to carry out an investigation of the unit or of her husband." I opened my mouth to argue, but he held up his hand to stop me. "Nothing more to be said; I'm going now and I'll see you tonight."

Tough luck, buster! "Ah, no you won't. I have surveillance to undertake tonight, and it could last until breakfast time." It wasn't too far from the truth. I was thinking of making a start on the insurance case… although I hadn't worked out what that 'start' might be. The supercilious sod could find someone else's house to eat at tonight. Ben had the knack of dismissing me like some teenage bimbo when he didn't agree with me. That might be one of the reasons we never made it beyond being friends.

A few minutes after Ben left, I gathered up my files, snagged my bag off the spare chair as I went past, and went home.

Chapter 14

Time to check out the upmarket part of town and the damage to the well-to-do family's property. As I prepared snacks and coffee for a night away from home, I tried to work up a plan. The house was unlikely to be hit again so soon, and parking for any length of time in that part of town would bring security and/or the Police. However, a slow drive through the neighbourhood wouldn't hurt to refresh my memory of the house and grounds, and identify other potential targets in the area.

While not an avid reader of the local newspaper, I do manage to skim through it each day. I couldn't remember reports of recent similar robberies. Until almost six o'clock was spent checking previous editions of the local paper online. No mention of any similar incidents in residential areas, although there had been a spate of robberies of commercial premises.

Traffic was light as I drove to the leafy area that was home to many of the wealthy local residents. As expected, a look at the crime scene told me nothing, although the scars of damage to the grounds were visible from the street as I crawled past. I hadn't gone much further when the sound of a vehicle caught my attention. I pulled over and grabbed my phone. A silver coloured sports car with the top down roared out of the crime scene driveway and flew past me as I sat pretending to be on a phone call.

With no plan for what to do next, I abandoned the phone and followed the sports car. Sports cars must be immune to traffic calming devices. This one careered over speed bumps and other calming devices installed along the street, ignoring Give Way signs and speed limits. As a result, the gap between us increased as I made some attempt at driving responsibly.

The car headed towards town. On entering the commercial area, it slowed to a legal speed. By then, I was far behind it. I lost sight of the sports car after I entered the city centre. At this time, shops were closed, diners weren't flocking to restaurants yet, and it was too early for the many nightclubs in the city heart to open. How could I lose a flashy sports car amid so little activity and almost no traffic?

I drove to the end of the main street and checked out traffic heading out towards the beachside suburbs. No sign of the sports car, so I turned and began cruising the meticulous grid pattern of streets in the city centre area. I found myself back at the point where I entered the city centre about half an hour earlier. With no better ideas on what to do next, I again drove the length of the main street and across the road that led to the bridge. This took me into an area that, although still considered part of the city's commercial precinct, was a much lesser animal than the city heart.

Dotted along both sides of the street were a number of pawn shops and 'greasy spoon' type diners. Motor mechanics and panel and paint shops seemed to predominate in what was more of a light industrial area than a shopping precinct. The eastern end of the street presented two options. Straight ahead was the huge parking lot servicing the local boat ramp used by recreational fishermen, or continue along the street to where it made a sharp right-hand turn into what looked like a seedy residential area. I wasn't going fishing, so I followed the road around the bend.

This was one of the earliest residential areas established in Millhaven. Cottages were small and old. Modifications to some of them served the needs of their residents but ignored aesthetics. None of the buildings had seen fresh paint in a long time. This, coupled with the high proportion of derelict buildings, gave the place a ticky-tacky look that screamed 'slum'. Graffiti was everywhere. Some derelict buildings, although apparently boarded up, showed signs of habitation. This was a squatters' paradise.

A flashy silver sports car, incongruous with this area, would stand out like the proverbial. I would not undertake night time surveillance in the area. Just driving through it gave me an uneasy feeling. At not much above a crawl, I drove through looking for somewhere to turn and head back into the city centre. With the opportunity for a carjacking at the forefront of my mind, I wanted somewhere to turn around without having to make a 44-point turn. Places where I could describe a wide arc to drive out the way I came in were in short supply.

About to abandon my search for a safe place to turn, I went around a bend and encountered what was once a park. In one corner, the rusting skeletons remained of what were once children's playground equipment. That long grass covering the area didn't deter use by the locals was evidenced by discarded garbage littering the place. A couple of house-proud residents dumped unwanted vehicles in the park rather than allow them to clutter their front yards. The vehicles, now nothing more than rusting hulks, added to the neglect and desolation of the park.

For several metres along the road, the kerb beside the park had crumbled and disappeared. I took advantage of the non-existent kerb and drove into the park. The slight bump that was all that remained of the former kerb posed no challenge for my SUV. As I described a wide circle through the long grass, I hoped my tyres would stand up to syringes or other unmentionable sharps discarded in the grass. After several seconds, I was back on the street and breathing normally again. Focused on getting out of this place as quickly as possible, I increased speed to almost the legal limit… and then jumped hard on the brake pedal.

Some distance up ahead, a silver sports car bumped out from behind a building and roared off down the street away from me. The driver, talking on her phone, didn't check for other traffic. A few metres ahead of where I stopped, what was once a bougainvillea hedge along a property boundary line had escaped the confines of its yard and roamed free. The tangled mass of colour and thorns now crossed the footpath to encroach on the bitumen. I pulled off the bitumen and eased up to the rampant greenery. Although not hidden from view, the bougainvillea provided me partial cover.

I sat studying the building that Cynthia and her sports car had left. It was difficult to tell whether the building was once a block of units or something else. Abandoned long ago, the derelict building, featuring curling paint and bare weatherboards, was adorned with graffiti. Although boarded up, there were signs of life. It wasn't clear whether squatters had taken it over, or if it served as a venue for occasional get-togethers by a few locals. My interest focused on what the overindulged Cynthia and her sports car were doing here.

What am I waiting for, I asked myself as I remained parked

behind my bougainvillea screen. I had taken photos of the property and scribbled notes for my case file while I waited, but no one else appeared and nothing seemed to be happening at the building. But my gut told me to continue to wait. I hope it comes up with something creative for me to tell the locals who come to investigate why I'm parked here for so long.

An intense darkness began to set in. A tiny sliver of a new moon crawled above the horizon but failed to add much light to this part of the world. Five more minutes, I told myself. That would be half an hour, more than enough time for something to happen if anything were going to happen. About two minutes after giving myself the five-minute deadline, headlights lit up the street.

They slowed and turned into the derelict building's yard. A second set of lights coming along the street lit up the first vehicle. Cynthia and her sports car had returned. The sports car bumped its way over the rough driveway and around behind the building. Although the car had disappeared, the glare of its headlights remained visible for a while. The second set of headlights now reached the derelict building, turned in and negotiated the driveway.

There is something familiar about that vehicle. I wish I knew what. At last, the vehicle reached the end of the driveway, turned and was lit up by the sports car's headlights. "What the...?" I yelped, and snatched my camera off the passenger seat. A couple of quick shots before the truck disappeared. It too parked behind the building.

I tried to make sense of what I'd seen. That is 'my' truck with the high canopy that is now parked behind the derelict building. It appears whatever is happening over there requires the vehicles to keep their headlights on. Although I can't see the vehicles, their headlights light up the backyard of the building, revealing cluttered rubbish including drums and car bodies along the back fence.

Now two questions occupied my mind... or the same question relating to two different situations. I'd already spent time wondering what Cynthia and her sports car were doing here. Why the truck was here was the new question nagging at me. After my discussion with Ben earlier today, I suspected the truck – and Terry – might be involved in the trafficking the Police were investigating. The truck's presence at the derelict building tended to add weight to my suspicion.

For about 40 minutes after the truck arrived, I sat intrigued by thoughts of what might be happening. Then headlights began moving behind the building. The truck reappeared and headed back towards town. A couple of minutes later, as I was preparing to follow the truck, the sports car came down the driveway. Cynthia had three passengers on board. They followed the truck.

The lack of traffic through the area made it difficult to follow the vehicles after they left the derelict building. I waited as long as I could bear before following at a distance. As we neared the town centre, traffic increased, allowing me to close up a little on the sports car. From the back of the procession, I watched the truck turn off at the main intersection before the city heart and head over the bridge. I knew where it was going. I chose to stay with the sports car. It crossed the intersection and drove into the business centre.

It had come alive. Restaurants were busy and the nightclubs were crowded. Traffic and pedestrians packed the street. Parking was at a premium and presented something of a problem. The sports car disappeared into an underground carpark. Not wanting to follow it, but needing to watch what might happen, I drove around looking for somewhere to park. On my second circuit, a car pulled out of a parking spot ahead of me. I slid into the space it vacated. It couldn't have worked out better. I was parked directly across from the underground carpark that swallowed the sports car.

This time, the wait was short. Cynthia and her three friends went into the nightclub above the carpark. She was slumming it tonight. The chosen nightclub was one of the less salubrious establishments along the strip. It was known for things other than good music. Regular Police raids added to the entertainment some nights. As none of the quartet had 'dressed up' for their night out, I guessed they were familiar with the place and its reputation.

No point in hanging around. Cynthia and her friends would settle in for a long night. I went to check Blondie's house to see if anything worth noting was happening there. I knew sufficient time had elapsed for the truck to be back there by now.

After turning onto Grevillea Crescent, I eased back to a slow speed. The truck was parked outside the open shed. Lights were on in the shed. I caught a glimpse of two men carrying boxes. They seemed to be moving the boxes out of the way to allow the truck to park in the shed. I drove from Grevillea into the main street and parked in front of a hairdressing salon. The main street was deserted. After about five minutes of 'thinking', it was 9.32p.m. I eased onto the street and made a hands-free call as I drove out of Sandlands. Ten minutes later, I was ringing Ben's doorbell.

He didn't look ready for bed so I wasn't guilty about calling so late. "Hope I'm not disturbing you," I chirped as he showed me in, "But I have something I want to run past you. Perhaps more like share with you I think."

"Fire away. By the way, have you eaten?" I was tempted to say I had, but this was Ben and he would see through the lie.

"Now that you mention it, no I haven't. I took snacks with me but I've been too engrossed in everything to give eating a thought."

Ben motioned for me to follow him. He spoke over his shoulder as we headed for his kitchen. "I'm just about finished making a wok full of Thai. Grab a couple of bowls and chopsticks and we shall eat."

I glanced at the wok on the stove. "You're just making dinner at this hour?"

"I intended spending a few minutes at the precinct this evening. Then you think 'just a few minutes more', and before you know it, a great lump of the night has disappeared, it's late and you are starving."

"Okay, that's enough conversation. I realise I'm starving too. Let's eat first and then I'll tell you why I came."

The food was good, the white wine cold and crisp and, by the time we finished eating, I was impatient to tell him about my evening. He insisted on making coffee and taking it through to the lounge before we embarked on any serious discussion. The background to my insurance case and report on tonight's surveillance took longer than I expected. Most of the surveillance details I read from my notes to ensure I got the sequence of events, times, and places correct.

I snapped my notebook closed. "Yeah, I think that's about it.

What do you think?" I asked as I looked over at him for the first time in a few minutes. Ben was leaning forward, his hands resting on his knees. He didn't respond in any way. "Ben... Ben, I asked you what..."

"Interesting; very interesting," he murmured barely above a whisper as he stared at some indeterminate point in the distance... and then the cross examination began.

Tedious and frustrating though it was, his questions made me think more deeply about my own case. My research earlier today hadn't found any other incidents where the same degree of damage was caused as happened in my insurance case. However, there were several robberies from high-end residences where the usual expensive electronic gear and valuable artworks were taken. So, why was the insurance case crime different from the others? It wasn't the robbery, but the apparent rage involved in creating that level of damage to the building and the grounds.

'Rage' is the keyword in this case, with the level of rage or hatred involved approaching the extreme end of the scale. Any number of people had been offended by Cynthia's father in the course of his business dealings. The likes of him have to be ruthless to be as successful as they are, and people get trodden on in the process. However, in this case, something more bitter and vindictive was behind the damage. I shared this thinking with Ben when he exhausted his questions about tonight's surveillance.

"From the insurance company's photos of the damage, your thoughts about some form of personal vendetta being involved seem about right. Has your investigation uncovered any potential suspects?"

"Not suspects as such, although I imagine further digging might uncover a long list of possible candidates. While it's still too early to point the finger, my initial focus is on Cynthia. She had a hard time of it after her mother died and, from newspaper articles, she appears not too enamoured with her new stepmother. I believe it was the new stepmother's appearance on the scene that sent Cynthia off the rails."

"A dramatic change in the girl occurred soon after her father remarried. It triggered poor behaviour that led to run-ins with the law… or, it it's just a phase where the spoilt little rich girl wants to kick over the traces. While Cynthia's involvement might prove significant, it's the involvement of your truck that has my interest. I'm beginning to think your two cases – the Fielding case and the insurance case – are connected."

Ben's last comment about the cases being connected sent my thinking off in another direction. What if my Inneston case also had connection in some way with the other two cases? Although I had suppressed the thought, somewhere in the back of my mind was a half-formed question about Gloria Purtell's regular visits to Geoff Inneston.

She was perfect to continue the drug trafficking that put Inneston behind bars. As a public servant, she would have easy access to others within the department who escaped detection when Police rounded up key players, including Inneston. Her position provided convenient travel all over the state. Although Purtell and Inneston's relationship appeared close and personal, I always suspected the pair of them of somehow continuing the trafficking operation. I won't share these thoughts with Ben. I don't need the derision I feel sure would follow. I was mulling over thoughts on the Inneston case when I realised Ben had spoken.

"Hello, earth to Sonoma Whittington, are you receiving? Over…"

"What… what are you on about?"

"Well, I did ask you a question. I didn't get an answer and you didn't look as though you were on this planet. Shall I ask the question again?"

Smart arse! "Please do; I promise to give it my undivided attention."

"I asked you if you felt like a drive. I thought you might show me the derelict building in the slum area that captured your interest tonight."

A few minutes later, Ben drove past the boat ramp area and into that depressing neighbourhood I discovered earlier tonight. I pointed out the derelict building and we drove slowly past. After a quick circuit of the place, we parked in the area with the rusting playground equipment and car bodies. "Stay in the car and don't do anything to alarm me," Ben commanded.

He slid out of the car and tramped off through the long grass until he reached a rusting climbing structure in the playground area. Although there was no moon, I could make out Ben talking on his phone. It was clear I wasn't to hear or know what it was about. I didn't have to think too long or too hard to work out that it was police business and he wasn't going to share it with me. That's the problem with Ben – one of them anyway. He expects you to give and is happy to take, but he never feels compelled to reciprocate.

It was dark and cosy in the vehicle. I reclined the seat a little, got comfortable and let my mind roam free. And roam it did across a host of topics. In the process, it visited the break and enters of other high end residences. The people in those residences belonged to the same social set as Cynthia's family. Some had offspring of about the same age as Cynthia. She would have been to their homes and socialised with their children. My mind was in hyperdrive. I wanted to go home to interrogate Google about those other robberies.

The sound of Ben returning to the car made me sit up. He climbed in behind the wheel without a word, and sat drumming his fingers on the steering wheel for a few moments. His words, when they came, were a bit left field. "Right, while we are out and about, how about you show me that Sandlands property. 'Blondies house', isn't that what you called it?"

We were out on the street already and heading out of the slum area. He sped to Sandlands before slowing to crawl along Grevillea Crescent. "That's it over there; the second house. See the shed up the back; that's where the truck lives when it's not doing whatever it does." As I finished speaking, I realised we were stationary. "I don't think the locals will welcome a strange vehicle parked on their street at this hour of the night. Shouldn't we move on before someone comes to ask the question?"

"Hmm... perhaps... What backs on to that house? What's behind it in the next side street?"

"It's a construction site. Looks like a new block of units is being built."

"Feeling energetic...?" That was a question I didn't like the sound of and didn't want to answer. I chose to look at him in anticipation of what came next instead of answering. "I thought it was a nice night for a walk, or a jog if you prefer. Let's park the car somewhere away from prying eyes and wander around the place a bit."

I showed him where I parked when I wheeled my pram through the parkland beyond the side streets to allow me to wander down past Blondie's house.

"Does the parkland extend to the next street beyond Blondie's, the street where the new units are under construction?"

"Yes, it does, but it becomes a much narrower strip of parkland." He was exiting the car by the time I finished speaking.

"Okay, come on, let's go. If you don't hurry up, the sun will come up before we go anywhere."

It wasn't yet midnight, although close to it. I was tempted to tell him there was no fear of the sun coming up any time soon, but Ben was some distance ahead along the road. I caught up to him. "Oh, good, you've made it. Let's jog or we will be here all night." Without waiting for a reply, he took off and I had no choice except to jog with him.

We went down the street before Blondie's with me in the lead. The parkland was more tricky and intimidating at night. Some moonlight would be good, but the new moon didn't help. Ben must have built in radar. He negotiated the parkland without mishap, while I found every root and fallen branch to stumble over. We were travelling at something between a fast walk and a slow jog. I stopped when we reached the entrance to Blondie's street. "Are we going down this street?" I didn't need to ask. I had my answer.

Ben didn't stop, but stated the obvious over his shoulder. "No, we'll go down the next street. Come on, keep up."

The last comment came after I trod in a hole and stopped to wait for the pain to tell me how much I had damaged my ankle. It didn't appear serious, so I picked up my speed a little and caught up to him again. I almost heaved a sigh of relief when we reached the entrance to the required street and we moved from the parkland to its sealed surface. Then we became a couple out for a late night stroll around the neighbourhood.

"There's the new block of units under construction," I whispered as we neared the Grevillea Crescent end of the side street. "What do you plan to do?"

"Dunno yet; I won't know until I have a look around. I didn't notice a back fence running along behind the shed on Blondie's block. That might be a good thing."

At the construction site, Ben veered off the street and picked his way across the block towards Blondie's place. There was nothing to indicate the rear boundary of the construction site. However, the blocks on either side of Blondie's did have boundary fences, so it wasn't too hard to gauge where the boundary line should be. "You can't go wandering around in there," I hissed. "You don't have a warrant, and I don't want my professional reputation ruined by being caught trespassing with a senior police officer."

He turned on his heel and marched back across the construction site to the street. "I wasn't going to 'wander' on Blondie's block. I was checking for any windows in the shed. There weren't, so we still don't know what goes on in there. I did see the red car parked on the back lawn when I peered around the corner of the shed. At a guess, I would say Terry doesn't go home too often these days."

"Maybe because he knows Trish is not there anymore... and that is what's worrying me. Has she cleared out or has something happened to her? That's the question I have been trying to get you interested in."

By the time I said my piece, we were back at Ben's vehicle. A police patrol car turned onto Grevillea Crescent as we were knocking the remnants of the parkland from our boots before getting back into the car. The patrol car spun around and stopped with its nose across the front of Ben's car and its rear end effectively blocking Grevillea Crescent. Its red and blue lights continued flashing as the two officers strode towards us.

Ben lowered his window and smiled. "Evening officers, what seems to be the problem?"

"Turn it off and step out of the car please, Sir," the male officer requested. "Hand me the key please."

"No, I don't think so." Ben still wearing his best smile, reached into his pocket.

"Show me your hands. Put your hands on the window where I can see them, and slowly get out of the car."

Oh, charming... now we look like being arrested. That's all I need. I smiled at the female officer who now stood beside my door. That didn't work.

"You too... out!" she demanded. She tried wrenching the door open, but it was locked. She kicked the door. "Open this fucking door and get out of the car before I shoot you." I was now looking at the snubby end of the barrel of her service weapon pressed up against my window.

Her kicking the door caused a momentary distraction during which Ben managed to extract his warrant card from his pocket. He opened his door a couple of centimetres. The interior light came on at about the same time as the officer standing outside tried to wrench his door open. With one firm hand preventing the door being opened, Ben brought up his warrant card, almost slapping it on the officer's nose. The officer froze for a moment; then raised his hands. "Step back," Ben rasped, and then turned in his seat and flashed his warrant card at the female officer, who still stood outside my door with her weapon trained on me.

She stepped away from the vehicle and the weapon disappeared. "Over against your vehicle; the pair of you," Ben shouted. The male officer took a few steps backwards to stand beside the patrol car. The female officer scrambled around the front of Ben's car to stand beside her colleague. Ben was out of the vehicle in a flash and herded the two officers around to the far side of the patrol car. I couldn't hear what was being said, but body language told me the two officers were not enjoying the interlude.

I saw Ben writing something in his notebook. The officers' names and numbers I guessed. They had not followed protocol this evening, had not done things by the book and were likely to hear more about it in the near future.

We drove back to Ben's place in silence. Ben remained furious and it showed. Out of politeness, he asked if I would like a nightcap before I left. Not bloody likely in the mood you're in, I thought, and begged off going inside with him. I drove home in something of a confused state.

Chapter 15

Sunday morning is my time unless I'm in the middle of an investigation requiring me to be on the job. I'm not sure where I'm at with my current job, but last night's thoughts of interrogating Google about other robberies of high-end residences lured me into my office before I even made coffee this morning.

I found reports of several similar thefts, but none involving damage. With printouts of everything I found spread out on the desk in front of me, I looked for similarities and differences between the crimes. If there were variations, they weren't obvious. As I sat scanning printouts, something occurred to me. All these crimes involved high-end houses in 'money belt' areas of Millhaven.

The first thing owners of such properties do is install the best possible security system. Systems with intruder alarms and CCTV cameras included. I'd heard one installed 24-hour computer monitoring of the house and grounds. Given this state of the art technology, how could a break and enter occur when no one was home without tripping the alarm and being captured by CCTV? To my mind, the only way that could happen was if the system wasn't armed when the residents went out.

If we ignore my case, the almost total absence of damage was intriguing. Other premises suffered no damage to grounds and 'minor' damage to buildings at the point of entry, providing little evidence anyone had been there while the family was absent. In a couple of instances, it was thought a credit card was used to pop the lock on a conservatory or sunroom door.

All through breakfast my mind kept going over what little information I had. Mental exhaustion set in. For want of anything better to do, I took myself for a drive past all the properties I identified as having been robbed. As I approached the driveway of the last house on the list, I was cut off by a Corvette which shot out of a driveway and roared off up the street. The young bloke driving it followed the latest fashion trend and wore oversized sunglasses. I watched him tear along the street and ignore the stop sign at the end, before disappearing around the corner and onto one of the main arterial roads. "Spoilt little darlings think they have some God given right to ignore all the rules that apply to the rest of us," I murmured as I followed the Corvette out of the suburb.

What else could I do today to progress the case? The short answer was 'nothing', so I went home. However, my thought about the Corvette driver's attitude to road rules triggered something. It triggered the memory of a shiny silver-coloured sports car careering out of a driveway in a similar fashion yesterday evening. Both those drivers looked to be about the same age. How many of the places robbed were home to similar aged offspring? Maybe I need to talk to Google again.

I sat back to consider the results of an hour's intensive research. Cynthia was 18 going on 19 now. All the households robbed included offspring around that age. Two had more than one kid that fell in the 17 to 21 years age group. It was probable all those youngsters knew each other. Their families attended the same social events. Some might have attended the same school. Okay, apart from a disregard for road rules, being overly indulged, belonging to the same age group, being acquainted and all having been robbed, was there any other connection?

Connection! Yes, that's what this case is about. But connection to what, that's the big question. My gut was telling me there had to be something more, the big end game that connected them all. Was that connection something to do with the robberies? The phone interrupted my deliberations: Emily.

"Hi Sonny, what are you up to today?"

"Today is Sunday, the Lord's designated day of rest."

"Yes, but what are you working on today? Whatever it is, can you tear yourself away to lunch with me at the waterfront?"

Lunch at the waterfront in one of the eateries overlooking the marina sounded alluring. "Sounds wonderful; what time do you want to meet?"

"I'm in town now. I'll come by to pick you up. I'll be there in about ten minutes. In the meantime, think about what your tastebuds fancy so we can work out where to eat."

I swapped my usual work clobber of jeans and tee shirt for casual slacks and top, and topped off the transformation with a strappy pair of low wedge sandals. My wardrobe doesn't run to much apart from work clothes, but I saw this outfit in a shop and couldn't resist it. What to eat for lunch was proving more difficult. My tastebuds weren't sending me any suggestions. Spot on with her timing, Emily arrived as I combed my hair.

As neither of us had any firm ideas about what we wanted to eat, we opted for a tapas bar, sat outside and watched the boating activity in the marina. "So, what have you been working on since I last saw you," Emily asked as we waited for our first dish to arrive.

"Nothing very exciting, it's another insurance case. Before you ask, no I still haven't been able to contact Trish Fielding."

Emily's question reminded me I hadn't done anything more on the Inneston case, and had made precious little progress on the Fielding case. "How much longer are you planning to stay in Millhaven?"

"I don't know. I didn't expect to stay this long. As soon as Mum's outlook improved, I intended going home. Sonny, she hasn't improved. In fact, I think she is getting worse. Whatever is bothering her is crawling on top of her. She is so down. I don't know what to do. And, being here all day every day with her is starting to drive me up the wall. If you haven't anything I can do for you, can I just come on occasions and sit in your office for a while?"

"That's okay with me, but your mother might have a problem with your disappearing for hours on end."

"She's not at home this week. There's a craft show kicking off in Ralston this afternoon. It runs till the end of next weekend, with lots of demonstrations, workshops and the likes, as well as trade stalls. One of the women she does craft with wanted Mum to go to the show with her, so I helped her talk Mum into going. So, if you should have something I can help with, I will be at a loose end all week."

With Sandra Inneston out of town all week, it gave me a little breathing space on the Inneston case. Nevertheless, I needed something concrete for her when she returned. Depending on what else my investigation turned up, Emily's presence in Millhaven could be a blessing, or it could turn into a problem if Sandra wanted to keep everything from her daughter. However, Emily's comment about being available should I need some help with a case created an idea. I need to progress things further though before I bring her in on any investigation.

Our time beside the water lulled us into such a relaxed state that the afternoon slipped by without our noticing it was getting late. After I promised to call her if I had something for her to do, we parted company at about 4.30p.m. Too late to start anything, I took coffee and my book out onto the deck and settled down for a long read. I must have dozed off. The phone woke me with a start. My voice was thick with sleep when I answered. I recognised Ben's laugh.

"It is still daylight. What are you doing sleeping at this hour of the day?"

My response is best left unrecorded, but I did manage to rasp out, "Did you want something?"

"Well, I was thinking about apologising for being a bit unsociable at the end of last night, and I was going to ask if you were working on something today. Oh yes, and I wondered whether you were cooking dinner or if I should bring something."

"I'll cook… see you when you get here, but don't be too late."

Good one, Sonny; now that you've said you will cook dinner, what is it you plan to make? I scrambled out of my comfortable lounger to find my leg had gone to sleep. With book and coffee mug in hand, I hobbled to the kitchen and began a search of the freezer. "Ah-hah, chicken pieces," I yelped. "They will do." While the microwave helped them thaw a little, I raided the pantry for other ingredients. An hour later, a Moroccan chicken dish was simmering on the cooktop and a packet of lemon and herb flavoured couscous was at the ready on the bench. Just about have time for a shower, I told myself, and went to freshen up before setting the table for dinner.

Ben arrived as I finished the table. He brought wine which, by amazing coincidence, would go perfectly with dinner. "Something smells good," he said as he put the wine in the fridge, before wandering over to peer in the pot of simmering chicken. We decided on drinks before I made the couscous, and took them out onto the deck. After dinner, we returned to the deck, this time with mineral water. The night was cool but not unpleasant. Talk found its way around to work and what each of us did today.

Ben kept checking his watch every few minutes. It was irritating and got the better of me. "Is there somewhere you need to be? Don't let me keep you if you need to go."

"Eh? No, I don't have to be anywhere. It's just…er… well, there's something going down this evening and I'm waiting to hear how it went."

"And what time was this 'something' supposed to happen?"

"About an hour ago; I should have heard something by now."

"Is the silence cause for concern… like something might have gone wrong, for instance?"

"Do you feel like going for a drive? It won't take long and shouldn't result in a late night."

What a rare invitation this is, to accompany Ben to a police operation. Of course I would go with him. Five minutes ago, sleep was top of my priorities list. "I'm in. Where are we going, and do I need hiking boots or other special equipment?"

He was already out the door and yelled back at me, "No, you'll do as you are. Come on, hurry up and get in the car."

We should be married. I'm sure many wives are familiar with this. I bit my tongue, climbed in and buckled up as he started the car. We were on our way to some mystery destination. There was a tension in Ben, heightened expectation perhaps, or trepidation. I wasn't sure which, but his focus was not in this car or with me, so I kept quiet and banked on all being revealed 'in the goodness of time' as they say. 'The goodness of time' wasn't too long coming.

Ben drove through the city centre, crossed the street leading to the bridge and headed for the eastern end of town. One street before we reached the boat ramp and the bend in the road that led into the slum area, Ben turned off to the right. I figured this street ran parallel to the one that ran through the slum. The street was dark. Although there were street lights, none of them worked. It wasn't a residential area. From what little I could see, it looked like it was the tail end of the light industrial stuff we passed through earlier.

Although I didn't know where we were going, instinct told me we would end up somewhere near that derelict building that held my interest last night. Ben wove his way through dark deserted streets. Then, up ahead on the left hand side of the street, I recognised the neglected park I visited twice last night. Now I knew where we were. I saw the bougainvillea screen I hid behind last night … and I also saw the sea of red and blue flashing lights up ahead.

Tonight had a high degree of familiarity. That is, apart from all the police vehicles blocking the street up ahead. Once again, I found myself in a car parked behind the bougainvillea barricade. "Stay in the car. Lock it when I leave. Do not get out and do not unlock it for anyone except me." He crossed the road and strode off towards the roadblock and the derelict building. I had no hesitation in complying with Ben's 'lock the doors' command after I saw him reach under his seat before exiting the car. The handgun that lived under the driver's seat was now tucked in the waistband of his jeans.

The darkness seemed more intense tonight. It made the flashing lights on the police cars seem so bright. I risked lowering my window a few centimetres. Silence greeted me. That's strange. Whatever is happening at the derelict building should be creating some sound, even if they are not forcing their way in. I left the gap in the window. The night air that drifted in was welcome even if it didn't have the sweetest aroma.

At first, I was focused on the scene up ahead and anxious about what might be happening, but I hate waiting. My mind drifted onto other things and I found myself mulling over my own cases as I sat there alone in the dark. A scream split the still night air. Gunshots followed. No longer lost in my own world, I sat bolt upright, my eyes straining through the blackness for any indication of what was happening. I closed my window properly and reached under my seat.

I was interrupted by an apparition that seemed to materialise from midst of the bougainvillea. The longhaired skinny individual sneaking towards me either had poor eyesight or wasn't paying attention. He crouched behind the car for a moment before sliding along the side until he reached my door. I froze. I wish I explored under my seat sooner. I yelped in fright as a face appeared at my window. Two solitary teeth occupied the black hole of a mouth open in surprise but uttering no sound. He stumbled backwards, regained his feet and took off across the street. He managed to grab hold of his trousers before they reached his knees, but not before I had a glorious view of his skinny white arse.

Thank you, Ben. My hand found the spare handgun strapped under the passenger's seat. I wrenched it free, and then felt around for the ammunition I knew should be under the seat. I found the small package. It came free with one hard yank. I checked the weapon: not loaded. The slider on the Glock worked freely. I placed the weapon and the box of shells on the floor at my feet and, using my phone as a torch, loaded the gun.

My pulse was racing. I took a few deep breaths to steady it. No need to get excited back here so far away from the action, I told myself. 'Skinny Arse' is gone and I am now armed. But something resembling World War III now replaced the earlier silence. The sound of gunfire, shouting, swearing and the occasional scream drifted my way. This was not right. The operation had turned sour; things had gone wrong. It didn't matter how many people were in the building at the time, storming the house should take only several minutes… and not require the use of weapons.

They weren't just police weapons I could hear. The thump of shotgun blasts punctuated the crack of shots from rifles and handguns. What should I do? Did Ben really expect me to sit here and let it all happen without getting involved? Perhaps he did, but that wasn't my style. A moment or two of hesitation while I debated the wisdom of my next move was interrupted when a shadow passed between me and the flashing lights. One uninvited visitor tonight was enough. Instinct kicked in.

I unlocked the car, slid out and quietly pushed the door closed before locking the vehicle again. With the key safely in my pocket, I moved over to the tangle of bougainvillea and crouched in as close to it as I dared without skewering myself on its prickles. Feet drumming on the bitumen were coming fast in my direction. I pulled back the slider on the Glock and took a couple of breaths to steady myself.

A dark figure ran past the end of the bougainvillea screen. It appeared to be looking back at the derelict building as it ran, but then it straightened up to look ahead… and that's when it saw Ben's vehicle. The runner hopped and skipped for a couple of steps as he tried to prevent over-running and stop. Then, with one quick backward glance over his shoulder, he bounded over to Ben's car. He tried the driver's door, then the rear passenger's door before moving around to the rear to try the SUV's rear door. He crouched behind the vehicle for the length of a few of heartbeats. Checking that no one followed him, I guessed.

With my breathing reduced to shallow slow breaths, I froze as the dark figure moved around to the passenger side of the vehicle. This one is not very bright. If all the other doors are locked, there is every chance all the ones on this side will be too. That fact seemed to escape the dark figure as he tried the rear passenger's door first, and then moved to my door. He tried the handle, found it locked, and then mashed his face up against the window in an attempted to scope out the interior. That was my cue for action.

As he stood there with his face plastered to the window, he cupped his hands around the sides of his eyes for a better view. Then he scrabbled around in the dirt with his foot and took a half step back and to one side before bending down to pick up something. I couldn't see what it was, but he hefted it in his hand a couple of times as if to feel the weight of it before quickly moving back to his original position beside my window. He seemed to decide he was too close and took a small step back. A quick look in all directions (except behind him thank goodness), and he raised his arm above and back behind his head. In his hand was a rock the size of a frozen chicken.

No you don't. I dashed as quietly as I could from my position in the corner where the bougainvillea broke free from its yard. He must have sensed my presence rather than heard me, my best efforts at stealth and the noise from the derelict building not enough to masque my presence.

Still holding the rock aloft, he stepped back from the car and spun around to face me. His chest made the acquaintance of the Glock's barrel. I didn't move away. He dropped the rock. It clipped his toe. Expletives mingled with the sound of World War III.

"Turn around slowly and place your hands on the hood of the vehicle." He smiled and stood his ground. "Look Sunshine, I've had a really shitty night. You know how you feel like kicking something when you're fed up and angry? Well, I feel the urge to shoot something instead. Any excuse will do. Please provide me with one."

There was an attempt at laughter. It didn't work. "You wouldn't dare. You would end up behind bars, and I don't think they would be kind to you in there."

"What are you talking about? There would be no questions asked. You are just another one of that mob from that building. And that's where your body would be found, along with any others that might be lying around at the end of tonight." I waved the Glock to indicate he needed to turn around. After a further moment of indecision, he complied.

I was pleased he chose not to argue. My courage was evaporating by the second. A quick and inexperienced frisk (I must learn how to do that properly and with more conviction), and I was marching him towards the derelict building, with only an occasional prod in the back with the Glock to keep him moving. As we neared the building, his demeanour changed. He became agitated. I assessed him as looking to make a break for it. Determined that should not happen, I grabbed him by the shoulder with a firm left hand and shoved the Glock hard against his spine. "Don't even think about it. Remember what I said about wanting to shoot something? That still applies."

With every step closer to the building, the noise from the action happening there became louder. I was forced to shout above the racket to deliver the reminder about wanting to shoot something. He wasn't the only one who heard.

"Who's there? Hands in the air... Identify yourself." Ben barked from behind a parked patrol vehicle.

"It's only me and some lost property."

"What the ...? What are you doing here?"

"You misplaced something. I found it. I thought you might want it back, so I'm returning it."

Ben, wearing a bulletproof jacket he didn't have on when he

left me, eased out from behind a vehicle. After relieving me of my captive, Ben slammed him up against the patrol car. Then the lad experienced a proper frisking before he was cuffed and shoved into the patrol car. As soon as Ben took charge of the lad, I thought it prudent not to have the Glock visible. I stuffed it into my waistband behind my back... and waited for the fallout that I knew would follow.

"What the hell did you think you were doing?" Ben snarled as he strode towards me. "I told you to stay in the car. You could hear what was going on here, and yet you march one of that mob back here to where it is all happening."

I smiled sweetly and said nothing. There was more to come yet... and Ben didn't disappoint. When the ranting and roaring subsided, it was my turn to speak. "Well, I must say, that's gratitude for you. I brought you back your escapee, and that was after he developed a keen interest in your car, and that's all the thanks I get."

"Go back to the car and wait there. We'll discuss this later."

"No, I think I prefer to stay here. It feels safer than being stuck back there on my own in the dark."

The look on his face told me I would not enjoy being on the receiving end of what he was about to say. However, I was saved from the tirade when one of his officers called him. "Stay here," he snarled at me before going closer to the building to join his men.

It could be a long wait, so it makes sense to get as comfortable as possible. I wandered over to the nearest patrol car and boosted myself up to sit on a mudguard. From that more elevated position, I could see more of what was going on. After checking out who and what was where for a minute or so, I noticed a significant drop in the noise and activity. A 'paddy wagon' arrived.

Three blokes in cuffs were bustled forward and unceremoniously loaded into the wagon. A new wave of screaming, more like screeching, erupted from somewhere in the building. It was female. Two uniformed officers, one under each arm, dragged a screaming and kicking female out the front door which now was open. The girl refused to walk and a third officer was called in to help. He picked up the girl's legs. The three officers carried her to the wagon and bundled her inside.

An undignified heap on the floor of the wagon, she continued to scream abuse, and tried for one final lash out at the officers. Her kick found only air. Before they slammed the wagon's doors shut, I got a good look at the female prisoner. Along with some of her friends, Cynthia was off to the cells in the Millhaven precinct.

A few officers wandered over to one of the patrol cars and drove off. After several minutes, Ben walked out with what I assumed were detectives in plain clothes. They stood beside an unmarked car talking for a couple of minutes. Then they too drove off, and Ben was walking towards me. Here we go I thought. Better prepare for the next round of tongue-lashing.

That's not what happened. As he reached the patrol car I perched on, Ben ripped off his bulletproof jacket and threw it into the vehicle. He looked weary and leant back against the car. "It's all over except for the mopping up. I'll need to stay on for some time while we try to tie up loose ends. Take my car and go home. I'll get a ride home with someone. That reminds me, I've got two vehicles out the back to be impounded. I better organise for them to be taken in."

"One of those vehicles wouldn't happen to be a silver-coloured sports car would it?"

"Y-e-s; what do you know about it?"

"Uhmm… what's the other vehicle? Can I see it?" Ben shrugged and led the way around to the back of the building. From the corner of the building, I could see all I needed to see. The two vehicles were reverse parked neatly side by side over to one side of the back yard. A male body lay on the concrete slab outside the backdoor of the building. I didn't need to go any closer.

"That's all I need, thanks Ben. The silver sports car is associated with my insurance case. It belongs to Cynthia. I can't remember the name of the driver of the Corvette, but I can give you his address." On our way back out to the street, I explained how I knew about the vehicles, how they related to my insurance case, and their possible relevance to the Fielding investigation.

Ben remained insistent that I should take his car and go home. I realised arguing with him was going to get me nowhere, so I walked back to the car. By the time I reached the car, my foot gave me a clear reminder of the bougainvillea prickle I stood on while crouched up against our makeshift screen earlier in the night. The prickle went through the leather sole of my sandal and pierced my foot. It now hurt like hell. When I climbed into the car and took the weight off my foot, it throbbed something fierce.

To leave without knowing what went on at the derelict building didn't sit well with me. The body by the back door was a clue to some of the action, but it didn't tell me why a simple raid turned into a firefight. And it didn't tell me what they found in that building that the occupants were prepared to wage war to protect.

Nevertheless, told in no uncertain terms to go home, I started Ben's car and eased it around the bougainvillea and onto the street.

Chapter 16

Part of the roadblock at the derelict building cleared making it possible to drive past the crime scene, so I crawled up the street to where police remained busy at the site. Since getting behind the wheel, I nurtured the wild idea of leaving Ben's car at the crime scene and getting a patrol car that was leaving to take me home. As I reached the cluster of cars parked on the street, two uniforms walked towards the cars. They looked like they were about to leave. I'll ask them if they wouldn't mind going via my place to drop me off. I pulled in behind the police cars but didn't get out of the car.

A new idea that sprung from nowhere the moment I pulled up had more appeal than getting a lift home in a patrol car. By the time I decided to run with the new idea, the officers drove off. I followed them out of the slum area. As I approached the city centre, I pulled over and checked my bag. I had the key. When I moved off, I wasn't headed for my house. A few minutes later, I drove into the carport at Ben's place.

After pausing on the doorstep for a moment to make sure I remembered the code. I let myself in, punched the code into the security system, and breathed a sigh of relief when I heard the long wheezing beeps of the security system disarming. Thank goodness Ben hadn't changed the code. With nothing to indicate how long it might be before Ben arrived home, I curled up on the sofa and tried to sleep.

Sleep didn't come easily. Tonight's events, or what little I knew about them, kept my mind active and my frustration mounting. My decision to go to Ben's instead of going home was based on the assumption that he would come home sometime before daylight and I would be able to quiz him about what they found at the derelict building. It seemed like a sound move at the time but, as I lay there and time ticked by, I began to reassess the situation.

It was now quite late – early morning actually – and Ben still wasn't home. The reality was that, when Ben did come home, he would be too tired to discuss anything and would not take kindly to being questioned. Perhaps I should have gone home. The longer I considered it, the more convinced I became that was a better option.

I crawled off the sofa, turned on a light and went to the bathroom to splash water on my face. Then, turning lights off behind me as I made my way through the apartment, I picked up my bag and made my way to the door. I paused to make sure I remembered the code to re-arm the security system before keying it in and slipping out the door. I froze.

A car door thumped closed. It was close. A brief snatch of voices drifted my way. A car drove away. I moved to the door, arming the security system abandoned. Footsteps approached. I flattened myself against the wall where I would be hidden when the door opened. A key rattled in the lock. The wheezing squeak of the security system arming began. I raced to the security system control panel and cancelled the arming process. The neighbours would not appreciate Ben's intruder alarm going off at this hour of the morning. "Come in; don't use the remote," I yelled through the door at him.

The door opened a fraction and Ben peered around it. Confident there was only me inside, he opened the door fully and strode in. "What the bloody hell are you doing here? I thought I told you to go home."

In quick succession, I gave him my most contrite look followed by my sweetest little girl smile... and then launched into an explanation. I explained about my change of mind and how I thought I was doing him a good turn. "So, you see, I thought it would be more convenient for you if you had your car to go into work tomorrow. Tomorrow, or should I say, today, being your first official day back at work after your overseas jaunt, it would not do to have you arriving late, or having to ring the precinct for someone to collect you because you didn't have a car.

Ben grunted in response, but I could see my words had worked. "I don't feel like driving you home at this hour. In fact, all I feel like right now is a shower."

"That's okay. You go for a shower and I'll curl up on the sofa again."

"No. Coffee and something to eat would go down well. While I take a shower, make coffee and see if you can rustle up toast of some sort."

Coffee and toast seemed a good idea. I went to make the acquaintance of Ben's kitchen and his larder. His coffee machine was similar to mine and posed no challenges. I put a batch on to brew before tackling the fridge for something to turn into toast. A sliced fruit loaf in the freezer solved the problem and eliminated the need to work out what to put on it. By the time Ben joined me in the kitchen, the smell of fresh brewed coffee and raisin toast permeated the place. We sat at his breakfast bar. It was 4.00a.m. A bit earlier than my usual breakfast, but it was good, and it required another couple of trips to the toaster before we satisfied our appetites.

Now, with our need for sleep dispelled for the moment, it seemed a good time to talk about what happened at the derelict house. As I had tipped Ben off about the possibility of the place being involved in something interesting, I felt entitled to know what they found there. There were indications the building might be connected to my case. I needed to know whether there was a connection or not. I asked the first question in the hope of initiating discussion. The hope being full disclosure of last night's events would follow.

"What did your men discover at that building to trigger the firefight?"

"The officers were caught out. They weren't expecting such a violent response to the raid. It was as well they followed protocols and were prepared to deal with what happened. Our only casualty was one of our guys who received a flesh wound to his upper arm. The other side of the ledger tells a different story. I counted four bodies but there might be a couple more I didn't see. In addition, there are two wounded in hospital, and there are others who are enjoying the hospitality of our cells until their court appearances."

"They made no secret of their displeasure at being raided, but what was it they were protecting? What was in the building that they didn't want you to know about?"

"I think your insurance company will be pleased they don't have to pay out on what happened at Cynthia's parents place. I'm sure they will find some of the stolen stuff is amongst the hoard uncovered in that building, along with stuff from a few other properties, I suspect."

"Okay, so the robberies of high end residences were inside jobs.

I get that, but I don't understand the motivation. Cynthia and the bloke in the Corvette don't look like they are short of a dollar. Why would…"

"Brenton…"

"What…?"

"Brenton Crosland; that's the name of the lad with the Corvette."

"Oh, excuse me for not knowing. Who cares what his bloody name is, the question remains the same: why did they need to do it?" I'm not the most affable person when I'm sleep deprived. "It could only be for money, or to satisfy some vindictive streak. Did their parents suddenly cut of their allowances? Although they lifted high quality expensive stuff, its illegal sale wouldn't result in too many dollars in their pockets. And they would need a reliable fence to get rid of it for them."

"That could explain what your truck was doing at the building. Perhaps it's being used to move the stuff on."

An idea that hatched a little earlier wriggled its way to the forefront of my mind. The risk of Ben dismissing it out of hand made me cautious. I decided to give it air anyway, but worked my way up to the core of the issue. "Might the stuff you found in the building constitute a 'secondary commodity' in the context of one of our earlier conversations?"

Ben sat looking at me for a few moments before replying. "Hmm, that's a distinct possibility. It doesn't change the fact that it wouldn't attract a massive amount of dollars, but it would bring in more than an empty back loading for a truck does."

"Did you find any evidence of drugs at the building?"

"Not so far, but they are bringing in sniffer dogs to go over the place this morning."

At that point, Ben's phone rang. He moved away to take the call and didn't share any details later. His only comment was that he needed to go into the precinct and that he would drop me home first. After a flurry of rinsing our breakfast things, I picked up my bag and followed Ben out to his car. His silence and the set of his jaw coupled with his perfunctory goodbye as he dropped me off suggested something was not right at the police station. It wasn't too difficult to surmise whatever it might be was associated with last night's operation at the derelict building.

I decided sleep topped my list of things to do before going to my office in town today. It was a good idea that didn't work. By the time I had a shower and was ready to crash for a while, I was wide awake and not interested in sleep. I knew that would change sometime during the day, so I opted to go to my office until such time as the need for sleep descended again.

That damned Fielding case, never far out of my thoughts, had me driving to Sandlands again this morning. At a few minutes before seven o'clock, I turned onto Grevillea Crescent… and almost ran slap bang into a little red car hurtling out of the Crescent.

The car, belting down the centre of the road, showed no inclination to pull back onto its correct side. Evasive action called for, I veered off onto the shoulder of the road. We passed without either of us losing our side mirror, but I'm not sure how with such little gap between us. Although I was busy trying to avoid a collision, I did manage to note Blondie was Terry's passenger.

After the near-miss, I parked on the shoulder until I my breathing returned to normal. In my rear view mirror, I watched Terry Fielding exit Grevillea Crescent without slowing down, and turn towards town. Since I was pointing in the right direction, it was easier to drive to the other end to exit the Crescent rather than trying to turn around and go out the way I came in. Anyway, something interesting that I wouldn't want to miss might be happening at Blondie's house.

There was something going on but I'm not sure how interesting it might be. The shed was open, the lights were on, and the truck was parked outside with its nose in the shed doorway. What did strike me as interesting at the time was the frantic activity involving the truck and the shed. The truck driver and another man who I hadn't seen before scurried about as though Armageddon was imminent.

Sandlands came to life. While some residents drove out of the suburb on their way to start work, some of those with a later start time walked or jogged around the streets, including along Grevillea Crescent. It wasn't possible to stop to observe the activity at the shed without drawing too much attention. I drove at the slowest speed possible. It didn't help. I still wasn't sure whether they were loading or unloading the truck. Whatever was going on, it was happening at a feverish pace.

A stroll in Melaleuca Grove might be nice at this time of the morning, I told myself as I circumnavigated the big roundabout and drove through the suburb's shopping area. Another car occupied my usual spot in the park. I saw two people on the other side of the park heading down to the beach. After parking a short distance further along, I got out of the car and began my rendition of a walker out for an early morning stroll.

Sometime later, I abandoned the charade and returned to the car. I spotted the high canopy of the truck turning out of Grevillea Crescent. A nearby log was useful for hamstring stretches while I tracked the truck's departure from Sandlands. It seemed in an almighty hurry to get to wherever it was going. If I want to know where it's going, I had better follow it.

By the time I was ready to leave the park, three more cars departed Sandlands. I slipped into the queue behind the third car and soon, another two vehicles trailed me. My thinking was that the truck would go to the warehouse-type building in the industrial estate. That suited me. It was only a short distance from Thornton Transport to confirm where the little red car went in such a rush this morning. The only problem I had was that the truck driver had other ideas about where he was going.

After crossing the bridge, instead of crossing the main street and continuing straight ahead to the industrial estate, the truck turned left and travelled sedately towards the boat ramp end of the main street. It wasn't inconceivable the truck had to pick up or drop off at one of the light industrial establishments dotted along this end of the street, except that proved not to be the case.

At the boat ramp end of the street, the truck followed the street around the bend into the slum area. Now an expert on that particular part of town, I knew it would be impossible to follow the truck in there without the driver realising he was being tailed. Why would the truck risk visiting the area after last night? The speed at which it drove out of Sandlands suggested a significant degree of urgency attached to this morning's trip. If they knew about last night's raid, they must realise there was a strong likelihood police would still be in the area.

My knowledge of the area and its lack of turning places along that road meant I couldn't follow the truck into the slum. Instead of following the road around the bend, I drove into the car park at the boat ramp and parked amongst the SUVs and boat trailers. After a few minutes of watching the seagulls and the pelicans doing their thing, a troubling thought occurred to me. The lack of sleep made my thinking sluggish. I cursed aloud as I started the car and drove out of the boat ramp car park.

Given what I knew about what lay along the street beyond the boat ramp area, there was a good chance the truck would not emerge from in there via the same route it used to enter the area. If the driver were a regular visitor, he would make it his business to know the area well as part of his safety and survival strategy. Even Ben, who had never been to the area before, knew of a less obvious route to that mass of tangled bougainvillea than I did. No doubt, the truck driver also knew of other less direct routes to use in case of emergencies.

I retraced my drive along this end of the main street until I reached a point close to where I thought Ben had turned off the street to enter the slum area last night. A café two doors back from the intersection had a carpark along one side. Although big enough for about five cars, the area was empty at this hour. I drove in and messed about a bit until I found a space offering the best view of the intersection up ahead. From here, it was possible to watch passing traffic on the street as well as traffic emerging from the slum area.

It would be rude to occupy the café's parking lot without bringing any custom to the business. While keeping an eye on the street, I went into the café and emerged s few minutes later with a large cappuccino and today's newspaper. Back in the car, I got comfortable for what I hoped wouldn't be a long wait. To my surprise, the coffee was excellent. As usual, the local paper was a waste of money. It seems it was a 'no-news' weekend. With any luck, the police raid on the derelict building might make it into tomorrow's paper.

After throwing the paper and the empty coffee container in a bin, I sat drumming my fingers on the steering wheel. A suspicion started gnawing at me. What was taking the truck so long to exit the slum area? Had the driver been silly enough to go to the building and now found himself 'helping the police with their enquiries', or had he gone somewhere else… found another way out of the area perhaps?

A drive through the slum would prove whether the truck was still somewhere in there. I started the car and idled out to the kerb. A set of lights changed somewhere further along the street and a string of traffic now streamed past me as I waited for an opportunity to drive out onto the street. There wasn't a plan. My thinking was to drive into the area from the boat ramp and complete a circuit by exiting along the route that Ben had used last night to enter the place.

As the last car approached where I waited, I again checked the intersection where I imagined the truck would emerge. It did. At that precise moment, it moved out of the side street in readiness to tag onto the tail end of the string of passing vehicles. After checking I wasn't going to run over or give anyone a coronary, I reversed into the café's parking lot. By then, the last of the traffic had passed me and I watched the truck slide in behind the last vehicle. Not wanting to tailgate my target, I waited until it was some distance along the street, which allowed a couple vehicles to fall in behind the truck, before I drove out onto the street and joined the end of the cavalcade.

The truck had two options at the next major intersection. It could turn right and head for Blondie's house, or it could turn left for the warehouse on the industrial estate. It turned left. The following cars continued straight ahead into the city centre. That left me exposed should the truck driver check his mirrors. I followed the two cars across the intersection and wound my way through the inner city area to re-join the road into the industrial estate several blocks further along from where I left it.

The truck made good progress and was now quite some distance ahead of me. Lights at the next intersection it came to helped narrow the gap between us, although I stayed well back. From a distance, I watched it turn off onto the side street that provided access to that warehouse type building. As I drove past that side street intersection, the truck was disappearing into the building. I drove on and navigated my way back to the street running past Thornton Transport.

Everyone was at work by then, and the little red car was invisible as I drove past. Further along the street, I made a U-turn and slowly came back along the street. From this different angle, I spotted the red car in the front row of the carpark. It must have been one of the first, if not the first, car to arrive today. I conceded that the morning had provided no new information, but it had posed a new question to nag at me: where did the truck go when it entered the slum area?

With nothing more concrete to investigate, I drove to the boat ramp and followed the street around into the slum area. What I expected to find was as much a mystery to me as it was to the rest of the universe. By driving slowly and continually looking right and left, I tried creating the impression of someone searching for a particular address. The street was devoid of life. No vehicles moved about. No kids on bikes or walking to school. A short distance before the derelict building, I pulled over and flapped a map about a bit.

No police or any other vehicle was obvious at the building. I drove up to the building, stopped in the middle of the street in front of it, checked the map and then peered at the building. From here, the area along the side of the building and a small part of the backyard were visible. No vehicles there either. I drove on. Why weren't police and forensics still processing the building? Their investigations couldn't be completed already.

"Well, that didn't tell you anything more than you knew before," I told myself aloud as I continued along the street at a snail's pace. No one thoughtfully installed a sign announcing 'the truck was here'. That's about what it would take for me to know where the truck went and what it did when it came in here this morning. I focused on finding the route Ben used to enter the place last night. The map wasn't much help. I explored a couple of dead-end streets before emerging on the eastern end of the main street. No excuse for putting it off any longer, I drove to my office and flopped down behind my desk.

Messages from Emily, a potential client and another insurance company greeted me. I dealt with the potential client and the insurance company inquiries before calling Emily. I wasn't sure I had anything for her to do, but a chat probably wouldn't go astray.

"How's being alone at mum's house going?"

"Please tell me you have something for me to do."

"…That good, eh? There might be something you could do. Drop into my office if you are coming into town today."

"I'll see you for lunch."

There were several things I might use Emily for, but I wasn't sure about involving her. Although there wasn't a high degree of danger, there always is some element of danger involved. By the time she arrived early for lunch, I had decided. Over the chicken and salad lunch boxes from the local deli, we discussed a plan for the afternoon. In my mind, the now critical stage of the Fielding case required a massive input of effort… and possibly a reasonable degree of risk.

"I thought we might try to get into Trish Fielding's unit this afternoon while we know Terry is at work and unlikely to surprise us with a visit."

"You think he has been there in the last week? I get the impression he hasn't bothered to go 'home', if he still considers the unit his home, since Trish disappeared."

"I can't argue with that. Our first approach should be to chat to the neighbour again. I'll think of a story to cover why I'm interested in what's happened to Trish. You could be an ardent dog lover concerned about Trish's poor little dog ever since you found out about its apparent abandonment."

"I didn't get the impression she knew anything more than she said. What's your fall-back plan if she isn't able to tell us anything more?"

"It's likely she doesn't think she knows anything, but her answers to a few questions I have could prove enlightening. Development of a follow up strategy depends on her answers… and whether you are involved or not." Regardless of what the neighbour had to say, I still wanted to monitor what all the players in the Fielding case were up to. That might be something for Emily to do. However, first things first; focus on visiting the Fieldings' neighbour.

Lunch was over by 12.30p.m. "Now might be a good time to visit the Fieldings' unit. The neighbour is elderly. She might have a nap after lunch. We can't leave a visit until late in the afternoon in case the little red car decides to visit that general store across the road from the unit. It's safe enough to assume he won't come to the unit. However, it would be best if he didn't see us talking to the neighbour." We were out of the office moments later.

"I'll go to the Post Office to check my mail first." Emily ready to argue, spun around to face me. I kept talking. "While I'm checking my mailbox, you can watch the other side of the road for any sign of activity at the units." She relaxed again and we drove the rest of the way to the Post Office in silence.

"Nothing happening over the road," Emily said as I dumped my few bits of mail on the back seat. "What's next?"

I took a few moments to go over my plan with her before driving from the Post Office to pull up on the opposite side of the street in front of the Fieldings' unit. We rang the bell a couple of times before pounding on the door. We didn't expect anyone to come to the door, and received no surprises. What we hoped would happen was that the elderly neighbour would come out to investigate all the fuss. I was beginning to think I had misjudged the timing of the visit. Perhaps, the woman was out.

"Thump on the door once more," I told Emily. "If the woman doesn't appear, we will abandon the operation." While Emily pounded the door with some gusto, I called out Trish's name. That did the trick.

As I was about to walk away, the door to the next unit opened. A harassed-looking elderly woman stood in the doorway. "She's gone away. I don't know if she's coming back."

Time for me to go into another of my Oscar-winning performances; I hoped Emily would pick up the thread and ad-lib along.

Chapter 17

"I'm sorry we disturbed you. I was becoming worried something might have happened to Trish and she couldn't come to the door."

"I heard you ringing the bell but I was on the phone. I don't know what's happened nextdoor, but Mrs Fielding hasn't been around for a few days now. It's strange. We always told one another if we were going to be away so the other person could keep an eye on our place."

"We had arranged to meet. I tried ringing her a few times to confirm the time and place but got no answer. It's not like her not to ring and cancel the arrangement before going away. If something did happen and she had to leave in a hurry, she would ring as soon as possible to let me know things had changed. She was like that, considerate of other people."

"I was going to put the kettle on as soon as I made my phone call. Would you like to come in and have a cup with me?"

Silly question! Of course I want to come in to quiz her about what she knows about all things 'nextdoor'. After introducing ourselves – first names only, we followed her into a small dark kitchen that retained the smell of her morning toast… or, maybe it was lunch. "I'm Margaret, but please call me Peggy. Everyone does." Emily and I sat at the small kitchen table as Peggy bustled about making tea and chatting all the while. "I'm sorry it took me so long to answer the door before, but I was on hold on a call to the airline. I was booked on the late flight this evening. I got a message that the flight was cancelled and I needed to find out what was happening. Now, I'm on the mid-morning flight tomorrow. It's not as convenient, but it will have to do."

I was sympathetic and asked whether the change of flight made things difficult for her. "Well yes, it does a bit. My daughter usually collects me from the plane on her way home from work. My new flight time means I will have to take a cab or bus into town and then wait around for her to finish work for the day. I go down south to stay with my daughter for a couple of weeks at this time every year.

She and my granddaughter have their birthdays while I'm there. Then, I go down again to spend the Christmas/New Year break with them."

More kind words from me, "When they live so far away, it must be lovely to spend those important family times together. I'd like to get away more often, but it is so difficult with the house and everything else to consider."

"That's the beauty of living in a set of units like this… and having great neighbours like Trish. We look out for each other. Trish has a key and comes in to look after my plants whenever I'm away. I don't know what will happen while I'm away this time. I suppose I'll just have to put them outside and hope they survive somehow."

"Yes, I could see Trish doing that for you. She is that sort of person. Did she take her little dog with her when she went?"

Peggy looked confused in response to my question and gave Emily a quizzical look. Terrific! She remembers Emily coming to the unit yesterday. I could have bitten my tongue the moment I asked the question, but Emily rose to the occasion.

"No Sonny. Remember, I told you she left the dog behind."

"Gee, I do remember, now that you've reminded me. I hadn't paid much attention to it at the time because we had arranged to meet today. I thought she must be away just for the day. She would never go away for any length of time without taking care of her dog."

Our responses must have been acceptable. Peggy relaxed again. "She doted on that dog. If she was only going away for a weekend or something like that, I looked after Goldie for her. She didn't go away much but, a couple of times, she went somewhere for a week or so. She took Goldie with her on those occasions. The poor little thing was distraught when I rescued it. I can't understand her going off like that and leaving it behind unattended."

"Maybe she thought her husband would look after it while she was gone," I suggested.

"I don't think she would trust him to look after anything other than himself. He's a strange animal that one. I don't think things have been too good there lately."

"Trish and I have known each other for a long time. I never got to know her husband. – Terry, isn't it? I met him once or twice, just to say hello when I picked Trish up to go for lunch. We always met up during the day when he was at work I found him a bit strange too but, as I said, I didn't know him. I remember thinking he wasn't what I expected Trish to end up with."

"I don't think he would be easy to get to know. In my day, he's what we might have called a 'wrong-un'. It's just a feeling I have. I don't know that he's ever done anything wrong, although I think he used to knock Trish about sometimes. She always denied it and tried to hide it, but I lived with one like that for a long time. I recognise the signs."

"If she didn't ask you to look after Goldie, she must have been confident the dog would be okay with Terry. But, it seems Terry wasn't taking care of Goldie. I can accept that he might not have time or inclination to take it for walks, but it wouldn't take much for him to give the dog a bit of food and water every night when he came home from work."

"No, it wouldn't. Of course, that is if he came home from work. I don't remember seeing him at the unit since before Trish left. I tried to convince myself he went with her and, somehow, the dog got left behind by accident. But I know that's not true. I've seen him driving around in his car… and he hasn't been alone."

It seems Terry and Blondie often go to the general store across from the unit. An observant neighbour like Peggy notices these things. She avoided mentioning Blondie directly, or making any comment about a possible cause of the deterioration in the Fieldings' relationship, so I asked the question. "Do you mean he had another woman with him? Are you suggesting Trish cleared out because Terry was cheating on her? That doesn't sound like the Trish I know. If he was playing up, she would have thrown him out, not walked out leaving Goldie behind."

"I think there might have been some problem like that involved. Nothing specific, just a comment Trish made in passing."

"Will you take Goldie with you tomorrow?"

"No. I don't know what I'm going to do about the dog. My

daughter lives in an apartment block; no pets allowed. I'm only a pensioner and it's expensive to put it into the kennels even for two weeks. …And then what? I don't know if Trish is coming back."

"What makes you think she might not be back? If she's having a problem at home, she might have gone away to clear her head or to think things through for a while."

"No, I don't think so. The way their place was left makes me think a different situation occurred."

Emily had been quiet throughout most of the discussions. She now found her voice. "I'll tell you what we can do with the dog. I'll take Goldie home with me while you are away. I'll have spare time on my hands and I would enjoy the company. We could come round here to water your plants. That way, Goldie wouldn't fret too much about being away from home, and we could keep a bit of an eye on things here. Who knows, by the time you get back, we might have some news about Trish. What do you think, Sonny?"

What could I say? I'm thinking this girl has real potential. I enthused over her bright idea and Peggy was almost beside herself with relief.

"Come through to the back with me and I'll show you where things are." We followed Peggy out to a carport attached to the rear of the unit. She showed Emily where she would put the plants so she could water them. "See this here," she said, indicating a couple of grubby empty pots on a shelf beside a pair of gardening gloves and a bottle of seaweed plant food extract. "I'll hide the spare keys to both my unit and Trish's in there in case you need to get in for any reason while I'm away."

Goldie came bounding up to us from across the backyard of the complex. Emily went down on her haunches and ruffled his ears. He took to her straight away. It was agreed Goldie and his various bowls and food supply would go with us when we left. As Peggy had nothing to offer, as soon as good manners allowed, we left with our precious cargo. Goldie didn't mind the ride. He curled up in the back and went to sleep as soon as we drove off.

"Are you sure about what you are doing with the dog? What's your mother going to say about Goldie when she gets home?"

"No problems; everything will be fine."

"Well, I was going to ask you to do some surveillance tonight, but now you have the dog to look after."

"Goldie can come with me. It will be company."

"No. Terry and his associates might recognise Goldie… or Goldie might recognise them. Either way, the risk is too great."

"Okay, there are two options: I can take Goldie and leave him at home while I'm out and about, or you can take him home with you until I'm finished surveillance tonight."

"My place isn't set up for dogs; no fence and no door flaps. You take him home. Pray he doesn't howl the house down and annoy the neighbours when he's left alone."

I pulled into my parking space and walked around to open the rear door. Before Emily could clip on his leash, the fur ball jumped out and sat at Emily's feet. He then trotted along beside her as she walked to her car parked out in the street. At least Goldie is well trained, I thought. That should help make him more acceptable to Sandra when she arrives home and finds she has inherited a dog.

The long night without sleep was taking its toll. I was flagging fast. No point trying to push myself to do anything when I'm like this. I needed to sleep for a while. If I went home to sleep now, I would probably sleep until 10 or 11 o'clock and then be awake for the rest of the night. A better option was to take a nap in my office. It wasn't nearly as comfortable as my bed, but I knew a nap would last no more than a couple of hours. With the lights off and the door locked, I fully reclined one of the old lounge chairs and settled down for the rest of the afternoon.

Somewhere in the distance, a phone rang. I tried clawing my way back out of the darkness. The phone stopped ringing. I gave up on trying to wake up and started sliding back into the black oblivion. The jangling of my mobile phone, loud and close to my ear, brought me back from the brink of sleep again. There was a moment or two of confusion as I groped for my phone and tried to orientate myself with what seemed like foreign surroundings. My mouth was thick and dry but I managed to croak, "Hello, this is Sonny."

"Good, that's who I have been looking for. Where are you? You're not at home and your office is locked, but your car is where it was when I left earlier this afternoon. I'm outside your office. What's the surveillance you wanted me to do tonight?"

Oh God, I'd forgotten all about asking Emily to do some surveillance. Phone still connected to Emily, I unlocked the office door. "Coffee...!" I croaked as she walked past me. She kept walking and started the coffee machine while I managed to get myself together enough to turn on the lights.

I flopped onto one of the chairs in front of my desk and Emily plonked a glass of water on the desk in front of me. "Drink...! It might start the humanising process while we wait for the coffee. By the way, Goldie is happy in his holiday house. The dog flap is still in the back door and he has all the toys from Mum's previous dog to amuse him."

"It's getting late. You will need to go as soon as you have coffee. The first thing I want you to do is to see where Terry's little red car goes when he leaves work. No doubt, he will go to Blondie's house. Find a good spot in Melaleuca Grove, that little park at the approach to Sandlands. Watch for any movement by the red car or that truck with the high canopy. If you see either of them go past, call me straight away."

A few minutes later, Emily was on her way to the industrial estate while I sat nursing the last of my coffee. With tonight's surveillance organised, what did that leave me to do? That warehouse building on the industrial estate is begging me to investigate further, but entry is difficult. It is impossible when the roller door is closed, and the entrance is far too exposed and well-lit to slip in unnoticed when the door is up. I wanted to look around inside that derelict building, but I know Ben won't agree to that. The only other place that interests me is the Fieldings' unit, and that's a job for tomorrow or the next day now that Emily has a key.

No phone call from Ben so far today, so I might as well work on the assumption that he's not planning to eat with me this evening... and that means he won't be sharing any details of the raid on the derelict building. Okay, that makes decisions easier. The derelict building is the place to be. I raided the kitchenette for chocolate bars, made a sandwich and grabbed a bottle of water before heading for my car. It wasn't yet dark but, after night fell, I would need to use a torch inside the building and that was bound to attract attention.

The slum area seemed deserted. Maybe its citizens disappear inside early to eat dinner in front of TV. Where to park and leave the car…? Leaving it unattended anywhere in this neighbourhood was a worry. I entered the area via Ben's route and soon found myself at the overgrown parkland. The two buildings across the street from the park appeared unoccupied. I could see lights on in only two houses.

Just as I decided this was the right place to leave the car, a small group of teenagers descended on one of the unoccupied buildings across the street. They were rowdy and carried six packs of beer. It sounded as though they had sampled a few ales before their arrival. No, I don't think this is the right place to leave the car. I drove to that now familiar spot with the tangled bougainvillea. My oilskin jacket was on the back seat. I slipped it on and added a chocolate bar and bottle of water to one of its pockets and a heavy torch and my phone to the other before setting off on foot for the derelict building.

If anyone noticed my presence, nobody made a fuss. I crossed the street, ducked under the police tape and carefully picked my way around to the rear of the building. How to get into the building was the big question. Although the police busted open the boarded up front door, the sheet of plywood covering the door still hung in place. Any messing about to get in through that door was bound to arouse interest and could attract a bevy of spectators.

The way around to the back of the house was a mass of wheel ruts and littered with rubbish. Careful to avoid stepping in what I was sure was a pool of dried blood, I stepped up onto the concrete slab at the back door. Police tape crisscrossed the entrance. The door, although pulled to, didn't close properly after the hammering it received from the police's ram. I reached through the tape and gave the door a gentle shove. It might have moved a few millimetres.

Access was possible but it required more than a gentle shove. I freed one end of one of the tapes, ducked under it and put my shoulder against the door. The door scraped minimally across the concrete floor. It needed lifting a little to enable it to move more freely. With both hands firmly on the large doorhandle, I heaved the heavy wooden monster a whisker off the floor. My weight against it as I lifted swung the door open about third of the way. That was enough. I eased myself through the gap and stood still behind the door.

No sounds from anywhere inside and no one rushing to the back door to investigate what was happening. I inched forward, sliding my feet across the floor, not daring to step out until my eyes adjusted to the gloom. Although there was still a bit of light left outside, the darkness inside the building was intense. It didn't take long to work out my eyes couldn't adjust enough to be able to see what was around me. I dug the torch out of my pocket and flicked through its various settings until it provide a dim light. I began my tour of inspection.

With no idea how long I might have before someone came to investigate my presence, I couldn't stand around wasting time. A quick arc with the torch revealed a two-storey building with a corridor running through the centre of the ground floor between the front and back doors. A number of doorways, now with open doors, led off both sides of the corridor. In its last iteration, the ground floor appears to have served as residential accommodation, probably as bed-sit rentals. However, the placed looked as though, at the outset, it was intended for some other use. I set off down the left hand side of the corridor, checking each room as I went.

The rooms were small, filthy and home to the abandoned detritus of a long line of squatters. Located just inside the front door, a worn and somewhat unsafe looking staircase led to the upper floor. I do want to go up there but, I needed to pluck up the courage to risk that staircase. There were still the rooms on the right hand side of the corridor to inspect. Maybe after that I'll feel brave enough to venture upstairs.

This side of the corridor was different. Although its initial construction mirrored the small rooms across the corridor, changes had been made... and not professionally. In the first room I entered, the dividing wall between it and the next room sported a gaping hole. The rudimentary arch formed by the hole looked more like a sledgehammer job than a planned modification. However, there remained enough structural integrity to prevent a collapse. No evidence of squatters in these rooms, but there was evidence of recent use. Dust and cobwebs everywhere suggested a lack of use. The floor told a different story. Areas of the floor were virtually dust free and drag marks decorated the dark bare concrete floor.

All of the rooms along this side of the corridor presented the same picture. It was a different picture from their counterparts across the corridor. The story on this side suggested used for storage; a sort of warehousing arrangement.

I spent longer than planned on the ground floor. I needed to negotiate that staircase to see what story the upper floor had to tell. Somehow, I didn't think it would say much. I shone my torch on each stair tread as I climbed it. A thick, undisturbed layer of dust covered each tread. About halfway up the stairs I stopped. "This can't be right," I told the empty building. "The Police raided this place. Surely they checked the top floor too." Yet, the evidence suggested no one had climbed these stairs in days, if not weeks.

People – probably squatters – had been up here in the past, a long time in the past judging by the look of the place. There was rubbish lying around, but less than downstairs. In support of my assessment, the dust and cobwebs showed no sign of having been disturbed. The rooms were larger up here. Again, they suggested their original intended use was not residential.

A quick tour of the upper floor rooms produced nothing to alter my original assessment of this floor. I braved the staircase once more for a closer look at the ground floor area on my way out. I zig-zagged from side to side along the corridor, checking each room on my way to the back door. It was in the last room before the back door that my pulse stepped up a notch.

My interest in the place was waning. I stood in the doorway of that last room and swept my torch over it. Nothing; just as empty as all the others on this side of the corridor. Or was it…? My torch lit up something on the floor in the corner along the wall from the door. "Probably just dirt or rubbish," I said aloud as I trudged over to investigate.

Some of it was rubbish. It looked like a few splinters of wood had broken off something. I picked up a couple of pieces: rough, unfinished wood with a hint of red spray paint on one piece. Splinters from a pallet, was what came to mind as I turned the wood over and over in my hand. Three other pieces about the size of ten cent coins remained on the floor. I squatted down, and rolled them over with my finger to examine them more closely. They seemed to come from the same source as their larger counterparts.

As I stirred them around with my finger, something else became visible. It looked as though these splinters were swept here sometime in the past to get them out of the way. Now that I had disturbed them, they revealed another secret: a few white grains beneath them. I'm no expert on drugs but, if I had to hazard a guess about that white stuff, I would say it was 'Ice'. Had the police found this? If they did, why was it still here?

Deep in thought, I started to climb up off my haunches. My phone rang, frightening years off my life. I wrestled it out of my jacket pocket and answered it without checking the caller ID. My immediate thought was that it would be Emily ringing about some development at Sandlands. "Yeah, Sonny speaking…"

"Are you going to be home and would Thai for dinner be okay?" Ben asked without preamble.

I hadn't planned on seeing Ben this evening – hadn't wanted to see him tonight – but now I did want to talk to him. "Yeah, That would be great. I'll be home shortly, say, in about 20 minutes."

"I'll be a bit longer than that. I'm hoping there's something cold in your fridge to go with the food."

Something to drink with dinner was not a problem, but not wasting any more time getting home was a priority. I put the splinters back where I found them and hurried to the back door. After a cautious check for anybody lurking about outside, I was wrestling the door back to where it was when I arrived. The police tape I had pulled off was a little more uncooperative. Persistence paid off and I got the end to stick to the wall again. I knew it wouldn't stay there but, as long as it was where it was supposed to be when I left, I didn't care.

The temptation to jog back to my car took some resisting. A galloping figure would attract attention, so I settled for a brisk walk instead. My car was still where I left and appeared unmolested and with all four wheels still attached, all of which surprised me. I had

an interesting mental picture of reporting my car stolen from here…
and all the questions that would follow about what I was doing in
this area.

My memory of the drive home is foggy. So many questions
occupied my mind, not just about the derelict building, but about
both my current cases. Somehow, I knew they were connected but
I couldn't see the common denominator. What was the connecting
factor? My concern was that, until I identified that connection, I
wouldn't be able to crack either case. And looming large over
everything else was the question of what has happened to Trish
Fielding.

Ben arrived soon after I arrived home. As I opened a bottle of
white wine, I explained, "The wine is for you. I'm on mineral water
tonight. I am sort of on-call and might have to dash off if I get a
phone call… wouldn't want to get picked up for 'driving-under-the-
influence'. That stirred Ben's interest. He wanted to know about the
case I was working on. I was looking for a subtle way of introducing
mention of that derelict building in the hope it would allow me to
work up to talking about what I found in the corner of that last room
I inspected.

A deep breath and a moment of reflection, and then I was
discussing my Fielding case in a way I hoped encouraged Ben to
reveal what they found derelict building.

Chapter 18

"So you see, I have a vague idea about the operation Terry Fielding is mixed up in, but I can't quite get a handle on it. I know my case was to investigate Terry Fielding's possible infidelity and not whatever else he might be up to but, once my client disappeared, it all became relevant. And that also makes the derelict building you raided last night important."

"I don't see how you make that connection."

"You knew about that building because I told you about my truck being there. If you want the truth, I think that truck might be part of the Police's current investigation. We might be investigating the same thing, but coming at it from different angles. What you uncovered in the raid on the derelict building could confirm, or totally disprove, my ideas about what Terry Fielding is mixed up in. It could shed some light on what has happened to my client."

Ben remained silent when I finished speaking. I knew he was weighing up what he would or wouldn't share with me. With my hands in my lap to stop them from drumming on the table while I waited, I sat back in my chair and gave him all the time he needed to consider his options. It was while this process was happening that my phone rang... and ruined the moment I feared. It was Emily.

"Sonny, I'm still sitting here watching Thornton's and haven't been out to Sandlands yet. What do you want me to do... should I stay here?"

"Why are you still outside Thornton's? Is something interesting happening there?"

"The little red car is still in the car park, although I can't see any sign of activity in there."

"Okay, I'm on my way. Stay where you are until I get there."

Now focused on me, Ben had dismissed all thoughts about the Police's investigation and that derelict building. All my groundwork was for nought. He looked at me expectantly as I ended Emily's call. "As I said earlier, I am on-call tonight. That call means I have to leave now. You're welcome to stay or go home, whichever suits you. I don't know how long I'll be gone."

"There is another option: I could go with you." He looked like an excited puppy when a treat is on offer. His attempt at a beguiling grin wasn't necessary. The moment he suggested coming with me, I could see there might be advantage in getting him involved. He might develop a more constructive interest in my case and my missing client.

Emily was parked out front of the diner. I drove past her and parked against the kerb further along the street but with a clear view of Thornton's. I rang her for a report on what had happened since she began surveillance earlier this afternoon. If anyone should happen to be interested, walking over to talk to her would look suspicious. Her report was brief. Nothing of any interest had happened. The only interesting thing was the fact that nothing appeared to be happening but the little red car was one of four vehicles still in Thornton's car park.

The last time we knew Terry Fielding had 'worked' late into the night was when a late-arriving semitrailer's strange behaviour caught our attention. Was tonight to be a repeat of that? If it were, I wanted to be here to see it and, more importantly, I wanted my passenger to witness it. "Emily, I'll take over watching Thornton's. You head over to Sandlands. Take a drive along Grevillea Crescent. Look for any activity, any sign of human presence, at Blondie's house. Let me know what you find, and then go home for the night."

She mounted a token argument for continuing surveillance at Sandlands on the off chance something might happen there. I insisted that after checking out Blondie's, she go home to Goldie. She drove off. I knew she was unhappy and I would need to square it with her sometime soon.

We watched Emily's taillights until they disappeared around the corner at the end of the street before settling back for what we knew could be a long and futile wait. About 20 minutes after Emily left, a semitrailer entered the far end of the street. I glanced across as Ben to see if he was aware of the development. He was slumped against the window and dozing with his mouth slightly open. A none too gentle prod had him awake and upright again.

The semi driver seemed unsure of his surroundings. He crawled his rig down the street, almost stopping in front of properties a couple of times along the way. In my peripheral vision, I spotted a figure emerge from one of the buildings and make its way to Thornton's gates. Not having noticed it until it was halfway across to the gates, I didn't know which building it came from. I grabbed my night glasses from the glove compartment and focused on the advancing figure.

"Terry Fielding…!" I squawked in a stage whisper. Ben grunted in response, but I noticed him now perched on the edge of his seat. Terry reached the gates and they slid open a few moments before the rig arrived. "Must be a new driver," I whispered. "He mustn't have a remote device to open the gates. Terry had to open them for him." Everything about the semitrailer's arrival at Thornton's followed that previous routine Emily and I witnessed. The rig drove along the front of the building, past what we knew to be the loading dock area, and around the far corner of the complex.

Ben's seatbelt catch snapped, drawing my attention back to the car. He had climbed out of the seatbelt and sprung his door open by the time I managed to work out what was happening. "What are you doing… where are you going?"

"You want to know what's happening with that semi, don't you? You're not going to find out anything sitting out here." He slammed his door closed and started walking around the car. I hit speed dial for Emily and scrambled out of the car with my phone to my ear.

"Emily, where are you?"

"…Just leaving Sandlands. I was going to call…"

"Tell me later. Head back to town please. Park somewhere near the end of Thornton's street, somewhere near the corner or just around the corner. Anywhere there as long as you can see anything that comes along the street from Thornton's direction." By the time I finished speaking to Emily, Ben and I were standing outside Thornton's huge gates.

"Now what…?" I asked. "There aren't any convenient gaps in the fence and those rolls of barbed wire on top of the fence aren't exactly inviting. I assume the plan is to get in there somehow."

"How else are we going to find out anything? And if you look closely, there is no barbed wire on top of the gates. It would tangle with the wire on top of the fence when the gates slid open."

"Nice idea. But those gates aren't designed to be climbed and, like the fence, they are tall. I couldn't reach that top bar even if I jumped up."

"Empty the pockets of your jacket. I'm not going to boost up any excess weight. Come on, hurry up."

He took my torch and slipped it into his own pocket. The bottle of water he tossed on the ground to one side of the entrance. Then he bent over and motioned for me to put my foot in his clasped hands so he could boost me up. "Hang on a minute. How do we know the area isn't monitored, and what happens when I am inside? How do I get out again, and what will you be doing while I'm stuck in there?" I could just see myself standing in the dock explaining to the magistrate that 'a policeman made me do it'. If I went over that gate, I probably could kiss my private investigator's license goodbye.

"Stop mucking about and get over the gate. We haven't got all night to discuss it. Once you are inside, you will go to that box on the post to open the gate for me."

"I don't know anything about that box. What if there is a code or something that has to be entered?"

"There won't be. That's why it's positioned so you can't reach it from outside. Besides, if it required a code, it would be too restrictive. Only a handful of people who knew the code would be able to open the gate. For Christ's sake, stop mucking about and put your foot in my hands."

I grabbed hold of the top bar and hauled myself up and over the gate to drop to the driveway on the other side. "Give me the torch so I can see what to do in this control box."

Ben passed the torch through between the bars of the gate. "You need to go on a diet, or lose some weight somehow. How heavy are you anyway?"

"How do you fancy walking home? You might have to if you keep that up. Anyway, it was your harebrained idea to toss me over the fence, so stop moaning. I need to concentrate on how to make this gate open."

It wasn't that complicated. There wasn't a lot on the control panel to confuse me. And the two large buttons on the middle of the board clearly indicated they were for opening and closing the gates. A large red button suggested it was for use in some sort of emergency. Best I give that a wide berth in case it triggers an alarm somewhere in the bowels of the Thornton complex.

"Now what's the hold-up?"

"No hold-up; just being cautious." The gates slid open with nothing more than a faint swishing sound.

"Okay, I'm in. Now close them again."

I didn't fancy trying that. I could see the button that closed the gates, but I didn't know what would happen if I pressed it while they were still opening. I opted to wait until they were fully open before hitting the 'close' button. Cool! They began their reverse travel without bringing the world down around me. Ben had reached the few cars in the parking lot. I put my triumph with the gates behind me and rushed to join him.

"It would not do my career any good to be caught in here without a warrant, so don't do anything stupid that could get me into hot water."

"Oh, I get the message. Your career is important but it doesn't matter about mine…" I was wasting my voice. Ben, running in a crouch, was halfway across to the main building. I followed his example but just a little faster to enable me to catch up to him.

With our backs pressed hard against the brick front wall, we waited for any indication our presence had been detected. Nothing happened. Everything was still and quiet. We slid ourselves along the wall and past the closed loading dock area to reach the corner of the building, the same corner the semitrailer went around after it arrived. Ben risked a look down the side of the building. "No sign of the rig and nowhere along this side for it to enter the building. It must have continued around to the rear."

Ben's observation was right. There were no openings along this side of the building and also no windows at ground floor level. Stealth seemed a waste of time given we couldn't be seen. We broke into a run staying in close to the wall. A few metres before the back corner of the building, caution kicked in again. We picked our way to the end of the wall.

It appears Ben thinks he is in charge of this operation. He led all the way from the gates. Still in the lead, he reached the corner first and took a quick look along the back wall. He snapped back and pressed himself against the wall. I didn't need any prompting. I was right there with him. My back was pressed so hard against the wall, it's a miracle it didn't open up and swallow me.

Ben leaned over to whisper in my ear. "…Light shining out through an opening about halfway along the back wall. The semi has reversed in. Prime mover remains outside the building. There are shadows dancing about; people being busy in there. There is a shadow of another funny shape."

"Let's get out of here. I know what's happening in there. That other shadow is the truck with the high canopy on the back. We need to be in the car to follow what happens next. Come on, hurry up. Let's get back to the car before the vehicles start moving."

I sensed his reluctance. A hard yank on his arm and briefly dragging him along after me had us both heading in the right direction. Our trip back to the gates seemed to take less time than before. At the gates, I hit the button to open them and prepared to dash out through them. Ben grabbed my arm to stop me. "Wait till they are about half open and then hit the 'close' button. Let's see what happens. They take so long to open completely and then close, those vehicles could be on the move again before they shut. We don't want to give the game away at this stage."

A small voice in my head warned me anything could happen if we did that, and it might not be a good move. Ben guessed I wasn't going to do it. The gates had opened about halfway. Ben's grip on my arm had loosened. I flicked his hand free and bolted towards the opening between the gates. Without hesitating, I raced out onto the pavement. I heard something behind me. I looked back. Ben was two paces further back but also outside the gates. The gap between the gates now reduced to about a metre as the two gates slid together.

"The car…," I yelped, but need not have bothered. We both already were at full gallop crossing the street. I fumbled the key out of my pocket as we ran and unlocked the car when we were still metres away. There followed a few seconds of feverish activity. In a flurry of arms, legs and breathlessness, two bodies hurled themselves into my car and buckled up in readiness for whatever might come next. Nothing came next… well, not for about 15 minutes anyway. Then the program got underway again.

"Lights…" I hissed. The glow from headlights shone out from somewhere down the side of Thornton's building. At the same time as I saw them, I noticed the gates had started to move.

"Y-e-s, I… can… see… lights." Ben added an exaggerated way for effect

"If everything happens as before, that will be the truck with the high canopy on its way out of the complex."

As I spoke, the truck emerged and headed for the gates as they started to open. They were about half open when the truck, continuing at full speed, raced through the gap between the gates, and out onto the street. Without pausing at the edge of the pavement to check for other traffic or anything else, it turned right onto the street and sped off into the distance. "Well, come on. Are we going to follow it, or are we going to sit here and watch it disappear?"

"We are going to continue to sit here. Relax Ben, there is more to happen here." I called Emily and gave her a quiet heads-up that our truck was coming her way.

"I'm certain they transhipped material from the semi to that truck. Don't you want to know where it's taking the stuff? I know I would very much like to follow it to see what happens next."

"That's being taken care of. Look, the next stage of the performance is about to start."

Lights came on in the now open loading dock as the semi, following the truck's earlier route, appeared from around the side of the building. It travelled along the front of the building and reversed into the loading dock.

"I can't image there is much left on the semi to unload after all the frantic work that happened at the rear of the building. Why would they unload it in two different places? I suppose if they have two different types of material on board, special stuff might need special handling facilities." Ben said, answering his own question about the two unloading locations.

"I suspect that 'special stuff' requiring 'special handling' might just about describe the situation. The special stuff was transhipped to that truck around the back, away from prying eyes. Now, the legitimate material is being unloaded in the normal fashion, out front in the loading dock area."

After giving me a hard look, Ben replied. "By 'special stuff', I assume you mean illegal material of some sort that is then whisked away to the next stage of its journey."

"That's my suspicion. And, from what I found in that derelict building, I think I'm right on the money." Oops, maybe that wasn't the wisest statement to make. It didn't go past Ben unnoticed.

"You will explain that statement to me later." His tone told me he would ensure that happened.

My phone vibrated: Emily. I took the call while my eyes remained fixed on the activities in the loading dock area.

"The truck headed deeper into another part of the industrial estate. I drove past the street it turned into, drove on, and then doubled back to drive past that street again. The truck was reversing into a building towards the far end of that street. Do you want me to take a closer look, or hang around to see what happens next?"

"No thanks. Get the hell away from there. I know where it went and it is impossible to take a closer look without being seen. Go home now and tuck Goldie in for the night. I'll talk to you sometime tomorrow morning."

"Anything I should know about?" Ben asked. His expectant face was as phony as a seven dollar note.

"Not really; the truck did exactly what I expected it to do… although, in hindsight, I realise it might have chosen the other option."

"Thank you very much. That was most enlightening. Now maybe you might care to explain."

"Yeah, I will. But look, the semi is moving out. Do we want to follow it to see where it goes?"

"Nah, I don't think so. At this hour, it probably will spend the rest of the night at one of the local truck stops. If it's now empty, it will go somewhere in the morning to pick up a new load. If it still has a reasonable load on board, it will continue to the next delivery point in the morning. So, what other entertainment have you got for us this evening?"

"Fancy a ride out to Sandlands with me?"

"Are we going to take another look at that house?"

"I wasn't planning to. I was only interested in whether the truck returned and at what time."

He shrugged and nodded and I took that as his support for my plan. There was one more phase to this performance. I waited until the semi had cleared the street. It turned left at the end of the street, away from the industrial estate. Then I watched Thornton's and waited. I could feel Ben's eyes burning into the back of my head as I sat watching Thornton's carpark. I knew he would be busting to ask me why the hell I was still sitting here, but he managed to restrain himself... and I enjoyed delivering the torture.

In reality, the wait was only about three or four minutes. A small group of people straggled out to the carpark. As on the previous occasion, Terry Fielding and Blondie were the last to reach their car. Again, Terry got the door for Blondie, and they followed the other three vehicles out onto the street.

"Now we can go for a drive," I told Ben. He didn't respond but settled back in his seat.

At the end of the street, I turned right. "I thought we were going to Sandlands. Why the change of plan...?"

"Not a change of plan; I want to show you something – somewhere, I mean – that might be of interest to you." I drove to what was becoming a familiar area and crawled past the street with the warehouse type building at the far end. As I approached the street's intersection, I clued Ben in. "This street coming up on your left; look down the left hand side of the street towards its end." I risked a quick glance as we drove past the intersection.

The warehouse roller door was open. Light spilled out into the street, along with the unmistakable shadow of a high canopied truck. "There's a bit of activity happening down the end there," Ben commented.

"Make a note of the address. You and your blokes might find it useful in the near future."

There wasn't much conversation on the drive to Sandlands. I parked amongst the trees in Melaleuca Grove and got comfortable for what I figured might be a long wait. I was wrong. About ten minutes after we arrived, the truck drove past at speed and turned onto Grevillea Crescent. "What now…?" Ben asked. This was good. He now recognises this is my stake out, my case, and is not trying to take charge.

"Let's give them a couple of minutes to open the shed and all that, and then we will drive past. It will have to be at normal speed so our presence doesn't stand out in the quiet neighbourhood. Keep your eyes open."

I had a quick look and was pleased to see my hunch was right The shed was open and lit up. Three figures were near the truck, one of whom looked female. "Everyone present and accounted for," I announced as we continued along Grevillea Crescent.

With nothing more to be achieved tonight, my intention was to go home. Ben could collect his vehicle and then he too could go home. I pointed the car towards town and drove out of Sandlands. As we approached to turnoff to the shortest route to my house, I started to slow down.

"Where are you going?"

"Home; I thought we both might be looking forward to a relatively early night. So, I'm going home so you can collect your car and go home too."

"No. We're going to the derelict building so you can show me what you found there, and you seem to believe my men didn't find."

"It's the middle of the night. Don't you think a visit at this hour of the night might raise the odd spark of interest from the locals?"

Since nothing would dissuade him, I drove to the eastern end of town and entered the slum area via the direct route. As we drove towards our target, a light moving about inside the building caught our attention. "Drive on and park behind that tangle of bougainvillea," Ben commanded. To park behind the bougainvillea required a U-turn a bit further along in the narrow street. I executed something akin to a 10-point-turn to idle up to and park behind the prickly barricade.

As I backed and filled in the narrow street, the light, which we decided was a torch, moved to the backyard of the building. "For God's sake woman, hurry up. Our friends up there are getting ready to vacate the property." Ignore the sod, I told myself and continued messing about until I finally parked in the designated place.

"I'm going to wander up to see what's going on," Ben announced as soon as we stopped. "You wait here in the car until I give you a call to join me."

Not bloody likely! My feet hit the ground at about the same time as his. We stopped at the end of the bougainvillea. Ben peered around it to check there were no surprises waiting for us out on the street. He snapped back, pushing me back against the bougainvillea as he did so. I yelped as a prickle went through my jacket and jabbed me in the shoulder blade.

"Sssh...!" Ben hissed. A moment later, a vehicle flashed past us. "Bugger! Plates are obscured." I hadn't noticed. I was too busy trying to reach around to investigate my injury.

The absence of streetlights made it impossible to identify the make and colour of the vehicle with any accuracy. However, we agreed it was big, dark – possibly black or dark blue – and sufficiently boxy-looking to be a large model SUV.

Once the vehicle was out of sight, Ben risked another look along the street... nothing happening and no lights at the derelict building. We strode out onto the street, Ben full of confidence and me with as much bravado as I could muster. The sounds of gunfire at the building last night remained clear memories. I wasn't convinced tonight wouldn't end in a repeat performance. The fact that it was a Police crime scene didn't deter the bloke who just drove past us. Why would it deter his associates from returning to the building?

I marched along the street beside Ben. When we reached the building, he roughly shoved me behind him, almost tripping me in the process. "Stay behind me. I don't suppose you brought a weapon with you."

"I wasn't planning on being here at all tonight, let alone indulging in some target practice. Of course I don't have a weapon. I don't make a habit of carrying one around with me." I should have saved my breath. He wasn't listening. By the end of that exchange, we were three parts of the way along the side of the building.

Ben again pushed me back against the wall, and signalled me to stay there. He reached the corner of the building without making a sound and, after checking out the backyard area, beckoned me to join him. Still hugging the wall, I raced up to the corner. Ben was no longer there. He was halfway to the backdoor.

One strand of police crime scene tape dangled loosely down one side of the doorway. It was the same piece I removed and replaced previously. I suffered a moment of guilt as I wondered whether it was my interference that had it dangling now, or whether the recently departed visitor was responsible. After reassuring myself the latter was the case, I got over the guilt. I told myself he would have removed it to enter the building.

The door hadn't been closed properly and stood about half open. Once more, I got the signal 'to stay' before Ben cautiously slipped around the open door to enter the building. A few moments later, he poked his head around the door and invited me in. Ben still had the torch he took from me at Thornton's. Before getting out of the car, I remembered to grab my small spare torch from the side pocket on the door. I dragged it out of my pocket now and was pleased to see there was plenty of charge in the batteries.

"Right, where is this thing you want to show me?"

I led the way to the far corner of the back room. It didn't look as though anything had been disturbed since I left. Ben went down on his haunches beside me. With both our torches trained on the small pile of wood splinters on the floor, I gently moved a couple of bits to reveal what lay beneath. The few grains of white powder stood out starkly against the dark floor. Ben pulled out his phone. "Record this for me, please."

After a quick scan, I found the camera app and focused it on the pile of rubbish on the floor. "Move back further so the first few frames are of me down here beside the stuff on the floor. Oh, hang on a minute. I need to put those bigger slivers of wood back where they were."

"Allow me; I've had practice." I returned everything to the way it was and then moved back to fit Ben's large hulk in the frame. "I'm guessing you want this on video and not as still images." He nodded. "Okay, action! The camera is rolling."

"Move in for closer shots of my hands as I move the bits of wood."

Within a few seconds, the whole process of uncovering the white substances was captured, including shots of Ben using adhesive tape to collect the white material from the floor. He produced a plastic evidence bag from his jacket pocket and sealed the tape in it. After writing something on the bag with a felt tipped pen, he requested a shot of the label on the bag. "Okay, that's it. You can turn the camera off now."

As we had finished what we came for, I expected we would leave. Ben had other ideas and decided to take a look around. We went in and out of rooms, working our way along that side of the building and across to the staircase. "Did you look up there? I don't fancy testing my weight on those stairs if I don't need to."

My report on the upper floor was brief, and emphasised the fact that it didn't look as though anyone had been up there in a long time. "Good; let's take a quick look at the rest of the rooms down here and leave." He got no argument from me… no argument that is, until we were in the last of the rooms.

Chapter 19

"Sssh, stand still; I think I heard something." I closed my eyes and opened my mouth slightly to sharpen my hearing. Nothing. Ben started to say something. "Sssh, just listen for a minute; I'm sure I heard something."

"Like what…?" At least he had decided to whisper now. I saw him open his mouth to say something else, but closed it immediately.

The sound came again, faint and from some indeterminate direction. "That's it," I mouthed to Ben. He heard it too and wasn't looking at me. His head swivelled in all directions as he tried to pinpoint the source of the sound, but it had stopped. Whatever it was, the sound only lasted a second or two before disappearing.

I slid over to stand next to Ben and whispered, "What was it?" He shrugged. I noted he was tense, on high alert. That's good, so am I. Last night's firefight loomed large in my mind again. I jerked my head in the direction of the door to suggest we should leave. Ben shook his head. I gave his arm a couple of impatient tugs as I jerked my head towards the door again. More negative head shaking from Ben.

He put his mouth close to my ear and whispered, "I want to know what it is, don't you?"

My turn to shrug. Yes, I want to know what it is and where it is coming from, but I'm not sure that trumps my survival instinct. We stood still for what felt like an eternity. Just when I was convinced the sound wasn't coming again, there it was once more. It was weak and not a sound either of us could identify. Again, it lasted only a couple of seconds. "Sounds muffled somehow," I said, "But I can't fix its direction. Have you any ideas?"

Ben gave one half-hearted shake of his head before starting to move across the room. He motioned me to follow. I copied his example. A cat would make more noise than the short silent steps we took to cross the room. We planted our backs against the brick wall. It felt cold through my jacket. I realised this was the external side wall of the building. After standing there for a few heartbeats,

I raised my eyebrows in question at Ben. Why we stood against the wall like this was beyond me.

The rubbish strewn backyard seemed a better option to me. I wanted to bolt for the backdoor. Ben sensed it and gave me a 'stay' signal. Although reluctant, I remained plastered to the wall. We had turned off our torches. I'm sure I would feel happier if I could see what is around me. With my torch back on, and ignoring Ben's scowl, I played its beam around the room, over the floor and walls, and the various rubbish cluttering the space. Something drew my attention back to the floor. Something was not right here… but what? What was trying to prod my subconscious into action? Nothing floated to the surface.

Perhaps the room as it looks now is confusing the process. I turned my torch off and focused my mind on my previous visit to this room. That visit was brief, no more than a quick scan of the room and its abandoned contents. Then it hit me. The floor and that old rusted chest freezer, something was different. I turned my torch on and played its light across the floor and over the freezer. Nothing! Nothing jumped out at me, but something kept urging me to look closer. Inspect the freezer, I told myself. Then, a movement pushed all thoughts of what was different about the room from my mind.

Out of the corner of my eye, I caught Ben shaking his head at some private thought bothering him. Before I could inquire about what was baffling him, he grabbed my arm and, with a jerk of his head, signalled for me to follow him. He put a finger to his lips. Does this bloke think I'm such an amateur at this sleuthing game? As if I'm likely to go clattering about the place encouraging the hounds of hell, or whatever lurks here, to come find me.

On our slow and silent tour of inspection, we stopped at the doorway of every room on the ground floor to give each one a cursory check. We had worked our way about halfway along the opposite side of the central corridor when the sound came again, halting us mid-stride. It lasted a split second but was different this time. A quite different sound from those we heard earlier. We waited for it to come again. I've no idea how long we stood there frozen to the spot. There were no further sounds.

At last Ben abandoned the waiting and, grabbing my arm dragged me towards the staircase to the upper floor. "Take a look up there. I don't think it came from up there but we can't be sure."

"Hang about. What if there is something or someone up there. If you're so curious about what's up there, you go and take a look yourself."

"If you run into trouble, scream. I will risk life and limb to climb those fragile looking stairs to rescue you."

"…Be a waste of time. I'll be the blur passing you on my way down." Nevertheless, heart thumping, I picked my way up the stairs. Nothing moving and nothing appeared disturbed since my earlier visit.

Back on the ground floor, I again motioned towards the backdoor. The place was beginning to creep me out. Ben nodded and padded off towards the backdoor. He stopped suddenly at the door. I spun around to look behind us. Had he heard something I didn't? The corridor was empty. The only sound was my elevated pulse pounding in my head. I looked back at Ben for explanation. He shrugged and ducked out around the door.

There was something comforting about being outside. Ben seemed to have lost interest in the building and strode off along the side of the place, leaving the backdoor ajar as we had found it and the police tape waving in the gentle night breeze. I fell into step beside him for a silent trek back to my car.

Ben broke the silence a short distance before we reached the car. "Something you want to share?"

"Eh…? What's to share?"

"Whatever you've been worrying to death all the way back from that building."

"I don't know what it is. It's complicated. When I sort it out a bit, I'll tell you about it."

"Well, do you think you can put it out of your mind so you can concentrate on driving us back to your place?"

I shot him a hard look but it was lost in the darkness. He was right about concentrating on the driving, only a part of my mind focused on that while the remainder wrestled with what it was about that building tonight that wasn't right. However, traffic was almost non-existent and resulted in a speedy and safe trip to my house.

When we arrived at my place, I expected he would say good night, go to his car and go home. It didn't happen. "Coffee…?" He suggested. Coffee at this hour would keep me awake for the rest of the night, but somehow it seemed a good idea. We traipsed inside and I got busy with the coffee machine.

While I rattled about with mugs and the like, Ben sat waiting at the dining room table. "Cake…?"

"What…? Cake is an unknown commodity in this house."

"Something to go with would be nice. Even raisin toast would be good."

I scrabbled about in the freezer and found half a fruit loaf. The tray loaded with coffee and toast was plonked on the dining room table. I was determined not to take it through to the lounge room where he might get comfortable and stay even longer. While the thought of coffee and toast was tempting, I longed for sleep. However, the late-night indulgence seemed to work some sort of miracle, and I found myself slipping into relaxed mode. Maybe it was a precursor to ending up with my head on the table and sound asleep. Ben prevented that happening.

"Something's been gnawing at you since we were at that derelict building. You said you can't identify what it is but, maybe if you talk about it, it will start to unravel itself. Don't worry about making sense, just tell me what's on your mind."

This has worked for us before, but there's a bit of a ritual involved. I turned off the light in the lounge room and dimmed the kitchen and dining room lights. We got comfortable in the lounge room. I laid my head back on the plush cushioning of my chair and let my mind drift. When I started speaking, a jumble of rubbish came out, but coherent thought soon followed.

"I can't put my finger on it, but my gut tells me something inside that building is different tonight. It must not be anything major or I would be able to identify it. I think it's more a sense of it having changed in some way…"

"When did you first start to feel something had changed?"

"Uhmm, let me think. Yes, it was while we were standing up against the wall in that back room that I first felt something was different. I switched my torch on expecting to see something major, but there was nothing. Still, I'm sure something had changed in that room. The same feeling screamed at me when we looked into a couple of the other rooms as well. I've been trying to convince myself it was just the sound we heard that was unnerving me, but I know that isn't true. Something was different. What do you think that noise was anyway? It couldn't be anything as simple as the wind flapping something around."

"…Could have been anything, even rats. I'm more interested in your belief that something changed since your previous visit. Walk me through each room where you experienced that feeling. Close your eyes, open your mind, and take yourself back to earlier tonight. Think of yourself standing in one of those rooms and describe what you see. Start with that back room where we stood against the wall and listened for the sound."

It sounds dopey, but this process has worked in the past. Nevertheless, I always struggle to get myself into the right frame of mind for it to work. Tonight was no different. But it only took a couple of minutes before my mind was replaying visions from earlier in the evening. I did as I was told and started describing what I could see when I turned on my torch in that back room. A rambling inventory of what was in the room began. Then it came to me.

"Some stuff was missing. There was less rubbish in the room than previously… And that rusty freezer had been moved. Even though it was a mess with all sorts of rubbish piled up down the back end, last time it looked as though it was in use. It wasn't exactly set out properly, but the rubbish seemed organised in some particular way."

"That's good. Now look around the room again. Don't focus on the rubbish this time. Look at the room itself; the walls, the floor, everything about the room."

"I don't think I paid attention to the walls on either occasion. They were just walls and I didn't notice anything special about them. Ooh, yes I did. On my first visit, there was something taped to that wall we were standing against. It wasn't paper. It looked more like that light cardboard they use for craft projects. I think there was writing of some sort on it. It wasn't there tonight. Give me a moment to think … about … that … thing … taped … to the wall. Yes; it was drawn up as a table of some sort, maybe a schedule."

"Excellent; if there is nothing more about the walls, what about the floor? Is there anything specific on or about the floor in that room?"

"Yes! Yes, it was different. On the first occasion, the floor wasn't clean but there wasn't a lot of dust on it. It looked as though it was in regular use, and had traffic in and out of the place. That was still the case tonight, but there were drag marks, scratches if you like, in a couple of places that looked like something heavy was dragged across the floor. I don't think there's anything else about that room, so I'll try to focus on another room."

"Okay; as we moved through the building, which was the next room where you felt something was different?"

Each of the rooms I commented on carried much the same story: items had been removed or moved about. In every case, the change was subtle, but it was there and finally I was seeing the changes clearly. For a few moments, I sat silent, letting my mind drift back over everything I had seen and spoken about. "You know, Ben, if I had to summarise the changes I saw tonight, I would say what had been removed was evidence of people who I believe squatted there until – maybe up until the raid on the place."

"You've gone deep in thought again. Is there something else we haven't covered?"

"N-o-o, but that rusty freezer in that back room keeps calling to me." I shrugged and shook my head in frustration. And then another thought hit me. "And those noises… there were no noises in the place on my first visit. If there had been, I would have been out of there like a shot and wouldn't have found that little pile of rubbish in the corner of that other back room."

We were both exhausted and struggling to keep our eyelids open. "There are only a couple of hours until dawn. You can either go home or catch a few hours of sleep in my spare room. If you stay, I don't run to pyjamas in your size." Ben elected to sleep on the couch in the lounge room. Although it folds out into a full size bed, his feet hung over the end of it. He was asleep by the time I had showered. I threw a blanket over him before I fell into bed.

Neither of us surfaced before eight o'clock next morning. After a 'make do' breakfast, Ben left to shower and change before going in to work. Over breakfast, he asked what my plans were for the day.

"I don't have anything resembling a plan. I need to spend some time in my office catching up with where I'm at with my cases. Why do you ask?"

"I think we should go back to that building. It's probably a good idea to take a closer look at those rooms where we think changes happened. The problem is, I'll be busy at the precinct for most of the day. They created a new office for me in that refurbished wing and I'm supposed to be shifting in to it today. I moved a few bits yesterday. You could just about hold a dance in my current office now that some of the stuff is gone. There's plenty of wide open space… with a scruffy looking carpet from things being dragged across it. So, as soon as I'm done shifting offices, if you're free, we might take another trip out to that derelict building."

"I should be free, or will be able to free myself from whatever I'm doing. Have the police finished with that building? It doesn't appear any of your officers have been there since first thing the morning after the raid."

"Nah, they gave the place a good going over on the night and then picked up a few extra bits the next morning. Everything is still being looked at, but they don't think there's anything to be had by going back to the building. It remains a crime site until all of the legalities surrounding the gunfight are finalised. That could take a while, as I don't think it'll be before the court for a few weeks."

It was around ten o'clock before I finally made it into my office. Emily tried to ring me. She didn't leave a message. Two other messages came in, one of which was a hang-up and the other was a follow-up query on an insurance job. Nothing required my immediate attention, so I made coffee and sat down to think. I was about halfway through my coffee when the sound of the door opening startled me. I looked up to see Emily standing in the doorway hands on hips.

"Come in, come in. I've only been here about half an hour and I was going to ring you as soon as I got coffee into me. How is Goldie settling in?" As she marched in, I pointed to the coffee machine. She detoured and fetched herself a mug before collapsing into a chair in front of my desk. Up to this point, she hadn't said a word, but it was obvious she was a bit off side. I half expected something after sending her home last night, but not this level of angst. It took a few minutes of fancy footwork on my part before normal relations resumed and Emily was asking about the outcome of last night's surveillance.

I gave her a brief overview of my night's activities, leaving out any mention of Ben or our visit to the derelict building. As expected, her next question was, "Okay, so where do we go from here? What's our next move? I am available for whatever you want me to do between now and when Mum comes home. It might get a bit tricky after that." If only it was as easy as allocating her something to do to progress my cases, life would be wonderful.

A change of tack might be called for, I decided. There had been little progress on Sandra Inneston's request to investigate her husband's infidelity. For professional confidentiality reasons, and to spare Emily any unnecessary upset, I had not told her about that investigation. However, there were two questions bothering me that I felt Emily might help with. One was whether anything ever was said at home about her father's potential 'bit on the side', and the other was whether Emily got to know any of her father's more recent associates… 'more recent' meaning the immediate period prior to his arrest. It was going to take some delicate questioning, but today seemed like a good time to do it.

I eased in gently. "Does your mother have much contact with any of your father's former work colleagues?"

"No, I don't think she has had any. Why do you ask?"

"I thought that, while they might not be classed as friends, they might rally around her a bit. You know the sort of thing I mean: give her a call occasionally and keep of an eye out that she was okay."

"No, I'm sure nothing like that happens. She didn't know too many of the local staff. Mainly knew two or three of the head office staff from when she and dad attended dinners with them. I think that's part of why she wants to leave Millhaven. She doesn't have much of a support base here."

Okay, now I feel guilty about neglecting Sandra. Time to find another subject not so close to home for Emily. "Are you still thinking of going to the Fieldings' unit complex sometime today?"

"Yeah, I want to check that Peggy left everything as she said she would. We need to make sure Terry Fielding is at work before we go there though... could be embarrassing if he turns up at the unit while we are snooping around in there."

"Good thinking. I'm not sure what time he will go to work today, if at all, after being at Thornton's until so late last night. It's not likely he will turn up at the unit. I don't think he has been there in days. It suggests he knows what happened and that Trish is no longer there. However, I wouldn't want him to call in to that store over the road and become curious about our car being parked outside his unit."

"I might go for a drive now to see if a certain little red car is in Thornton's carpark. And, I wasn't planning on parking out in the street. I was going to drive in and park behind the complex. I have a legitimate reason to do that, thanks to Peggy."

Emily went off to check at Thornton's leaving me alone with my thoughts on the Fielding case, and my deepening conviction that Terry knew what happened to Trish... and might have been involved in some way. As each day passed, I became more convinced Trish would not be found alive. I don't know what I expected to find by searching the Fieldings' unit. There probably would be nothing there to shed light on her disappearance. I consoled myself with the hope that we might find something – anything – that might be a clue about what Terry and his associates were involved in.

Somehow, my mind made the leap from the Fielding case to the derelict building in the slum area and our visit there last night. My session with Ben afterwards helped me focus on what bothered me about the place, but it also spurred Ben to investigating further. That noise we heard kept nagging at me. There was something about it I couldn't put my finger on, something that had me replaying it in my mind over and over again.

Less than an hour after she left, Emily bounced back into my office and announced, "Peggy seems to have gone on holidays as planned. I stopped and rang the bell a few times on my way to Thornton's but got no response. I couldn't see the little red car in the car park when I drove past, so I did a U-turn and came back to park in front of the diner. I don't know why I did that, but I'm pleased I did. A couple of minutes after I pulled up, the red car beetled down the street and drove into Thornton's. His lady friend was with him."

"If Terry has just gone into work, he is unlikely to leave again before about four o'clock. It's almost lunchtime. Let's have lunch and then take ourselves to water Peggy's plants."

It was nearly two o'clock when we parked behind Peggy's unit. A quick check of the carport confirmed the plants and keys were there. She watered the plants before she left. No need to waste time on them. Emily found the Fieldings' key and, a few seconds later, the door opened without a sound. We tiptoed in. No movement or sound greeted us.

Our time in the unit extended beyond my expectations. We searched the place systematically without finding anything of use. Someone had been there before us. Drawers were pulled out and contents displaced. Small pieces of furniture were knocked over or upended. A terrible stench pervaded the place. At the kitchen, we just about gagged. The stench was so strong there. Finding its source was a no-brainer. The kitchen bin was alive. Maggots spilled out from under the slightly ajar lid and wriggled across the floor.

I felt bile burn the back of my throat. Emily looked decidedly green. "Wait outside in the fresh air. I'll finish up in here."

"No, if I give you a hand, it'll halve the time it takes to check out this room. Let's get on with it."

"Okay, if you're sure you can handle it. Just don't throw up in here."

The kitchen didn't reveal anything either. But there was the question of what to do about that bin: should we leave it, or try to get rid of the contents. We agreed that, if Peggy had come in and found the bin in this condition, she would have removed it. It seemed logical then that we should do the same. I sent Emily to hold the back door open while I held my breath and gingerly carried the seething mass outside.

"What do we do with it now?" Emily asked.

A large green wheelie bin with the unit's number painted on it was parked up against the back fence. I bolted for it with the kitchen bin held out in front of me as though it might explode at any moment. My initial thought was to dump the lot, bin and all, into the wheelie bin, but something told me that's not what Peggy would do. Peggy would empty the contents into the wheelie bin before hosing out the kitchen bin and leaving it somewhere to dry. There was some merit in doing likewise

By the time I decided what to do, I was at the wheelie bin. I upended the kitchen bin into it. Maggots crawled all over my hands and started crawling up my forearms. I dumped the kitchen bin on the ground and shook and flicked the maggots off me. A final inspection of my hands and arms to ensure no strays lingered anywhere, and I reached over to close the wheelie bin's lid. As I did so, I glanced into the bin. Something caught my eye. I hesitated.

On top of all the rubbish festooned with writhing maggots was a polythene envelope tightly closed with packaging tape. I knew instinctively this wasn't rubbish. It shrieked 'important' at me. Gritting my teeth, I reached in and retrieved the packet, shaking it as I picked it up to dislodge its passengers.

I looked around for Emily. She stood near the carport and held a garden hose with a spray nozzle attached. She is definitely proving her worth! With the packet held out in front of me by two fingers, I headed for the hose. Emily met me halfway, hosed off the packet and then turned the spray on me, giving my hands and arms a good hosing. In spite of the fact that I knew I was carrying no livestock and I had received a thorough hosing down, I could still feel those things crawling on me. I shuddered. Emily looked alarmed. She grabbed the packet from me. "It's okay. It's okay, just a delayed reaction," I reassured her.

She thrust the packet back into my hand before hurrying to hose out the kitchen bin. I shook the droplets of water from the packet. It was my first close look at it. I hoped I hadn't endured all that to end up with nothing more than a packet of genuine household rubbish.

The polythene envelope had become cloudy making it difficult to see its contents. However, from what I could see, it appeared to contain what looked like documents. I didn't want to open the package here. In fact, I just wanted to get the hell away and go back to my office. With the kitchen bin hosed out and left upside down to drain, Emily checked the hose was turned off and stowed properly, before replacing the Fieldings' key back where she found it. She scrambled into the car and looked at the packet. "You haven't opened it yet. I thought you would have done that by now."

"Not yet; I want to open it in the office. Before we go there though, I think I'll check for mail at the post office."

"I'll come and check your mailbox later. Let's just see what's in that packet first. It might be important; could answer a lot of questions."

"I'm hoping it does. I feel it was deliberately hidden at the bottom of that kitchen bin. If I'm right, it has to be important. But before we go back to the office, I want to park at the Post Office, check my mailbox, and just sit for a couple of minutes to see if there's anyone interested in anything that was going on over at those units."

Emily remained in the car on lookout duty while I collected my mail and went into the Post Office to collect a parcel. Back in the car, I handed Emily some junk mail and told her to look like she was interested in whatever she was reading. While keeping an eye on the surrounding area for any interested spectators, I flicked through my mail without opening any of it. With no one much around and confident no one was showing any interest in us or the units across the road, we returned to the office.

Chapter 20

The packet lay in a cleared area in the centre of my desk as I rummaged in the drawer for scissors. I wasn't too concerned about messing up any latent fingerprints. They would have disappeared long before we retrieved it. Nevertheless, I donned gloves to remove its contents. Emily slit the tape holding the flap closed. I held the packet by the bottom corners and upended it. Its contents tumbled out to lie in a heap. With the polythene envelope parked to one side, it was time for the moment of truth. Did we have something important, or not?

As I spread the contents out on the desk, I realised there were more bits of paper involved than I expected. Some pieces were clipped together, while others remained as loose sheets. Some were typed, others were handwritten. I thanked whoever for having sealed the thing so well. Its recent hosing hadn't impacted on the contents. I didn't know if the contents had been stacked in any particular order. When I upended the packet, heavier clumps of paper fell out before single sheets, but some single sheets were caught up in the heavier material as it tumbled out.

Although I knew Emily was excited about the find and anxious to see what the contents might tell us, I wanted to look through it alone and in my own time. I was wondering how I might achieve that, if at all possible, when my phone rang. It was Ben. I didn't use his name when I answered.

"I'm established in my new accommodation. If you're still interested in having another look at that building, I'll pick you up in about half an hour."

Silly question; of course I wanted another look at that building. It also provided the solution to how to ask Emily to leave. Again, without using his name, I told Ben I would be ready to go when he was ready. Then I set about apologising to Emily. "I'm sorry Emily, work calls. I have someone coming and then we'll be going to look at the scene of a possible investigation. I need to prepare. I'll probably be gone for a while. I'll give you a call later if I need you for surveillance tonight. Now I need to put this stuff from the Fieldings' unit into the safe and do some preparation for what comes next. If I don't call you later, I'll talk to you tomorrow."

Yes, I do feel mean. But, while Emily is a willing helper and showing real promise, there are times when I need to be alone with what I do. This is one of them. Going through that stuff from the Fieldings' unit will take time and concentration. Maybe Emily will be useful after I do some preliminary work on it. And, depending on what I find, there might be merit in showing it to Ben. In the meantime, there is this niggling realisation that I am not devoting the time I should to my 'real' cases.

We took the direct route to the derelict house. I was surprised when Ben drove up beside it and parked in the middle of the rutted ground that was once the building's driveway. I raised a questioning eyebrow at Ben. "It will prevent anyone parked out the back making a getaway. Now, go and see if there is anything happening in the backyard."

With some degree of trepidation, I crept along the wall and looked around the corner of the building. The backyard was empty. I stood up and motioned Ben to drive around to the back. Moments later, we were once more in that back room with the rusty freezer. "The first time I came, that freezer was over there, not exactly against the wall, but close to it. It's been dragged more into the middle. See, there are drag marks and a couple of tears in that rubbishy bit of carpet it's on."

"The floor in this room is strange. Every other room has a concrete floor. They probably had some floor coverings sometime in the past, but they have long since disappeared. This room has a timber floor, probably laid over the concrete one. Maybe it was the boss' office or something and needed to be a bit more upmarket."

"That bit of carpet that's on this floor isn't laid properly. It's just a stray piece that's been thrown down on top of the timber flooring. The other thing that's different about this room is that rubbish over against the end wall behind the freezer. Those broken chairs and that fragile looking table were set out as though they were being used. Now, they are thrown on top of the heap of other rubbish."

After a few minutes, and having identified the obvious changes in the room, we moved on to the next room where I noticed changes. It was across the corridor and near the front of the building. Most notable change was the removal of much of the clutter that was strewn around before. An old table that looked as though it once graced a boardroom stood in the middle of the room. Against the side wall and immediately opposite the doorway stood a large old cupboard and a rusty four-drawer filing cabinet.

We sat with our backsides resting on the edge of the table and slowly scanned the room. Scratch marks on the concrete floor were evidence of heavy things being moved or removed. I ran my hand across the smooth unvarnished tabletop beside me. This table was old-style oiled timber, not shrouded in many coats of varnish. I checked my hand … no dust. "Ben, this table has been in recent use. There is no dust on the surface."

I watched him swipe his hand in a wide arc across the tabletop. "Now isn't that an interesting situation to find in a place that's otherwise covered in dust and the crap of ages?"

"There wasn't much in this room before. I can't remember exactly what was here, but it looked more recent and personal. What can you tell me about those who were involved in the gunfight with the Police … or maybe I should say what are you prepared to share with me?"

"Uhmm, probably not a lot at this stage; but I can tell you that there was evidence that at least some of them were squatting here. What's that got to do with anything anyway?"

"I'm not sure yet; maybe nothing. I've a half-formed idea that's begging for attention. But, here's a question for you: can you see any evidence of squatters on this ground floor now? Even if your officers took most of the evidence away with them, I still would expect to see something that tells of the squatters' presence and what they were doing here. There wouldn't have been a gunfight to protect their territory if they were the 'regular' breed of squatters."

He agreed they were not the 'normal' type of squatter you found in a local slum area, but offered nothing more. We moved to the last of the rooms where I felt things had changed. The story there was much the same as in the other rooms. I couldn't get past the fact that all evidence of squatters had vanished. I could understand the Police removing some critical bits and pieces, but everything having vanished was beyond my comprehension. While I had a whole string of questions I wanted to ask, I knew Ben well enough not to ask them now.

Once we toured all the rooms and I had pointed out the perceived changes, Ben suggested there wasn't much else to do and that we might leave. I couldn't agree. My gut kept telling me there was more to discover here. The trouble was, it wasn't suggesting what or where. However, Ben having decided we were leaving was on his way to the back door. I trailed along behind him until I reached the doorway of that back room where the rusty freezer held pride of place. My instinct screamed in my ear, 'look in there'. So, I detoured into the back room and walked around the whole room before stopping in front of the freezer.

What's threatening about it? For some reason, I hesitated before lifting the lid on the huge chest type freezer. For God's sake open the lid, I told myself and reefed it open at the same time as Ben entered the room. I caught my breath... and then gagged on the lungful of stench I'd sucked in. Ben coughed as the smell wafted across to meet him. He joined me at the freezer.

The lid went down with a thump the moment the smell hit me. The stench was cloying, sickly sweet and overpowering. As I tried to control my heaving stomach, in something of an automatic response, I stepped back from the freezer a couple of paces. Ben, now standing beside me, looked down at me and asked, "...That good is it?" Not game to open my mouth, I just nodded.

As he went to lift the lid, I attempted to back another couple of paces away from the freezer, and stumbled on some of the debris stacked against the end wall. More hardened to such things than I, Ben stood peering down into the freezer. I stood as far back from it as I could and held a tissue over my nose and mouth. At last, the lid thumped closed again. Ben remained standing at the freezer with his hands splayed out on top of the lid. I moved the tissue far enough away from my face to ask, "Is it female?"

"N-o-o, I don't think so. Hard to tell, but no I don't think so." I felt relief surge through me. My mind had connected Trish Fielding's disappearance with the gruesome sight in the freezer.

"Let's go back to that other room with the big table. I think I want to inspect the furniture in there." Ben was on his way out of the back room as he spoke, and I was right behind him, happy to be as far away as possible from the ripe contents of that freezer. We strode across the corridor to the room near the front of the building. Ben marched in and went straight to the cupboard against the side wall.

It was locked. An over-enthusiastic tug on the door handles sprung the cupboard doors while almost dislodging one of the handles. Ben stood, hands on hips, examining the cupboard's contents. I peered around him to see what his efforts revealed. There wasn't much to see, but what was there was interesting. Some of it, I didn't recognise, but I did recognise the couple of sets of electronic scales and a jumble of various sized spoons. A light dusting of fine white powder adorned shelves. This allowed us to see clear outlines of where other equipment once sat in the cupboard.

"Don't touch anything," Ben warned. "The forensic boys will have to dust all of this. We might as well see if there is anything in the filing cabinet while we're here."

There wasn't much in any of the four drawers. An empty box for one of the electronic scales, and its operating instructions, were the only items in the bottom drawer. The next two drawers above it contained packets of various sizes of small zip lock plastic bags. A bit disappointing, the top drawer held only a few torn scraps of paper yellowed with age and looking as though they were left over from its original owner. I heeded yet another warning not to touch anything and stood back as Ben slammed closed each of the drawers in turn.

Then we were on our way to the backdoor. Once we were outside, I strode to the vehicle while Ben, his phone to his ear, remained on the doorstep. I knew the place would soon swarm with forensic officers... and heavy lifting gear to remove that freezer and take it back to the lab.

Ben snapped his phone shut, scrambled into the driver's seat and wasted no time driving away from the place. His set jaw and the focused told me this was not a good time to ask silly questions – like where we were going and what would happen next. I didn't have long to wait to find out. We pulled into the carpark behind my office building. Ben kept the car idling. "I have something to do back at the precinct for a while. Do you think you could organise something for dinner. I'll come around when I'm finished at work, but I don't know what time that will be."

The set of his jaw suggested any comment was a waste of time. There wasn't opportunity anyway for, as soon as he finished speaking, he drove off. Oh well, at least I knew he was coming around later. I might be able to ease information out of him over dinner or over drinks after dinner. In the meantime, I had to think about what we might eat tonight and whether I should do anything in my office before heading home. The building was in darkness as I made my way to my office, most 'normal' people having gone for the day. I decided to follow their example.

After collecting my bag and the Inneston folder, I called at the supermarket and bought the fixings for a chicken pasta dish before driving home. A shower to clean up after where I had been today and remove the cloying aroma that clung to me and my clothes was essential before I made the sauce. I let it simmer while I sat at my office and went through the Inneston file. It was easier to think about cooking dinner than trying to develop a strategy to progress that investigation.

Something about this case is nagging me. It's not just that I can't make any progress with it, there is something more to it than Geoff Inneston's having a bit on the side. The case could be closed. We established that his relationship with Gloria Purtell was something other than professional, and that's what Sandra asked me to investigate. I'll talk to her when she's back at the end of the week, but I suspect she will end the investigation. I need to talk to Emily between now and when her mother returns. She needs to know what's going on and what might be lurking in her parents' future.

While turning those thoughts over in my mind, I flicked through the Inneston file. The CCTV image of Gloria Purtell on her first visit to the prison had somehow floated to the top of the file. I held it loosely in two fingers and was about to turn it over onto the other documents when an alarm bell clanged. It drew my attention back to the photo of a woman disguised in a wig and heavy make-up. My mind compared the photo with the Gloria Purtell I observed in the prison car park last Thursday.

Last Thursday's version wore an elaborate hairdo and was well made-up, but looked natural. The other interesting thing that came to mind about her on that day was her outfit. Her business suit was fitted – very well fitted – and its skirt ended well above the knee. In another situation, her killer-heeled stilettos would add to her overall well-dressed appearance, but something kept telling me they were inappropriate for this situation. I put the CCTV image aside and rifled through the file for a document I remembered reading early in this investigation.

"Yes!" I yelped aloud. The document set out the requirements for anyone visiting inmates of Tulloch Correctional Centre. Comprehensive and to the point, it covered such issues as dress standards, shoe heel heights for women, and even such personal matters as deodorant, perfume and jewellery use. It contained the warning that any visitor found to be non-compliant would be barred from entering the Centre.

The CCTV image of Gloria Purtell on that first visit showed a woman brazenly in contravention of those requirements. In spite of this, she was allowed in. I cast my mind back to the Gloria Purtell in the prison car park last week. Her outfit, and definitely the shoes, came nowhere near complying with requirements. I wasn't sure about the make-up and the hairdo, but I suspected enough products were involved in both of those to render them in contravention of the standards required. Why was she allowed to enter when other women wearing deodorant could be turned away?

Ben's car pulled up in the driveway. I had left the pasta sauce simmering unattended for about half an hour. It shouldn't have suffered any damage yet, but I rushed to check on it.

After breathing a sigh of relief, I busied myself finishing off dinner. Ben, showered and changed, looked tired. He sat on a stool at the breakfast bar. We both sipped glasses of chilled white wine while I fussed with dinner.

In the few minutes it took to finish preparing dinner and setting the table, he seemed to relax. That's encouraging. It might make him more amenable to sharing information with me. The pasta was good. Conversation was light and covered wide ranging topics. We took coffee out onto the deck and let the intense blackness of night cocoon us from the real world. The moon had grown bigger but, still a long way from full, its gentle light was unobtrusive.

I tried manoeuvring the conversation around to today's events. "How did the rest of your day pan out, and how is your new office?" I encountered some initial resistance.

"The new office is fine. It's bigger and brighter than the old one, but who cares? I don't spend much time there anyway. There wasn't much of the day left by the time I got back there, which was a good thing. It didn't allow much time for anything else to crop up today."

Persistence is the best approach, I decided. "Yeah, I didn't spend any time in my office after you left, although I did bring a file home to think about overnight. I'm beginning to wonder if I've developed paranoia. I'm seeing connections everywhere, connections between cases that are in no way related and where those connections fall outside the scope of my briefs. But, those suspicions have haunted me for days. Likewise, something keeps suggesting that derelict building is involved in it all."

"I don't see how it could be. I know that truck that you've been following was there on one occasion, but that could have been for a legitimate reason. The truck belongs to a registered carrier firm. It could be seen anywhere in town carrying on its legitimate business."

"What legitimate business would have it call at a derelict building in a slum area and which soon after is the scene of a shootout with police, and where a body – a badly decomposed body – is found in an abandoned freezer?"

"You have a point. Oh, and while I think of it, the lab says the body is definitely male. It has been in the freezer for seven to ten days, and they believe it is a foreign national."

"I don't suppose the bloke just happened to fall in by accident and the lid just happened to close on him."

"No. Evidence shows he was beyond knowing or caring about the freezer when he went into it. The bullet hole in the back of the skull is a giveaway."

"Execution style...?" Ben nodded in reply. I continued with what was nothing more than my version of thinking aloud – accompanied by the hope that Ben might join in. "Why has that building become such a notorious landmark in Millhaven? What happened there over the last few days is unknown in this town. We have crime, but not this kind of criminal activity. There has to be a new 'game' in town that's at the root of it all. What that 'game' is and its scope are critical to understanding what's happening. Millhaven hasn't had the calibre of criminals responsible for this before. If my assumption is right, the catalyst has to come from outside, from out of town."

"The way your brain works fascinates me. It's no surprise you do so well as an investigator. You are right. Those involved in the shootout were not locals. We haven't been able to interview the two wounded members yet."

"I accept everything you've said tonight, but I still feel there are connections and, if I'm right, those connections extend to your case too. Argh, I wish I could sort it out and move on. The whole thing is getting in the way of other things I should be doing."

"You're convinced there is relevance to the Police's investigation...?"

"As convinced as I am about any of it. But, yes, I think there is a connection between your investigation and two of my cases."

"Two of your cases...? Maybe we should spend some time going over those cases tonight. You weren't planning on an early night, were you?"

Not bloody likely if he is going to show some interest in my cases at last, I thought. I assured him I wasn't looking for an early night and I agreed we needed to investigate possible intersections between our investigations. We dropped our coffee mugs in the kitchen on our way to my office. I spent the trek from the deck trying to work out how to approach this 'show and tell' session. It was more difficult than I imagined, but I had a plan by the time we were settled in my office.

I retrieved the Fielding file from my bag and took it to my desk. Ben was going through my Inneston case file. "Is this one of the cases you think is connected to other happenings?" He spoke slowly and thoughtfully, putting all my senses on high alert.

"Yes. The brief was limited to investigating whether Geoff Inneston had another woman in his life. That was confirmed by the end of last week. But, factors that emerged in the course of the investigation raise a whole lot of other questions. Those questions might not be of interest to my client, Sandra Inneston, but I think their answers might point to illegal activities." I looked up at him as I finished speaking. He was hooked.

Now perched on the front of his chair, he studied the Inneston file. Then the question and answer session began. I outlined all I had discovered, including everything I knew about Gloria Purtell. When I finished that, I showed him the Tulloch Correctional Centre's 'Advice to Visitors' document. After he read it, I asked the question that has bothered me. "How does someone who doesn't comply with the required standards get to visit an inmate on a regular basis?"

"Perhaps she does meet the requirements." I shot him an 'aw-come-on type' look which he ignored.

"No she doesn't. For a start, there is a two centimetre heel height limit for women. Then there is the no deodorant, no perfume or anything else that might confuse the sniffer dogs or the body scan gadget. Most visitors find the actual entrance process quite degrading. They feel they are being treated as being as guilty as the person they have come to visit... or so I have been told. I can't see Ms Purtell accepting that treatment every month when other mere mortals find it degrading."

"I see your point, but what 'illegal activities' do you think she – or they – might be involved with?"

"I don't know, but my gut suggests that somehow they are maintaining the drug trafficking activities that landed Inneston in gaol I don't know how that could happen. However, Purtell's job does require travel over much of the state. It would provide the opportunity for distribution."

"You have no evidence of that. And all the visitors' cars in the Correctional Centre's carpark are scanned for any trace of drugs. If your assumptions were correct, her car should send the sniffer dogs wild. Did it?"

"Uhmm… n-o-o… but that's because they didn't go all over her car like they did the rest of the vehicles, including mine. They didn't go near it. Is it possible she isn't subjected to the same screening process inside the Centre as everyone else?" I don't need more questions, but this one had started the synapses firing. I feel I am tantalisingly close to seeing the whole picture. Just the last bit is missing.

We sat in silence considering the Inneston case for a couple of minutes. Ben ended the silence. "Okay, let's leave that for now. You said you thought two of your cases were connected to my investigation. What's the other one?"

"It's my Fielding case. Again, the case was to investigate whether a husband was being unfaithful. I still don't have evidence he is, but it looks like there is a fair chance that's what is happening. The husband, Terry Fielding, seems to be spending most of his time at that house we took a moonlight hike to look at the other night."

"I know why we were interested in that house, but – refresh my memory – what is the connection to your Fielding case?" I spent some minutes explaining my interest in Blondie's place, that truck, and their connection with Terry Fielding. "You don't think you might be reading too much into this? It might be that Mr Fielding is playing away from home, and might even have thoughts of making it a permanent arrangement."

"No, I don't think it's that simple because, as I have been trying to draw to your attention, my client, Terry Fielding's wife, disappeared under suspicious circumstances soon after she hired me to look into her husband's late night work schedule."

"Disappeared…? Exactly what do you mean by 'disappeared'?"

What's so hard to understand about 'disappeared' I wondered, but I smiled and set about describing the condition of the Fieldings' unit and how Trish's beloved dog, Goldie, was found abandoned.

We discussed scenarios that might explain what happened. None of them convinced me. At the point when we ran out of ideas, I remembered the packet of documents found buried at the bottom of the kitchen bin. "Why are we wasting time on guessing games?" Ben demanded. "Trot this stuff out and let's have a look at it."

"…Can't; it's in my safe in town. And, before you ask, I can't tell you what it contains, because I haven't had a chance to look at it yet. …And no, I am not going to go and open my safe at this hour of the night."

"What time will you be at your office in the morning?" This question I didn't mind. I had finally managed to generate some interest in my missing client.

After arranging to meet at my office early tomorrow morning, Ben went home and I wasted no time in taking myself off to bed. It felt like the first time forever I had been in bed by eleven o'clock.

Chapter 21

As I unlocked my office door this morning, Ben arrived. Neither of us was inclined to waste time on niceties. I went straight to the safe and retrieved the packet of documents discovered at the bottom of Trish Fielding's kitchen bin. While I wanted Ben to look at the documents and for us to discuss them, I felt a bit put out that I couldn't go through them alone first. I had arrived at my office about half an hour before the agreed time to peruse the documents before sharing them with Ben. However, whatever his motivation, Ben decided to arrive early.

I spread everything out in rows across the desk. One row contained the few handwritten documents, while the other row contained all of the typed material. "Was this the order they were in when you found them?" Ben asked.

"No, I don't know what order they were in. When they fell out of the plastic envelope, all order was lost. I suppose the first thing we need to do is work out what goes with which."

Ben agreed and we set about scanning the contents of each document and trying to locate something that it matched up with. This was no easy task but, after about half an hour, we had it all arranged in what we thought was its original order. Then came the interesting part of the exercise: reading every word on every document and trying to make sense of it all. Silence reigned as we selected a bundle of paper, read it, swapped it, and moved on to the next bundle.

It was slow going. Although I scribbled notes as I read through documents, I knew I wasn't absorbing everything I read. Like everything else in life, there came an end to it all. At almost the same time, we both laid down the last bundle we read, and exchanged stunned looks. "Coffee...?" I suggested. "This seems like a good time to take a break before we try to make sense of what we read." Ben nodded his agreement and I took myself off to the kitchen to make coffee.

We didn't talk about or look at the documents until we finished our coffee. We drank in silence, each one alone with their thoughts on what Trish thought to leave behind. But a mug of coffee doesn't last forever and, when they were empty, we shoved the mugs aside and returned to the issues contained in the documents spread out on the desk between us. Ben waved his hand over the documents and said, "If this stuff proves to be true, it's a time bomb waiting to go off. I don't think there can be any doubt Trish knew too much about what was going on around her. It's probably what contributed to her mysterious disappearance."

The possibility hadn't escaped me, but a different question nagged me. Why had Trish Fielding hired me to investigate her husband's strange behaviour when she had all this? Why approach me under the guise of concern about an unfaithful husband when it seems clear she knew he was involved in something much worse? Ben brought me back to earth with a thump. "I need to take these with me. Forensics will need to check them out and we'll need to work on what's contained in the documents."

"O-o-h, no you don't... not until I've copied them. She was my client and these documents probably have some relevance to my case. I'd go so far as to say she probably left them in the hope that I would find them. Sure, you can take them with you – just as soon as I finished copying them." In a couple of sweeping moves I gathered them all up and moved to my photocopier. It took a while to copy them all, as just removing all the staples from those clipped together bundles took time. We set up a production line: Ben removed staples, I photocopied and then gave them back to Ben to restaple.

With the copying finished, Ben was on his way to his own office. I took the photocopies and spread them out on my desk. Lunchtime came and went while I was still poring over the documents and scribbling notes. As I put the last of them aside, my phone rang. Emily was down in the street and asked if she could come up. "Only if you bring me something to eat... I haven't had lunch yet and I'm starving."

I put the coffee machine on to make a fresh brew while I waited. She arrived ten minutes later with wonderful chicken and salad rolls from the deli two doors down. It seems she hadn't had lunch either, so we devoted our full attention to eating before anything else.

Then, armed with a fresh coffee each, we got down to the business of discussing Trish's documents.

While Emily scanned them, I read through my notes and made a start on typing them up. Just before three o'clock, Emily checked her watch and jumped up in alarm. "I have a dentist's appointment in about five minutes from now. Will it be all right for me to come back here when that's finished?"

"Perhaps not; I have to go out and might not be back for a while. Let's try to get together tomorrow. I'll give you a call either tonight or in the morning to arrange something." Now, why did I say I would do that? I didn't have anything I needed to talk to Emily about. If truth be told, it's because I feel guilty about not having treated her well over the last few days. God, I have so much squaring off to do, it could take a lifetime to fix things.

There wasn't anywhere I needed to go, but I was developing an urge to go for a drive, a drive to a certain derelict building in a slum area of town. It took a few minutes after Emily left for the urge to get me out of my office and into my car. I didn't have a plan. I just knew I needed to go back to that building. I entered the street at the boat ramp, drove straight to the building and around to the back.

The forensic crew or whoever was there last installed new crime scene tape across the rear doorway. It hadn't been disturbed in any way and I was loath to interfere with it. So, I ducked under the tape and slid in around the back door which stood slightly ajar. After only a few seconds inside the building, I had only made it as far as that back room doorway when a sobering realisation hit me.

Whoever was responsible for installing the new tape would not have left the back door ajar. They would have made sure it was closed as part of the process of securing the crime scene. A vision of that big SUV leaving the building the other night flashed through my mind. Not everyone associated with this building had been rounded up or neutralised in some way.

I raced to the door, slipped around it and bounded across the backyard to my car, unlocking it as I went. I dived into my car and sped out from behind the building and down the street away from it. My hasty departure took me down the road some way before my nerves settled down, and I realised I was near that overgrown park with the rusty children's playground equipment. I used the parkland to turn around and paused, as you do, before entering back onto the street to make sure I wasn't going to run over anything.

As I looked along the street towards the derelict building, a large black SUV came into the street from the boat ramp end. I grabbed my phone and hit speed dial. Ben answered on the first ring. "A big black SUV has just driven around to the rear of the derelict building. I…" Ben ended the call before I could say any more. I had intended to tell him that I just happened to be in the area and noticed the vehicle, but I didn't get a chance. He had saved me from the little white lie I was about to deliver.

While I made the call, I watched the vehicle drive up to the building and, without any hesitation, drive around the back. It was only a minute or so after I spoke to Ben that a patrol car, without lights or siren, drove in and parked across the end of the derelict building's driveway. A few seconds later, two unmarked vehicles arrived and parked one at either end of the patrol car. I decided to idle quietly along the street to my favourite patch of bougainvillea.

My parking place provided a ringside seat for everything unfolding at the derelict building. As I made myself comfortable, I sensed movement. I swung my head around to face it at the same time as I reached for the ignition. The skinny-arsed drunk I had encountered in this area previously staggered through the long grass of the park towards me. I hit the button and heard the reassuring clunks as all doors locked. He seemed to cover the ground with surprising speed and reached my car within moments.

He didn't waste time trying all the doors, but made his way around the rear of the car to come up beside my window. At least I didn't have to smell him this time. The window was closed and was staying that way. "I'se knew ya would come back ta me. You'se jusht can't resist me, can ya? Open ya door an lemme in."

I should have shot him the first time. He's just going to make a bloody nuisance of himself. "Go away," I bellowed at him through the glass. At the same time, in my wing mirror, I caught sight of a car coming up behind me. "Go away. I didn't come here for you."

"Why'd ya come then, Shweetie?" He had to put a hand on the side of the car to support himself as he asked the question. Talk about swaying in the breeze... he was barely able to remain upright.

"I'm meeting my boyfriend, so go away." As he made his way around to my window earlier, I had dragged my bag over and placed it on my lap. Now, I thrust my hand into the bag and closed it around my Glock.

"Boyfriend... here...? Why ya meeting him here? Not much of a good time in this prickly place. Come with me, I'll show you a good time." Definitely should have shot him.

"He's married. We can't be seen together." Ben pulled up a short distance behind me.

"Boyfriend ... heh, heh ...married ... heh, heh ...Oh shit... copper!" Skinny Arse suddenly morphed into Usain Bolt and streaked off across the road to disappear between two houses.

Ben tapped on my window and I lowered it. "You seem to have terrified your drunken Casanova. Did you show him your Glock again?"

"No, and it was you who terrified him, not me. He recognised you the moment you stepped out of your car. And, although he does a great imitation, he wasn't drunk. He was stone cold sober when he realised who you were."

"Interesting; I wonder ..."

"Look there he is. He's just come out from behind that house over there, and he's in a hurry to go somewhere." On the other side of the street, the would-be drunk emerged from behind one of the houses he disappeared behind, picked his way through the junk cluttering the space to the next house and disappeared behind it.

A big, fit bloke, Ben surprised me with his speed as he thundered off at an angle across the road. As he took off, he mentioned something about a cockatoo. Why would he be interested in a bird at a time like this? I checked the sky and the surrounding trees, but I couldn't see a cockatoo anywhere. It will have to be a question for later. I did notice another patrol car arrive while I was otherwise distracted. It was parked across the street, effectively blocking all traffic coming in from the boat ramp end.

The next time I saw Skinny Arse, he was cuffed and being

prodded in the back by Ben as he was marched towards the patrol car blocking the street. My would-be lover screamed and shouted, and hurled abuse in all directions until he was unceremoniously bundled into the back of the patrol car. Then Ben and a uniformed officer went around to the rear of the vehicle. Ben removed a vest from the boot. As he began squeezing himself into it, I thought, good luck with getting one that fits. The uniformed officer offered Ben a rifle, but he refused it.

Ben wandered back to where the patrol car and the two unmarked vehicles blocked the building's driveway. He had almost reached the first of the unmarked vehicles when the sound of a vehicle shattered the prevailing silence. The Black SUV rounded the corner of the building at speed and stopped. It hesitated at the top of the driveway before the driver slammed it into reverse and sped towards the back fence as far as the rubbish allowed. All those out on the street took up defensive positions. The powerful V8 roared down the driveway at top speed.

I tensed, expecting it to barrel into the patrol car blocking the end of the driveway. At the last moment, the driver reefed the SUV to the right in an attempt to go around the front corner of the building. The gap between the building and the parked vehicles can't be wide enough for the SUV, I thought. It wasn't wide enough... well, not quite. A front corner of the SUV clipped the patrol car and bounced off it to continue at high speed between the front of the building and the rear unmarked vehicle. A barrage of shots happened when the SUV bounced off the patrol car. They seemed to have no effect. Then, the crack of a rifle rang out above the rest of the racket, and the SUV's windscreen crazed.

The driver rolled out of the vehicle unhurt and hit the ground running. Bent over and trying to use the unmarked as a shield, he ran towards the street. From out of nowhere, four burly officers fell on him. The struggle was brief and was over when the paddy wagon arrived. One almighty heave-ho by two officers sent the now cuffed driver sailing into the back of the paddy wagon and it drove off. The scene out front of the building was a bit like a jigsaw puzzle being pulled apart.

One by one, the vehicles departed. The patrol car with Skinny

Arse as a passenger was first to leave, followed in quick succession by one of the unmarked vehicles. Two plain clothes and one uniformed officer walked around to the back of the building, leaving one uniformed officer talking to Ben beside the damaged patrol car. A truck arrived, winched the damaged car on board and drove off with it. The officers returned from their inspection of the building or whatever they went to do. They all climbed into the remaining unmarked. I started my engine as they drove off, and slowly made my way to where Ben stood alone in front of the derelict building.

"...Like a lift back to your car?" He climbed in and we drove back to that patch of bougainvillea. I couldn't help myself. I wanted to know the details of what went down at the building. Although I had watched it from a distance, I wanted it explained. My question and answer session on the way back to Ben's car didn't produce much.

"Who was the bloke in that SUV?"

"Dunno."

"What was he doing at the house? Was it the same vehicle we saw the other night?"

"Dunno... probably... yeah, I think it might be." That's an improvement.

"What's the story with Skinny Arse? He wasn't involved was he?"

"Dunno yet. You were right, he wasn't drunk. The alcohol fumes came off his shirt which I think he must have soaked in rum."

"Why the sudden interest in birds at a time like this?"

"Eh...? What birds?"

"As you went dashing off after Skinny Arse, you said something about a cockatoo. I couldn't see one anywhere. What was that all about?"

When he finally stopped laughing, he explained... adopting a 'words of one syllable' approach. "Not a bird; your suitor was a cockatoo – a lookout – for those involved with the building. If there was trouble, his job was to warn those in the building. He was on his way to warn the SUV driver that a copper – me – was around. That's what all the shouting and swearing was about when I was trying to take him to the patrol car."

Do I feel stupid? Yeah, pretty much… and no doubt I will hear more about it at my expense later. And, the next time I saw him, Ben would remember to quiz me about how I came to be in the area to see the SUV. I was unlocking my office when my phone chirped: Ben.

"Are we on for dinner tonight? I'll pick something up and bring it round." It seemed it was too bad if I had planned to work tonight.

'Work', that seemed a foreign concept at the moment. The machine told me I had three messages waiting. They could wait until tomorrow. I wanted to go home. It was still early, so it gave me time to sit and think about a few things before Ben arrived. I picked up the Fielding case file, including Trish's documents, and added them to the Inneston one already in my bag. About ten minutes after I arrived at my office, I was heading home.

My early departure gave me about an hour and a half of solitude before Ben arrived. I spent the time poring over Trish Fielding's documents and my notes. A few ideas were baying to be let out, but they were vague. Perhaps another long session discussing the Fieldings with Ben would help. I hoped so as I wanted to put the whole business to bed and move on with other things… like the Inneston case for instance.

Dinner turned out to be boxed roast dinners with all the trimmings Ben bought from a new place that opened up this week. With no preparation to do and not wanting to let them go cold, we sat down to eat as soon as he arrived. Tonight was different from the outset. Tonight, Ben wanted to talk work and led in with some generalities over dinner. By the time we had cleaned our plates, we were down to the serious stuff. We shoved our dinner things to one end of the table, and remained sitting where we had eaten.

It goes without saying that my first questions were about today's operation at the derelict house. Feedback was a bit disappointing. Skinny Arse opted not to co-operate, and his identity remained a mystery. The identity of the SUV driver had been established but little else about him was known, including his possible connection to the mob involved in the earlier raid on that building. I turned my questions to the two men wounded in that earlier raid and who remained under guard in hospital. The Police hoped to interview them tomorrow. So far, my questioning had returned zilch in terms of new information.

Then it was Ben's turn to ask questions, and he started with the big one: why was I in the neighbourhood when the SUV arrived at the derelict building? I thought about giving him a story about wanting to get a look at the neighbourhood in daylight but weakened at the last moment and came clean. "I thought I'd like another look at the building."

"You went inside our crime scene?"

"Hell no; I wouldn't do that. When we couldn't find the source of that noise inside the building, I wanted to see if I could hear it outside somewhere. Perhaps it wasn't coming from inside the building at all. Maybe something harmless outside caused it." One little white lie is allowed isn't it, especially if it avoids a tongue lashing.

"I would recommend you don't go there again… and definitely not on your own. Were you armed when you went there today?"

"The question is irrelevant, Ben. I wasn't at the building when the SUV arrived. I was driving along the street." Ben let the topic drop, although I doubt he bought my story.

Without any prompting, Ben moved on to a new topic and provided me with the evening's first piece of interesting information. "We checked out your truck with the high canopy on the back. It is registered to a legitimate carrying business. When we dug a bit deeper, we found the bloke who drives it is the bloke who owns the truck and the business." That wasn't useful. The next bit was.

Ben consulted his pocket notebook before continuing. "The driver/owner's name is Vincenzo Fanucci. The woman who owns the house with the shed – and whom you have taken to calling Blondie – is Lorenza Passmore. She is Fanucci's sister. Passmore is her married name. Mr Passmore seems to have disappeared some time ago, but she kept his name."

"Those are not local names. I wonder how long they have been in Millhaven."

"We're working on that. What we know so far is that Vincenzo, both on his own and with his brother-in-law Passmore, has a long history of being involved in shady operations in the past. Both did time in Victoria a few years ago, along with a few of their associates.

There was some sort of bust up between the two men after their release. After that, Passmore dropped off the radar. Fanucci was hauled in a couple of times for questioning but not arrested."

"That doesn't mean he went straight. He just got smarter. Is the criminal record stuff all from Victoria, or did one or both continue their wicked ways in Queensland?"

"…Nothing on record for either in Queensland or any other states, nothing we've found yet anyway."

"That's interesting, as is Mr Passmore's disappearance. I would like to know more about that. It could be v-e-r-y interesting." Ben shot me a look and shook his head.

"Whatever happened to Passmore has nothing to do with your case."

"You don't know that. What's Lorenza's marital status now? Is she married, divorced, widowed…? In the report I give my client, she will expect to find such information." I doubted that was true but it was worth thinking about. "Huh… you may treat that comment as hypothetical. At the moment, I am not sure I have a client any longer, or that she is still alive."

"You seem hell-bent on convincing yourself she has met with foul play. So far, you haven't given me any solid reason to think that might be the case."

"…Want to come and have a look at the Fieldings' unit? It might change your mind about the fate of my client. We don't have to break in, I have a key." That's not strictly accurate, but Ben doesn't need to know that… anyway, being able to access a key means much the same thing.

A moment of indecision; Ben went to say something but changed his mind and studied the tabletop for a couple of seconds. I'm patient. I let him work it out without interrupting the processes.

There it was: the look of satisfaction at having reached a decision. "I am not going to ask how you came by a key, but I suppose it might be worthwhile having a look at the unit. It might help me convince you nothing untoward happened there and that your client probably just changed her mind about having her husband investigated… and didn't want to pay for work you might have already undertaken."

I didn't argue. I knew better. I had been in that unit. And there was the abandoned dog, Goldie, which I hadn't mentioned to Ben and probably wouldn't yet. "If you do want to have a look inside, we need to make sure Terry is at work. The likelihood of him coming to the unit while we were there is slim, but I would rather avoid it if possible." Ben said he would think about it and that brought the topic to an end. I wanted to return to the topic of another visit to that derelict building.

Something still bothered me about that sound we heard while we were in the building. I felt that sound was critical, and that sourcing it required some urgency. I refrained from sharing those thoughts with Ben as I knew he would dismiss them as fanciful. After my near miss encounter with that black SUV today, I agreed with Ben's edict that I should not go there alone. Who knows how many other people who are still at large might be involved and have occasion to visit the building. That thought brought another question to mind.

"Ben, given that your raid dealt with the mob from the derelict building, and that we know there is nothing of any interest left in the place, why would the SUV go there? What could he have been looking for, or what was he hoping to do?"

"They are good questions, and ones we can't answer yet. We could speculate that he might have gone to see what was still there, or to retrieve anything that might be incriminating. That seems unlikely though, and I don't think either of us believes that was the case. So, if we eliminate those possibilities, what else is there? A thought just occurred to me. What if the driver was scavenging? Perhaps his first visit was to check out what was left in the place, and today's visit was to collect whatever he thought was worth taking."

"…Like what? There's nothing there worth taking, except maybe that boardroom table. I quite like that and would be interested in it if it was being thrown out."

"And you would put it where?" He had a point, but I wasn't going to concede that fact, and there wasn't any chance I'd get the table and have to work out what to do with it.

"Before you go tonight, can we agree there are two things we need to do with some urgency? One is to visit the Fieldings' unit, and the other is a visit to that derelict building. Don't argue about the latter. If you don't come to the building with me, I will go alone.

I have to find out about that sound. I can't think of anywhere in the building that we haven't checked, but my gut is telling me we have missed something."

There wasn't any argument. Ben just threw his hands up in resignation and agreed to another visit. The intention was to visit both places tomorrow if possible, but Ben needed to check things out at the precinct before setting times for the visits. It was more than I dared hope for. By the end of the evening, I was more than pleased with what I'd achieved. The other pleasing thing about the evening was that Ben didn't stay late.

It was my intention to make the most of the opportunity for an early night, but it didn't work out that way. After I went to bed, my mind wouldn't stop, and worked its way into top gear instead. Within a few minutes, I was out of bed again and sitting in my office with my computer booting up.

Ben hadn't given me much new information this evening but what he did share took on mammoth significance. What he gave me was about connections. Connections between Blondie – oops, I mean Lorenza – and the truck driver, and between her husband and her brother. Without know why it was important, I knew I needed to know more about the Fanucci offspring. I searched the web. My first couple of attempts brought up nothing. Then I managed to find the right way to ask Google my question. It brought up pages of articles.

Regardless of what I found, Lorenza would remain Blondie to me. I found newspaper reports of the truck driver's involvement in a couple of petty crimes. Newspapers had committed another few column inches to his being taken in for questioning about other crimes. Then I found what I was looking for... and there was heaps of it. The newspapers had a field day covering the crime that put the truck driver and his brother-in-law behind bars for a fair stretch. Almost every Victorian paper and a few interstate ones ran the story... most of them with the same content.

I was elated. The search was worthwhile. Connections became clearer and took on substance. It appears the pair ended up behind bars together on more than one occasion. The first occasion was for a petty crime that brought a three-month sentence. The papers thought the men's individual past records influenced the magistrate in handing down the maximum sentence. The second occasion was for something more significant and, in accordance with the crime, resulted in more significant sentences. This bit of the pair's criminal history had me intrigued. But a little voice in my head kept urging me to find out when the Passmores were married before I did anything else.

Although it wasn't easy, I heeded that voice and spent the next few minutes searching for a marriage record for the Passmores. My jaw dropped. There it was: Lorenza Fanucci marrying Gary Passmore in a small agricultural town in Victoria. "They were married when?" I yelped and reached for the printout I made of details of that major crime involving the two men.

The Passmores were married for only two weeks when Gary Passmore went to prison for two years. However, of more interest was the fact that Vincenzo Fanucci was sentenced to five years. I went back to researching the crime that put the pair away. The sentences those involved received were interesting. A couple of others involved in the same crime received even longer sentences. Did Passmore only play a bit part in the crime? Why else would he receive such a light sentence compared to the others?

I could hear a little voice in my ear repeating over and over again, "Connections, connections; look at the connections." So, as I had learned to do long ago, I listened to that voice.

Chapter 22

What connections could I detect in my pile of printouts about Fanucci and Passmore crimes? It appears they were small part of a much bigger operation that resulted in multiple arrests across a number of states. The crime involved drugs and every aspect of that trade: growing, manufacturing, importing and distribution. It appeared the small Victorian group operating out of a base in a horticultural area played a major role.

I made a list of the names and sentences of those in the Victorian operation. Another connection leapt out at me. With the exception of Passmore and one other, all had foreign sounding names. Damn! What were the names of those involved in the shootout at the derelict building? Were they foreign too? And why didn't I press Ben for the name of that SUV driver? I'm either getting old or losing my touch, or both.

No point in beating myself up about it, I reached for my phone to call Ben. My phone showed midnight had slipped by a few minutes earlier. Not wise calling Ben at this hour. I'll suffer the frustration until I talk to him tomorrow.

Having hit a brick wall, my mind hurtled off elsewhere. When did Gary Passmore disappear… and how did he disappear? I realised it might be that the Passmores separated or divorced. Two years in gaol so soon after they married couldn't do the marriage much good. Did Lorenza know what her brother and others were up to, and accepted the situation? Maybe she even accepted her husband's involvement in it.

This new problem was about Gary Passmore's disappearance. If it was due to a marriage breakdown, there wouldn't be any record of it other than as a divorce record. Was I clutching at straws in the hope it was something more dramatic that would merit mention in a newspaper? I typed Passmore's name into Google. Bad move; apparently there were quite a few people by that name all over the place. I added 'disappearance' to the search parameters and waited.

It worked. The new search produced four entries. I didn't hold much hope any of them would be useful. All four articles appeared in regional Victorian newspapers over a one-week period. The gist of it was that the police were looking to interview Passmore as a suspect in a recent crime. The fact that he couldn't be found reinforced Police's belief he was guilty and had gone to ground to avoid arrest.

Dramatic, but I still didn't know when it happened. I checked the dates of the articles, and checked for correlation between that and other events involving this mob. This all occurred several years after he received that two year gaol sentence. I did some calculations and came up with an answer of five years and three months after he was sentenced. 'Five years' rang a bell. More flicking through my notes revealed that five years was the sentence Vincenzo Fanucci received at the same time as Gary Passmore received a two-year sentence.

Was there another connection here… a major connection in this case? Intuition told there was. But my eyes were becoming heavy, and I was aware my thought processes had become slower and muddled. Time to go to bed and, hopefully, to sleep through what remained of the night.

I soon drifted off to sleep, but it was a restless sleep. Morning found me feeling below par. I pushed myself through a sluggish start. Coffee brought some of me back to life and a second cup taken through to my office with me aided the process. My first decision for the day was whether to stay home and work in my office there, or to pack up everything and head to my office in town. Why have an office in the city heart and work from home? I collected all my paperwork and hit the road. It was early, traffic was light and I was in my office before the city heart came to life.

My next major decision: deal with my messages first, or resume my research from where I had left off last night. The messages could wait. Anyway, it was too early to be returning calls. After pushing everything to the edges of my desk, I spread out my research notes on the clear space I created. Although I now knew when the police were searching for Passmore, I still didn't know when he disappeared. He might have 'disappeared' from rural Victoria soon after his release from gaol, or at any time between then and when the police searched for him. Somehow, I think I would put my money on the latter situation.

There was no way of narrowing it down. His body hadn't turned up anywhere, and he didn't appear to have been involved in any further crimes. There was no report of his death. In fact, there was nothing to suggest he disappeared at all except that he was no longer around and the police hadn't been able to locate him back then. In spite of that, I believed there was some connection between his disappearance and his brother-in-law's release from gaol. I needed to know more about the trial that put them both away. A transcript of the trial might not answer my questions but it might eliminate a suspected connection.

The next half hour of searching the Internet didn't locate a transcript or even a detailed report on the trial's proceedings. Much of the proceedings were held in a closed court. That heightened my suspicion that something unusual happened during the trial. Well, if I couldn't find out what went on, I'd have to call a friend. I wondered what time Ben might call to arrange times to visit the Fieldings' unit and the derelict building.

By lunchtime, I cleared the messages, interviewed a new client and had a new case, but I hadn't had a call from Ben. I knew that was due to whatever was happening at the precinct keeping him occupied. And he wouldn't be available to take a call from me. At six o'clock, I put in a quick call to Emily to ask if she would like to meet up for dinner somewhere. She was cooking dinner for herself and thought she produced enough to feed the Chinese army, so I joined her for dinner at the Inneston residence.

It had all the makings of a very pleasant evening: Goldie bounced out to meet me, and we dined on excellent lasagne washed down with a decent wine. But then, dinner was over and we were mellowing out with coffee and a slice of cake she had bought in town. It was at that point that she threw restraint to the wind and began what developed into a long conversation about my current cases.

Although no formal arrangement to the contrary exists, Emily was offended I hadn't involved her more in my investigations over the last few days. I did feel guilty about it. There was plenty she could do to help out on lesser cases that I am neglecting. We agreed she would come into the office first thing the next morning to work out her schedule of work for the next few days. Goldie had settled in and appeared happy. Nevertheless, Emily was concerned about his future and, I suspect, also the fact that she was becoming quite attached to him. I had nothing new to offer on the whereabouts of his owner. Emily took the news well but it prompted speculative discussion about what happened to Trish Fielding.

Conversation moved on to Emily's mother, Sandra, and her return from the week-long craft show in Ralston. "She wasn't going to leave Ralston until next Monday. The craft show finishes Sunday lunchtime, but she and her friends were going to stay and come home the next day. She rang earlier today to say things had changed. She now will arrive home around lunchtime on Sunday."

I queried what prompted them to leave before the show finishes."

"It's not about the craft show. Only she and her mate, Grace, are leaving early. Grace's husband has to go the Brisbane on Monday for his work. He and Grace are driving down and will stay with their daughter while there. Grace suggested Mum might like to go with them to visit my sister who also lives in Brisbane. Mum thought it a good idea and is going with them. They leave around lunchtime on Monday, will spend the night in Ralston and head on to Brisbane on Tuesday. I think Mum is coming home to do some washing and repack her bag."

That gave me food for thought. I needed to talk with Sandra again about her case, but it didn't appear there would be opportunity during the short period she would be back in Millhaven. It wasn't a late night. I begged off early, citing the few hours' sleep last night as justification. When I was a couple of blocks away from the Inneston house, I pulled over and rang Sandra. She was out at dinner with a group and wandered outside to take the call. Although she wouldn't be home long before leaving for Brisbane, she suggested a meeting first thing Monday morning. That gave me a little time to work out what to say to her and make a start on a preliminary report.

A final check of my phone before I collapsed into bed showed I hadn't missed any calls. Ben's silence continued. While sometimes nice to have a whole day without contact, today I found it frustrating and intriguing. I spent the few minutes before I fell asleep pondering everything I said and did over the last couple of days to see if I could find anything that might have upset him and sever communications. Nothing came to mind. I fell asleep wondering.

The thoughts occupying my mind over breakfast on Friday morning concerned Ben and his lack of a call yesterday. While I accept he has an important job that keeps him busy, I couldn't help wondering why the silence. Another thought close to the front of my mind was that something big had broken in their investigation. If that were the case, what was it and was there a connection with my cases?

My mind was preoccupied all the way to work this morning. Things didn't improve much once I reached my office. In some kind of funk, I couldn't get started until my phone reinstated some sense of reality. "I'm just leaving home now, so I'll see you in about 20 minutes. Anything you want me to bring or do on my way in?" I had forgotten about Emily.

"If you wouldn't mind going via Sandlands to see if anyone is around, and then taking a drive past Thornton's to see if the red car is there."

Those two things gave me an hour to put together a schedule of work for her for today and tomorrow. With her mother home for part of Sunday and Monday, Emily needed to be at home and not running around for me. My mind snapped into gear. When Sandra went to Brisbane for an extended stay, would Emily return to her job at Moxton? Emily's reason for being in Millhaven is to watch over her mother and help Sandra with whatever is bothering her. That's something else to add to the list of things to discuss when she arrives.

Emily arrived a few minutes before nine o'clock and went straight to the kitchenette to make coffee. Our meeting didn't last long. She would do some research in the newspaper's archives this morning before spending the afternoon on a surveillance job. Tomorrow would see her on surveillance for a different case. That could take up most of the day. She looked through details of the work I gave her, shoved it all in her bag and left to start work. I need to devote some time to working out her contribution to my cases so I could pay her. She doesn't expect payment, but it's only fair that she is paid for helping out. I started making a few notes about it. A phone call halted everything.

"How are you fixed for a visit to the Fieldings' unit in about half an hour's time?"

"Okay, that suits me." No mention of the fact he didn't call me yesterday I notice.

"Good, I'll come by to pick you up." Almost 30 minutes later, Ben called me from the tenants' carpark behind my building. He followed my directions to the Fieldings' unit and parked out of sight behind it. I let him into the unit with the key retrieved from its hiding place in Peggy's carport.

"Should we have checked first that Mr Fielding wasn't likely to drop in on us?" Ben asked as he followed me in through the unit's back door.

"Not necessary; as of an hour ago, he was at work."

Ben's inspection lasted over an hour. He checked every drawer, cupboard and shelf, and even checked in all the canisters and containers in the kitchen. It was during this last stage of his inspection that the only interesting thing happened. The last kitchen cupboard Ben opened contained a flock of brightly coloured plastic containers with snap-on lids. Some sported labels scrawled in permanent marker on the outside. Over Ben's shoulder, I could see ones marked salt, sugar, tea and rice.

Each container came in for thorough inspection as he worked his way up to the top shelf which held only two large opaque red plastic containers. All the other containers were of a translucent plastic. Ben's approach was to lift the lid, shake the contents around a bit, replace the lid, and then shake and roll the contents around while watching them through the plastic of the container.

Then, there were only the two large ones on the top shelf left to check. I struggled to reach these but Trish, who was taller than I, might reach them. Why would you put them up there? There was plenty of room on lower shelves. As they were opaque, I though Ben would take a quick peek in each one and maybe give it a bit of a shake before replacing it on the shelf.

The first of those containers held flour and was less than half full. I was surprised when Ben used a large spoon to stir the contents of the container, lifting and turning the flour over on itself. His excavations having produced nothing, he returned the flour container to the shelf and took down the other one from the top shelf.

This one contained breakfast cereal. It was mostly cornflakes but it looked as though the dregs of a different packet of cereal were mixed in with it. I expected to see the spoon pressed into service again to rifle through the contents. I picked up the spoon and held it towards Ben. He shook his head and plunged his gloved hand into the container. After a few moments of stirring, he stopped. His hand remained buried in the cornflakes, but a smug look spread across his face. Ever so slowly, he withdrew his hand. I leaned forward to watch it exit the cornflakes. I gasped. His hand held something sealed in a small zip-lock plastic packet.

"What's that... what have you found?"

"Take my phone out of my top pocket and takes some photos, please." I retrieved the phone and turned on the camera app. "Now, see if you can get a good shot of my hand emerging from the cornflakes."

He thrust his hand back into the cereal and slowly withdrew it until it remained partially covered with cornflakes but with the package it held clearly visible. I snapped off a couple of shots, then a couple more of his hand fully withdrawn with the package in it but now minus the cornflakes. Then there were a few close-up shots of the package as Ben held it up by a top corner and turned it through every angle. The package went into his pocket and the container returned to the top shelf. I tore off a length of paper towel, wiped the flour off the bench top, and off the spoon and put it back in the drawer.

"Right, I think that takes care of everything here. Let's go. I want a look at what was in that container." I still hadn't managed a good look at what was in the packet, but it looked like a memory stick of some sort. It occurred to me as I returned the key to its hiding place that Ben probably intended dropping me at my office before haring off back to the precinct with his precious find, effectively preventing me from knowing anymore about it.

Back in his car, I addressed that issue. "When were you planning on letting me see what's on that thing?" I pointed to the pocket that held the packet.

"Why would you expect to see what's on it?"

Yep, I was right. "Let me remind you. For starters, I took you to that unit. I have been granted access to the place but, as a policeman, you were in there and removed something without a warrant. The Fieldings and their unit are relevant to me as an investigator and, whatever can be gleaned from that thing may well be relevant too... as well as being critical to knowing the fate of my client. Shall I go on?"

By the time I said my piece, I found myself sharing the vehicle with a none too happy Police Superintendent. Who cares, as long as I get to see what's on that stick. There was no response for a few seconds. Although he had started the car, we hadn't moved. "Of course, one solution would be for you to come up to my office with me when we leave here. We could look at it on my computer before you take it to the precinct and give it to your people."

His reply was a grunt – or a snarl, I'm not sure which – but I was relieved when he didn't just bundle me out of the car in my building's parking lot, but parked and got out of the car with me. We locked ourselves into my office, and Ben freed the memory stick from its packaging... more photos before anything else was allowed to happen. Then, while we waited for my computer to boot up, I suggested Ben make us a coffee. There was no argument and he retired to the kitchen.

While he fussed with the coffee machine and clattered mugs about, I quickly downloaded a copy of the stick and removed it from the machine again. I joined Ben in the kitchen as he was pouring the coffee. I took a bottle of water out of the fridge for each of us and we returned to my desk. The memory stick was lying on my desk exactly where it was when he went to make coffee. "Okay, now for the big moment; do you want to move around here beside me so you can see the screen?"

The big moment didn't disappoint either of us. There appeared to be only two documents on the stick. In the opening paragraph of the first one, Trish stated she believed her life was in danger and that she believed her husband was implicated in that threat. It wasn't exactly a 'last will and testament' type document, but it did suggest what to do in the event anything happened to her. I felt the hairs on the back of my neck stand up as I read through it. The final paragraph of that document just about did me in. I struggled with the lump in my throat as I read it, and then reread it.

Even Ben seemed a little unsettled by that final paragraph, squarely directed at me. It read, "Sonoma Whittington, I hope all I have heard about you is true and, should anything happen to me, you will not let it rest until those responsible are brought to account. My reason for employing you was not because I suspected my husband of cheating on me. He is, and I know it. He makes no effort to hide the fact. I have become a problem for him, not because of his extramarital activities, but for other more serious reasons which I believe also pose a major problem for others."

"Jesus... I wasn't expecting that," was all I could manage after reading that final paragraph. "Why didn't she tell me straight out what was going on? ...Why she believed her life was threatened?" I felt the tears welling up in my eyes. I grabbed my bottle of water and gulped down about half the contents. If Ben noticed, he was polite enough not to let on. While I tried getting myself under control again, he brought up the second and only other document on the stick. It was set out in tabular form and read like a running report.

This document contained names, dates, places and activities, all set out in a brief factual way that caught my attention, and immediately had me wondering about Trish Fielding's background. A few of the names mentioned we already knew. Vince (Vincenzo) Fanucci and his sister Lorena Passmore rated strong mention. Ben pointed out another name, he tried to convince me I knew from happenings over the last couple of days. I kept denying any knowledge of the name. "For Christ's sake, Sonny, think about the driver of the big black SUV we took in the other day. What was his name?"

...So he had intended to tell me. "I don't know. You never told me." I tried looking hurt, but I was wasting my talent.

"Of course you know... I didn't tell you? You sure I never mentioned Gino Pasquale to you?" Vigorous shaking of my head

231

convinced him of his oversight. "Huh, I was sure I told you his name. Anyway, that's him she mentions in this document."

We read through the second document again. I put my hand to my chin to check my mouth wasn't hanging open. "Do you think all this is kosher?" I was having trouble believing the activities documented here were happening in Millhaven or involved people associated with Millhaven.

"Yeah, unfortunately I do. It's a long story I'll tell you when this is over. Suffice to say at the moment, it fits with part of the reason for my return to Millhaven. For now, the most important thing is for me to get this back to the precinct for people to work on. I should go."

"We were going to visit that derelict building again. I'm more determined than ever to go back there now. Are you free any time this afternoon?"

"Yes, I think I have some time late in the afternoon. I'll give you a call about when I can get away."

Emily dropped into my office after finishing her research at the newspaper's archives and lunched with me. Once she was on her way to her surveillance job, I settled down to return calls. I hope Emily will stick around Millhaven for a while. I look like having a work overload for the next couple of weeks at least.

Ben's call came at three o'clock. He couldn't get away to go to the derelict building before about five o'clock. "I'll come by to pick you up a few minutes before five o'clock if that suits."

"N-o-o, don't bother picking me up. I'll meet you at the building at five o'clock." That suited him. Afterwards, I sat wondering why I suggested that arrangement. I wasn't doing anything this afternoon to prevent me going with Ben. But, at that moment, a little voice in my head suggested a better arrangement. Without understanding my motivation any better, I moved on to thinking about the visit to the derelict building.

A planned approach to what to do when we were at the building was essential. I suspect this will be the last chance I get to investigate the place. Ben was unlikely to come with me again, so it was critical that today's visit produced a definite outcome – whatever that might be. I doodled and scribbled random words on a jotter as I tried to cobble together a plan of action.

The last word I wrote stopped me in my tracks: Goldie. What possessed me to write the dog's name? Whatever triggered thought of the dog took my mind off in a new direction. A call from Emily interrupted the process. She was finished the surveillance and was heading home. "Could I call around to borrow Goldie for a while?"

"Goldie...? I suppose it will be okay if he doesn't get too upset by it. He seems to have settled in well and I would like things to stay that way."

"I won't do anything to upset him. I might have him for about half an hour, and then I'll bring him back." Emily was reluctant to relinquish her protection of Goldie for even such a short period of time. However, she agreed and I arranged to collect the dog at about 4.30p.m. That gave me about 45 minutes before arriving at the Inneston residence. I had no idea what I was going to do with the dog. Somehow, taking Goldie with me seemed like a good idea and, Goldie was happy to ride along with me.

As I expected to be battling the first of the heavy afternoon traffic on my way to the derelict building, I allowed plenty of time to be there to meet Ben at five o'clock. Things went better than expected and I drove up beside the derelict building ten minutes before the scheduled time. Ben, already parked behind the building, sat talking on his phone. I reverse parked beside him, snapped Goldie's leash onto his collar, and we jumped out of the car together.

"What's with the dog? I'm not sure a dog is allowed at a crime scene."

"It's part of a long story, and I think Goldie here might be part of today's story. Shall we go in?"

The building's back door was closed properly and remained festooned with police crime scene tape. Ben ducked under the tape and put a shoulder to the door which scraped open across the concrete floor creating what seemed like an inordinate amount of noise in an otherwise silent environment. Goldie was hesitant, but a gentle tug on the leash persuaded him to follow me. Once inside, I closed the door behind us and slipped the leash to allow Goldie to roam throughout the building. He didn't seem keen to go off on his own, staying close to Ben and I as we wandered around in the building.

Our first move was to check that nothing had changed since our last visit. No surprises were encountered. I led the way to that back room where the rusty freezer had been. Something about that room kept calling me back. I knew I was prepared to go in and sit on the floor for the rest of the afternoon if needs be until whatever was nagging me became clear. When Ben and I entered the room, Goldie wasn't with us. Something had caught his attention and he was busy snuffling around out in the corridor. While Ben and I stood scanning the room, I kept an ear open to make sure Goldie didn't wander off.

"Ben, at the risk of sounding silly, there is something about that piece of carpet on the floor at the other end of this room that isn't right. It hasn't been laid properly. It's more like a rug that's been thrown down." The carpet was filthy and torn, and the nearest edge was ragged and frayed. Its sides were neat and straight cut. The back edge, under the pile of rubbish against the back wall, wasn't visible.

"I'll grant you, it's a toxic looking piece of carpet, but squatters are as keen on creature comforts as the rest of us. Where the carpet came from is a mystery, but I can accept that the squatters might have thrown it down in a bid to make the place more hospitable, particularly in winter when even the timber floor would have been cold."

"Okay, but why put it on the floor up that end where all the rubbish and clutter is when this end of the room is empty and would have provided a nicer space?" I could see Ben wasn't interested in my fixation on the carpet, so I left him standing there and marched over to subject the offending piece of floor covering to closer scrutiny. It seemed important to check the back edge of the carpet. To achieve that meant moving some of the rubbish out of the way. I was standing in the middle of the room, so I simply marched forward and started throwing anything in front of me off to one side or the other.

While the rubbish on either side was densely packed, the stuff in front of me was more loosely piled up. Its arrangement looked a bit superficial, as though it had been placed there rather than simply thrown onto a heap. It didn't take long for me to clear a narrow path to the back wall. I went down on my haunches to take a closer look at the edge of the carpet which stopped about 100mm short of the wall. The edge of the carpet wasn't the only thing I found. The other thing was much more interesting.

I eased myself upright and was about to call Ben over to look at my discovery. A noise behind me caught my attention. Goldie decided to join us and was now prancing around Ben's feet as he scratched its ears and patted its back. "If you can tear yourself away from the dog for a moment, come and take a look at this."

Ben, with Goldie padding along behind him, started towards me. Goldie suddenly went mad. He scurried about giving funny little yips as he snuffled and scratched at the carpet. "What's got into him?" Ben asked. He looked concerned as he watched Goldie. "Perhaps he can smell what we found in that freezer. What do you think?"

"That's possible, but I think it is something else. My experience as a dog owner for a large part of my life is that, if he smelled that freezer's contents, he would back off, not react like that."

Chapter 23

We stood entranced by the dog's wild behaviour. Then that noise came again. Ben and I froze. Goldie became frantic, gave a strange little bark and renewed his efforts to claw a hole in the carpet. The noise came again, audible over all Goldie noise. I reefed the dog's leash out of my pocket and clipped it to his collar. He planted all four paws and refused to leave the room. I dragged him out squirming and bucking on the end of the leash and tied him up to the bannister of the staircase. With the dog out of the way, I raced back to the room and attacked the carpet.

"What the hell are you doing?" Ben demanded.

"I want to find out what's under this carpet and why it's here. Go over to that cleared area at the end wall. Have a look at what I found at the base of the wall. I wish I brought a mask with me." Without gloves, there is no way I would touch that carpet, but the prospect of what I might inhale in the process of rolling it up didn't thrill me either. The carpet was so thick with dirt, it was stiff and unco-operative. It took some effort to start rolling it up. Ben came back from inspecting my find and helped with the carpet. After a while of sweating and swearing, we had it rolled back as far as the rubbish. It didn't want to stay rolled. Ben piled a bit of rubbish on top to help anchor it.

"I might be wrong, but it looks like a section of this timber flooring lifts up. It looks like it's a hatch of some sort, but I can't see how you could get it open. It is so tightly fitted into the flooring." Ben, having finished subduing the roll of carpet, stood beside me looking down on the section of floor I was discussing.

"I think I saw something in amongst the rubbish that might do the trick." He came back brandishing a short-handled spade. "The blade of this should fit in the crack to help lever up that section of the floor."

I glanced at the spade... and then took a better look. "Look at the end of the blade. It's polished. There is no dirt or rust on the last three or four centimetres of the blade. It has been used recently, and used often by the look of it."

After giving the blade a brief inspection, Ben tried shoving it down the side of the section of floor we wanted to lift. The blade didn't go into the crack more than a couple of millimetres. "Come around to this end. The gap seems a bit wider here."

This time the blade went in without too much trouble almost to the depth of its polished area. Ben bore down on the handle and a whole section of flooring dislodged and rose up a few centimetres. Between the two of us, we managed to lever it up and moved it out of the way. With the section of flooring now leaning against the side wall, we move back to inspect what we had uncovered.

Below the timber flooring, a trapdoor was set into the original concrete floor. Of slightly small dimensions than the section of timber floor we removed, it looked heavy. Nestled in a circular recess close to the front end of the trapdoor was a sturdy steel ring. "Well, that looks like what you use to lift the thing, but I don't know what you do with this lump of concrete once you lift it," Ben observed.

"Perhaps that matching eyebolt that I found squarely set into the end wall has something to do with it. Once the trapdoor is lifted, a chain or something through its ring might anchor it back to that eyebolt in the wall."

"It would need to be a sturdy chain. You would not want this lump of concrete falling on you. If you are right, Sonny, the chain or whatever they used should be lying about amongst the rubbish just as the spade was."

I didn't need it spelled out for me. I was on my way to where the eyebolt was set in the wall. If they used a chain, it might be close to the eyebolt. It wasn't; at least, it wasn't obvious. "I might have thrown rubbish on top of it when I cleared a path through to the wall," I called over my shoulder to Ben as I started picking up the top bits of rubbish and hurling them out of the way. Ben came to join me and began likewise on the other side of the cleared area. A few moments later, I yelped, "Got it! At least, I think this might be what we are looking for."

A heavy duty rusty chain snaked out from under the rubbish. Ben stepped over and grabbed hold to help me with it. I didn't complain.

It was heavy but, with his help, it took no time to free the chain. We stretched it out to inspect it. A hook was welded to each end of the chain. Eyeball measuring suggested it might be long enough to connect the concrete trapdoor to the eyebolt in the wall once the trapdoor was fully raised.

"You are aware, I'm sure, that neither of us has any idea what we might find down there. I'm not sure we should try this without some form of backup present." Ben had a point. We didn't know what – if anything – might be down there, but I wasn't in a mood to hang about while he organised backup. I had a better and more urgent idea.

I race out to the staircase and untied Goldie's leash. The dog bolted for the backroom, towing me along behind him. He didn't stop, but rushed straight to the trapdoor and started pawing at it and barking excitedly. I looked up at Ben who stood hands on hips watching the performance. "You're right, Ben. We don't know what's down there, but I think Goldie does. I've a strong suspicion about what we might find, and I'm not sure whether it will be good or bad news."

With Goldie lashed to the bannister again, I returned to Ben and what I hoped would be the raising of the trapdoor. After what felt like an eternity of fussing around, Ben announced it was time to have a go at lifting 'that thing'. We attached one of the chain's hooks to the ring recessed in the trapdoor. Then everything came to a standstill. Ben stood there with the chain in his hands discussing how the next stage of lifting the thing should happen.

"Oh, for Christ's sake, Ben, let's get the thing up. We both know what we have to do and how to do it. There's nothing more to discuss. Let's just get on with it." I thought he was about to argue, but changed his mind.

Ben hauled on the chain. The trapdoor swung up. I race around to the other end of the chain. As soon as the trapdoor was high enough for the chain to reach the wall, I slammed the chain's hook through the eyebolt in the wall. The chain held the slab of concrete erect. We stood looking down on the rectangular black hole in the floor.

At last, inertia overcome, we moved over to inspect what we

uncovered. In the light from our torches, it was possible to make out a concrete staircase running down along the side wall of a cellar of some sort. From what little I could see, the underground room looked large… and dark. "No point standing around," Ben announced. "We're not going to learn anything more from up here. I'm going down. You are on guard."

"On guard for what…?"

"…Anything or anyone who appears without an invitation."

"Isn't it safer if you don't go down there alone? …What about if something happens to you?"

"I'll scream and you will take appropriate action to save me."

His levity was wasted on me, but he had started his descent into the underground chamber, so I took a deep breath and pretended I was brave and not terrified of what he might find down there. There was nothing but silence emanating from the cellar for at least five minutes. I couldn't even hear Ben moving about down there. A couple of times, I shone my torch down into the black abyss. That told me nothing.

Then, there was contact with Ben. "Sonny, can you hear me okay?" I yelled back that I could hear him loud and clear. The underground chamber seemed to amplifying his voice. "Okay, I'm going to give you a phone number and a code. It's important you get both of them right." I keyed in the phone number as he called it to me and committed the code to memory. "Right, now I want you to call that number. You will need to give that code straight after you identify yourself. Then, tell them an urgent medical evacuation is required, and give them the address of this place. Tell them to send the crash rescue truck as well."

That all sounded simple enough, but I doubted it would be in reality. As soon as Ben finished giving me instructions, I pressed TALK on my phone and the number he gave began dialling. It was answered on the third ring. I followed Ben's instructions to the letter, but got the third degree about every fact I gave them. It didn't take long for my patience to run out. "Superintendent Ben Richards' instruction was that this required medical evacuation was urgent. Stop wasting time asking me useless questions. Get your arse into gear and make this evacuation happen."

The call ended abruptly. I found myself hoping my outburst hadn't blown the whole thing. I cast a cautious look at the black opening in the floor, half expecting to see an angry Ben emerging to deal with me. There was no Ben coming for me and nothing else happened for about five minutes. Then Ben called out again. "Did you make the call?"

"Yes, but they didn't seem in any particular hurry to deal with it."

"They will be. Just remember, if anyone not dressed in a teal paramedics uniform comes through that door, shoot them. Don't second guess yourself, just shoot. The way you shoot, there probably will be opportunity to ask questions later."

"I am a good shot. If I...," Geez, why am I wasting my breath, I asked myself and let the matter drop. It was about then I heard the sirens approaching. My phone chirped. A voice asked if I was Sonoma Whittington and whether I had just requested a medical evacuation. Once we confirmed the facts, I gave 'the voice' instructions on how to access the building, including asking them to park at the rear of the building and enter through the back door.

A couple of minutes later, I heard a vehicle pull up and, within seconds, two paramedics loaded with various bags of gear clattered in. I moved to the doorway and signalled to them. They wasted no time in descending into the blackness below the floor. Almost as soon as they disappeared from sight, another vehicle arrived. At about the same time, the female paramedic clambered out of the hole in the floor and dashed outside. Three uniformed men accompanied her on her return.

The three men from the crash truck carried large unwieldy looking pieces of equipment. The paramedic carried a lighting rig fitted with two large lights. I felt obliged to point out that the building was not connected to the power grid and there was no electricity supply to the cellar. The paramedic grinned and pointed to the large pack on her back. "Battery pack...," she informed me as she started down into the hole. It seemed only a few seconds before the cellar was ablaze with light. Whatever was happening down there was happening where I couldn't see it.

While the paramedics were busy below ground, the three men from the crash truck rigged up a hoist arrangement that spanned the opening to the cellar. They attached a basket-like long plastic cradle. Then the hoist lowered the cradle through the hole in the floor. Nothing much happened for a while until a shout from below had the hoist in action again.

With nerve-wracking slow speed, it winched the cradle up to the surface. The female paramedic rode up with her patient. The three men at the hoist swung the cradle across to one side to place it safely on the floor a short distance from the edge of the opening. Next to emerge from the cellar was the other paramedic. He joined his colleague in fussing over their patient. So far, I hadn't been able to see who came up in the cradle. As I was about to move around to get a better look, Ben's head appeared above floor level. He gave me a look that I was sure was intended to send me a message. I couldn't interpret it.

One paramedic disappeared outside. With surprising speed, the three men from the crash truck detached the cradle from the hoist's cables and disassembled the hoist. They began returning their equipment to their truck. Ben disappeared into the cellar again to retrieve the lighting rig set up earlier by the paramedics. This left only the female paramedic kneeling beside the cradle. I moved closer... and caught my breath.

Christ, it's Trish Fielding! Now almost unrecognisable, she was covered in grime. Her hair was matted and filthy and her clothes reflected so many days in an inhospitable environment. The most horrifying aspect of her appearance was that she had been knocked about. She was agitated and fought the straps holding her in the cradle. I turned on my heel and raced out of the room.

An excited Goldie straining against the leash tugged me back into the room. As I reached the doorway to the backroom, I called to the female paramedic. "Free her arms." The paramedic looked at me but made no move to do anything. I yelled, "Free her arms; free her arms now." Although my tone didn't allow her too much to wonder about, she showed a high degree of reluctance but complied.

With a restraining firm hand on the leash, I managed to slow Goldie's approach. He reached the side of the cradle and stuck his head over the edge at about the same time as Trish's arms were freed. The change in her was dramatic. The agitation vanished. With difficulty, Trish lifted her right arm to gently stroke Goldie's head. I knelt down beside Goldie at the cradle to speak to Trish. "Goldie is fine, Trish. You don't need to worry about him. He is being well looked after."

She gave me a weak half nod in response, then raised her arm slightly and extended it towards me. Her fingers waggled at me. I leaned forward and grasped it with both hands. After holding her hand for a few seconds, I gently patted it and spoke softly to her. "You're safe now. They will take good care of you and keep you safe."

Another half nod and she opened her eyes wider to give me a meaningful look. Then, through cracked, parched and blackened lips she croaked, "I... knew... you'd... come." The effort exhausted her. She closed her eyes and lay back in the cradle. I was pleased she wasn't looking. Her comment finished me. My eyes brimmed and tears escaped to roll down my cheeks.

Ben was off to one side speaking with the crash truck officers and the other paramedic who had returned with a gurney. Their conference over, Ben came to join us at the cradle. I quickly wiped my face on my sleeve. No point in having him see what he didn't need to see. Trish, sensing his presence, opened her eyes to look at him. Uncertainty clouded her face. I stepped in to reassure her. "You can trust this one. I do. He has saved my hide a few times. His name is Ben and he's a copper." She gave me a fleeting hint of a smile, closed her eyes and relaxed again.

Things happened in quick succession after that. The three men from the crash truck helped the paramedics load the cradle and its delicate contents onto the gurney before they climbed aboard their truck and left. Ben followed the gurney out to the ambulance to see it loaded on board the ambulance. I remained in the back room with Goldie who wasn't too happy to see his mistress disappearing again.

I waited until I heard the ambulance drive off before venturing to the backdoor to look for Ben. He was standing in the backyard with his phone to his ear. When he saw Goldie and me at the back door, he continued his phone conversation as he walked towards us. The three of us returned to the back room. Ben ended his call along the way. "Do we need to retrieve anything from the cellar," I asked in the hope I might get to look around down there.

"No, forensics will need to give it the once over."

"I'll tie Goldie up and then I'll give you a hand to lower that trapdoor."

"No, we'll leave that up for the others when they come. We're finished here but we'll hang around until the others arrive."

"Did Trish say anything when you found her?"

"I don't think she was in any condition to speak. When she saw me I think her initial reaction was fear."

The sound of vehicles arriving brought our conversation to an end. We went to meet to newcomers. Goldie and I stayed outside while Ben took his officers in to show them the back room. It wasn't long before he came out again. As we walked to our vehicles, I asked about Trish. "Which hospital will they take Trish to?" I didn't get an answer. I thought maybe he hadn't heard, so I asked the question again. There are a number of hospitals in the Millhaven area and I hoped to visit her as soon as she was allowed visitors.

"Oh, I don't know. They will have their instructions about that."

I know a fob-off when I hear one so, while I felt the red mist rising, I didn't pursue it to give him opportunity for more of the same. I loaded Goldie into my car, climbed in after him and drove off leaving Ben standing next to his vehicle. A short distance from the building, I pulled off to answer my phone.

"Where are you… is everything all right?" Emily demanded. Oh hell, I told her I was borrowing Goldie about half an hour and that was over two hours ago.

"All is well. I'm on my way to your place now to return Goldie and tell you about our afternoon out."

"Okay, see you soon… there are left-overs for dinner if you are interested."

That created a problem. I needed to spend some time with Emily explaining what had happened this afternoon and why I had Goldie for so long, but I was hoping Ben might want to come around for dinner. I did not want to miss an opportunity to quiz Ben about Trish's whereabouts, and what would happen next. But, in all honesty, I didn't expect to see Ben tonight. He would be involved in everything that followed Trish's rescue. I settled for left-overs with Emily and Goldie.

As we sipped a cold drink before dinner, Emily made a confession. "I forgot to mention something earlier. After you collected Goldie, I realised I needed milk and there were a few other groceries running low. I took a trip to the supermarket... and then I couldn't help myself. I took a drive past Thornton Transport. It was a few minutes past five o'clock, but five cars remained in the carpark, including the little red car. I wondered whether there might be something funny happening tonight."

"Excuse me. I need to make a call." I hit the speed dial key for Ben as I wandered out onto the Innestons' back deck. He took a while to answer and I was about to give up. "What's up? Is it urgent, I'm a bit busy at the moment?"

"Yes, I guessed you would be but I thought you might be interested in what's happening at Thornton's."

Of course he was interested. It didn't take me long to relay Emily's information. It proved to be a short call. There was nothing more for me to do apart from sharing left-overs with Emily. As I went back inside to join Emily, the aroma of our dinner reheating in the oven convinced me staying was the right decision. It wasn't a late night. We discussed the work she would do for me tomorrow, and I promised to keep her updated on Trish's situation. As she walked me to my car, she commented, "I hope Goldie is okay. He seems a bit quiet since you brought him back. The pair of you didn't do anything to overtire him, did you?"

I hadn't told her of Goldie's role in locating his mistress, so I couldn't explain that his mood tonight was a result of losing her again. In fact, I hadn't alluded to my involvement in Trish's rescue. I had told it as second-hand information I was passing on. I planned to be more expansive – more honest perhaps – when I knew a little more about Trish's condition and her incarceration in that derelict building.

Although I intended an early night, by the time I was ready for bed, I found I wasn't tired enough. I worked on a draft report for Sandra Inneston. That led me to a new line of thinking. Gloria Purtell's apparent condoned breach of visitors' requirements at the Correctional Centre and her obvious lack of scrutiny by the Centre's staff continued to intrigue me. After staring off into space while I pondered it for about half an hour, I found I kept coming back to one plausible explanation.

With the Inneston case file spread out on my desk and glass of red wine in hand, I began a careful scan of every document not generated by me. Anything that seemed relevant to my current thinking, I pulled out and set to one side. At the end of the exercise, I found that the only documents set aside were those from Sam Keller, and there weren't many of them. I pored over each one, and found my pulse quickening with each document. There it was. The missing factor – the connection – I had been looking for.

On every occasion of Purtell's visits to the Centre, the same staff member was on duty to scan and scrutinise intending visitors. Was there a connection between the staff member and Purtell? There had to be of some sort – possibly a significant connection – to explain her exceptional treatment. "Okay, so what's the connection... and is it to Purtell or Inneston?" I asked the empty room. Oh, that was a possibility I hadn't seen when I started down this line of thinking: that the connection might have been between Inneston and the staff member.

It was all very well to come up with these ideas, but proving them, or unravelling them, was the challenge. Why break with tradition? I embarked on my customary first line of enquiry and asked Google what it knew of that particular staff member. To my surprise, my enquiry found several hits. After more printing and a bit of scanning, I at least had the gist of why the Centre's staff member was worth considering and why.

The connection was uncovered, or so I thought, but my eyes were tired and my mind was fuzzy. I thought I'd solved the mystery. Relaxed about leaving things as they were until the morning when I was fresh, I found a deep and untroubled sleep within seconds of falling into bed.

Saturday morning got off to a late start as I slept way past my usual wake-up time. The night's sleep refreshed me and I was eager to return to my research. Coffee and toast accompanied me to my office and was dispatched as I read through the material I'd printed last night. It appears our corrections officer was a long-standing member of the public service who changed departments soon after the drug trafficking trial that put Inneston behind bars. Although his name was unfamiliar to me, he had worked for the same department as Inneston and I.

Towards the latter part of his time with that department, he spent quite a few years in some obscure position at the Department's head office. That probably explains why I'd never heard of him. Inneston, who spent a great deal of time at head office, had every opportunity to get to know the man. The third person I associated with this trio, Gloria Purtell, also was based at head office and possibly worked closely with this man on occasions. I already had evidence of what appeared to be an 'up close and personal' connection between Purtell and Inneston. The Centre's correctional officer was a common denominator that completed the connections in this triumvirate.

This otherwise obscure public servant only merited mention on Google because he featured in reports on the demise of that drug trafficking network. He was hauled in to 'help police with their enquiries' on a few occasions, and was questioned during some of the participants' trials, including Inneston's. It appears he maintained a position of 'I know nothing' throughout. At Inneston's trial, the man was questioned about his association with Inneston. He never denied knowing who Inneston was, but claimed he didn't know him beyond saying good morning in the corridor on occasions.

My gut was screaming at me. It believed what I suspected from early in this case. That Inneston's lucrative sideline enterprise was alive and well despite his incarceration. And it required all three of these players to maintain it. The theory was great, proving it was something else, and something beyond my resources.

Under other circumstances, I would call Ben to discuss it with him. Given the reception I received last evening when I called him, and the fact that I knew he had a bit happening at the moment, calling Ben was not an option. That meant my investigation was stalled again at least until the next time Ben called me. With Sandra Inneston coming to see me for an update on her case first thing Monday morning, it was frustrating not to be able to resolve the whole thing beforehand.

There was nothing for it but to divert my attention to domestic chores. I checked my pantry and fridge. Not much of anything in either of those. A trip to the supermarket seemed wise before starvation set in. I was tired of eating bought meals but that's how I survive when I'm busy. Not tonight, I told myself. Tonight we will have home cooking. 'We'…? I was kidding myself if I thought Ben would spend time with me this evening. I could repay Emily's hospitality by inviting her to dinner. Tonight was still hours away. Before then, I had to shop.

Prior to the supermarket, I stopped by my office in town. As I unlocked the door, I told myself I was there to check my messages and to start focusing on my other cases. There were no new messages but, during my absence, someone slid an envelope under my door. I stepped over it and donned a pair of gloves before picking it up. It was a thin envelope. No more than one page in it I guessed, or it wouldn't have slid under the door.

It lay in the centre of my desk while I decided whether it was safe to open it or not. There couldn't be anything too sinister in it. It wasn't thick enough. It is probably from a client who intended to put it in the letter slot I used to have near the door. It might even be a cheque… except I don't think I have any clients who pay by cheque who owe me money at the moment. Decision taken, I grabbed the letter opener and slit the envelope open. One sheet of paper fell out.

I opened the sheet of paper out and shoved it and the envelope in a plastic bag before bothering to read any of it. Once the bag was sealed, I checked the envelope. Nothing enlightening gained from that, only 'Sonoma Whittington' written across the front. I turned the bag over to read the note. It was handwritten and neat. A female's handwriting I guessed. Its message was intriguing and more than a little confusing. In a couple of brief paragraphs, it gave me the following advice:

Don't waste time on Terry Fielding's extramarital activities. His wife has always known what he was up to. Put your efforts into taking a REAL close look at Terry Fielding.

You might find Trish Fielding's background interesting.

There was no signature, no date and it was hand delivered. None of that would help in tracing its origins. But it brought to the fore a question I had been trying to ignore since my brief conversation with Trish yesterday. When she recognised me, she said, 'I knew you would come'. What did that mean? Why did she think I would help rescue her? I knew I wouldn't be able to talk to Trish for several days, so I tried not to tie myself in knots over her comment. However, this note opened that door. Whoever wrote it knew more of what was going on than I believed the case was all about at its outset.

My initial reaction was to call Ben. I resisted the temptation. The fact that I hadn't heard from him meant he was still busy with what went down yesterday and last night. I slipped the plastic bag with its intriguing contents into my bag and headed for the supermarket… there was no point in starving while the mysteries associated with the Fielding case increased. Well, that was what I told myself, but I had a speedy gallop through the supermarket before rushing home. The groceries were put away with lightning speed. I had work to do in my office.

Urgent research required my attention. I was losing my edge. I hadn't looked into Trish Fielding but, in my defence, I don't usually look into the backgrounds of my clients without good reason. If I must be honest, I had good reason when I first became curious about what Terry Fielding might be involved in. Time to remedy that situation; I booted up my computer and called on my friend Google.

Chapter 24

Google didn't have much to say about Trish Fielding. Not surprising I suppose given that whatever was interesting in her background probably occurred before her marriage to Fielding. Okay, so I need to find a marriage for the Fieldings before going any further with Trish's background research. In keeping with my motto of start with the obvious, I searched the Queensland marriage records. When nothing turned up there, an idea occurred to me.

I switched to the Victorian PRO site's marriage records index. With only the Fielding name to search on, I wasn't confident of finding the required record. I got lucky. It didn't take long to find an entry for the marriage of one Terence John Fielding and Patricia Irene Wenham. More recent than I expected, the marriage was less than ten years ago. The fact that it occurred in an area of rural Victoria, not far from that frequented by Fanucci and Passmore in the past, was interesting.

Little of interest about Terry Fielding turned up but, now I had a maiden name for Trish, I might have more success digging up information on her past. I typed 'Patricia Wenham' into the search field and sent Google off to do its thing. My enquiry brought up a wealth of hits, some of them dating back quite a few years, and very interesting it all was.

The lady had a fascinating life before marrying Terry Fielding. I found entries relating to Patricia Wenham as dux of her class at the Queensland Police Academy, followed by mentions of her associated with a number of high profile cases as she rose through the ranks to Sergeant. It was unclear whether left the Queensland Police Service to join the Federal Police, or if she was seconded in some way.

A while after she joined the Feds, there was a sketchy report on a case in which Trish was involved. It didn't go well for her. An inquiry into her handling of the investigation followed. Although cleared, the mud appears to have stuck. For quite a period after that,

I found no mention of Trish. The next mention of her was when she was being questioned during a drugs related case. At that time, she worked as an investigator for a prominent legal firm. I found only one other mention of her sometime after that. It was an article in a regional Queensland newspaper featuring an interview with Trish about the new private investigator service she established in the South East Queensland hinterland. That would have been a year or two before she married Fielding.

After their marriage, the Fieldings appear to have led ordinary lives that never merited mention in any newspaper or anywhere else. That's all there was on Trish Fielding. It was tantalising, especially the bit about her setting herself up as a private investigator. Female investigators were rare back then, especially those who set up their own business.

My rumbling stomach told me lunchtime had been and gone long ago. I was on my way to the kitchen to make a sandwich and coffee when my phone interrupted.

"Are you home tonight? I should finish up here about six o'clock. Should I pick up something for dinner?"

My hunt for groceries earlier today was prompted by the desire for a home-cooked meal after all the take-away stuff we had eaten lately. "Don't worry about dinner. I'll make something," I assured Ben and then wondered what that might be. There was that nice little leg of lamb occupying space in the fridge, and there was enough time to have it and all the trimmings ready for a roast dinner tonight if it was in the oven within the next half hour. Not a problem, it would be roast dinner tonight.

It was closer to seven o'clock when Ben arrived, which was a good thing as it allowed me time to have everything prepared and the table set by the time he did. "That smells absolutely divine," Ben announced as he came through the door. "I hope it's ready to eat. I missed lunch today and I'm starving."

Dinner was wonderful and was dispatched with due reverence and concentration. Afterwards, armed with coffee and liqueur, we moved to the comfort of the lounge. I was trying to work out how to initiate conversation about Trish Fielding and everything that had happened since her rescue, when Ben surprised me by opening our conversation with an update on Trish. The ambulance took her from the derelict building to the Millhaven General Hospital. There, still on the gurney, she had a quick trip through the corridors of the hospital to another ambulance waiting in the staff carpark behind the hospital. It took her across town to a private hospital which was mainly the haunt of Millhaven's medical specialists, but was better known by the locals as a rehabilitation centre.

This convoluted trip and the secrecy surrounding her whereabouts were deemed essential for her safety. Ben promised he would let me know when and how I could visit her. No, he hadn't been able to interview her yet. That seemed to be all there was to tell about Trish for the moment, so I let the topic slide away and turned my attention to other matters. "The Fieldings are keeping you blokes busy. Did anything happen at Thornton Transport last night?"

"Every man I could round up was busy last night. Thanks for tip off; it was just what we needed. I sent an officer around to watch the place as soon as you called. It was a late night exercise again, which gave me time to have the warrants ready."

I noticed the use of the plural but didn't want to interrupt by questioning it. I hoped it all would become clear as we went along. "I assume last night followed the previous pattern of activities."

"Yeah, my observer let me know as soon as the semi arrived. He slipped in behind the semi before the gates closed, and opened them later to let a group of us into Thornton's. We waited until your truck with the high canopy left before we raided that area at the rear of the complex."

"Argh, you let the truck get away…"

"No… it was all part of our strategy. Once the officer let us in at Thornton's, he moved to a new location in the industrial precinct to watch for the truck. After the truck arrived, another group of officers raided that warehouse place. It was a busy night with about ten people arrested, including Fanucci, his sister and Terry Fielding. While they were being questioned, I took a lot of officers out to Grevillea Crescent. We tore Blondie's house and shed apart."

"I hope it all paid off. I would be disappointed if any of them managed to avoid prosecution through technicalities."

"Oh, it was even better than that. I had one of the detectives checking with managements of the local truck-stop places. One of them remembered occasional visits during early morning hours by a truck with a high canopy. Although not strictly a truckie like the rest of them, he was given honorary status which allowed him access to the truckers'-only facilities. We had an officer who, at a distance and in the dark, would pass for Fanucci drive the truck out to the truck-stop. A number of other officers travelled under that canopy."

"I like the sound of where this is heading."

"The boxes marked for various people that we found in the truck when we confiscated it remained in the truck with the officers. As soon as the truck arrived at the truck-stop, the relevant semi drivers swarmed over to collect their parcels. So, there were more arrests and more interviews to conduct."

"It seems like you cleaned up in a big way. It should upset the network for a while at least."

"It gets better than that. The boxes were marked for delivery to various locations in outlying centres. Officers from the Transport Division drove the semis to those locations and the recipients of those parcels also were arrested."

Over fresh mugs of coffee, we discussed the finer points of the night's operations. It must be one of Ben's finest hours career-wise. He has every right to feel ecstatic about the outcomes. But, as we discussed all the nuances of each stage of the operation, something began nudging a half-formed thought in the back of my mind to the forefront of my thinking. At last, what bothered me about Ben's operation became clear.

"Ben, everything you did last night neutralised a well-planned operation. The logistics behind having Thornton's, the warehouse and distribution systems come together at exactly the right times and places required extensive careful planning. I don't know all the players you rounded up, but I suspect the brains required for that doesn't exist among them. To my mind, there has to be someone outside the physical operation who is orchestrating it. Someone so removed and so isolated in some way as to be safe from incrimination.

…Someone so deeply buried as to eliminate any hint of suspicion."

"I hadn't overlooked that aspect. To kill the monster – not just wound it – you have to cut off its head. My problem is, I can't see the head to attack it."

Should I share half-baked ideas that plagued me for the last few days and risk bringing scorn down on myself, or should I play it safe for a change and say nothing? Always my own worst enemy, I opted to rush in when common sense warned not to.

"I know I've been banging on about possible connections in the cases I've been working on, connections that fall outside the briefs I've been given by my clients. Please bear with me while I hypothesise a little more." Ben gave me one of 'those' looks, followed by a resigned shrug and a nod. "Although, at the outset, some of those suspicions seemed a bit ethereal, those potential connections I saw in my Fielding case are now confirmed. I've also suspected there are wider connections associated with one of my other cases, but outside my brief."

"Could we at least finalise all the Fielding stuff before you come up with anything else to create work for me and my officers?"

"That's just the thing, I think these connections are what you need to finalise your Fielding stuff. I'm sure I mentioned that Sandra Inneston asked me to investigate whether her husband, Geoff Inneston, who is an inmate of Tulloch Correctional Centre, was involved with another woman. The woman in question is a regular visitor to the Centre, but doesn't seem to be subjected to the same standards and scrutiny as other visitors. As we discussed your last night's operation, the suspicions I held about Inneston clarified, maybe even crystallised."

"I remember you wondering whether he and his lady friend might somehow be continuing to some extent the drug trafficking operation that landed Inneston behind bars. Are you suggesting now that there is a connection between your Inneston and Fielding cases?"

"Yep, I think that is what I'm suggesting. I think there is a strong and direct connection. Inneston has the brains and the time to do the planning. His lady friend, Gloria Purtell, is ideally placed to coordinate the operation from outside, while remaining at arm's length from everything that goes on. Some of this is made possible by a Centre staff member who manages to be on duty whenever Purtell visits, and who knew both Inneston and Purtell in a former life."

"You are right about Inneston having the wherewithal to undertake the planning, but I'm not sure how he manages to get away with it without raising the suspicions of some of the Correctional Centre's staff."

"Maybe it's not just about connections. Connections are a big part of it, but I think it's about networks… more specifically, networks within networks. Inneston, Purtell and the staff member are something of an 'old boys' network that allows the planning and logistics aspects of the operation to occur. The Fielding-Fanucci local network comprising however many people is part of wider trafficking network. There is also another lesser network involved here. That group of spoiled rich kids. Cynthia and her friends, who knock off rich estates around the Millhaven area, operate as a discrete network supplying the Fielding-Fanucci network with a 'secondary commodity' for back loading and to increase cash flow for all involved."

While staring off into the distance, I cobbled my thoughts together as I spoke. Now, with nothing more to add, I looked at Ben to gauge his reaction to my guesswork. He was leaning forward in his chair, elbows resting on knees, while staring hard at some undefined spot on the carpet. There didn't seem to be any reaction and he made no comment. In the hope he was considering what I'd said, and that his mind hadn't wandered off onto something else, I sat and waited.

It was probably only a few seconds later, but it felt like half an hour, when I got a response. "You didn't happen to bring your Inneston case file home with you did you?" I nodded and jerked my thumb towards the office. "Maybe we should adjourn to your office to spend some time with that file. You don't happen to have something that might be construed as a dessert, do you?"

"Dessert…? That's another foreign word in this household. However, I did buy a six-pack of cupcakes from a fund raising stall.

How about one of those with a fresh coffee?"

I took the pack of cakes through to the office. When Ben works late into the night, I know what he's like when the 'late night munchies' strike. He becomes a deep pit that's hard to fill. By the time I arrived with coffee and cakes, he had the Inneston case file spread out across my desk. Before he became too engrossed in that file, I thought I would show him something else.

"Take a moment to have a look at this stuff first. It's some research I did after I found this note slipped under the door of my office in town." I plonked the printouts of information on Trish (Wenham) Fielding in front of him and placed the plastic bag containing the note on top. I didn't think he would show much interest in it and expected him to dismiss it after a quick glance. He had almost all he needed on the Fielding-Fanucci situation. Anything to do with Trish probably was surplus to his needs.

That's not what happened. Ben was interested to the extent that, after checking the time, and deciding to risk it, he called his brother Neil. He wandered out onto the deck to talk to Neil so I don't know what was said. However, I guessed Ben would ask Neil, who is a Federal Police officer, to dredge up more information on Trish Fielding's time with the Feds. Ben looked pleased with himself when he returned to the office, although not inclined to share anything about his phone call with me. Our focus returned to the Inneston file.

By about 2.00a.m., and in spite of all the coffee, I struggled to keep my eyes open. I tried stifling a couple of yawns before Ben noticed I wasn't paying much attention. He was reaching for a cupcake when he saw me yawn. "There's none left," I mumbled.

"Eh... where did they all go?"

"Ben, you have eaten five cupcakes since we moved in here. That's where they've gone. And, while we are talking about 'gone', shouldn't you be gone? I need sleep." We had discussed the Fielding and now the Inneston cases from every possible angle and reached the point some time ago where nothing new was being added to our thinking. There was little point in continuing when we could be sleeping

"Well, go to bed. I'll be all right here for a bit longer and I'll lock up when I leave."

"Not bloody likely; I'm not leaving you alone with my file. I'd get up in the morning to find I no longer had a file."

"I could confiscate it as evidence in an ongoing investigation."

"Not without a warrant and, by the time you get one, this file will have disappeared." I swept all the bits of paper off the desk into the Inneston case file folder. "Now, the office is closed for the night. You can piss off back to your own place, or you can sleep in the spare room for what's left of tonight, but this file is going into the safe." I marched to the safe set in the floor of my office and made a show of stashing the folder in it.

Ben's rumbling chuckle filled the room as I stalked back to the desk. "I know when I've worn out my welcome, I'm going home." Thank God, I thought. "I'll see you for breakfast; say, seven o'clock?" I groaned but agreed.

Why would he want to come back so early tomorrow? I doubt anything new will miraculously emerge overnight. And, no doubt he will expect a full English breakfast in the morning. This is like being married, but without the benefits – whatever they might be. That was the last thing I remember thinking before falling asleep.

*****

I woke at my usual time this morning but dearly would have loved to roll over and sleep for another hour or so. There was no time for that. Ben's threat to be here for breakfast at seven o'clock this morning had me out of bed and bustling about in the kitchen by a little after six o'clock. Although the dishes went in the dishwasher after dinner last night, the kitchen and my desk still bore testimony to the night's events. Ben's usual style is to arrive earlier than arranged. With that in mind, I made a point of being ready to deal with breakfast by a little before seven o'clock.

Seven o'clock came and went and there was no sign of Ben. After taking care of a few domestic chores, I went to my office, retrieved the Inneston file from the safe and settled in at my desk. I don't know what I was hoping to achieve by looking at the file again this morning but, in reality, I was filling in time until Ben arrived.

When nine o'clock rolled around and there was still no sign of Ben, I abandoned my office in favour of the weekend newspapers. I wasn't long comfortable on the sofa when my phone rang.

"It's too late for breakfast, but how about if I come around for coffee?" My response was something less than enthusiastic. "Okay, I'll see you in about 20 minutes. See if you can have a coffee ready when I arrive." Bloody cheek! I don't know why I let him get away with it. However, as he seems determined to come here this morning, I hope it's a sign he has something new to contribute to my cases.

I realised it was Sunday. Sandra Inneston was expected home around lunchtime today and I still hadn't done much preparation for our meeting tomorrow morning. Another worrying thought crept into my mind while I was thinking about my meeting with Sandra. Emily had been on surveillance duties for another of my cases all day yesterday. If we had followed our usual practice, we would catch up in some way after she finished work for the day. She hadn't called me, and I had been so busy being domesticated, I never thought to call her. That is highly unusual and, now that I'm aware of it, it worries me.

To hell with Ben and his coffee; I need to know if everything is all right with Emily. With coffee making abandoned, I went to my office and called her. She was a long time answering the phone and I felt my stomach tightening with every ring. I was about to end the call and ring Ben to tell him to forget about coffee this morning when she answered. She sounded strange, maybe out of breath or something.

"Sorry I took so long to answer. I was just turning into the driveway when the phone started to ring. It took a while for me to get to the carport and find my phone before I could answer. I didn't ring last night because it was late when I got home. I felt there was something strange going on at that place that I was keeping an eye on and I wanted to be out there again early this morning to see if I could work out what it was."

"I didn't want you staying on the job till late last night. You didn't run into any trouble did you?"

"No. No, I was fine. It's just that something seemed a bit odd and

I thought it might make sense if I stayed a bit longer to see what eventuated. I didn't resolve anything. This morning, I took Goldie for an early morning walk in that area of town. I now think I know what's going on. Mum is coming back today and then leaving again tomorrow. I'll wait until after she goes tomorrow and then I'll come to talk to you about my surveillance work."

Somewhere towards the end of that conversation, Ben arrived and let himself in. By the time my call to Emily ended, the kitchen was filled with the heady aromas of fresh coffee and warm Danish. "… Thought I'd better bring a peace offering since I missed breakfast this morning. And, as you don't seem to have much of anything decent to eat in this place, I picked up some freshly baked pastries on my way through town." The pastries were wonderful, so I chose to ignore the barb rather than honour it with a response.

The sod made me wait until after we finished morning tea before announcing he had received some news from his brother, Neil. It appears the then Patricia Wenham played a key role in the Feds operation to bust a drug importation racket. By the end of the trials of those arrested, quite a body of 'evidence' implicating Wenham in the racket had been accumulated. The so-called evidence came from comments by the accused during their hearings.

Although sceptical about its veracity, the Feds were compelled to run an investigation into Wenham's handling of the operation and her private life. Some within the Feds resented a female holding such a high position within their ranks, and waged their own covert rear-guard action to bring her down. The investigation was brutal and just about broke Trish. Although it cleared her of any misconduct, she knew that, in the eyes of some of her fellow officers, she was tainted. On the verge of a breakdown, she resigned.

Some time towards the end of it all, but before she resigned, she appears to have developed a friendship with a man. It seems it was his support that helped prevent her going over the edge. At the time, that relationship raised a few eyebrows among some of her colleagues. They suspected the bloke of being involved in the illicit drug industry. They had him under scrutiny for a couple of years, but he always came up clean. For some, her relationship with the bloke cast doubts on the findings of the investigation into her activities.

Ben was reading from his notes. When he came to the end of them, he looked up. "That's about it, but I don't know whether it provides answers or poses more questions. I know I now have some doubts about the accuracy of the findings of that investigation."

"When did all this happen? Do we have a date for when she resigned?" He flicked through the pages of his notebook before giving me the date of Trish's resignation from the Feds. "I reckon I know who the bloke was that supported her. She married Terry Fielding about 18 months after she resigned." I watched as Ben added that new piece of information to his notes. While he scribbled, I went over in my mind everything he told me about Trish Wenham's time with the Federal Police.

"Ben, it would be useful if we knew the name of the bloke those Feds were interested in, as well as where and what they thought he was up to."

"Gee, I would never have thought of that. I've only been a copper for a long time."

Sarcastic sod! "Okay, point taken. Anyway, today I have to focus my attention on the Inneston file. My client is coming to see me first thing tomorrow morning, and I feel I haven't got the whole story to tell her."

"I thought you had achieved what the brief called for."

"Y-e-s, but it's a bit circumstantial. It's fair to say there probably was an affair happening before her husband ended up behind bars, but there is little opportunity for him and Ms Purtell to get up to no good during her subsequent noncontact visits. If the pair is involved in some sort of illegal activities although he remains in gaol and, if I have conducted a thorough investigation, I would need to report on that aspect of their relationship as well."

"Most of the stuff you do is based on circumstantial evidence. How long will your client be in Brisbane? Perhaps you could give her a preliminary report tomorrow and ask her then if she wants to know the rest of the story – so to speak. If she is interested, you could arrange for another meeting when she returns to Millhaven. I suspect we will have sorted it all out before then."

He was right, I could do that. It was only my frustration at not being able to wrap up the investigation that was a problem. As he was leaving to spend the rest of Sunday in his office, he remembered something he had forgotten to tell me. "If you're interested, we will be interviewing Trish Fielding tomorrow morning. I could arrange for you to be able to visit any time from tomorrow afternoon."

"Yes, please. That would be great. I would like to visit her whenever I can fit it in while she is in hospital… just to be a friendly face after the grilling you blokes will give her." Ben can be a pain in the proverbial, but he has his uses and, right now, I could hug him for his offer to organise for me to have access to Trish.

A big slab of the rest of the day was devoted to tidying up my report for Sandra and reading the weekend newspapers. I didn't hear from Ben again today, so didn't have to fuss about organising too much for dinner. At about 8.00p.m., I was eating a salad in front of the evening TV news when my phone rang: Emily. With her mother at home this evening, her call came as a surprise.

"Can I come in to see you at lunchtime tomorrow?" she asked without any pre-amble. "I think Mum's lost the plot altogether. They are picking her up at 11 o'clock tomorrow. I'll come in as soon as she leaves."

I managed to say 'okay' before she ended the call. It didn't take too much to work out she did not want her mother knowing she had called me. Things did not bode well for my meeting with Sandra if, as Emily put it, she had 'lost the plot'.

As I drove in to my office on Monday morning, I was aware my stomach already had tied itself into a tight knot. Sandra was expected at eight o'clock. She arrived soon after half seven and almost followed me into my office. This is not what I had planned. I wanted to have everything ready and to have settled myself before she arrived. Her early arrival had me wrong-footed, and our meeting was not as smooth as I intended at the outset. But that proved to be because of my build-up of nervous tension following Emily's call last night. I soon realised Sandra was okay. She was the 'normal' Sandra I knew, although I did detect a touch of tightness on occasions as we discussed her husband.

Sandra agreed there wasn't much else required to prove her husband's infidelity prior to his being sent to gaol. As far as she was concerned, his continued association with the woman in question indicated a continuation of that relationship. I gave her the option of closing down the investigation now, while hinting that I might have more to tell her by the time she returned from Brisbane. Sandra was undecided, but admitted she wanted to know all there was to know. We agreed that I would continue to dig around but, unless I managed to dig up something significant in the following couple of weeks, there would be no further cost to her.

Our meeting didn't last long. Sandra was anxious to prepare for her trip. After she left, I sat at my desk wondering whether it might be Emily who was losing touch with reality. Sandra seemed fine to me. I didn't have to wait long to find out. I'm sure Emily jumped in her car and drove to my office the moment she waved Sandra off on her Brisbane trip. Emily painted a different picture of her mother's behaviour after returning from the Ralston craft show. "Sonny, she didn't ask me anything about Goldie, not even how I came to have him." That definitely was not like Sandra.

Emily's account of her mother's behaviour rang alarm bells for me too. After only a few moments consideration, I decided to tell Emily about the case Sandra engaged me to investigate. I confined it to a simple statement about the nature of the investigation. Emily sat shaking her head in disbelief for a few moments before commenting. "That explains a few things, especially some of the strange statements she has made. Can you tell me what you have discovered?"

"I'm breaching client confidentiality even mentioning it to you, but I felt it justified in this instance. All I will say is that there is evidence of an affair before your father went to gaol, and there is evidence they have maintained regular contact since then. The woman involved calls herself Sandra Inneston and passes herself off as your father's wife when she visits the prison. What are you planning to do now that your mother isn't around to require your attention? Will you stay in Millhaven or head back to Moxton?"

"I was half thinking I would return to Moxton. But I discovered the long-running industrial dispute at the mine has escalated into a major strike. I called my boss to find out what they wanted me to do. I have about six months' leave owing to me, so he recommended I remain in Millhaven until things sort themselves out at Moxton. So, if you need any help with anything, I'm ready, willing and desperate for something to do to maintain my sanity."

Mindful of my opportunity to visit Trish in hospital sometime this afternoon, I didn't encourage Emily to hang around. I promised to give her a call tomorrow after I had a look at my case load. After she left, I spent time until about two o'clock trying to get my head around how my conversation with Trish might go.

Chapter 25

As I made my way from the carpark to the Chigwell Private Hospital reception desk, I encountered Ben Richards on his way out of the place. He dragged me off to one side for a quiet word. "…You've come to see Trish Fielding?" Silly question; why else would I be here? I bit my tongue and just nodded. "I'll take you to her in a moment and introduce you to those on duty, but I wanted a word first. I think her interview with us proved a bit stressful. I've sorted out much of that background stuff you were interested in. I'll share it with you later. My advice is to keep your discussions with her light and on general topics, at least for today."

That wasn't how I planned today's visit but I could see the logic in what Ben said. Trish was in a separate small area at the end of one of the wings of the hospital. After my introduction to officers and nursing staff, Ben disappeared and I went in to find Trish propped up in bed. She looked pale and tired, but so much better than when I last saw her. In line with the nurse's instructions, I kept my visit short.

We talk about Goldie and how my 'associate' was caring for him, and of how we met Peggy and came to take Goldie home with us. Apart from brief comments about how she was recovering, there wasn't much. As I was leaving, a nurse called me aside.

"From tomorrow, we will be taking her out to that attached small sunroom. We'll see how she handles it, but we will leave her there for an hour or so each day from about ten o'clock. You might find that a nice time to come and sit with her."

I thanked her and, as I left, I made a mental note to clear an hour or so in my diary for tomorrow and the next few days. After spending the rest of the afternoon in my office, I left for home at about six o'clock. Ben called as I pulled into my garage. "I'll see you about seven o'clock with something for dinner." Good! I don't have to make dinner and I should get to hear what he learned about Trish's background.

Dinner was nothing exotic: fish and chips from our favourite place. I plated up, made a salad, and plonked condiments on the table with lightning speed. I was keen to get to the part where Ben shared information from his interview with Trish. We were both hungry, so dinner wasn't a long affair. Afterwards, we went straight from dining table to my office and got on with the business of information sharing.

"From the information I gained from my brother, Neil, I've been able to confirm a lot of what Trish told me today. She is adamant she was not involved in any of the drugs stuff she was investigated for. But, she did meet Terry Fielding during the investigation. Although she didn't know much about him at the time, he was kind and supportive. Their relationship developed and led to marriage a short while after the investigation."

"That confirms some of what we already knew, and I presume Neil confirmed Terry Fielding was the bloke they were interested in but couldn't prove anything against." Ben nodded his confirmation and continued.

"They remained in Sydney for a while before moving to Victoria, ostensibly for Terry's work as a 'salesman'. She never knew who he worked for or what products he sold. She claims to have been a wreck after the investigation and wasn't functioning too well. Anyway, after about 12 months in Victoria, they moved to Queensland. Then, when Terry secured a job with Thornton Transport, they moved to Millhaven."

"Somehow meeting Terry and all that followed seems just a little too convenient. She is no fool. How could she be suckered in so easily... or remain so ignorant of all that was going on around her?"

"She admits the 'happily ever after' bit had begun to fall apart by the time they moved to Victoria, and things got worse over the years. There were a string of other women along the way and, although they were the cause of a few rows on occasions, she tended to turn a blind eye to them. She sometimes wondered about what else there was in Terry's life. It was over the last 12 months, when he started working 'late night shifts', that she became suspicious. A bit of sleuthing of her own uncovered stuff she didn't like. She admits she probably got too close and they decided to eliminate the risk."

"I can understand Fanucci and his friends needing to neutralise her, but why keep her alive? The end they planned for her probably was the same regardless of when it happened. So, why keep her alive – if that's what you can call it – instead of getting rid of her at the outset?"

"Ah yes, she did explain that too. It seems that prior to the start of their relationship, Terry Fielding was Lorenza Passmore's personal property. They were engaged. Trish now believes the 'mob' ordered their foot soldier, Fielding, to start the relationship with Trish. Lorenza kicked up an almighty fuss but lost the battle. The mob thought Trish could prove useful if Terry could sway her to move to the dark side and use her skills to their advantage. It wasn't until a long way down the track that they realised they had misjudged the situation. After they moved to Millhaven – she thinks Lorenza was instrumental in that – Lorenza gradually got her claws into Terry again."

"That explains a few things, but it doesn't answer the question of why they didn't get rid of Trish instead of keeping her alive."

"I was coming to that. When they realised she as getting too close, they told Terry about it and suggested a fatal accident of some sort. There must be some good in Terry. He opposed the move. They thought he might bolt and leave them without a major piece in their transport arrangements. Fanucci ordered Trish be taken hostage for some indefinite period to ensure Terry didn't try to abscond. Once Terry settled down again and forgot about her, she could be eliminated permanently. After Trish was abducted, Lorenza wasn't happy with that arrangement and ordered one of the mob, Gino Pasquale, to get rid of her. For some time, Gino had sought to be more than Lorenza's friend but Terry Fielding was in his way. Apart from getting a better appreciation of what Lorenza was like, he also realised he couldn't oblige her. So, after Trish was knocked about by the abductors, he hid her in the cellar, taking her food and water whenever he could."

"It was a noble gesture on Pasquale's part, but I doubt he believed it was a long-term solution."

"Yeah, Trish believed that he would realise the futility of it all and eventually do what he was supposed to do in the first place. An alternative scenario as she saw it was for the both of them to be eliminated when they discovered what Pasquale was up to."

"If the raid and everything that followed hadn't happened, I think the latter scenario would have applied. My question now is where was Terry in all this? Did he know what was happening? He seemed happy enough in his renewed relationship with Lorenza. Did he know, and did he care about what was happening to Trish?"

"Trish seems to think he did. Most of the other stuff she told us we have been able to confirm through other sources. Terry hasn't been quite so co-operative. However, Gino Pasquale says Terry knew what had happened when the initial abduction took place, and later did become aware of Lorenza's directive to get rid of Trish. Gino claims that, by then, Terry was so far under Lorenza's spell, he went along with it."

"Do you believe that?"

"Gino is trying to be as helpful as possible, so I'm not sure. He is happy to co-operate and believes his co-operation coupled with his actions to save Trish will result in a lighter sentence than that handed down to other members of the mob."

"Okay, I have a couple of things I will try to follow up with Trish. What's your next move?"

"We now know how the local networks operated and who the players are, most of whom have been arrested. What we haven't been able to determine is where the stuff is coming in from. We know that some of the stuff is coming up from interstate via the various networks, but there is some stuff that's coming in from somewhere else. Everyone is confident it is coming in from overseas, but can't find its origins, or how and where it comes into the country."

"It seems my Fielding investigation is all but over. Now, if I can achieve the same with the Inneston case, I'll be able to put them both behind me."

"Oh, speaking of your Inneston case, there's been a bit happening in that regard as well. There was a covert opportunity for the sniffer dogs to give Ms Purtell's vehicle a good going over. Not even a hint of drugs found. We've had a word to the Correctional Centre and a certain staff member has had his work roster changed as of yesterday. Things could get interesting when Ms Purtell arrives at Tulloch Correctional Centre for her regular monthly visit next Thursday."

"Gee, I might just happen to be in the Centre's carpark that day."

After Ben left, I spent a couple of hours going over everything we had discussed. The most worrying aspect was how Trish Fielding knew in such detail what they planned for her. I had a few questions I wanted to put to her, but they would take careful handling given her delicate condition.

My visit the following morning coincided with Trish being taken out to the sunroom. I waited until the nurse came back in. "How is she doing? She doesn't look too bright. Is it all right for me to talk to her this morning?"

"Yes, but I don't know how much you'll get out of the visit. Her physical injuries are mending well and, under other circumstances, she might be allowed out in a day or so. Mentally she is not doing so well. She seems to be slipping further away from us."

I didn't like the sound of that but, after a couple of deep breaths, I went to the sunroom and did my best to engage Trish in conversation. The nurse was right. Her mental state seemed to have deteriorated. Trish was listless. It was impossible to establish a conversation. I managed to fill a half hour by babbling about everything from the weather to the local football scores. She showed no interest in any of it. I could have been speaking Klingon for all the good it was.

As I was taking my leave, an idea occurred to me. After first dismissing it, I decided it might be worth a try. The head nurse was alone, so I took my chance. "You were right about her deteriorating mental state. I have an idea that might bring her back to us. This is a hospital, right? And dogs are not allowed in hospitals...?" I got the negative response I expected. Then I floated my idea.

"Ooh, I don't think...." She tapped her pen on the counter for a few moments. "You know, mornings are a busy time for us. Sponge baths, all the vitals to be taken and everything else. Once I get Trish settled in the sunroom, I'm all over the place dealing with patients. If a little well-behaved dog that didn't make a nuisance of itself came in through that end door, I wouldn't see it come in. In fact, if it were gone by the time I came to take Trish back to her room, I wouldn't know it had been here."

"True; but the coppers on guard duty probably would notice… unless the dog was really sneaky and had a good plan."

She tapped the side of her nose and went off to do whatever nurses do. I churned that conversation over in my mind for the rest of the day whenever I had a moment to spare. By the time I sat down to dinner alone that night, I still hadn't come up with a plan of how to smuggle a dog past the coppers on guard duty. That situation still hadn't changed as I drove to the Inneston residence the next morning.

Emily thought I was mad and was reluctant to let me take Goldie, but admitted Goldie seemed a bit subdued since I brought him back the other day. After delivering a lecture about looking after him, she snapped the leash to his collar and I set off along the short track from the Innestons' house to the private hospital.

Bugger! I thought the coast was clear but, when I was a couple of metres from the end door, a copper doing his rounds of the place wandered outside to check on things. He gave me a quizzical look. What could I do? I placed a finger to my lips, signalling him to keep quiet while I kept walking towards the end door. The officer put a hand up to shield his eyes and turned his head away before walking back inside. "See that; that is one good copper," I told Goldie as I opened the door and was towed inside.

Goldie bounced around the great padded bed-like thing Trish was in. I pulled one of the visitors' chairs over next to Trish and hoisted Goldie onto it. From that moment on, there were two very happy bodies in that room. Trish's eyes lit up at the sight of the dog and, for the first time, I saw her smile properly – not just with her mouth but it was there in her eyes as well. Goldie laid his head on Trish's armrest and she spent our visit fondling his ears and rubbing his nose.

The transformation in Trish was unbelievable. She came alive and wanted to chat. I took a gamble and posed my first question. "When you saw me after they brought you out of that cellar, you said something like 'I knew you'd come'. It has intrigued me ever since. What did you mean by it, and why would you think I would come to that derelict building?"

"I didn't engage you because you're the only private investigator in town. I wanted you because you are like me. Once you start digging, you don't stop until you know it all – until you have uncovered everything. I had been gathering evidence on Terry and his friends for some time and I thought they were getting suspicious. I had no illusions about what might happen to me if they found out. That's why I needed someone else to start digging too. Someone who would discover the anomalies, and wouldn't be content until they followed them back to their source. A bit like chasing a rabbit back to its burrow."

"But you engaged me to look into whether your husband was playing away from home."

"Yes, I arranged that little scene at the Post Office, and then engineered it so that I would eventually engage you on the pretext of finding out if my husband were cheating. Of course he was cheating. I knew he was. It had been like that throughout our marriage. But I needed you to start investigating what he was up to and to become intrigued by what you found. I studied you long and hard before deciding you were the only one I thought capable of it. I took a gamble on it."

"It was a bit of a long shot. Okay, I accept that the whole scene at the Post Office was staged, but then you disappeared. I might have suspended the investigation since I no longer appeared to have a client... and was unlikely to be paid for what I already had done."

"Yeah, the situation escalated, and things moved faster than I expected. That was a bad weekend. Lorenza came to see me..."

"Lorenza came to the unit to see you...? What did she want?"

"Yes. She turned up at the unit the day after I engaged you. She told me I was becoming a nuisance – a liability – and that I should leave town, go a long way away and get lost. I played dumb; said we couldn't just up and leave like that. Terry's job was here. She made it clear she wasn't there to give me a piece of friendly advice, and that I should start packing. I pretended to be nervous and said I would talk it over with Terry when he came home. She just laughed and walked out."

"That would have started alarm bells ringing for you. Did Terry come home after that?"

"No, I haven't seen him since then. The game was up, so I started securing my evidence. They didn't waste time. They came that night, went through the place and took me with them when they left. They didn't get this little fellow because I'd let him go out for a bit before we went to bed. The backdoor was slightly ajar to let him come back in. I saw him slip back in as I was struggling to prevent them taking me. There were four of them. Three carried me out and dumped me in the back of a truck. I heard the other bloke slam the back door and then pull the front door closed behind him. I don't know where they took me. I think that fourth bloke might have been the driver and it might have been his truck."

"How did you get from where they took you that night to that cellar in the derelict house?"

"Oh, that was Gino." I shook my head to indicate I didn't know what she meant. "After they knocked me around for a couple of days trying to find out what I knew and what I had done with evidence, Lorenza came to visit. Gino was with her and she was all over him like a suntan. There was only the two of them. They thought I was unconscious and couldn't hear their conversation. Nothing happened and they left, but the pair of them came back early the next day. Things had changed between them... not on friendly terms anymore. There was another conversation. I heard enough of to know that Gino had been ordered to get rid of me."

"Jesus, you listened to all that?"

"Well, there wasn't much else I could do. After that, they both left and Gino came back a bit later and started dragging me out to a vehicle. Lorenza returned while this was happening and demanded to know what he was doing and why he hadn't finished me yet. He snarled at her that he thought she wouldn't want a mess on her own doorstep, so he would do it elsewhere. Lorenza didn't say anything. He loaded me in the vehicle and took me to that place and locked me in the cellar."

"I can't understand him doing that. He was taking a hell of a risk defying Lorenza… although I don't know what Lorenza's place was in the overall operation. I guess she had some influence if her brother was the local head honcho. Do you think Gino was just waiting for the right time to carry out his orders?"

"No, he was trying to protect me, trying to keep me alive. There were others using the building. I could hear them moving about. Then, every so often, it would go quiet. I presumed they all went somewhere. It wasn't like they kept normal work hours. Whenever they weren't around, Gino would bring me food and water. It wasn't much but it kept me going. After his first couple of visits, he began spending a bit of time instead of just dropping the food and water and leaving. We – well, he more than me – started chatting and I got to understand things a bit more."

"Are you suggesting that Gino is an all-round good guy?"

"I think that underneath everything he is a basic good guy. He's had a bit of a wake-up call and sees things more clearly now. He sees that his loyalty was misplaced. Once his eyes were opened, he could see that Lorenza was working on building up a power base with a view to toppling her brother. She was using all her wiles to draw people into her camp. Gino was one of those she snared with a honey trap. At about the same time as she ordered him to get rid of me, he realised she was using him, and that Terry was all that mattered to her. Lorenza's mantra was that their operation needed to expand. Vince, her brother, was more cautious and vetoed any expansion."

"So, seeing how Terry's continued participation was critical to the network, was her involvement with Terry just another honey trap to woo him to her side – and away from Vince – or was there more to it?"

"Terry was the real thing. They were engaged – officially or otherwise I don't know – before I came along. In reality, Terry was instructed to win me over so I would join them. It seems Lorenza never forgave them, and that includes Vince, for taking Terry away from her. Terry and Lorenza are the real thing. They have resumed from where they left off."

"Without knowing too much about any of the people involved, I don't see anyone in the local gang who has the wherewithal to organise and run the operation. I can't help feeling there has to be someone – some higher being if you will – who plans, organises and controls not just the local gang but perhaps an operation over a much wider area. That's speculation on my part as I have no evidence, no names, and I'm a bit short on suspects."

Trish seemed deep in thought for a moment before she answered. "You might be right. I heard odd snatches of conversation about a person. Even Gino mentioned him, now that I come to think of it. They all spoke of him as if he were God. I only ever heard him referred to as 'The Director', so I can't help you with the name or anything else, other than the person seemed to be male."

I felt a bit guilty about setting Trish up on that one. She might believe she knows not much, but she was most helpful. I checked my watch, and realised that they would soon come to take Trish back to her room. I explained I needed to get Goldie out of the place before that happened, so there was a hurried goodbye and I left after promising to bring the dog again. I was so preoccupied, I almost walked past the Inneston house until Goldie started pulling towards the driveway.

Emily was looking for us to arrive and rushed out to meet us before we reached the front door. She led us into the house and fussed over Goldie a bit. "Come through to the kitchen. I've made coffee." As I followed her into the kitchen, I realised something was not quite right. Emily was tense and there seemed to be an undercurrent of agitation. In no time, coffee was poured and we were sitting at the breakfast bar.

"I don't know what's going on, but something strange arrived today. Would you have a look at it please? Should I ring someone and asked them what it's all about and, more importantly, should I call Mum and tell her about it?"

As I took the letter from Emily, I could feel a knot starting to develop in my stomach. The Tulloch Correctional Centre's name and logo at the head of the letter suggested it was not going to be good news. Addressed to Mrs Sandra Inneston, it was brief. In a few short sentences, it advised that Geoff Inneston is being transferred to another prison this week. It didn't name the new facility, but indicated she would be advised further in the near future. I suspect Ben's fair hand is behind this, and I have to admit he is thorough.

Damn! Tomorrow is Thursday and it's the fourth Thursday of the month. The day Gloria Purtell visits Geoff Inneston at the Tulloch Centre. Things will be interesting tomorrow when she discovers the accommodating staff member is no longer on duty and also discovers Geoff Inneston is no longer an inmate at that Centre. I must be at the Tulloch Correctional Centre to see what happens. But I promised to bring Goldie back to see Trish again tomorrow.

"Emily, do you have anything pressing you need to take care of right now?" She looked surprised but shook her head. "How about coming for a walk to that private hospital with me? Leave Goldie here this time. I'll talk to you about this letter as we walk to the hospital."

A few minutes later we were on the track that I'd walked along with Goldie about half an hour earlier. "What you do about that letter is up to you. My suggestion is that you do nothing, at least for a day or two. I think there is a long story behind it, but I won't be sure until at least the end of the week. Once I know a bit more, I would be happy to sit down with you and go over everything. As far as calling your mother goes, and given her current view of her husband, I don't think she'll be concerned about him being relocated. Therefore, I suggest leaving it until we know more before calling her about it."

Our visit to the hospital was short. I introduced Emily as my 'associate' to the nurses and the police officers on duty and explained that Emily would be visiting Trish when I was unavailable. Then we went in to see Trish and I went through the same routine with her. She looked at me anxiously and, when I finished speaking, I could see something bothered her. I leaned in close and whispered, "Emily will bring Goldie when she comes."

The look of relief that crossed her face was wonderful, and the startled look that crossed Emily's face was almost laughable. With the major part of my mission completed, all that remained for me to do was show Emily the sunroom where Trish would be in the morning and its back door for Goldie's entry. All the way back to the Inneston residence, Emily went over details of her and Goldie's impending visit to Trish tomorrow. I didn't go in when we got back to the house, electing instead to drive back to my office. The rest of the day was taken up with clearing my desk to allow me a free day to be out of town tomorrow.

I had a casserole ready for dinner when Ben arrived. Conversation that evening focused mainly on what Trish told me earlier in the day. It provided Ben with information he didn't have and helped provide an insight into the gang's operation and internal allegiances. Ben proved particularly interested in Trish's comments about Gino Pasquale. I think he saw Gino as a weak link that might be exploited further for information about 'The Director'. Although I could follow his thinking, I had my doubts. "I'm sure the network employs a need-to-know basis, and Gino might not have been high enough up the order to know anything more than the bloke's assigned name."

"…Still worth a try. He might not know The Director's name, but I'll bet he know who does."

Conversation then swung back to Geoff Inneston and the likelihood my suspicions were correct. "What has he got to gain by keeping the trafficking operation going? He's been put away for a lot of years. If we assume he is doing it for financial gain, how is the money being handled? Where is the money going while he is locked up, and who is putting it there?"

"That's something we still have to sort out. It might take us a while to unravel it all or, by the weekend, we might know some of those answers." As he finished speaking, he gave me a knowing wink and tapped the side of his nose. Looks like I'm in for more frustration before I hear anything else on that subject.

It occurred to me as we spoke that my trip to Tulloch Correctional Centre tomorrow might be a fizzer. If Gloria Purtell knows Inneston has been moved, she is unlikely to turn up at Tulloch for a visit. He assured me Gloria Purtell had not received notification of Geoff Inneston's relocation. They made sure notification only went to the address for the Sandra Inneston they had at the time Geoff was committed.

"Okay, it looks like I am making the long drive to Tulloch in the morning. I need to get cameras and other gear ready… and have an early night. So Ben, go home."

He laughed, but was gone a few minutes later. About 20 minutes after that, my gear was in my car, the alarm was set for an ungodly hour of the morning, and I was in bed with the light off.

Chapter 26

Thanks to light traffic and few roadworks delays, I would arrive too early. I stopped at a small diner near Tulloch Centre for take-away coffee and doughnuts for breakfast. I still arrived at Tulloch earlier than the intending visitors. As I finished breakfast, the first of the visitors arrived.

As on the previous occasion, Gloria Purtell was last to arrive, and barely made it by the allowed cut-off arrival time for visitors. Again, she was a picture of sartorial elegance in a burgundy coloured business suit, stiletto heels, and with the same elaborately styled hairdo. As I watched her totter across the car park and disappear through the sliding doors of the Centre's reception area, I longed to be a fly on the wall in there.

Purtell had barely disappeared inside when a sniffer dog and its handler arrived in the car park. This time they went directly to Gloria Purtell's vehicle. I was disappointed. The dog showed no interest and it didn't excite the handler either. It made sense. Purtell and Inneston wouldn't get their hands dirty. They hadn't done so before, why would they do so now? Their role was planning and administration. That kept them at arm's length from the grubby end of the business. It's unlikely Purtell would have allowed drugs anywhere near her vehicle.

Well, that wasn't particularly exciting. The sniffer dog and its handler moved on to work their way around all the other vehicles in the car park. It was likely the exciting action would take place inside the reception area. I couldn't help myself. It would be too bad to miss it completely. As nonchalantly as possible, I sauntered towards the reception area, avoiding being seen through the glass doors as I did so. When I reached the building, I angled myself against the wall outside so I could peer in through the glass doors.

Due to the antiglare coating on the doors, it was difficult to see what was going on inside. However, Purtell's distinctly coloured suit stood out in sharp contrast to the otherwise drab surroundings of the reception area. I could make out at least two Correctional Centre staff members trying to deal with Purtell. She was agitated and, as I watched, she became aggressive towards the staff members when one of them tried to run the handheld scanner over her. The scuffle that ensued lasted a couple of minutes and ended with Purtell in handcuffs.

A third person, possibly a guard, entered the reception area and took charge of Purtell. She hurled abuse and struggled against his restraining grip. It took him a fair amount of brute force to finally manhandle her through the doors and out into the car park. I watched proceedings from my new vantage point behind some shrubbery growing close to the building's front wall. As he frogmarched her towards her vehicle, I heard the guard tell Purtell she would be charged with a string of offences, and she would find herself in court in the near future. After bundling her none too gently into her vehicle and removing the handcuffs, the guard turned on his heel and marched back into the reception area.

I expected Purtell to roar out of the car park in a fit of rage and humiliation. I misjudged the woman. I planned to edge my way to the end of the shrubbery closest to the reception area doors and, when Purtell wasn't looking, saunter over to my car as though I had just exited the reception area. I peered around the end of the shrubbery to watch for the appropriate moment. I didn't have to wait.

Purtell was gripping the steering wheel with both hands and had her forehead resting on her forearms. At first, I couldn't decipher what I was seeing. Then realisation dawned. She was distressed and sobbing her heart out. For a moment or two I hesitated, not quite sure what to do next. Common sense kicked in. I couldn't hide behind the shrubbery for much longer. Those leaving at the end of visiting time would wonder what was happening.

I stepped out from behind the shrubbery and started across the car park. I was about halfway between the building and the first of the parked vehicles when Purtell looked up and glanced in my direction. Her mascara had run down her cheeks and the front of her hairdo was in disarray. Now what do I do, should I go to my car, or do the neighbourly thing and go and ask her if she is okay?

The neighbourly option won out. I tapped gently on the window. My reception wasn't great. She looked up and glared at me for a moment before waving me away with a few frantic flaps of a hand. Always happy to oblige, I shrugged in response and walked over to my own vehicle. I sat in my car for a while, pretending to drink coffee from an empty cup and feigning making phone calls. The first of the visitors exited the reception area, and others soon followed as visiting time came to an end. Some glanced in Purtell's direction. None approached her vehicle.

With Purtell in no apparent hurry to do anything or go anywhere, I ran the risk of attracting attention if I remained the only car other than Purtell's in the car park. I drove out and headed for home. As I wasn't shadowing Purtell after she left the correctional centre today, the trip home would be a lot quicker than the last time. After arriving back in Millhaven around mid-afternoon, I resisted the temptation to slope off for the rest of the day and went to my office in town instead. The sound of the phone greeted me.

As is often the way, I made a grab for it just as it stopped ringing. There were three missed calls recorded: one from Emily earlier today and two from Ben, including the one I just missed. Coffee had top priority. It wasn't until I was comfortable with a freshly brewed coffee and sandwich half eaten that I thought about returning Ben's calls.

I wondered why he had rung my office twice. If I don't answer when he rings the office, he gives my mobile a try. He hadn't called on my mobile… my mobile! I turned it off when I pulled into the Tulloch Centre's car park and had forgotten to turn it back on. I turned it on and set it to one side as I hit Ben's speed dial on my office phone. As I waited for him to answer, I heard all the missed call messages pinging on my mobile.

"I've been trying to get you all day. Where are you? Are you all right?"

"Thank you for your concern. You know where I went today. I do work for a living, and there are times during that work when I can't be contacted. Now that we have sorted that out, what were you calling about that was so important?"

"I had something to tell you, but it can wait now. If you are going to be home tonight, I'll see you about six o'clock, if that's okay."

"It's okay if you bring food. I don't feel like cooking tonight."

Truth is, I couldn't remember what I had in the fridge.

Ben and dinner taken care of, I checked on the missed call from Emily. Her message said there was nothing urgent. She only wanted to report on her visit to Trish. I called the Inneston house phone. No answer; so I left a message that I would give her a call first thing in the morning. It was a touch after four o'clock, but I decided my working day had come to an end.

A shower brightened me up a bit. I booted up my computer and typed up notes of my observations at the Tulloch Centre and filled in the rest of the time until Ben's arrival watching a local news broadcast on TV. Dinner tonight is Chinese. He had made a good selection and brought a crisp white wine to wash it down. Although it was early, we ate as soon as he arrived. With the table still littered, we abandoned the dining room in favour of my office.

Although almost bursting to know what Ben discovered that was so important he had tried to call me several times during the day, I had to be patient and endure Ben's questioning about what transpired at the Tulloch Centre first. Based on the information about Gino that Trish gave me, first thing this morning, Ben and his men resumed questioning the man. Still anxious to 'assist the Police with their enquiries', Gino gave them all he knew. With a bit of skilful questioning, the police – and Gino himself – discovered he knew more than he thought he did.

"He remembered another man from some time back. Gino thought Lorenza was his exclusive property and became upset when he thought another bloke was creating some competition for her affections. Gino heard Lorenza mention a surname during conversation with Vince. By questioning other gang members about the name, he established that this might be the person they heard referred to as The Controller. I knew the name from my time in Ralston. A few years ago when we were rounding up the drug trafficking network that put Inneston and others behind bars, Aldo Rabonne was high on our list of suspects. However, try as we may, we couldn't find enough evidence to make anything stick."

"The name doesn't mean anything to me. I doubt I've heard it before, and I'm sure Trish didn't mention it."

"I passed what we knew onto Pete Messell who replaced me at Ralston. His guys worked fast but found nothing helpful in Rabonne's phone records. Sam – you remember Sam Keller – well, Sam decided to get hold of the Rabonne family financials. Nothing jumped out at her until, on a whim, she checked an account in the name of Rabonne's daughter. Although not yet four years old, the girl's account showed a number of transactions which turned out to be payments for a prepaid mobile phone, also registered in her name. Back to the phone accounts, and the only traffic on that phone was with one other prepaid mobile number. That phone was in Gloria Purtell's sister's name. The sister, aged 16, died in a car accident several years ago."

"Oh, I do like where this is going. Please tell me the connections are now complete."

"We were able to correlate the timing of calls from Inneston in Tulloch Correctional Centre to Purtell's main mobile phone with calls made soon after from the prepaid to Rabonne's daughter's phone. Rabonne ran this area's hub from Ralston. He is now helping us with our enquiries at the Ralston Station. He hasn't been told of the evidence we gathered against him, and has been digging a very deep hole for himself during questioning. I doubt there is one grain of truth in anything he has said so far."

"I'm surprised Inneston didn't ring Purtell as soon as he was told he was being relocated. He would be aware she was due to visit the day after his relocation."

"He is allowed only one call per month and he used this month's allocation to call Purtell at the end of the previous week. When he couldn't make a call, he demanded to see his solicitor... on the pretext of challenging his relocation. Inmates are allowed calls to their legal representative. However, Inneston's man, although a high flyer in the legal fraternity, has long been suspected of passing on messages for his client. When Inneston rang him late Tuesday afternoon, the solicitor wasn't available. Inneston didn't know it was his solicitor's golf afternoon. A request for an urgent visit by the solicitor first thing Wednesday morning was left with the solicitor's secretary. By the time the solicitor received the message, Inneston was on his way elsewhere."

"You might say Geoff Inneston had a large dose of bad luck at that particular point in time. Did he get to speak with his solicitor in the end?"

"No. By the time things sorted themselves out and the solicitor established where his client was, there was nothing for it but to pass Inneston on to one of the solicitors in another of the legal firm's offices closer to Inneston's new location. The new bloke, a young chap not long admitted to the Bar, was not about to get off to a bad start by breaking the rules. He refused to take Inneston's message and, on his way out, advised authorities of Inneston's request. Desperate by that time, when the new bloke refused to play the game, Inneston made the mistake of telling him that his 'real' solicitor always ferried messages for him."

"Oh dear, now you have a solicitor caught in your net along with all the other miscreants. I assume there is a flourishing legal career about to go down the tube."

"I'm afraid so… and Inneston looks like spending a long time in a special solitary confinement wing. Our 'net' also managed to catch a couple of bent coppers, one here and one at Ralston. There is still more digging into that side of things happening."

"Although all the connections are now complete, there is one factor I don't understand: the money. For Geoff Inneston, this isn't just some all-consuming hobby. It has to be for financial gain. Why else would he risk so much? So, where is the money, how does it get there, and who is managing it for him?"

"Ah, some things take a bit longer to unravel. That next episode of the story might take a while to complete, but people are working on it."

I left a message for Emily that I would talk to her in the morning. Given the letter she showed me about her father's relocation and everything else I knew had happened since I last spoke to her, I felt I owed it to her to bring her up to date. After Ben and I discussed what I could and shouldn't tell her, I was left struggling with how to go about it. Emily was resilient. I had given her a heads-up about unpleasant things happening within her family on a couple of occasions. Although she responded well to the news on every occasion, I still hated being the bearer of disturbing news.

This time, I felt sure I would be sharing the news that would precipitate her parents' divorce… and maybe the sale of their Millhaven property. I felt genuine regret at the thought of the Innestons bidding farewell to Millhaven. I like Sandra and we had been friends for quite a few years. Although my association with Emily was more recent, it would be sad if she slipped out of my life.

My internal struggle with something troubling my mind must have been obvious to Ben. Silence descended over us until Ben broke it by announcing he might have an early night. I didn't argue. I whittled away as much time as possible on every imaginable chore before taking myself off to bed. I knew I was in for a restless night.

The morning found me with a thick head and not ready to face the day. After dragging myself out of bed, I headed out intending to go to my office. Somewhere between my house and the end of the street, I changed my mind, and drove across town to the Inneston residence. Emily was out the back feeding Goldie when I arrived.

She hadn't had breakfast but had made fresh coffee. I accepted a mug of the steaming brew. Another cup so soon after my last one might help start my juices flowing. I decided there was no delicate way of telling Emily the latest news about her father, so I dived straight in. By the time I finished, she was staring at the tabletop as she shook her head from side to side.

"I'm so sorry, Emily. My role in life seems to be to deliver you bad news. Your mother knows nothing of any of this as yet. Whether you share it with her is up to you, as is how you go about it. I've given the police her current address and they will advise her in due course of what's happened regarding your father. She will not be apprised of anything else regarding the Fielding case, and you should not disclose information about it either."

"I came home to support her when you told me they were about to arrest Dad. I'll try for a flight to Brisbane today so I can prepare her for what comes next. Oh God, what about Goldie? I can't abandon him here alone, not so soon after he was abandoned before."

"Go and book a flight now. I'll take you to the airport… and I'll take Goldie home with me." I had no idea how I was going to look after Goldie but I would have to manage.

After about 20 minutes, Emily returned to the kitchen. "I'm booked on a flight at eleven o'clock. Is that okay for you to take me to the airport?" I said yes while still churning over the logistics in my mind. "Oh, I forgot to tell you. Yesterday's visit to Trish went well. The nurse told me as we were leaving that they would be changing Trish's routine. She is getting stronger and, from today, she will be spending two hours per day in the sunroom, from nine to eleven o'clock."

That sorted out the logistics. "Go and get ready for you flight. It's almost nine o'clock. Goldie and I will walk to the hospital for a short visit with Trish. Then we will come back here to collect you and take you to the airport." Emily hugged me and handed me Goldie's leash.

Everything went according to plan. Trish caught her plane and Goldie, along with his water bowl, came into the office with me. His food bowl, toys and what seemed like mountains of dogfood I left in the car. I shouldn't have worried about having Goldie in the office. He curled up and slept on one of the old lounge chairs for most of the morning and then went for a walk with me when I went to buy lunch.

*****

My routine over the next few days changed to incorporate at least an hour long visit to Trish. On the third day, the nurse took me aside to tell me they were letting her go home the next day. I argued that it wasn't safe for her to go home, but the nurse insisted Ben had approved it. Damn, I couldn't let her go back to the unit in the state it was in… and I wasn't convinced she would be safe there. Although I was happy to have both Trish and Goldie stay with me for a few days, she wouldn't be safe there either. My house would be an obvious target for anyone looking for her. If any of the gang remained on the loose, they would look to silence her.

I tried calling Ben a few times but he was unavailable. As I drove home that afternoon, an idea occurred to me. No time wasted, I rushed into the house, dumped my bag and hit the speed dial for Emily. She sat with her mother as soon as she arrived in Brisbane and told Sandra the whole story of Geoff's latest criminal activities.

A detective from one of the metropolitan branches called that afternoon to officially talk to Sandra. Emily assured me she and her mother were okay and were coping. She thought her mother had improved dramatically since finding out everything. I floated my idea past her to gain an initial reaction.

Emily thought my idea brilliant, and handed her phone to Sandra. I was a little surprised at how readily Sandra agreed. I slept well that night and was eager to set my plan in motion the next morning. There had been no contact with Ben for nearly three days. It was odd, but I didn't read too much into it. We both had lives that dropped us off the radar for periods of time every so often... and nothing I had planned required his approval.

Trish was due to be released at ten o'clock, so I faffed about until it was time to collect her. Goldie came with me along with all his paraphernalia. I pulled up at the door and a police officer, after a careful check of the area, escorted Trish out to my car. Goldie bounded over from the back seat and landed in her lap, where he stayed for the rest of the short trip. I drove to the Inneston house, parked around the back, and let myself in with the spare key that Emily told me about. "Welcome to what will be your home for the immediate future. I don't know how long you might be here, but I don't intend letting you go anywhere until I'm sure it is safe for you to be out and about."

About halfway through my explanation of whose house it was and what my plan for her safety entailed, her tears started to flow. I don't class dealing with crying females as one of my strong points, but I could understand her relief and gratitude. After unloading all Goldie's stuff and promising to come back later with the groceries she had asked for, I left her and her dog to settle in.

With the Fielding case and all its associated dramas wrapped up, I needed to finalise the file and write my report. It felt strange to be writing a report to Trish when she knew more about the case than I did but, in the interest of thoroughness and professionalism, that's what I did. And it took me the rest of the day and well into the evening to finish it.

Just after eight o'clock, as I was putting the Fielding case file away, my stomach rumbled. Lunch hadn't happened today and it was now well past dinner time. As I dug around in the fridge for something quick and easy for dinner, a stray thought stopped me in my tracks. I hadn't heard from Ben again today. So what, I told myself. I am not his keeper, and we both have our own separate lives to live. But the uneasiness about the lack of contact persisted.

After a toasted ham and cheese sandwich washed down with mineral water, I succumbed and tried his phone again. Still no response; it wasn't even going to messages. This was not normal. There was no one local I could call to find out about Ben's current state of incommunicado. I felt a knot developing in the pit of my stomach. This wasn't curiosity. It was concern. Ben had been dealing with some ruthless people lately and – yet again – had been instrumental in dismantling a lucrative trafficking network.

The round-up of those associated with my Fielding case effectively dismantled the network from the top down. It also extended to involve the Ralston area. An old friend, Pete Messell, now in charge of that precinct, along with his officers were mopping up the Ralston end of things. I searched my contacts list for Pete's number. That produced the same result as Ben's number and, in my mind, confirmed something unusual was happening. After a few moments of heavy thinking, another name popped into my mind: Sam Keller.

Sam impressed from day one and had developed into a damned good detective. It was her insightful investigation of things at the Ralston end of the trafficking network that uncovered the final critical connection. That needed acknowledgment. I called her number. She hadn't long arrived home from work and was keen for a chat. After congratulating her on her part in the investigation, followed by some brief discussion of the case and my involvement, I slid the conversation to the lack of communication with Ben and Pete.

"Pete had an urgent call to Brisbane. He's been gone a couple of days now. He didn't give me much in the way of details but I got the impression it had something to do with the case, possibly to advise other areas on what action to take to achieve a similar result. I would be surprised if that wasn't where Ben is too. After all, he was the one who engineered the whole take-down in our region. Whatever they are doing is all very hush-hush. When Pete told me I was in charge of detectives in his absence, he said that if anything came up, I would have to wing it as he would not be contactable while he was away."

That settled my anxiety and we moved on to other topics about what each of was doing, why Sam still hadn't found herself a romantic interest, and other girlie matters. By the end of the call, my earlier anxiety about Ben was replaced by pure unadulterated curiosity about what was happening at that get-together in Brisbane. Nevertheless, my call to Sam resulted in a sound night's sleep. The last thing I thought about as I drifted off was wrapping up the Inneston case file tomorrow.

Next morning, I awoke to a grey and drizzly day. As I started work on the report for Sandra Inneston, it was a case of déjà vu. I felt the same lack of necessity as yesterday when I was writing the report on the Fielding case. The wind got up during the morning and the drizzle turned into heavy rain. For a long time, I have suspected I am solar powered. Unlike other people who long for a rainy day to be able to settle down with their favourite pastime, I have difficulty settling to anything on such days. So, it was a good thing I had finished the Inneston report by lunchtime... and lunchtime was a good excuse to leave the office for a few minutes.

Out on the street, the rain, whipped along parallel to the ground by the strong wind, stung any exposed flesh. Umbrellas were useless, and raincoats weren't much better. But it was revitalising to be out in the fresh air, even if I was being soaked as I fought my way along the street to the bakery halfway along the block. The mouth-watering aromas of meat pies and sausage rolls combined with those of Danish pastries and doughnuts rushed to me as I opened the door. With my pie and Danish protected as best I could against the elements, I rushed back to my office and sunk into the sublime delight of a steaming hot, gravy laden meat pie. I convinced myself that, as I hadn't eaten much yesterday, today's overload of carbs and calories probably would be okay.

I was halfway through indulging in my pie when the office phone rang. The temptation was to ignore it until I finished the pie, but a glance at the caller ID showed it was Emily. In a shower of flakes of pastry, I managed to remove some of the pie from my hands before grabbing the phone.

"Hi Sonny, I just wanted to catch up with what's happened since I've been away, and to let you know I will be flying back to Millhaven tomorrow. Are Trish and Goldie still at the house?" I confirmed they were and wondered whether that might be a problem. "Good, I'll be able to spend time with both of them. Are you able to collect me from the airport? That way, we'll have a chance to talk on the way home so I'm aware of everything I need to know before I get there." After arranging to meet her flight, the call ended. It wasn't until then that I realised I hadn't asked what Sandra's movements over the next few days might be. It might prove difficult if Trish and Goldie were still domiciled in the Inneston residence when the mistress of the house came home.

That reminded me of something else I had been meaning to do for the last couple of days: ring the scene-of-crime clean up mob to have Trish's unit clean and tidy for when she was able to move back home. ...And when might that be, I wondered. In the absence of Ben, I had no way of knowing whether it was safe or otherwise for Trish to return to her unit. Plenty of questions but no answers; I needed to keep busy or start climbing the wall.

By the time I left the office at five o'clock, I had drawn up an investigation plan for three new pending cases and done some preliminary research for one on them. Although the weather had improved and the squally weather of lunchtime had become drizzle, the steak on the barbeque I had planned for dinner was out of the question. I settled for pasta instead, and ate it from a bowl in my lap in the lounge as I watched the evening news on TV.

Chapter 27

There was something comfortable about spending evenings at home alone. But, if I had to be honest, a part of me – a small part – missed Ben's company. We had a comfortable friendship, and I enjoyed having dinner with him a couple of times a week. Our evenings together lately were a bit much, but I knew that was due to the fact we both were involved with the Fielding case. However, Emily was coming home tomorrow. There might be opportunity for both Emily and Trish to join me for a home cooked dinner one evening.

My phone rang, preventing me from sinking too far into melancholia. "I wondered if you were home and could stand some company," Ben asked. He had eaten already, so I didn't have to panic about what to feed him. I suspect he rang from the airport. Alarm bells began the moment he walked through the door. He looked so tired and drawn. Coffee seemed like a good idea. We took them through to the lounge for what I hoped would bring an end to my curiosity about Ben's recent absence.

"Apologies for not taking your calls; I've been in a 'no contact' situation for a few days. While I think of it, Pete Messell says hello. Has anything new happened here while I've been away?"

"I thought that was going to be my question. However, all that has happened here is that Trish Fielding was released from hospital. I have her stashed out of sight for the moment and I called the scene-of-crime cleaning mob to go over her unit. I suppose the main thing for me is that I have wrapped up both the Fielding and Inneston cases. The concern I had, and the reason I tried calling you so often, was whether it was safe for Trish to go home yet, or if there might still be some degree of danger in her going back to the unit."

"Ah yes, I see why you were concerned. What I can tell you is limited compared to what I suspect you want to know. That aside, I can tell you that I need to have a long discussion with Trish Fielding. There is every chance she might not be going back to that unit, but that will depend on the outcome of my discussion with her. I'd like…"

"Does that mean you are offering her something akin to witness protection? So, she's still not safe."

"N-o-o, it's not exactly that. I don't want to talk about it until after I speak to Trish, which I hope to do tomorrow morning… if you tell me where you have hidden her." I explained how the Inneston house being empty over the last few days provided an ideal place for Trish to lie low. Ben suggested it would be close to lunchtime by the time he took care of things at the precinct and was able to get away. That suited me, but he didn't need to know that.

I was due to collect Emily from the airport at nine o'clock to take her home. That would give me an opportunity to warn Trish about Ben's impending visit, although I couldn't tell her why he was coming or what he wanted to talk to her about. Ben made moves to leave after only a short visit. I didn't attempt to keep him longer. He looked done in and in need of a good long sleep.

*****

The chat with Emily on the drive home from the airport this morning was interesting. My first question was about how Sandra had coped with all the news about her husband. "She's holding up well. In fact, in some ways it seems to have come as a relief. After speaking to a solicitor, she is pressing ahead with divorce proceedings. The legal people say it almost will be a matter of form under the circumstances and should go through without any delays or problems. To begin with, they weren't quite so sure about the property settlement side of things. But, after checking with the authorities – whoever they are – the solicitors advised that the Crown would not be seizing property under the Proceeds of Crime provisions. The house and everything else was in place long before Dad was convicted and probably before he ever got involved in criminal activities."

"Has she given any indication of what she plans to do about the house? Is she still talking about selling up and moving?"

"Yes, I think that has been sorted, for the foreseeable future anyway. I think you could describe her time in Brisbane as 'disappointing'. Things are not as she remembered them when we lived there. People had changed or moved away. My sister and I talked her into going along to the local Senior Citizens Club. They meet every week and go on lots of day trips and occasional overnight outings. She wasn't impressed with the group and that decided her. Why move when, in spite of what she thought, she does have a strong support base in Millhaven. Mum is staying in Brisbane until the end of the week when she will come home with the couple she drove down with."

"I think that's a good outcome all round for you mother. Now, what about you, how are you coping and what are your plans?"

"I'm not sure. I arranged more time off from work. I want to hang around for a bit to make sure Mum settles down okay. Apart from that, I'm not sure I want to go back to Moxton to work at the mine. I've no real plan for what I'll do if I don't go back. I've been doing some extra studies. I could concentrate on finishing those, but they would require only about one term to complete. I'd be finished that degree by the end of the year, maybe sooner if credits accrue from my other degrees."

Goldie made no secret of his pleasure at seeing Emily again. Trish and I went onto the deck, leaving Goldie to supervise Emily as she made coffee. My conversation with Trish didn't take long. All I could tell her was that Ben would visit later this morning and that he had what I believed was some sort of proposition to put to her. Trish looked concerned I rushed in to reassure her Ben wouldn't try to force her into anything she didn't want to do. I didn't add that he would be dealing with me if he tried anything that wasn't in Trish's best interests.

The rest of my day was spent on office administrative chores. My preoccupation for so long with the Inneston and Fielding cases meant I now had a build-up of outstanding work. Maybe it was a good thing Emily would be in Millhaven for a while longer. I could use her help. Ben rang as I was preparing to leave the office for the day. He wanted to talk to me about a few things, and he would bring dinner. Seems like this might develop into a long night … I hope! There is plenty I want to know that only Ben can tell me.

Dinner proved no more than a slight delay in the evening's proceedings. We moved to my home office as soon as we had eaten. Ben wasted no time in launching into his information sharing session.

"I saw Trish as planned this morning. She agreed to a proposition I put to her, but I gave her a week to consider it fully to be sure. An arrangement is in place for Trish to return to the Queensland Police Service – under her maiden name. Although her record shows she resigned some years ago, she has worked covertly for the Service on a few occasions since then, even while she was with the Feds. Her return would involve a six-week' 'refresher' course as a first step, followed by a posting to headquarters in Brisbane. She would put the Fieldings' unit on the market and relocate to Brisbane immediately. Before you ask, we don't believe she will be in any danger. It has been recognised that she has special talents and they will be utilised in the Service's intelligence gathering section."

When he finished speaking, he raised his eyebrows at me in question. I knew he was asking me to roll out my questions. I was still digesting all he had told me. After a few moments, I shook my head. I didn't have any questions, just a comment. "You said Trish gave you tentative agreement and that you have allowed her a cooling off period before acting on it. Is there anything you need me to do in respect of the matter, and where do you see her living until such time as she leaves Millhaven?"

"If she confirms her acceptance of the offer I put to her, she will stay with Emily until Sandra's return. There will be only another couple of days after that before she departs for Brisbane. In the interim until her departure, we will install her in one of our apartments. She will be safe to come and go as she wants to clear her things out of her unit and collect her vehicle. If you are worried about her, and you have the time, you might consider accompanying her whenever she visits the unit. I don't think it's necessary, but it might put both your minds at ease."

Unnecessary or not, I would be accompanying Trish whenever she was out and about… and I would be armed. With that topic exhausted, Ben moved on to something else.

"I don't suppose I have to tell you that what happened here in terms of the Fielding/Inneston affair brought about the demise of only the local regional hub of a much wider network. They have established a task force to plan and orchestrate dismantling more of that network. Trish will work closely with that task force once she is in her new position. I will lead the task force and will liaise heavily with the Feds. It will mean I will be away from Millhaven for from three to six months. At this stage, it is only for three months, but there is provision for the task force to be active for up to six months."

"I thought the network was dismantled and there was nothing but mopping up to do."

"Yes... and no. There is more to do, and we still don't know where the imported drugs are coming in through. The thinking remains that they come in through somewhere up this way. If we don't sort that part out while the task force is operable, there might be ongoing work to do up here. Do you think you might make an effort to stay out of trouble while I'm away?"

I chose to ignore the barb. "What about the Millhaven precinct? Who is going to be running the show while you're away? Surely they don't intend leaving your seat vacant."

"No, of course not; Pete Messell will move up from Ralston to fill the gap until I get back. So, you still will have an ally in the camp the next time you get into a scrape."

"When do you leave?" It was all I could think to ask I was feeling an overwhelming loss already. Good God, is that an indication that Ben means more to me than I am prepared to admit? I shoved that thought aside as he answered my question.

"I don't know. There's no definite date yet. But, when it happens, it will be at short notice, and I will become uncontactable immediately. I will let you know as soon as I know."

"Will I be able to maintain contact with Trish when she moves to Brisbane, or will the same situation apply to her as well?"

"No, I think your friendship and whatever contact that involves will be able to continue. There will be certain restrictions on what Trish can mention, but otherwise it will be okay."

As soon as we exhausted all the topics he needed to discuss with me, I walked him out and he went home, leaving me with a deepening sense of loss and sadness. Smarten yourself up, Sonny, I told myself. Go and do something useful to make yourself tired or you won't sleep well tonight. I heeded my own advice and took myself back into my office and booted up my computer. I hadn't checked my personal emails for a few days, so that seemed a good place to start. My outlook brightened soon after.

Amongst the junk cluttering my inbox was an email sent a couple of days ago by Troy Donaldson. A few years ago when I took a sabbatical to undertake some extra studies in the UK, I found myself on an archaeological dig on Crete. Troy was my supervisor on the dig. We became firm friends and, if I hadn't returned home when I did, we might have become more than friends. Since then, we have maintained contact by email and the occasional Skype call. As I opened the email, I felt some guilt pangs. It must be at least three months since our last emails.

His news was astonishing. He is on the academic staff of York University and that University lodged a bid for the archaeological work associated with the opening up of a new mine site about three hours' drive from Millhaven. His email suggested they would know the outcome of their bid by the end of the week. Wow! Troy here in Oz and not too far from Millhaven; that is something to look forward to. I was contemplating whether his stay in Australia might allow us to spend time together when my computer pinged to announce the arrival of the Skype call.

"Hi Sonny, I'm pleased I caught you. Did you get my recent email?"

"Yeah, I just read it. So you might be coming to Oz sometime in the near future."

"No."

"Eh...? I thought there might be..."

"No Sonny, I AM coming to Australia. We got the contract. I'll oversee all the archaeological work on the new mine site. I should arrive in about three or four weeks' time. I plan to spend a few days in Millhaven getting myself set up before heading out to the site. The long days will begin once I'm on site."

"I hope you are planning to stay with me when you first arrive. It will be great to get together again. What's the story with the long days?"

"We will be working 12-hour days, but get four days off at the end of every two weeks."

"Good, you can make my place your base for your days off. I assume you will spend your days off in Millhaven."

The call lasted longer than I expected. We discussed the project and how he might not be able to take his days off at the end of each fortnight, but might have to accumulate them until a suitable time to be away from the site. His actual work schedule would be governed by the mine site developer's program of works.

It was so unexpected to be able to meet up with Troy again. Nevertheless, as I crawled into bed, an interesting thought occurred to me. How was I going to handle having both Troy and Ben in Millhaven at the same time? Geez, why does life have to be so complicated?

It turned out not to be a problem after all. The day before Troy arrived in Millhaven after having spent three days in Brisbane at the mine developer's head office, Ben gave me the news I had been dreading. Three weeks earlier, I had waved Trish Fielding off on her way to Brisbane to begin her new life. Ben said at the time he expected to follow her in the next few weeks. In my excitement and flurry of activity to prepare the spare room for Troy's arrival, I hadn't dwelled too much on Ben's imminent departure.

When he arrived that night, I knew something was on Ben's mind. It didn't take too much thought to work out what it might be. He was leaving on the early morning flight the next day and didn't know when he would be back or when we would be in contact again. I shared with him the news of Troy's likely arrival in the next couple of days. In spite of his efforts to hide his reaction, I saw his face fall. It wasn't as though Troy was any great secret. Ben knew of my involvement with Troy while I was overseas, and I had told him of Troy's work at the new mine site.

His visit ended early. It was with a heavy heart that I walked him out to his car and tried to put on a brave face when I said goodnight. I was taken by surprise. Ben wrapped me in a bear hug and whispered in my ear, "Please try to keep out of trouble and stay safe while I'm not here to look out for you." That did it. I felt the hot, salty tears trickling down my face as he released me. He jumped into his car and drove off.

The following day, Pete Messell called me to let me know he was in Millhaven and that he had promised Ben he would keep an eye on me. After his call, I spent some time looking back over the wonderful friendship I shared for so many years with both Ben and Pete. My reverie ended when Troy called to say he was booked on the mid-morning flight the next day.

Oh well, a new day will dawn and a new page in the story of my life will begin tomorrow. There's no point in worrying about what's gone before, I told myself. Just look forward to and embrace the future.

The End

ABOUT THE AUTHOR

Neive Denis is the creator of the series featuring the Private Investigator, Sonoma Whittington. Neive Denis is the pen name of a writer who was lured from her usual genre to focus on the mystery and excitement that are a part of Sonoma Whittington's world. Neive came into being specifically for this series and, for the moment at least, intends remaining faithful to only Sonny's stories.

This series of stories tells of the intrigue and scrapes – some on occasion life threatening – that are part of the life of Sonoma Whittington, an Australian Private Investigator based in a Central Queensland coastal city. However, Sonny doesn't confine her escapades to Australia, and that provides Neive with an opportunity to weave some of her other areas of interest into Sonny's hair-raising adventures.

See more about Neive Denis and her work at
www.neivedenis.com